TRAPPED

I had finished giving Greta's file the once over and started going over the others when the quiet was broken by a loud crash followed by the sound of glass raining from the casement. Before I found what had come through the window, smoke started filling the room. My only thought was to get out. The windows were the kind that had a lot of square panes with metal between them. I choked my way toward the door as the smoke thickened and I worked to tamp down the panic. As the smoke blinded me, I fumbled for locks or hasps or sliding bolts, but felt nothing. The door wouldn't push open. Something must have been jammed against it . . .

Other Fran Kirk Mysteries by
Ruthe Furie
from Avon Books

IF LOOKS COULD KILL

A NATURAL DEATH

RUTHE FURIE

AVON BOOKS NEW YORK

A NATURAL DEATH is an original publication of Avon Books. This work has never before appeared in book form. This work is a novel. Any similarity to actual persons or events is purely coincidental.

AVON BOOKS
A division of
The Hearst Corporation
1350 Avenue of the Americas
New York, New York 10019

First Avon Books Printing: January 1996

AVON TRADEMARK REG. U.S. PAT. OFF. AND IN OTHER COUNTRIES, MARCA REGISTRADA, HECHO EN U.S.A.

Printed in the U.S.A.

RA 10 9 8 7 6 5 4 3 2 1

One

There was a warm body in my bed, and for a change it wasn't my dog. In my morning haze I was reliving the night before. The warm thigh next to mine belonged to the person who starred in my musings.

But when the phone rang, the reverie stopped. The call was about another body, a cold one.

"Fran, wake up." It was Delia's voice I heard after the answering machine beeped. Delia Winston sells insurance and shares my office in Buffalo.

Reluctantly I picked up the phone. Delia is bossy.

"I'm awake," I said. Ted groaned, and I covered the mouthpiece and nudged him. It was hard enough to keep secrets from Delia.

"What was that?" she said.

"Just Horace," I lied. Horace, my dog, is part spaniel and part something else that sheds a lot of white hair. He is capable of making some noises like Ted Zwiatek. "He needs to go out. What's up?"

Ted had opened his eyes and then narrowed them at me.

"Sunset called the office," Delia said, "trying to get you. They've got a stiff over at a farm in Wyoming County."

Sunset Insurance was my first client. At one time, my only client. They still hired me to investigate claims, but now that I had my license, I got other work.

"Stiff?" I said.

Ted frowned.

"Accident maybe," she said, "but they want you there, pronto."

There went the cozy morning I was planning.

"Anything else?" I said.

"Umm, the name of the farm is Hickory Hills."

"Hickory Hills," I said, not yet firing on all cylinders. The name was familiar. "Did they leave a number? Who am I supposed to call on a Sunday?"

"Dresden is trying to show what a loyal employee he is. He left his home number." Delia had worked for Sunset but had seen the writing on the wall and taken a big buyout with a medical plan attached. The guy who took her place, Pete Dresden, had been breathing down her neck for a year before she made the break.

"What are you doing in the office on Sunday?" I said.

"I'm not in the office. I'm home."

"How—"

"The office phone rings here. Didn't I tell you?"

"You know damn well you didn't, Delia." You sneak.

Most of the time she wasn't trying to do me any harm. She just had this need to know everything that was going on. Besides, she was a technofreak. Always retooling.

"Well, don't you think it's a good idea? Here you're getting a job that you might have missed."

"Delia, you shouldn't have done that without telling me. But I haven't got time to talk to you about that now. Give me Dresden's number."

"I hate it when you talk to me like that," she said.

"The number, please," I said sweetly, or as sweetly as I could manage. I swore as I hung up.

"Do your mornings always start so abruptly?" Ted said, once the receiver was safely in its cradle.

I was already sitting on the edge of the bed and rooting in my night table for a piece of paper. The morning haze had dispersed. It was the morning after our first night together, and I guess a leisurely breakfast was in order, complete with sighs and smiles.

"No," I said, and wondered whether he was criticizing and whether I should feel guilty about the pace of my mornings. I'm not exactly a healthy mental specimen. A ten-year marriage to a guy who hit me when he was feeling inadequate hadn't stoked my self-image. "There's a body at a farm in Wyoming County. I have to call Sunset."

At the mention of a body, the haze dispersed for Ted as well. A cop is still a cop, even on the morning after. He got up and headed for the bathroom, wrapped in a sheet. We were both on the shy side.

Before I could dial Dresden's number, the phone rang again. I picked up, thinking Dresden had got my home number, and answered in a formal way: "Fran Tremaine Kirk speaking."

"Fran, it's me, Amy."

"Amy, can I call you back later?" Amy and I belonged to a battered women's group, which met in Buffalo every Tuesday night. We tried to remind each other that there were ways to relate to men that we had never experienced. Even ways that might make us happy.

"Don't hang up on me, Fran, please. I need your help." There was panic in her voice.

"What's the matter, Amy?"

"It's, it's . . . do you remember the man I told you about?"

My mind was not tuned in to Amy's life at that moment. "I'm hardly even awake, Amy. And I was just called in on a case." I didn't want to sound as if I were trying to brush her off, even though I was. I started to explain.

"He's dead." She sobbed, not hearing.

What a way to start a Sunday. Two phone calls, two death notices.

What I knew about Amy's life clicked in at that point. Amy was living and working out at Hickory Hills, and she had recently gotten involved with a man who also lived and worked there.

"It's Ben. It's Ben. He's dead."

"Oh, he's the one," I said stupidly. The two phone calls were about the same death, after all.

"Poor Ben. It's my fault. I shouldn't have gone out with him."

"What do you mean it's your fault?"

"I'm afraid," she said. "Afraid Greg found out about us and, well, did something crazy."

That was something all the women in the group lived with,

that fear that our opposite numbers would do something crazy. Amy had left her husband, Greg, after their baby was stillborn. He was one of those men who reacted to his wife's pregnancy by lashing out not only at the woman but also at the baby in the womb.

Amy had left, first for the shelter, and then for this job that she loved on an organic foods farm. She hadn't told Greg where she was, but she always worried he would find out.

"Can you stay out of sight? I'll be there soon."

"You're coming here? That's really nice of you, Fran. Really."

"I was coming out anyway, Amy. Sunset Insurance wants me to look into a death at Hickory Hills. I guess that's your friend."

Amy calmed down. "You said that a few seconds ago, didn't you?"

"Do you think you would feel safer at my place? You can come here if you want."

"Thanks, Fran," she said. "I don't know what to do. I won't feel safe anywhere if Greg did this. I'll see you when you get here. The cops have just arrived, so I should be all right."

"Keep your eyes open, cops or no cops."

As I hung up, Ted came out of the bathroom. He'd heard my remark about cops. He stood there with one hand on his hip, the other hand holding up the sheet. Besides the sheet, he was wearing a sarcastic smile on his face.

"What have the cops not done now, oh, lady detective?"

"Amy's afraid her husband's on the rampage. You've got to admit that cops don't have a terrific record on protecting women from irate spouses."

"How can cops win that one?" he said. "Half the time the women won't press charges. How can we tell the good guys from the bad guys?"

Ted and I had had this argument before. "Let's not rerun that one," I said, "not until we get some new ammunition." I smiled when I said it, but I meant it. And before he could start an argument about why we should or shouldn't argue, I dialed Dresden's number.

"Pete? Fran Kirk. You want me to go out to Hickory Hills?"

"Yes. A guy named Ben Grasse was found in a hay barn." I was taking notes. "What's Sunset's position in this?"

"Ah, yes. Cut to the chase. I was told that about you."

I didn't say anything. I just made a little humming sound.

"Sunset holds their liability insurance, also fire and theft, some life policies, auto and farm vehicles—just about everything except their medical."

"So what happened to the guy?"

"Impaled. On a pitchfork."

I swallowed. "Do they still use pitchforks?"

"I asked the same question," he said, as if he thought it was marvelous of me to think the way I did. "It was for a special project on collecting and storing hay the old-fashioned way. An experiment. I think they were getting special funding for it from some university. The hay in that particular barn is loose, not baled."

"So they use pitchforks, and Mr. Grasse fell on one. Or did someone run him through?" I said.

"If it's accidental death, our liability kicks in. If someone knocked him off, we don't cut the check."

Ah, yes, the sangfroid of the insurance company.

"What else do you know about this?" I said.

"Edith Baere—she and her husband own Hickory Hills—called the claims office about ten minutes ago. The call was routed to me, and I called your office and got Ms. Winston."

"What did Edith Baere say?"

"She was very agitated, as you can imagine. She said that they had discovered this fellow dead in the hay barn and that they had called the sheriff. How soon can you get there?"

My house is in Cheektowaga, a suburb east of Buffalo. I could get to Wyoming County faster then any claims man from Buffalo.

"In less than an hour if I step on it. I just woke up."

"Lucky you," he said. "I've been up since four. We've got a new baby, and—"

I interrupted him and hung up. Maybe the next time I talked to him I'd let him ramble about the new kid.

"I guess you're leaving," Ted said. He sounded disappointed.

"I'd like to get there before they clean up."

I walked over to him and kissed him, which wasn't too smart of me. "Can you come over tonight?" I whispered.

"On duty till midnight," he breathed back.

"I'll leave the light on for you." I pushed myself away and ran for the shower.

TWO

On the way out to Hickory Hills, my mind wouldn't stay on business. Ted kept intruding. Ted, when he arrived the night before, smiling, carrying beer and pizza and a big bouquet, flowers from the garden at his folks' house. Ted, after we finished eating and went out in the backyard to look at the stars. Ted, when we got so hot I was afraid the neighbors would come out with a fire extinguisher. Ted, when we got undressed in the dark and he stuttered something about birth control.

After much embarrassed stammering, we discovered that we both had provided for such an eventuality. And afterward, we giggled when we realized that neither of us was sure we'd ever get that close.

It wasn't anything like the movies. We were both too tentative, fumbling in the dark, literally. It was unfamiliar territory for me; my husband had made love to the bottle for years and our attempts at coupling could only be called disastrous if one were being kind.

I didn't know what Ted's love life had been, but I'd have to say, even though my information on the subject was mostly vicarious, that he was shy and insecure. I was hoping to get into that realm we call normal, whatever that is, so far as the opposite sex is concerned.

I had not only not had breakfast with Ted this morning, but I had left him the job of looking after Horace before he left. Horace needed breakfast and some exercise. Not exactly a romantic windup for a sexual encounter unless one's taste ran to other species.

My thoughts snapped back to the case when I saw the sign, ENTERING WYOMING COUNTY. According to the instructions that Pete Dresden had given me, Hickory Hills wouldn't be far off.

HICKORY HILLS FARM, NATURAL FOODS SINCE 1965, said a big wooden sign that would have been hard to miss. The driveway snaked through the trees, lush with the promise of June. Some of the trees had signs on them, telling their species and their age. There were also signs requesting visitors not to litter the landscape. The signs were made of wood and designed to look quaint, but they were too new to be genuine quaint.

Where the woods thinned out, a sheriff's car was parked across the road. The officer who got out to intercept me had been eating; his lip and chin and tie bore specks of unidentifiable foodstuffs.

After I showed him my ID, he gave me directions. He was a big beefy fellow, and his uniform was starched and ironed. His name tag said HENRY LAYTON.

"The body's in the barn over next to the hay field. Just follow Northeast Road. There's a few more of our fellas over there. You won't have any trouble findin' it."

"The body is still there?" I said.

"We're waitin' for Doc Farnham. He's the coroner. He's waitin' for his mare to drop her colt. Takin' her own sweet time about it."

"Sheriff, do you know what time they found the body?" I looked at the clock on the dash, nine forty-five. I had made good time on the way out, speeding. Lucky for me the local officers were engaged in activities other than policing the highways.

"I'm not the sheriff, I'm a deputy, but you can call me Hank."

"Hank," I said. "Were you the first one here?" I tried to sound chummy and a little awed.

He smiled. "No, I came over to do traffic, but I do know we got the call just before eight. Edith called, said a couple of the men had found a body in the hay barn."

"Edith. She's the owner?"

"Owns it with her husband, but she's the one to ask if you want to know anythin' about anythin'."

"Well, that's good to know. Thanks, Hank. Say, what's the sheriff's name?"

"Castle, Dick Castle. He's been sheriff here for ten years. Thought everybody knew him."

"Sorry. I don't get over this way too often. Thanks again."

"Ah, one thing you could do for me, Miss Kirk."

"What's that, Hank?"

"See if Edith's got more of that berry cobbler. It's darned good. I'll radio ahead and tell the sheriff you're comin'."

"Thanks. And I'll pass the word on the cobbler." I wondered why he didn't radio for more cobbler. Probably some protocol. I wasn't about to deliver food to him, but I'd pass on the message. Now I knew what was hanging from his chin.

Northeast Road was marked with another one of those quaint signs, and the landscape was all fields ahead. The woods had probably been cleared on this part of the farm for at least a century. The few trees that had been left standing in the hedgerows between the fields had huge trunks, and I imagined them in their lifetime giving shade to the farmers and oxen who worked the fields in the years before engines started roaring through the rows.

Looking for a barn by a hay field in that complex of barns and fields would have been impossible. I didn't know hay from barley or alfalfa. Cop cars I recognized, and there were several parked by the barn I was looking for. The cops, though, were all standing around the back of a van, where a big white-haired woman was handing out coffee and plates of what must have been that berry cobbler that Hank yearned for more of.

Everybody looked at my car as I drove in, but nobody left the little knot around the van to see who I was. Cobbler was cobbler. When I got out of my car, one of the officers waved at me to come over.

"I'm looking for Sheriff Castle," I said as I got within sniffing distance of the snacks. And I must say that the aroma of the cobbler made my mouth water.

A reedy-looking officer with eyes like new pennies raised

his arm while he finished chewing what was in his mouth. "Guilty," he finally said. "You the insurance lady?"

One thing I wasn't prepared for was the affability of the officers I'd met so far. Maybe a low crime rate made them more sociable. "Fran Tremaine Kirk," I said. "Sunset Insurance Companies sent me."

"Have some coffee and cobbler," the sheriff said. "The body's not going anywhere, and the coroner won't be here for a while. Edith, this is Miss Kirk from the insurance company."

Edith was busy dishing up cobbler in the way that good cooks have of dishing out their specialties. Although she seemed to be intent on what she was doing, I could tell that she had already sized me up. She wiped her hands on a towel and came over to shake hands with me. "We found him this morning. Poor man," she said, shaking her head. "He looked like he'd been dead awhile. Probably happened last night."

And then, with a slight shift in her weight, she had handed me a dish of cobbler. "How do you like your coffee?" she said.

"Thank you," I said. "With milk, no sugar."

I had some misgivings about eating before seeing the body, but I was hungry, and everybody else was eating except Edith, who looked like she had eaten her share of cobblers. But her flesh seemed tight and looked as if it covered muscle. She moved quickly and efficiently, cutting cobbler with one hand and pouring coffee with the other. Not one false move.

"What does it look like to you?" I asked the sheriff after swallowing the first bite of cobbler—every bit as good as Hank said it was.

"Looks like he threw himself down in the hay and landed on a pitchfork," Sheriff Castle said.

I put down my fork. "An accident, then?"

"That pitchfork should have been hung by the door. They're supposed to check on that every night," Edith said. "We went over all the rules when we started this experiment."

"Experiment?" I said.

"We're trying out some of the old growing and storing methods. Keeping track of the time it takes, the condition of the hay, the nutrition, the amount of waste. I don't know what this will do to the project." Edith's composure slipped briefly, and she fidgeted with her hands, smoothing the apron over her ample front.

"And the victim?" I said. "How long had he worked here?"

"About seven months. Started right after Thanksgiving. He's been computerizing our operations. It's been like shining a light down into water to see how much we can keep track of."

"So he knew the rules?" I said.

"Of course. Everybody did."

"It's early for hay, isn't it?" I said.

"Last year's," Edith said. "We're feeding it to the cows now. Aren't you going to eat your cobbler?"

"You bet I am," I said, trying to act hungry but knowing that the smell of death was just inside the barn. "By the way, the deputy down the road asked me to pass on the message that he'd like more."

"That Hank," the sheriff said, "he's probably madder than a wet hen that he's down there and the cobbler's up here."

A couple of the other officers laughed, and one volunteered to take another helping to Hank.

I stuffed down the cobbler and hoped it would stay there. Then I asked the sheriff if I could see the body. I hadn't seen Amy yet, but I didn't think I needed to worry about her since the sheriff was talking about accidental death.

The barn was dark, and the thick dusty air carried the faint odor of flesh returning to dust. Light angled in from the windows on either end and from the doorway we were standing in.

Sheriff Castle's flashlight was streaking over the mounds of hay. "There he is," he said, holding the light steady. "I don't want you to go any closer until Doc Farnham gets here."

The body was lying faceup, the eyes wide and the mouth open. Two tines of the fork stuck through his shirt at an angle. He was wearing what looked like a blue shirt with a button-down collar, no tie, dark slacks, loafers, argyle socks. He looked about forty, maybe six feet tall, sandy-colored hair receding slightly.

"What was he doing in the barn?" I said.

"Edith says he had a bad back and that sleeping in the hay gave him relief."

"He slept with his clothes on?"

"He would come in and lie in the hay for a couple of hours before he went to his rooms."

"Pretty fancy duds for sleeping in a hay barn."

"Yeah," Sheriff Castle said. "I was thinking the same thing."

Hearing the sheriff say that made me worry again about Amy.

"Where are the rest of the employees now?"

"We have most of them over in the store."

"Most of them?"

"Except those doing the milking. When they finish up, they'll go to the store, too."

"Do you know anything about this fellow? Do I have his name right? Ben Grasse?"

"Yeah, Grasse with an *e*. He moved here from Pennsylvania. Did the same kind of job there. Worked on a big farm, but worked in the office."

"Married?"

"No. Never been married. But he's no monk, if you get my meaning."

"Did Edith tell you that?"

"Didn't have to. There aren't a lot of people around here. And the people that do live here like to talk about the other people who live here. Mr. Grasse gave them something to talk about."

"Who was he seeing?" I asked, figuring that Amy's name had run the grapevine.

The sheriff smiled and his copper eyes gleamed. "If he slept with all the women I heard he was sleeping with, he wouldn't have time to hold down a job. I'm assuming he slept with some and that the rest was talk."

"Wouldn't it be good to know which was which?"

"If somebody did him in, you can bet we'll try and find out."

Edith's voice boomed across the open space between her van and the barn. "Doc's coming."

I followed the sheriff out of the barn and looked in the

direction Edith was pointing, where a dust cloud was being raised behind a rapidly moving long black vehicle.

"I'm fresh out of cobbler," Edith said. "I'll go back to the store and get some for Doc."

There were three roads leading away from the barn in different directions. One I came on, one the doctor was approaching on, and the other that Edith took.

"How big is this place?" I asked the sheriff.

"Better than ten thousand acres, and that's just what they farm. I don't know what they've got in woods and open field."

"So a stranger could find plenty of places to hide."

The sheriff looked at me and narrowed those glinty eyes. "Nobody said anything about any stranger."

I was wondering whether to blat out what Amy had told me and what Amy feared had happened. If Greg had found her and had killed Ben Grasse, then Amy would be in danger, too. But if it was an accident, there was no point in adding to Ben's list of conquests for everybody to recite. Unless, of course, Amy was already on the list everybody was reciting. I decided to go halfway.

"Sheriff, a friend of mine works here. Name's Amy Hastings. Blonde, about my height. Have you seen her this morning?" I watched the sheriff to see what he knew about Amy and Ben.

"That pretty thing a friend of yours?" The sheriff gave no hint that he knew anything, no half smile, no arch of the eyebrow. "She and the other gals at the store were a mite nervous about this."

"I'll go see her later," I said. "Maybe one of your men could contact the store and tell her I'm here and that I'll see her before I leave."

"Sure. We can do that for you. An' I know just the officer who'd like to do that." The sheriff smiled conspiratorially.

Before I could ask the sheriff which officer had eyes for Amy, a big, loose-limbed man, sporting a handlebar mustache that was the same salt-and-pepper color as the mop of loose curls that licked his collar and hung in his eyes, stalked into the barn. The sheriff and I followed.

"Finally got that mare bedded down. Had twin foals, both

stallions. Beauties. Sorry to keep you waiting. What have we here?''

His voice filled the air and bounced against every hard surface.

The sheriff shined his light across the hay to where the body lay.

''Haven't they got any damn lights in here?''

''We were waiting for you. We didn't even do fingerprints or anything. The only folks that have been in here since he died, as far as we know, were the two guys who opened the barn this morning.''

''Did they turn on the lights?''

''They said not.''

''How the hell did they see him?''

''The sun was coming through that east window. They saw him in the patch of sunlight. One of them went over to see if he was sleeping or what. Then they told Edith and she called us.''

''Well, I'll need some light. Get one of your ballerinas in here to tippie-toe around and turn on lights and not disturb the scene too much.'' The doctor put his bag down and pulled a pair of rubber gloves out of it. ''Here, give him these.'' Then the doctor withdrew another pair of gloves and put them on.

I didn't know how they were going to preserve the scene and go over the body. Hay just didn't stand still. And forget about little bits of fiber or any fancy stuff.

''Damn fool office workers,'' Doc Farnham said. ''Don't know enough to watch for pitchforks in the hay.''

''I thought pitchforks were becoming a rarity,'' I said, not wanting to leave all office workers undefended.

''And you are?'' Doc raised his eyebrows and cocked his head.

''Fran Tremaine Kirk,'' I said. ''Private investigator. The insurance company sent me.''

''One of those ladies with three names, eh?'' He curled his lip in distaste.

I was ready to find a pitchfork to ram into Doc Farnham. But I just giggled girlishly and said, ''Why, how many names do you have besides 'Doctor'?''

He gave me fish eyes, and a smile crinkled around the corner of his mouth. That's when I decided he was really a good guy and a big tease.

"We still use pitchforks," he said, "when we toss around hay that's been let loose from the bale or the roll." He picked up his bag and started to walk toward the body.

"Maybe you want to wait a little longer to get started," the sheriff said. "Edith's gone to get you some berry cobbler."

"You mean to say you guys have been hanging around eating Edith's cobbler while I was sweating over that mare and then came over here without so much as a piece of dry toast?"

I don't know how she got there without our hearing, but Edith made her entrance just then. Of course, Doc Farnham's voice was loud enough to drown out a locomotive, so maybe that explained why we didn't hear Edith drive up.

"Did I hear someone mention cobbler?" Edith said coyly, holding out a plate and a cup to the doctor.

With no hesitation Doc took coffee and cobbler and tucked into both in record time. Edith waited and took the cup and plate when he was done. She apparently was familiar with Doc's eating habits. "Holler when you want more," she said.

"Hell. I haven't had any breakfast. What's the matter with now?"

"Make up your mind whether you're going to work or eat," Edith said. "And take off those silly gloves if you're going to eat cobbler."

After the doctor had stuffed a couple more helpings into his face and gone to work on the body, Edith came over to me and said, "Amy said to tell you she's okay and that she'll be in the store."

"Thanks," I said, trying to read her face. But I saw no undercurrent.

After a few minutes, Doc called the sheriff over and indicated that I could come nearer to where the body was. "What do you think?" Doc asked the sheriff. "How did this fork get here like this?"

The doctor had pulled away some of the hay to reveal the fork handle, which was lying at a sharp angle to the body. Doc was rubbing his chin and moving his head first one way then another, looking at the fork and the body.

"Hmmmm," the sheriff said.

"Yeah," Doc said.

I could see what they were hmmmming and yeahing about. With the fork at that angle, it didn't seem that someone could throw himself down onto it.

"I'm going to go over this body before we move it," Doc said. "Sheriff, I'd like you to call my assistant and tell her to bring out the full set of tools. She'll know what I want."

"Right," the sheriff said. "I'll get right on it."

"I'm going to get the county forensic people over here, too," Doc said. "I guess you want to—"

Before the Doc could finish, Sheriff Castle said, "Yeah, you're right. I'll call them."

I frowned, and the sheriff explained that he thought it would be a good idea to call in the state police if foul play was suspected.

I stood there looking at the decomposing flesh that had been Ben Grasse. The doctor was right. It didn't look like he had fallen on the pitchfork. And if he hadn't, someone had thrust it into him and then turned the body over. I couldn't imagine someone doing that unless he or she was strong. But everybody on a farm is apt to be strong. Edith certainly didn't look like a weakling.

And then there was Greg. Would a city fellow like him think of a pitchfork as a weapon? Or was it just standing there, a weapon of opportunity?

And if Greg did this, would Amy be next on his list?

Three

I followed Edith to the store, which was about a mile from where I had driven into the Hickory Hills property. When she got out of her van, Edith came over to me and told me about the things we had passed.

"Did you see the dairy cows? They're raised on organic feed. So are the beef cattle. We've been doing it for years. Now people are realizing how important it is not to have all those chemicals and pesticides in their food."

"I'm not sure I can tell a dairy cow from a beef cow," I said.

"The beef cows we have are Black Angus and Herefords. Our dairy herd is all Guernsey. The Guernseys are the lighter brown with white patches all over them, while the Herefords are darker brown with white faces. The Angus are black. Remember seeing them?"

"Yes," I lied. I wondered whether every visitor got the lecture.

My lack of enthusiasm seemed to dull Edith's zest to continue. "Amy's inside," she said. "So's practically everybody else. We're supposed to wait until the police are finished with us. I hope it is soon. We've got work to do."

When I entered the store, Amy rushed to me and hugged me. "Fran, I'm so glad to see you." She stepped back and looked at me intently. "What did you find out?"

Edith was right beside me. "Doc's not sure that it was an accident," Edith said.

Amy gasped. The others reacted as if that were impossible.

17

"What do you mean, Edith?" A big man, maybe about sixty, said. He was large-boned and rangy; his skin was fair, and what was left of his hair was a yellowed gray.

"Just what I said, Heinz. Doc's called for his assistant and some people from the county coroner's office."

"I'm going to go talk to Doc," he said, and started toward the door.

A tall, thin officer with a red mustache stepped in front of him. "Sorry, Mr. Baere, you have to stay here."

"This is just a waste of time, keeping us all here, doing nothing," Edith said.

"Orders are orders," the officer said. "You can stay here or you can stay down at the jail. Your choice."

The officer obviously had been having the same argument with Heinz before.

Heinz harrumphed and swore and decided he would stay in the store. Then he noticed me. "Who's this? What's she doing here?"

"The insurance company sent her. What did you say your name was?" Edith said.

I handed her one of the cards I had just gotten printed. It was the first time I had handed one out, and it felt funny, as if I were an imposter.

" 'Fran Tremaine Kirk, private investigator,' " Edith read from the card.

I think my face got red, but I decided to ignore my insecurities. I extended my hand to Heinz and he shook it.

"I'm Heinz Baere," he said. "Edith and I started this place back in sixty-five. This is my son, Ernest. He wasn't even shaving yet when we came here."

Ernest was as tall as his father, but fleshed out, like Edith.

Heinz then introduced me to Ernest's wife, Theodora, and Ernest and Theodora's son, Eric. Eric, too, was tall, but thin like his mother and with her darker coloring.

"My granddaughter hasn't shown up yet this morning. Probably still sleeping," Heinz said. "Some day to wake up to."

"She ought to be here," the red-mustached officer said. "Is she over at the house?"

Heinz looked at Ernest, who looked at Theodora, who

ooked at Eric. Then they all looked at Edith, who took a deep
breath.

"We don't know where she is," Edith said. "We went to
her room and her bed was made and she was gone."

"Gone?" the officer said. "Gone like for the morning or
gone gone?"

Theodora started to cry. "She took some of her clothes."

"Why didn't you tell me before?" the officer shouted.

"We thought she would come back," Edith said. "She
never left like this before."

Four

"You're all under house arrest," the sheriff said when he came to the store in response to the call from the red-mustached officer.

He was miffed that no one had told him earlier that Greta was gone. I didn't blame him. Edith had been feeding the cops her cobbler and sitting on information that she knew the cops would want.

The sheriff's manner had changed; he had dropped the cordial deference and become scrappy and terse.

When the Baeres protested, he said, "No noise. Stay in your living quarters. We're taking over the store and all the phones. We're closing off all the roads into the farm. Any one of you breaks the rules, you get hauled off to the jailhouse."

Ernest, the son of Edith and Heinz, ventured a small request. "Can we milk the cows?"

"I don't want to see the animals suffer. But nobody goes anywhere without an officer or does anything without reporting to the officer in charge. Got it?"

The family members, chastened all, mumbled their assents and were escorted to their houses.

I went with Amy to her apartment, which was on the second floor of a cement building several hundred yards from the Baeres' family compound and separated from it by a stand of trees. The lower floor of the building was given over to storage, mostly old file cabinets and boxes. Most of the downstairs rooms weren't being used, Amy said, but they were clean. The bathroom down there did get a lot of use, because it was on the way between the store and the living quarters for the family and the farmhands. Amy had given me a rundown on the cast of characters at the farm and where they all lived.

"I hear people down in that john at all hours," Amy said. "Isn't that scary?"

"It wasn't up to now," she said. "I felt pretty safe here. You know, comfortable, until this."

I knew how fragile a thing like comfort was. I didn't remember having had many periods of my life when I felt comfortable and safe. "That must have been nice," I said.

"Darn it," she said. "You can help me, can't you, Fran? Find Greg. Find out if he did it. Can't you? I'll pay you, little by little, every cent."

"You're going to have to tell the sheriff about you and Ben Grasse. Then he'll have the cops looking for Greg. That'll save you some money." I smiled.

"Oh," she said. "He will have to find Greg, won't he?" Relief spread across her face like sudden sunshine. "But I still want to hire you," she said, as if she'd been disloyal.

"You may not have to, Amy. Really, I don't mind." I wanted to tell her that it would be nice to see her feeling safe again. I wanted to hug her. But most of the time, I'm too scrunched up to say the tender things I feel.

"Will you come with me? To see the sheriff?"

"Sure," I said, but I knew the sheriff wouldn't want me to stay while he questioned her.

The sheriff wasn't mad at Amy when she told him about her brief affair with Grasse. But when she told him her fears about Greg, he was ready to spit nails.

"If I had known about him sooner, little lady," he said, "we might have a suspect in jail."

"What do you mean?" Amy was saucer eyed.

"We had your husband in our jailhouse overnight. Picked him up drunk in the wee hours. But we let him go this morning. He's got a good start."

"Oh, God, I knew it. I knew it. He's going to kill me, too."

The sheriff wasn't listening. He was on the phone putting out an all-points bulletin on Greg.

We were in the store, where he had set up temporary headquarters. I saw Theodora, Greta's mother, being escorted by an officer into a back room. I guessed that the family was being interviewed one at a time so that the cops could get at some semblance of truth. The Baeres had all kept their mouths shut about Greta until Edith thought it was time to tell.

Amy was rocking back and forth in her chair and crying. "I should have told them sooner, I should have. I should have. I'm sorry, Sheriff. It's all my fault."

I was wishing she would shut up. But I didn't say anything. I try to act nicer than I really am.

"How long have you been seeing this Grasse fellow?" the sheriff asked Amy. At the same time, he gave me a look and a little wave of the hand that told me I was dismissed.

"Just a couple of weeks," Amy said. "I only met him a couple of times. He was so . . ."

"Don't leave the farm just yet, Ms. Kirk," the sheriff said as I took hold of the doorknob.

"I won't," I said. "I still have work to do here. That is, if it doesn't interfere with your investigation." I didn't like the way the sheriff was treating me, and I laced my remarks with a snippy tone.

He jerked his head to one side and squeezed his eyes into slits. But he didn't answer right away. Finally, he said, a little too sweetly, "Just keep the officers apprised of your whereabouts. I'm sure you know what's right and wrong in a criminal investigation."

"If I don't, I'm sure one of your deputies will help me," I said and flounced out like an outraged hen. I felt foolish and angry and didn't know whether either feeling was justified.

Deputy Hank was standing outside. "Where are you headed, Miss?"

"I'd like to talk to the Baeres so I can finish my report."

"I'll escort you over there," he said. "And thank you for havin' that cobbler sent down to me. Didn't I tell you it was somethin' special?"

"That you did."

Hank reported to someone on the other end of his walkie-talkie that he was taking me over to the family compound. On the way over, he talked about what a nice family the Baeres were, what a great place the farm was. But I was listening with one ear and letting most of the meaning fall out the other while I organized my thoughts to write the report for Sunset. Of course, they wouldn't pay off unless the death was ruled accidental. And that was starting to look unlikely. It didn't seem as if there was much more for me to do for Sunset.

It probably wouldn't be necessary for me to work for Amy. Greg would be picked up pretty soon. If he had killed Grasse and then got so drunk that the cops picked him up and put him in the cooler, it wasn't likely that he would be able to elude law enforcement for long. Or was he drunk when he killed Grasse? Or didn't he kill Grasse?

Maybe this young girl, Greta, had something to do with Grasse's death. Did the family think so and that's why they stonewalled the sheriff? Or did she see something that frightened her and then she bolted?

"Which Baere house you want?" Hank was saying.

"What?"

"This is where Edith and Heinz live," he said, pointing to a Cape Cod bungalow. "And the big house is where Theodora and Ernest and the kids live. Edith and Heinz used to live in the big house. When Eric and Greta came along, they moved out."

The big house was a standard two-story farmhouse with extensions built on the back and on one side. All the houses were painted gray with white trim. But the doors were a deep blue green.

"What's the other house?" A ranch house stood a bit apart from the family homes.

"That's where some of the help live. Ben Grasse had a couple of rooms down that end," Hank said, pointing to the back area of what was an ell extension to the house, where there was yellow tape stretched across the windows and circling the exterior. "We boarded up the rooms on the inside so's the men could use the rest of the house."

"Only men in that house?"

"Your friend is the only gal workin' here who doesn't live around here."

"How many men live there?" Amy had already told me, but I like to check.

"Four, countin' Grasse. I guess that makes it three now.

Those three do the milkin' and the daily chores. There's other guys from around here who work here, too, in the fields, in the office, in the warehouse.''

"How many people do they have working here?" I was beginning to realize that the farm was a big business.

"I guess they've got about thirty regulars. Then they take on help durin' harvest and for cannin' and whatever else.''

Just then, we heard a bunch of sirens. "That'll be the troopers," Hank said. "They like to make noise.''

I was getting the idea that there was an uneasy relationship between the sheriff's department and the state police, but I wasn't about to ask questions. "I wouldn't mind having one of those sirens," I said with a little laugh.

"Especially when you're going out for a pizza," Hank said with a big laugh.

Definitely an uneasy relationship.

Five

I talked to Edith and Heinz about the death of Ben Grasse as if it were an accident that Sunset might have to pay on. Edith repeated what she had said earlier about the rules on storing pitchforks.

Heinz said a few words of agreement and nodded as Edith answered my questions.

Edith complained when it was clear that I was finished: "Farm insurance is so expensive. So many farms have accidents, but we have so many safety drills. We try to be so careful. Our record has been so good, and now this."

"We should have made him stay out of the barn," Heinz said, looking at Edith and curling his lip and narrowing one eye. "There were other ways for him to cure his back." I noticed a slight German accent; his *w* sound was almost a *v*.

"Do you think Greta's disappearance had anything to do with Grasse's accident?" I said. "Is it possible that she saw what happened?"

"I don't know what time she left," Edith said.

"She is no angel," Heinz said. He stood up and waved his arm, dismissing the subject, and walked out of the living room. I heard footsteps going upstairs.

I waited for Edith to say something. It was a long wait, but I was learning how to hold my tongue and not rush to fill up the gaps in conversations. I had decided that people who do that are oiling the machinery of social interaction: Keep the party going, avoid awkward pauses.

When I am trying to get information out of people, making

the conversation flow easily is not always the best tactic.

"Greta," Edith finally said, "is young and—and very foolish."

"Sounds normal at seventeen."

"No," she said, "not so foolish as Greta."

I waited again.

"Do you think you could help us find her?" Edith said.

Whoa. That knocked me off my pins for a minute. "I'll need to know a whole lot more than you've told me so far," I said, "before I can decide."

"I can tell you what you need to know."

The woman was annoying me, but I swallowed. "Let me use your phone to call the insurance company," I said. "Then we'll talk."

"The sheriff has the phones tied up," she said. "We tried to make a business call."

"Maybe he'll let me call," I said. "He's not mad at me." I smiled, but Edith didn't smile back. Of course, I didn't know whether the sheriff was mad at me or not. Perhaps he thought I had encouraged Amy to hold back her story.

"We're recording outgoing calls," a woman on the line said, "but the sheriff said it's all right for you to call the insurance company. What's the number?"

There was nothing I had to tell Sunset that the cops couldn't hear.

Dresden was relieved when I told him the coroner suspected that the death wasn't an accident. You'd have thought it was his money.

"Dictate to the claims secretary, will you, Fran? I want to get this in early today," Dresden said. "Then you're done. We won't need you again unless they decide it was an accident after all."

As I put down the phone, Edith brought in a tray loaded with sandwiches and drinks.

"Organic, low-fat cheese," she said. "All organic vegetables, lettuce, relish. And organic apple juice and peach nectar. Also spring water from our well. Since we don't use pesticides or any other harmful chemicals on the soil, our well water is wonderful and pure."

She never stops with her pure routine. "I'm sure I'll be able to taste the difference," I said, not sure at all.

"If you eat meat," she said, "I have some organic hamburgers cooking."

Now you're talking. "I'd like a hamburger," I said. "Don't tell me you have organic ketchup."

"Of course we do," she said. "It's one of our best sellers." The proud smile suddenly faded. "Ben had set up such a good system for keeping track of sales and inventory," she said, shaking her head.

"Are you going to be able to run the system without him?"

"Not me. The computer is not for me. But the children, Eric and Greta, they took to it like little ducks to water. Greta is, I think, even better at it than Eric. Ben taught them, but they can do what he taught and more."

"What about your son and daughter-in-law, are they computer literate?"

"Ah, is that what they call it? Yes, well, they can do what they have to do to run the business systems."

"Was he finished setting up the system, then?"

"I think with the computer, he could always think of more things for it to do. I think we would have kept him here only a few more months."

"Did he know that?"

"Everybody knew that. That was the understanding when we hired him."

"What if Ben's death wasn't an accident?" I said.

"Who would want to kill him?"

"The line would go from here to the village," Heinz said, appearing in the doorway.

"Ah," Edith said. "You smelled the hamburgers cooking. I know you can't sleep when there is anything cooking." She said this fondly, as if he were a young boy. "I'll set the table in the back room. Miss Kirk, will you bring that tray?"

Heinz and I followed her, carrying the juices and sandwiches that she had brought into the living room before. I marveled at the way the woman was always producing food for people to eat.

She called back over her shoulder, "Maybe the sheriff

would let Amy come over for lunch. Why don't you call the store to see if that's allowed?"

What I really wanted to do was ask Heinz about the line of people who'd want to kill Grasse, but Edith had sent him to the cellar to get something or other.

"We have a wonderful fruit cellar in the basement," she started. I knew it was going to be another treatise.

"I guess Greta's in high school," I said.

"She's supposed to graduate."

The way she said it left me doubting. "Hasn't she been doing well in school?"

"No. Not well."

Heinz was back. "She doesn't go to school. Most of the time, she sits in front of the computer in her room."

Edith looked annoyed at Heinz.

"It's true," he said. "Why hide it? She's uncontrollable. I told you to do something. And now she's gone. It's no surprise."

There was something nasty in his tone, as if this territory had turned bitter.

"I'll call the sheriff about Amy coming to lunch," I said, not at all sure I wanted to stay.

By the time I returned to the room at the back of the house where Edith had set the table for lunch, she and Heinz were talking amiably about the fruit trees on the lawn behind the house. The table was in front of a picture window from which there was a view of the lawn and trees, sloping down to a narrow creek. A field rose on the other side of the creek, and beyond that were tree-covered hills with a break here and there for a house or a power line.

"Amy will be over in about ten minutes," I said. "May I help you with something?"

"No," Edith said. "I'll do it. Heinz will take you up to Greta's room. There are pictures."

"Up?" I said. "Does Greta live here? I thought—"

"She doesn't get along with her mother," Edith said. "She moved in here a couple of months ago."

Too bad all that organic food doesn't keep the poison out of relationships, I thought as I followed Heinz up the stairs.

One side of Greta's room was all frills and flowers, the other side, where the computer, desk, phone, printer, and shelves were installed, was stark by comparison. It was almost like looking at a split personality.

Her bed was covered with lavender quilt. The dust ruffle and pillow shams were a flowered lavender print. The curtains were white eyelet tied back with lavender ribbons, and on the floor were white throw rugs. A white wicker chair in the corner had a cushion on it with the same print as on the bed. The lamps were brass with flowered globes. The pictures on the wall were those sickeningly cute kittens and puppies. Guess what color ribbons on the little cuties.

The computer side of the room stood in derision to the frills. The desk and chair were Early Attic. Some of the bookshelves were of the brick-and-board variety. The floor was bare wood. It was almost as bad as the office space one sees in the back of gas stations.

Heinz watched me looking from one side of the room to the other, and he laughed. "Guess vich side Edith fixed up. Ha, ha, ha. Vat a vaste!" The *v* sound was getting more pronounced. Maybe he tried harder to say the *w* when he first met people.

"Which pictures did Edith want me to see?" I didn't think the kittens and puppies would do me any good.

"Not the ones on the inside of the closet," he said, laughing again.

Naturally, I went to the closet doors and opened them.

"Edith wouldn't let her hang them on the wall," he said. He was smiling. Although he had complained about Greta earlier, he seemed to enjoy her defiance of Edith.

Small wonder Edith didn't want the pictures in plain sight. The boys and girls in leather, with their earrings of safety pins and twisted nails and the holes for studs in other places on their faces, with their multicolored hair and death-mask makeup, would have clashed with Edith's flowers even more than the junk store motif that Greta had put together for her computer corner.

"I don't think these are the ones Edith meant, either," I said.

Heinz pulled a box out from under the bed. "Albums in here," he said. He handed me the box.

At that point, Edith appeared at the door. "Look at that mess," Edith said to me, pointing at the office. Then, as she directed me to look at the other side of the room, she walked behind me and closed the closets. "Bring the box of pictures down," she said. "Lunch is almost ready."

By the time lunch was over, I had managed to look at about half of one album and had gotten a rundown on Greta's friends and the places she went.

Also by the time lunch was over, I was getting tired of being around Edith. She had her hand on the controls all the time. Nobody moved without her knowledge and consent.

I was thinking that if I were a teenager, I would be thinking of ways to get out of there, even if I had managed to louse up my grandmother's idea of a perfect teenager's room.

Amy seemed to enjoy Edith's company, but Amy was used to being bossed around, and at least Edith didn't beat up on her.

Edith invited me to a small office on the first floor of the house where she officially hired me, that is, she wrote out a check.

When I told her my rates, she said, "You're reasonable." That's what Delia had told me, too, but she'd used the word "cheap." I didn't feel that I was a hotshot investigator, so I charged accordingly. That's what I'd told Delia, anyway. Her answer was always that hiring a cheap detective was like buying a cheap parachute.

When Edith and I had finished our business, Amy and I were escorted back to Amy's apartment by the officer with the red mustache whom I had seen before in the store. His name was Jeff, and he must have been the one that the sheriff meant when he said he knew someone who would be glad to take a message to Amy ("that pretty little thing"). Jeff practically fell over himself whenever Amy talked to him. Amy just smiled at him and didn't seem disturbed in the least that a grown man would act so silly.

At the door to the apartment, he asked her whether there was anything she needed, whether he could do anything for her, whether she was all right, whether she would be all right that evening.

Amy thanked him and said that she would call the sheriff's

office and ask for him if she thought of anything. At that point, he, of course, gave her his home number. He was giddy with excitement when he left. I half expected him to kick up his heels and start skipping.

With the sheriff's permission, I called Ted's house and left a message saying that I wouldn't be home that night. Then I called my paperboy, Wally Klune, and made arrangements for him to take care of Horace. Wally got along fine with Horace. He liked to take the dog with him on his paper route, something that Wally's mother liked, too. She worried about weirdos attacking her boy.

I never worried about Wally. He was such a resourceful little guy. Actually, he wasn't so little anymore. I'd guess he had grown about five inches in the last few months. The last time I saw him he was taller than his mom. I'm five seven, and he was looking me squarely in the eye. It wouldn't be long before I'd be looking up, maybe calling him sir.

I started putting together some notes about Greta—writing things down always helped me sort out what was important. Next I turned my attention to the pictures Edith had lent me.

Greta was tall, sturdy, and blond. She looked like she would grow up to be like her grandmother, as if she should wear a hat with horns on it and sing Wagner arias.

I asked Amy if she had noticed anything different about Greta recently.

"Only that she stopped wearing jeans and started wearing long skirts. But you know how styles change with teenage girls."

"How recently did she do that?"

"A couple of weeks ago, I think. I remember because Heinz made a big stink about it. He didn't like the change."

"You'd think an old-fashioned guy like him would like skirts better than jeans."

"He said she looked like those religious people. He said their outfits were ridiculous."

"What religious people? What outfits?"

"You know. The Amish people. Ben told me that Heinz didn't like the long skirts because Heinz lived in Amish country when he was young."

"Was he Amish?"

"I don't know. There was some connection, but Ben was sort of vague. Besides, I didn't really want to talk about Greta or Heinz while I was with Ben. He . . . I don't know. I really liked him . . . a lot."

"I guess he was a charmer," I said, before I realized that I shouldn't have. I bent over the pictures again and tried to look busy, hoping Amy would let it drop.

But she didn't. "What do you mean by that?"

I was wondering what kind of lie to hatch up. "Well, didn't you find him charming?" I said as aggressively as I could. Maybe I could shout her down—in a nice way, of course.

"Come on, Fran," she said. "What did you hear?"

The worst part about going to a therapy group with someone is that they get to know you too well. Amy and I had been sitting around that circle every week for almost a year. She knew I was holding back.

"The sheriff," I said, figuring I'd put the blame somewhere else, "said there were rumors that Ben Grasse was . . . well, what he said was that Ben was no monk."

Amy buried her face in her hands and began to wail. In between her sobs, she shouted at me. "How could you not tell me? What kind of friend are you?" And other recriminatory statements. I guess she figured she had to blame someone. But we had had a number of lessons on this kind of behavior at the battered women's group, and I knew she would snap out of it if I came up with the right counterattack.

"How much time have we had together since I've been here?" I said, loudly and assertively. "And how do I know whether the sheriff's a gossip or not?" Then I tried, "You ought to be thanking me for not telling the sheriff right away about you and Grasse."

The last one was the one that got to her and calmed her down.

She said, "I was looking for someone . . . to blame."

"To blame," I said along with her. We were both quoting Polly, the woman who ran the group and who was always furnishing us with words to live by.

"Now," I said, "could you tell me more about Greta?"

She told me and told me. Until suppertime.

Six

Dinner was at the house where Theodora, Ernest, and Eric lived, the house where Greta had lived, too, until she had a big blowup with her mother.

Amy had become an honorary Baere in that she ate dinner with the family every night. The other employees who lived on the farm—including Grasse, Amy had told me—ate at the ranch house where they lived. The meals at both houses were usually supplied by the queen of kitchen, Edith.

Theodora was a mousy brunette. Although she wasn't a small person, about my height, she seemed small next to Edith, and probably also next to her daughter. The differences in physique were more in width than in height. Theodora was narrow shouldered, thin, and wiry, and walked stooped over with her head down. Her posture, it seemed to me, told the story of her position on the farm: the outsider, a Baere by marriage, not by blood.

Although I couldn't imagine Theodora having a fight with anyone, I was assured by Amy that there had been a fight, a very loud and vicious one complete with hair pulling, scratching, and biting. The argument, according to Amy, was about Greta's curfew, to which she had not adhered.

Greta was mentioned only in passing during dinner, something about her liking the dish we had that night, a type of scalloped potatoes made with turnips sliced among the spuds. We also had a spinach quiche and a big salad with several kinds of greens. Dessert was vanilla pudding with blueberries. I made a mental note that if I stayed around here much longer that I would have to skip some of the meals, or I'd begin to resemble Edith.

During the meal, Eric, who was twenty-one, mouthed off a few times about the way the farm was run and the way the cops were conducting themselves. The adults in the family listened to him politely, as if what he was saying had merit.

I thought the kid was a blowhard and very impressed with himself. So far as I could see, he was another reason for Greta to have blown town. Eric did not have the blond sturdiness of his father and grandparents. He looked more like his mother, but taller and without the browbeaten stoop.

Ernest, with Heinz's ranginess and Edith's tendency to run to fat, was the biggest of the bunch, probably tipping the scales at close to three hundred pounds. Like his mother, he moved gracefully and efficiently, despite all the tonnage.

I tried once to ask about the last time they had seen Greta, but Edith immediately took over the conversation and everybody else clammed up. It was obvious that I would have to follow the same procedure that the sheriff used: divide and conquer.

On the wall in the dining room were several pictures of Greta with two women I recognized from the pictures in the albums. They wore skirts down to their ankles like the ones that, according to Amy, Greta had started wearing recently.

I waited until we were clearing off the table and followed Theodora into the kitchen to ask her who the women were.

"Her great-grandmother and her great-aunt, Heinz's mother and sister," Theodora said. "Greta used to spend vacations with them when she was younger."

Edith did not allow the conversation to last long. She walked in while Theodora was speaking, and Theodora barely mumbled the last of her sentence.

"We sent Greta there," Edith said, "when we were busy on the farm and she was too young to do the work."

"Do you think that's where she is now?" I ventured.

"I called them this morning," Edith said. "She is not there."

If Edith had been calling relatives this morning, she had been more worried about Greta's absence than she let on to the police.

"Where do they live?" I asked.

"In Paradise, Pennsylvania."

"How would she have gotten there?"

"She has her truck," Edith said.

"And that's gone, too?" I said.

"Yes."

"And the sheriff knows about the truck?"

"He does now."

I wondered whether the sheriff had put out an all-points on Greta. I wondered, too, whether the medical examiner had decided whether Grasse's death was accidental.

When I made noises about leaving, it was obvious that Amy wanted to stay longer at the farmhouse. I thanked the Baeres for dinner and excused myself. I wanted to see the sheriff or whoever was still minding the store.

When I went outside to pick up my escort, Jeff was waiting. It was easy to see he was disappointed that I was alone, but I told him that Amy would need an escort later and that took some length off his face.

When I got to the store, I found the sheriff sitting at the same table he had been using earlier when he was questioning Amy. Now, however, it had accumulated a few piles of paper.

He greeted me with a smile and motioned to a chair.

"Well, Ms. Kirk, did you enjoy the dinner?" He had stopped calling me "miss."

"Yes," I said, and then, after I had spied some paper plates with familiar looking colors and textures, I added, "Did you?"

"Ah, yes. No one goes hungry here."

"I noticed. A few days of this, you'll be able to make foie gras of my liver."

"Have you found out anything useful?" he asked. I didn't know whether he was being nosey or facetious.

"Actually, I came over to ask you what the ME had decided about Grasse's death," I said, ignoring his question.

"He didn't fall on the pitchfork. I can't repeat the explanation he gave me, but it was something about the angle and the fact that the body had been turned over after the fork had pierced the body. He's certain of his conclusions, so I guess that lets your insurance company off the hook and you can go home."

He had a gleam in his copper eyes. He was baiting me. My guess was that someone had told him that Edith had hired me to find Greta.

"The insurance company will be glad to hear that they don't have to pay off on an accident. I'm not sure whether they have a life policy on Grasse," I said. I knew they didn't, but that was enough to throw the sheriff off guard.

"Oh, I thought," he said "that Edith had . . ."

I was too quick to smile. We were both holding back and weren't fooling one another, but we were stuck with the posturing, so we both laughed.

"Have they picked up Amy's husband yet?"

"No, not yet," he said. "I'm guessing he's somewhere getting drunk again."

"I hope so. If they could find him . . ."

"We're checking all the gin mills, and we sent out information about his drinking habits, too."

"He's got some other nasty habits when he drinks," I said, and then told him about what Greg had done to Amy.

"Yeah. Bad guy. What did Amy see in him?"

"Maybe the same thing she saw in Grasse."

The sheriff shook his head. "Some women don't know how to stay away from guys like that."

"I've noticed that," I said, thinking of my own botched attempt at marital bliss, which I barely escaped with my life.

"I know a few things about you, too." The sheriff lifted his chin and looked down his nose at me.

"I guess you've been checking up on me," I said. "Well, it's no secret. The cops know who I am."

"Actually, they had some nice things to say. But you've had troubles of your own, not unlike your friend Amy."

"Guilty as charged," I said. I was getting uncomfortable with the discussion. "Anyway, I'm glad the cops are being kind."

"They did say, however, that you don't always give them all the information that they ask for."

That teed me off. "Not true. Not true. The problem is that they don't listen. They have their theories, and anything that doesn't fit is disregarded." I shouldn't have let him get to me. The sheriff, I realized, was setting the ground rules for my working in his county. "While I'm in your territory," I said, "I'll be sure to give you every thing you ask for." No problem. All he had to know was what to request. Theories were another matter. "You want to know what I know so far?" I said.

He sat back in his chair and folded his hands across his chest. I told him what I had heard about the family fights and what I'd noticed about the family dynamics. I gathered by the way he nodded as I went along that he had the same information and didn't disagree.

When I finished, I said, "Anything you know that I should know?"

"Don't take this any farther than this room," he said and paused for maximum drama, "but this may have some bearing on what happened to Grasse." His face was serious. No more glint in the eye. "One of the hired hands says he saw Theodora in the barn with Grasse one night."

"Whoo. Now that's interesting. Did the farmhand say what they were doing when he saw them?"

"As a matter of fact, he did."

"In flagrante delicto?"

"So he said."

"Which farmhand?"

"Terry, Terry Kurtz, the young guy with the bald head, always smiling. Makes him look stupid, always smiling like that. But he's not."

It took me a minute to remember him. Then, as long as the sheriff seemed to be in the mood to share information, I told him what he already knew. "Any other tidbit that would help me find Greta?"

He smiled. "We want to find her, too."

"But you don't think Greta did it," I said.

"No, but she might have seen something."

"Something that scared her enough to make her run?"

"Something like that," Sheriff Castle said. He had a funny look on his face. A look that said, you're not even close.

"Sheriff, who else was Grasse taking to the barn besides Amy and Theodora?" The sheriff looked less smug. "Would he have been fooling around with Greta, too?" No trace of smug left. "Would that have been the reason for the fight between Greta and Theodora?"

The sheriff nodded. "We're working on a theory that runs something like that," he said, "but it's only hearsay."

"If it were true," I said, "both Theodora and Greta could be suspects. Not to mention anyone who found out about it and wanted to teach him a lesson for fooling around with Greta. Or a jealous husband. Seems like there are a lot of suspects if that theory holds."

"You might say we have our work cut out for us." He chuckled and his eyes looked like two flames.

"But you can't just keep the farm closed down and question them one by one day after day."

"No, we're going to let them get back to work tomorrow, but we'll keep a couple of deputies here 'round the clock."

"Has Jeff already volunteered?"

The sheriff chuckled again. "It's pretty obvious, isn't it?"

"Is there anything else about Grasse that would inspire murderous feelings besides his sexual appetites?"

"From what we've learned he was a hell of an organizer. Heinz told us that with the system Grasse set up, the whole farm ought to run more efficiently, make more money, too. No, so far as his work went, no motive there."

"When you went through Greta's things, did you find any diary or any personal papers? All Edith gave me was a list of her friends and the places she hangs out and some pictures."

"No. I was wondering about that, too. Usually, young girls have some stuff around that tells you something about them."

"Unless she took that stuff with her."

"Possible," he said.

"Maybe she kept it in the computer," I said.

"Hmmm," he said. "I'd have to get someone from the state police to help us with that. When they were here earlier, they looked around and then left. Told us to call if we needed anything. They've got bigger fish to fry; they're working on something with the drug people."

"There's a woman who works with me who's pretty good around computers. Do you mind if I ask her to come over?"

"Will she be working for me or for you?"

"She'd be happy to work for both of us and charge us twice."

"The Baeres wouldn't argue with me about access to the computer. So I'll put out the word that she's working for me. You can hang over her shoulder and find out what you need."

"That would work," I said. It would also save me some money.

I called Delia and put the sheriff on the line to talk to her. He hired her for more than Edith was paying me per day. She would be arriving tomorrow.

Seven

Delia arrived at the farm Monday morning, trailing expense vouchers, which she submitted to the sheriff immediately, a practice, she told me pointedly, that sets the tone of the relationship. "If you wait till the end to turn in your expenses, they quibble. After all, by then, the job is done."

It has occurred to me that Delia, when she was working for Sunset and hiring me to work on some of the claims, was taking advantage of the fact that I didn't charge a lot for my services. Self-worth is another one of my struggles. Watching Delia was giving me some tips.

Besides, Delia has a proprietary interest in my career as a private detective. She was the one who pushed me and pulled the strings to get my license. And since she shares the office, the more money I make, the more secure the office is.

Delia got right to work in the office at the back of the store. Heinz, Ernest, and Eric told her about the files, the systems, and the passwords. They were loitering around the desk watching her for a while. I could see she didn't like it. They explained everything she called up on the screen. When she gave the sheriff the high sign, he sent the Baere men packing.

"It's a simple inventory system," Delia said. "They could have picked it up in night school instead of hiring a high-priced consultant. This system even has a pretty good tutorial."

"What about personal files?" the sheriff said, taking the words out of my mouth.

"The passwords they gave me were only for the business files. Let me check to see how much is stored in here."

Delia fooled around with the keys and made a few "uh-huh" noises. "This will take a while. There's a ton of other stuff in here and some devices that won't allow tampering. I'll have to go around the back way to get copies and printouts."

Delia kept her eyes glued to the screen while Edith and the workers descended on the store. Edith was in a bitchy mood and not happy to have Delia taking up space.

"We're a day behind on the mail orders," Edith said.

It was finally agreed that Delia would be set up in the office space downstairs from Amy's apartment. Delia would be staying in Amy's apartment that night, too, if she needed more time to finish mining the computer files.

While Delia was being relocated, I went to find Theodora to see if I could talk to her without the bullying presence of Edith. Amy was walking at Edith's elbow when I left.

The deputies were no longer escorting people from place to place, and the farmworkers were going about their business in a more or less normal manner. Three sheriff's cars and a trooper's unit were parked by the store, though, so normality had not really returned.

Theodora was hanging out sheets when I got to the farmhouse. I tried a down-home ploy to get her talking.

"They smell nice when they're dried outdoors, don't they?" I said, thinking I had hit the right note.

"Except when they're spreading manure, which is what they're supposed to do this afternoon." She was fast and deft with the clothespins.

I dropped my shoulder bag on the ground and grabbed a few pins. "Maybe if we get them up right away, they'll be dry before the manure spreaders get going."

Theodora smiled. "Thanks," she said.

I hoped I had a foot in the door. "Do you ever work in the store or in the office?" I said.

Theodora smiled again. "Not if Edith's there."

Maybe she wasn't so mousy after all, I thought. Maybe she was just outnumbered. It seemed that she was standing up straighter today. "You two don't get along?" I waited for her to say something like, "Is the pope Catholic?" or "Does a wild bear crap in the woods?"

"Never have," she said, "not from the first moment we laid eyes on each other. I think that's why Ernest wanted to marry me, because his mother hated me."

"How do you manage to live so close?" What I wanted to say was, How come you let Edith make so many of the decisions that affect your life?

Theodora looked at me as if I were a world-class dolt. "The farm," she said. "Edith and Heinz won't live forever. Ernest would never give up the farm."

How touching family life was. Such filial devotion. "And your children," I said, "are they looking forward to running the farm someday?" And waiting for you to die, I didn't say.

She either didn't notice or ignored the attempt at sarcasm. "Eric loves the farm, but Greta is another story altogether. She likes her music, her friends, and boys—lots of boys."

Was this mother telling me that her daughter was what they used to call oversexed? "She keeps late hours, you mean?"

"Early," she said. "She gets home early in the morning with her hair a mess, her lipstick smeared, bruises on her neck, and her clothes on backwards."

"And you haven't been able to persuade her to behave better?"

"That's a nice way to say it," Theodora said bitterly. She bent over and picked up the laundry basket, which we had emptied. "There's another load to hang," she said.

I followed her in the back door, where there was a big room that might be called a mudroom. There was a rack for boots and a grate in the floor in front of the back door, where dust and mud could fall off work shoes. A washer and dryer and clotheslines took up one side of the room, and a door near the back opened to a lavatory. While she loaded up the basket, she unloaded a few more nasty comments about her daughter's habits.

"Did she do any work on the farm at all?" I asked.

"The only things we could get her to do reliably were the computer entries. That she did. I'll give the she-devil her due."

"Has she been interested in computers for a long time?"

"No, not until we had the computers installed." Her face was full of unspoken emotion. "She learned very fast. That's why we got her one for her room. We thought that would keep her home. It did for a while."

"What did you know about this fellow who got killed?" I asked.

"What do you mean got killed? Wasn't it an accident?"

Damn. Did I shoot my mouth off? I didn't remember the sheriff telling me that it was a secret. Why hadn't anyone told Theodora? "Did I say it wasn't an accident? I just said he got killed. People get killed by cars. Most of the time by accident."

Theodora frowned. "He worked hard, and he set up a good record-keeping system for Edith."

It was not exactly what I expected to hear, but, then, I guess she wasn't going to give me the particulars of her tumbles in the hay with Grasse.

I stuck my neck out a little farther. "Did you see much of him?" I meant "much" in the sense of time spent, not in the sense of how many square inches of his body she had seen. But she blushed anyway.

"Why are you asking about him? I thought you were supposed to find my daughter." There was nothing mousy about her tone now. She was loaded for bear.

"Since she disappeared about the same time he died, it occurred to me that the events might be related," I said sweetly and calmly.

"Why would she have anything to do with Grasse?" She spat out the words like a riled-up cat.

"I didn't say she did. But maybe she saw what happened and got upset." Interesting that she would jump to the conclusion that I thought Greta had something to do with Grasse. I got the feeling that the sheriff was working on a sound theory.

"Greta probably went to a friend's house and got into some drugs and is passed out somewhere on somebody's couch with her clothes half off."

Whew. Some mother! "I thought that you and Edith had called all her friends."

"Do you think the kids she hangs out with would tell the truth?"

"Obviously, you don't. Well, thanks. I'll drive around to some of their places and see if I can find her. Thanks for your help."

Theodora had calmed down some, and the laundry had been hung up. "Thanks for your help, too," she said. "I'm sorry if I sounded rude. I guess I'm more worried and upset than I thought."

Sure you're upset. Probably your daughter stole your boyfriend. That's the nastiest kind of triangle. Now your boyfriend is dead and your daughter is missing. And you're upset. It sounded to me as if she had the sensitivity of a slug. And I thought she was mousy when she and her husband were just hanging around waiting for the old folks to die or become incapacitated.

"I guess I'd be, too," I said.

Edith had given me a list of four of Greta's friends, all girls that would be in school, if they went to school. I compared notes with the sheriff and he had the same list.

"We checked those girls," the sheriff said. "They're all in school today. Greta's truck isn't parked near any of them, and it's not in the high school parking lot, either."

"What about the great-grandmother and the great-aunt, Grace and Hildegarde? Did you check them?"

"We called them. They haven't seen her."

"Looks like you fellows are doing my work for me."

"Did you talk to Theodora?"

"Yes," I said, rolling my eyes. "She's not what she seems at first. I think she's hiding something, but it could just be her affair with Grasse. She got hostile when I asked about him."

"A woman like that," he said, "has a lot to put up with."

"Like what?" What did the sheriff know about Theodora's tribulations?

"You see what the family is like," he said, not telling me anything.

"You don't think she knows where Greta is, though, do you?"

Sheriff Castle shook his head. "No. And maybe I hope she doesn't."

"You think she's dangerous?"

"Not dangerous, just outraged at her daughter, no one else."

"You think Edith thought the same thing and that's why she had Greta move in with her?"

"Edith's no fool."

"I guess I agree with you, but that doesn't make her easy to take."

"But if Edith's your friend, you can rely on her absolutely. I'd trust her with my life."

"That's high praise," I said, thinking that if I knew what he knew about the Baeres, my job would be easier.

"I want you to be careful while you're here," he said. "I'm leaving a unit here, but they won't be able to be everywhere at once. Since we don't know who did this to Grasse or why, just watch out while you're poking around and stirring things up."

"Thanks," I said. "I'll be careful."

"And tell your friends to watch out, too. I don't want any more trouble."

"I will," I said. "Does that mean you think the killer is here? What about Amy's husband?"

"I'm not ruling out anybody yet. Except maybe you." He smiled.

"Maybe?"

"You can't be too careful. You got here pretty quick yesterday morning." More grinning and that copper glint.

When the sheriff left, he gave me his home number as well as his private line in the sheriff's office and told me again to be careful.

I went to the office that had been set up for Delia. She was surrounded by rolls of printouts.

"We're getting somewhere," she said. "I've gotten into most of the personal files." Delia waded through some of the paper. "Just a second," she said. "I've got Greta's here somewhere."

"Great," I said. "How'd you do it?"

"I'm a genius," she said, continuing her search. "Here."

She pulled on part of a long strip of paper with those perforations in the sides and moved it toward me. "Don't rip it. Pull it out and fold it."

"I would never have thought of that," I said. "Do you want me to fold up some of the others so you don't have such a mess?"

"Neatnik strikes again."

Delia knows me. I fold things, straighten things, dust things, line things up with the edges of desks. Compulsive.

"Actually," she said, "I'd like you to fold them up. And would you write in big letters on the top of each one whose file it is? You'll find out whose file it is at the end." She handed me a marker.

While I was putting order into the chaos of Delia's search, Eric came in and invited us over to the farmhouse for lunch.

When he left, I warned Delia about the meals and told her I was going to pass on lunch. I was still feeling the lump in my stomach from the organic French toast and sausages (turkey) that I'd had for breakfast. Not to mention the coffee cake. I know, I know; I didn't have to eat it, but it all looked good.

Delia and Amy went to lunch, and I stayed alone in the office. I figured it would be a good time to go over the files that Delia had unearthed.

I started with Greta's files, in which I recognized the names of the friends that Edith had given me and some names of entertainers that I'd heard on rock music stations. There were also some homework assignments and some short stories that I took to be English homework.

One was about a little girl who lived with adopted parents who hated her and she went to live with a fairy godmother. The parents were "vicious and spanked her all the time."

Another was about an unhappy girl who had to work "night and day until one day a handsome prince came and taught her magic things." Autobiography? I wondered. If it was, where had he taught her the magic things? On the computer or in the barn?

Some of her other stories didn't seem to relate to anything I knew, or thought I knew, about her.

She also had stored in her personal files some records that looked like they belonged in the farm business files.

And then there were little notes about girls she hated for one reason or another and boys she liked and what she liked about them. Some of the things she liked were intimate. I was blushing as I read them. She was obviously no novice when it came to things sexual. Where was I when young girls were getting so knowing?

I had finished giving Greta's file the once-over and had just started going over the other files when the quiet was broken by a loud crash followed by the tinkle of shards of glass raining from the casement.

I gasped and sprang to my feet, looking for the object that had made the gaping hole. The glass scattered on the floor crunched under my feet. Before I found what had come through the window, smoke started filling the room, making my eyes water and stifling my breath, and my only thought was to get out.

The windows were the kind that had a lot of square panes with metal in between them. I didn't know whether I would fit through them, and I didn't want to get cut up. I backed away from the windows and choked my way toward the door as the smoke thickened. As I groped in the direction of the door, I pulled my shirt up over my head. It seemed to take forever, and I worked to tamp down the panic. On reaching the door to the hallway, I pulled down my shirt, but the smoke still blinded me.

I remembered that the hall was blessedly short. Soon I would be outdoors.

Oh, no!

The door wouldn't push open. I fumbled for locks or hasps or sliding bolts, but felt nothing. Something must have been jammed against it. The only other way for me to go was up to Amy's rooms. Maybe the smoke had not penetrated there.

I began groping my way faster toward the stairs, coughing and crying. Thank heaven, the smoke was thinner as I reached the top, and the air was relatively clear once inside the apartment. I leaned against the closed door and took a deep breath. Being able to see made me calmer, but I still had to get out of the building. Where there's smoke, there's fire, was the thought that kept jingling through my brain.

I ran from window to window, looking for the best place to jump, and found one that had a tree growing next to it. That looked better than jumping directly to the ground. As a matter of fact, it looked almost inviting. A sturdy branch seemed to beckon. With the window open all the way, I thought I could sit on the windowsill and practically slide over to the branch.

It wasn't that close when I got out there. I needed to push myself off and hope I got a good hold. I pushed and grabbed, but I didn't end up sitting on the branch as I had planned. Instead, I was hanging from it like a baboon, arms and legs wrapped around the branch, which now was bending from my weight. I realized I was closer to the ground and probably could drop without breaking a leg. I released the scissors hold on the limb and looked down to see what I would land on. Weeds. Good. Just as I was about to drop, I heard a crack and the limb splintered. It broke so gradually that I was let down as if by a gentle hand.

Safe, I thought. But wait a minute. What just happened here? The realization changed my notion of how safe I was. Somebody had thrown a smoke bomb in the window where I was working. That someone could be nearby. I took off for the store, running as if I were in a sprint and going for a record. I didn't look behind me; that would have slowed me down.

There was only one car at the store, and it wasn't a sheriff's car. It was a Land Rover with tinted windows. The door to the store was closed and locked. I rattled the door and screamed. Where the hell were the deputies who were supposed to be watching this place? When the door to the car opened, I was ready to run again.

Then I saw it was Jeff, smiling, his red mustache catching the sunlight. When he got closer to me, he stopped smiling.

"What happened, Ms. Kirk? You look terrible."

I babbled out my story, tears and snot running down my face, which, I didn't know then, was streaked with soot. I pointed toward the office where I'd been working, and Jeff started toward it, shouting, "Is Amy in there?"

"No, no. She's having lunch at the farmhouse," I yelled, and he changed his course.

"Where are the deputies that are on duty?" he said.

"I don't know. I just got here."

"What I mean is, I've been here a half hour and I haven't seen anyone."

"Why don't we find a phone and call the sheriff," I said, remembering that there was a phone in Amy's apartment that I could have used if I hadn't been in such a hurry to jump out the window.

All the doors to the store and the warehouse behind it were locked. Jeff broke one of the panes on a side door with the handle of his pistol.

"This makes me a burglar," he said.

We saw the mess before we got to the phone.

Eight

The sheriff came back to the farm wearing a disgusted expression. His deputies had been stuffing themselves at Edith's table while someone was trashing the farm office and tossing a smoke bomb in the window of the office that had been set up for Delia.

It didn't take a genius to figure that somebody didn't want Delia digging into the computer files. Had that somebody tipped his or her hand and given us all the more reason to dig into the computer files? Or was it a ploy? Or was the somebody stupid? Or desperate?

The first thing I wanted to know was how much damage had been done. Maybe the somebody had, in effect, erased most of the farm data.

Edith almost lost her imperial stance when she saw the ruin of the office and the computer terminals, with the screens bashed in, the syrup poured on the keyboards, and the circuit boards axed.

Heinz said, with an arch of the eyebrow at Edith, "You see, Grasse didn't always have all the answers."

Theodora had not shown up at the store. Edith said she was back at the farmhouse cleaning up the lunch dishes.

Ernest scratched his head and made a move to start cleaning up before the sheriff stopped him.

"We'll see if we can pick up a few prints before we clean up," Sheriff Castle said.

Eric strutted up to the sheriff and said, "You've got to find out who's doing these things."

The sheriff raised his brows so that his copper-colored eyes flashed. "Let's find out where everybody was and when. We'll start with you, young fella," he said to Eric. "Follow me."

Eric's bluster faded, and the young man who followed the sheriff to the car was not the same one who exited the car fifteen minutes later carrying his head down in the fashion of his mother.

Delia and Amy arrived at the store while Eric was in the car. The deputies had not allowed Delia to go into her office, nor would they let Amy go into her apartment.

When Delia saw the mess of the store and heard my story about the smoke bomb, she got a funny look on her face, but she didn't say anything until she pulled me away from the group.

"What happened to the printouts?" she said.

"I don't know. I was going over them when the window broke. I guess they're on the desk where we left them."

"Whoever did this doesn't know what we've got. Those printouts may be all that's left of the system."

"They'll be valuable to the farm, then."

"But we can't let anyone know what we have until we find out what's in there that someone doesn't want us to know about."

I looked admiringly at Delia. "Do you think you got everything?"

Delia smiled. "Just about."

Delia and I cooked up a story about some medicine in my purse that Delia needed. It didn't fool the sheriff, but it seemed to work on everybody else. The sheriff went along with the story and sent me back to Delia's office with Deputy Hank Layton to fetch my purse.

The smoke bomb had left a coating of soot on everything. It had probably ruined this computer, too. My purse was on the desk right next to the printouts, but the printouts were too bulky to fit in the purse, big though it was.

"Hank," I said, after looking into my purse, "I can't find Delia's medicine in here. Would you check the downstairs john to see if I left it in there on the shelf for her, while I go upstairs and check the john up there?"

Hank had no problem with that. I bundled up the armload

of printouts and tucked them into a drawer, then I put some other papers in a pile next to my purse on the desk. Upstairs I found a bottle in Amy's bathroom that looked suitably pharmaceutical.

Hank was at the bottom of the stairs when I came out of the apartment. "No luck," he said.

"Found it," I said cheerfully flashing the bottle at him.

"Good," he said. "Let's get out of here. My wife's gonna complain like hell about the smell of my uniform."

Delia met us as we approached the store, where everyone was standing around waiting for instructions from the sheriff. Heinz was complaining about falling behind in the farmwork.

I gave Delia the medicine bottle and a smile.

She smiled back and pretended to take a pill.

The sheriff couldn't wait to find out what we were up to. I was next to get questioned.

Before he started on me, I jumped in with a question of my own. "What did you say to Eric to bust his bubble?"

"I reminded him about the smoke bomb that was tossed into his class at school a few years back."

"You think he did it?"

"Not if, as he said, he was eating with the others when it happened. But he has friends, and I suspected that he was in on the smoke bomb at school."

"But why would Eric do all this damage?"

"I don't know. Now suppose you tell me what you and Miss Winston are up to."

I told him about the printouts and where I had put them. "Ah," he said. "I think I'd better look at them."

He promised to copy the files and let me have a set. "We'll both go over them and see what we turn up," he said. "I'll have your copies to you this evening. Where will you be staying tonight?"

"In Amy's apartment, I guess."

"Remember what I said about being careful. You could have been hurt this afternoon."

"I don't know what I could have done about it. Besides, it's deceptively peaceful here. I got lulled into thinking this was some kind of Eden, I guess."

"Yesterday a murder. Today a smoke bomb and vandalism. It's no Eden."

I said, "I'll be suspicious of everybody, even the cows."

Suddenly it occurred to me that there was one more computer on the farm, the one in Greta's room. I didn't know how it was hooked up or whether it was hooked up to the computers at the store, but I did know that Greta did some of her farmwork in her room.

When I mentioned Greta's computer to the sheriff, he sent Hank over to Edith's place. Hank's wheels screeched as he left.

A couple more cars with deputies showed up, and the sheriff put them to work in the store. At that point, he had all of us go back to the farmhouse, where he intended to continue his questioning. It seemed that this routine was putting a strain on him, and I was wondering whether he would welcome some help from the troopers about now. There had to be other crimes being committed elsewhere in the county, and the affairs at Hickory Hills were using a lot of manpower.

When we got to the farmhouse, Hank was standing next to his car talking into his radio. The sheriff arrived and went into the Cape Cod where Edith and Heinz lived. The rest of us, the Baeres and Amy, Delia, and I, and the hired hands, were crowded onto the farmhouse porch, where we were told to wait. The deputies were running around but didn't seem to be accomplishing much.

Edith didn't wait for instructions. She left the porch and headed for her house. No one stopped her. Thinking that she had a good idea, I followed her. Sort of like an end picking up blockers on a football field.

Edith stormed in the front door and charged to the back of her house to her kitchen, where some deputies were on the phone. I made a detour and ran up the stairs and got a look into Greta's room, before anyone knew I was in the house. I knew what I would find, but I wanted to look anyway.

Greta's terminal was trashed in much the same way as those at the store. But the store smelled like maple syrup, while Greta's room was emitting far more offensive odors.

I looked at the other side of Greta's room and got another jolt. Someone had left feces in the middle of the lavender quilt, and there were yellow wet spots on the white rug.

Maybe the sheriff was on the right track, I thought. Maybe Eric's cronies were behind this. Some of the circumstances bespoke an excess of hormonal activity, the kind of excess found in young males. But why would Eric want to trash the computer?

I tiptoed down the stairs and could hear Edith still in her kitchen with the deputies. As I walked out the front door, the sheriff came around the side of the house, looking annoyed and something else. Amused, maybe?

"Did you see what you wanted?" he said.

"Not what I wanted, what was there. Nasty. It sure seems to point to Eric's friends, doesn't it?"

"Or someone who wants it to look like Eric's friends. Anyway, Hank got a partial on a pickup truck that was leaving here when he drove up. While everyone was at the store, they were here messing up."

"Didn't Theodora see anyone? Or hear anyone?"

"We haven't found Theodora, yet."

"What do you mean? She went for a walk? She was kidnapped? She was one of the vandals?"

"Could be anyone of those. But we can't find her."

"What does the kitchen look like in the farmhouse?" I said.

"We haven't looked at it yet," he said. "We're coping with the trashing of the room. I've got to get more deputies to go over the room upstairs."

"Are you running out of men?"

"Bingo," he said. "Give that lady a box of candy. Looks like I'm going to have to call in the troopers after all."

"If Theodora doesn't turn up, you'll be able to call in the FBI."

"Great," he said. "I'm looking forward to it."

"Mind if I look at the farm kitchen? I won't mess up any evidence."

"I'd rather send you in than some of what I have to work with," he said. "But you never heard me say that."

I went around the house to the mudroom door and walked in, using a hanky to turn the knob. There was a rather large sneaker tread mark on the mudroom floor that I stepped around, thinking that it might have been made by one of the vandals. When I got down on the floor close enough to sniff at it, I was sure that it was one of them. The tread smelled like the syrup that was poured over the keyboards at the store.

I tried to step only on the throw rugs as I made my way through the mudroom, which adjoined the kitchen. The kitchen sink had dishes in it, likewise the drainboard. The dishwasher was open and half loaded. Some of the food was still on the countertops and in pots on the stove. Nothing was thrown around, but on the kitchen table, there was a cake that looked like it had been mauled.

I took a quick tour through the house, looking for Theodora, but found nothing to indicate that she had been taken or that she wasn't just out for a walk. The beds were all made, and all the rooms were in order except for the kitchen and the dining room, where a few cups and saucers and dessert plates remained. There were no signs of violence or struggle.

Except for that sneaker print, there was nothing to give away what happened to Theodora. But on my way out, I took a closer look at the items in the sink and saw a knife with blood on it, a big knife, probably sharp. A knife with blood on it isn't necessarily cause for alarm in a kitchen where meat is being prepared, but the meal was long over, for one thing, and for another, there wasn't much meat prepared on this farm.

I bent over to take a closer look at the knife and then stooped to look at the floor, where I saw a spot that could have been blood on the rag rug in front of the sink. Those were the only traces of blood I saw.

As I walked through the mudroom, I saw Theodora's sweater, the one she had worn when we were hanging up the laundry. If she had gone for a walk, she would have worn her sweater, I thought. And even if she were miffed at Edith, she wouldn't have gone for a walk with the dishes half done. No. Something wasn't right.

When I told the sheriff what I found, he sent Hank around to hang the police line tape on the mudroom door. Then he bowed to the inevitable and called the state police.

"Drug busts or no, they're going to have to shake loose some personnel to help," he said.

*   *   *

By late afternoon, the place was swarming with cops, in uniform and in plainclothes. I was glad to see that the long arm of equal opportunity had reached into the rural areas, too. Some of the cops were female. One woman, a detective, wore a gray suit, a tailored blouse, and a necktie. Really. She carried a briefcase, too.

Even Edith could not by the force of her will and her strength serve supper as if nothing had happened. Delia, Amy, and I went to the apartment over the still-smoky office. I heard some discussions about where to send the Baeres, because there were cops everywhere collecting evidence. I didn't know until later where they ended up that night.

Apparently Edith did prevail upon the cops to let her get at one of the kitchens, maybe the kitchen that was set up at the back of the warehouse behind the store. Edith showed up at Amy's with plastic containers around suppertime. They bore the plenty that was Edith's trademark. She had whipped up a cold supper, complete with sliced meats and cheese, potato salad, bean salad, green salad, several breads, and juices. Dessert was rhubarb pie. I was grateful for Edith's provender; after all, I had skipped lunch. I ate enough supper to make up for it.

"I have a message for you from Mr. Dresden," Edith said. "I called him to report the damage. He wants another report from you."

"Of course," I said, wondering why I hadn't thought of it myself. "I'll call him."

Since I had seen the damage firsthand, Dresden had me dictate a report. He would send an appraiser out the next day to actually assess the damage, he said, and would call my office if he needed anything else from me.

Delia couldn't resist prompting me to quote my expenses and the hours, including travel, that I had already spent. She was right, and Dresden didn't argue at all. Consequently, I was paid better than I would have been without Delia's coaching. And Delia got some satisfaction out of the fact that Dresden had to reach down deeper into the corporate pockets.

Delia and Amy and I spent the evening going over the copies of the computer printouts that the sheriff, true to his word, had sent to us. Since Amy had been working at Hickory Hills and was familiar with the ordering routine, she was able to tell Delia and me what some of the names meant that appeared on the printouts.

The first thing we had to do was sort out orders from letters, invoices, and address lists. The printouts were dense with type—apparently a paper-saving setup—and, therefore, were hard to read. Amy separated each order and wrote the company names in dark ink in the margins. She separated the other paperwork in much the same way and then alphabetized each pile. A woman after my own heart. I could see why Edith liked her, too.

We worked late. The day sounds—the occasional low of a discomfitted cow, the growl of an engine, the caw of a crow, the clanks and rattles and bumps of the farm machinery—all had stopped.

Before we realized, the sounds of the police and sheriff cars going by had stopped, too. The headlights were no longer flashing by, and darkness and quiet had descended on the farm.

"I wonder if all the cops went home," I said.

"They wouldn't do that, would they, with all that's happened?" Amy said. "I wonder if there's been any word about Theodora."

For several hours we hadn't mentioned Theodora or the vandalism or Ben Grasse. But the darkness and the silence made us uneasy. Talking helped.

"There must be a couple of deputies on duty," I said, walking to a window that looked in the direction of the store. The store wasn't visible from the window, because it was around a bend and behind some trees. I thought maybe some light would be visible. "I can't see anything."

"I'll turn out the lights. You should be able to see the night-light at the store," Amy said. "There's a streetlamp right on the bend in the road; you ought to be able to see that, too." She turned off the lights and came over to the window.

"I guess I'll look, too," Delia said. "I can't work with no lights."

Amy and I laughed. We hadn't realized that Delia was still poring over the papers.

The three of us were staring into the inky night. No stars, no moon. I thought about being a kid and searching the sky for stars, for airplanes, for Santa Claus, for angels, for a good fairy that would make my dreams come true. It was always the cloudy nights that made me unhappy. Not even a star to wish on.

"I can't see any light at all," Amy whispered. "It's pitch-black out there."

"Why are you whispering?" I whispered.

"I'm scared," Amy said.

"I'm wondering why the lights are off," Delia said. "Are there any other lights that are usually on that you can see from here?" she said to Amy.

"You can see the lights from the family houses through the trees," she said. "And down the hill, you can see the light at the entrance. And there are lights over by the barns that flicker through the trees, too."

Amy went from window to window.

"I can't see any light at all." Her voice was shaking.

"Well, we have light," Delia said. "Turn them back on."

I heard the click, then another, then a little gasp.

"Let me try the bathroom," Amy said. More clicks and no results.

"Shit," Delia said. "This damn place is spooky."

"Where are the cops? What's going on?" Amy's voice.

"I have a flashlight," I said. "I just have to find my purse."

"I have some candles," Amy said.

Something went bump. "Damn, damn, damn." Amy again.

"Did you hurt yourself?" Delia said.

"My shin," Amy said. "Kicked into the table leg."

I was groping around for my purse when I touched something. It was Delia. We both shrieked.

"What's the matter?" Amy sounded frightened.

Delia explained, and I continued to grope.

Just as my hand found something that felt like my purse, footsteps sounded on the stairs.

"Lock the door," I whispered.

There was another bump and a curse, then the sound of a bolt sliding.

More footfalls continued up the stairs.

We said nothing. I know I was hunched over, trying to make myself small. I remember doing that when Dick hit me.

Every time I get afraid, I think of him.

Finally the footsteps were outside the apartment door. A few seconds of silence were followed by one loud thump.

"Oh, my God," Amy whispered. "Somebody's right outside the door."

"Who's there?" Delia said. Her tone was commanding. She had more guts than I had at that moment.

I was rooting in my purse for my flashlight. "Found it."

"Let's get him," Delia said as I turned on the flashlight. Rapid footsteps retreated.

"Get ready to fight," I said. "I'm opening the door." I didn't really mean that. I was trying to sound as tough as Delia. I was convinced that whoever it was was gone, anyway.

Amy opened the door and stood back as the door swung in. The hallway was empty, but there was a piece of paper stuck to the door. Delia grabbed it.

"Don't," I said, too late. "Fingerprints."

Delia dropped the paper, which landed upside down. When we finally read it, being careful not to obscure any more fingerprints and also after having relocked the door, it said: MIND YOUR OWN BUSINESS. GO HOME. OR ELSE.

"I'm going to call the sheriff," I said, but when I picked up the phone, Amy's line was dead. "No dial tone," I said.

"Oh, my God," Amy said for the second time. This time her voice was verging on a sob.

She wasn't the only one who was scared. If Amy hadn't been there to do the crying, I would have been doing it. My heart was pounding so hard I could hardly think.

"We've got to get out of here and call the sheriff," I said, thinking that it was a lousy idea. "Who knows if that creep will come back. Who knows if there's one or more creeps. We can sneak around in the dark as well as they can."

"We don't have to go anywhere," Delia said in a tone that only Delia can produce. A tone that said, Guess what I have up my sleeve.

She didn't have anything up her sleeve, but in her pocketbook she had a cellular phone. At that moment, she could have converted me to her passion for electronic gadgets.

"Delia, you're terrific," I said and meant it.

The sheriff arrived within ten minutes, by the end of which

power and phone service had been restored. The situation didn't even seem threatening when he arrived.

He listened carefully to us, asking us what time the lights had gone out, when we'd noticed the phone was dead, what the footsteps on the stairs had sounded like. Then he took the threatening note. We had put it in a plastic bag; I told him Delia's prints would be on it.

Then the sheriff told us what no one else had bothered to tell us: that Theodora had arrived home around supper time wearing a bandage on her right hand where she had gashed it trying to catch a knife that she dropped.

"Where was she all those hours?" Amy said.

"Why didn't she call?" I said.

"Hiram Cody, one of Eric's friends, took Theodora to the emergency room," the sheriff said. "I guess she expected him to call."

"Is that who was in the pickup truck that we saw speeding away? Hiram and Theodora?" Amy said.

"Yes," the sheriff said. "He was one of the boys on my suspect list for throwing that smoke bomb."

"And now he's not?" I said.

"Hmm, I didn't say that, but it seems less likely that he did it. You see, Hiram had seen the mess in the store and gone to the farmhouse to tell the Baeres."

"That's what he said? But why didn't we see him?" I said.

"He said he had stopped at the store to use the toilet and had gone inside a ways before he realized that maybe it was a good idea not to go any further. He went to the barns, he said, thinking that everybody would be working.

"When he didn't find anyone, he drove cross lots coming out by this place intending to use the toilet here. When he saw the smoke pouring out of the window, he headed for the farmhouse, to tell everybody what happened and to use the toilet.

"When he got to the farmhouse, Theodora came out of the kitchen into the back room holding bloody towels around her hand. So he raced her to the emergency room."

"When did he finally get to use the toilet?" Delia said.

The sheriff chuckled. "I didn't ask, but the rest of the story checks out."

I went through the string of events in my head and thought

that it sounded plausible. "Did someone question him?" I wanted to know whether one of the deputies had led him along or whether this was the story Hiram told without knowing what bases he'd have to cover.

"No. The story came bubbling out as soon as we started to talk to him. Seems he was worried about not telling the rest of the family about the vandalism before he left the farm. I think the kid needed a tranquilizer, he was that wound up when he brought Theodora home."

"Why didn't he call someone from the hospital," Delia said.

"Probably because he's a kid," Sheriff Castle said. "I don't think we have to worry any more about young Hi."

The sheriff was starting to worry me. He had his way of deciding who was a good guy and who was a bad guy. It made me wonder whether he was missing something. The kid could have made the whole mess and then done all the things he had told the sheriff he'd done. Nobody had asked him, apparently, what he had been doing before he supposedly saw the mess in the store for the first time.

"So the pickup truck Hank saw was Hiram speeding off with Theodora," I said.

The sheriff nodded.

"And the troopers left here because Theodora returned home and there was no kidnapping."

Another nod.

"So, where were the deputies that you were going to leave here all night?" I was miffed about the farm being unguarded.

The sheriff looked abashed. "Changing shifts at headquarters," he said. "They leave their own vehicles there. I feel bad about that. I'll work out some other way to change the shifts even if I have to cover the place myself."

I took a deep breath. The whole picture made me feel ill at ease. Somebody who knew the deputies were changing shifts had turned off the lights and the phones and put that note on the door. "So who do you think left us this note?" I said.

"Someone who wants you gone," the sheriff said.

"Have you got any idea who that might be?"

"More than likely, the same person who's behind the

wrecking of the computers.'' Sheriff Dick Castle wasn't giving anything away.

"In that case," I said, "maybe Delia and Amy and I ought to leave."

"But what about Greg?" Amy said. "Suppose he's in Buffalo."

"You can stay with me," I said. "And we can go to the group meeting tomorrow night. And Delia and I can go over the printouts and see what we can dig out of them."

"Be careful of those printouts," the sheriff said.

I didn't like what I heard in his voice and dreaded what he would say next.

"The originals," he said, "they're gone."

"From where?"

"My car."

"Your car? Jesus." I shut my mouth before I started saying what I thought. What I thought was that the sheriff was doing what he could with the resources he had. I was comfortable with that notion, but not with the position I was in because of it.

"I have an idea how and who. And when," he said. "But I figure that they were destroyed before I discovered they were gone. So I didn't say anything about them to anyone but you."

"Care to tell us who your suspect is?"

"Not right now," he said. "I don't think you have to worry. I don't think anyone knows about the copies."

"You don't think?"

"I had the department secretary make them in the county building. Someone might have seen her. It's possible word would get around. Someone might put two and two together."

"We'll make another copy," Delia said, "and put it on your bill."

Even though it was two in the morning, I insisted that we three leave. "We'll be able to see if anyone's following us," I said.

"And we won't go home," Delia said. "We'll take a motel room and put it on your bill, Sheriff."

The sheriff didn't say word one about that.

We packed quickly and left in the dark. Amy rode with

Delia and I followed them. The sheriff escorted us to the county line.

I would call Edith tomorrow and let her know what I was doing. I could go over the printouts of Greta's files carefully, and I could do that without being on the farm. It occurred to me that the computer that was destroyed in Greta's room could have contained data that wouldn't be in the printouts, and I was harboring the hope that Greta had backup disks somewhere. If I could find Greta, I could clear up a lot, I thought.

I had not yet decided when to return to the farm. The sheriff had enough to do without the added burden of guarding us. Maybe he would be able to ferret out some information to put him on the trail of whoever was behind events on the farm. Maybe it was more than one person. Maybe Grasse's death had nothing to do with Greta's disappearance. Maybe the computer wrecking had nothing to do with either. But who on earth took the original printouts from the sheriff's car? Whoever it was must have nerves of steel, I thought. Or be desperate. Or . . . what?

Nine

Delia led the way to a motel near the airport in Cheek-towaga, a busy place with people coming and going at all hours, and better yet, she informed me, a place that had its own private police force.

"Good work, Delia," Amy said. "Maybe we'll get some sleep."

We did. Until about ten in the morning when the maid knocked on the door.

"Should have put the DO NOT DISTURB sign out," Delia said and rolled over.

I got up and ate breakfast alone, leaving Delia and Amy peacefully somnolent in the darkened room—with the DO NOT DISTURB sign in place.

A phone in the lobby was my next stop. I had obligations, after all, not the least of these being a call to Ted, but I saved him for last anyway. I didn't go into my motives for putting it off.

Natasha was in the office taking the calls from the lovesick, the lusty, and the lonely. She ran the dating service, which was sort of bequeathed to me by the fellow who used to rent the office. The dating service wasn't my favorite kind of business, but the women who were the "dates" couldn't run it themselves. They begged me to run it when their old boss left town.

At the time, Natasha, another member of the battered women's group, was out of work, having quit her job to stay out of the clutches of her ex-boyfriend, who had almost killed her the last time she saw him. She had also given up an apartment that she loved. But she loved life better.

Natasha got along well with the dating service women, who all lived in a house on Ashland Avenue in Buffalo. I hasten to assure you that it was not a whorehouse, although the women themselves were not averse to bedding down their "dates." All the dates were elsewhere, no clients entered the house. That setup seemed to skirt (no pun intended) the law sufficiently so that the Buffalo police did not think it worth their while to pursue the gathering of evidence that might land one or more of the women in jail.

The women, themselves, were not what you might think. Several of them were graduate students, working their way through college, you might say.

Natasha told me that the office was running fine without me and gave me my messages, two from Ted, one from the appraiser at Sunset, and one from Polly, the leader of the battered women's group, who wouldn't arrive at the meeting until 8:30 instead of the usual 8:00 P.M.

"Do you have any messages for Delia? She's here with me. She's working for the Wyoming County sheriff."

"There's a bunch for Delia. I'm going to fax them to her house."

"What? Does she have a fax at home now, too?" I told Natasha about the office phone ringing at Delia's place.

"I knew she was thinking of doing that," Natasha said. "I told her to keep her mitts off the dating service."

"Good for you. I guess I'd better learn to tell Delia what I want and don't want."

"It ain't hard, honey."

"That's easy for you to say."

"You got to learn the magic word."

"Yeah? What's that?"

"No."

"It takes more than that to stop Delia." I was beginning to feel cranky, probably because Natasha was right.

Natasha, always sensitive to people's moods, backed off. "Yeah, Fran, Delia's tough."

"Sorry," I said. "I'll tell Delia about the messages."

We spent a few minutes more on business before I told her about the happenings at Hickory Hills.

"Do you think there's anything to worry about here at the office?" she said.

"It wouldn't hurt to take a few precautions," I said, "at least until we find out who's after the printouts. And we don't think anybody who might want them knows about the copies."

"I'll keep the office door locked, and I'll leave before the folks downstairs do." The office is upstairs from a beauty parlor called Looks, in a neighborhood that shuts down after business hours.

"Good plan," I said.

"Shall I tell Ted that you called? He's pretty persistent. He's called several times without telling me his name or leaving a message. I recognized his voice."

"No. I'll call him. Tell him you haven't heard from me. He'd like to think he's the first one I'd call."

"Hmmm," she said. It was full of meaning.

"Are you coming to the meeting tonight?" I asked, which was as good a segue as any.

"Yes," she said. "We'll have a full house. There'll be Amy, you, me, Minnie, Diane, Brenda, and a new member. That's why Polly's going to be late. She's picking up the new one."

Before I hung up, I gave her our motel room phone number and told her, although it wasn't necessary to tell her, not to let anyone else know where we were.

"You be careful," she said. "See you tonight."

I tried to get Ted at home and at work and left messages both places. I was relieved not to have to talk to him. But I still didn't examine what I was feeling and why.

The motel wasn't that far from my house on Maple Street in Cheektowaga. It was tempting to go over, get some clothes, and check on things, and it probably was safe. But so many weird things had happened out at the farm, I felt insecure about who might be watching me or following me. So I called Mrs. Klune, my paperboy's mother, just to check on Horace.

"He's here right now. Wally brought him over this morning. He's been chasing the cat all over the house, having a wonderful time."

I felt guilty about all the time I left Horace alone and was glad he was having fun, but also jealous about having his affections stolen from me. "Thanks for taking such good care of him," I said without a trace of irony. "I'm not coming home just yet. Can you look out for him another day or three?"

"Sure. He's a nice dog."

I went back to the room, and it was wide open and Amy and Delia were gone. I felt a catch in my throat in the instant that it took me to realize that the maid was inside cleaning the room. When I went in, I found the maid scrubbing out the tub.

"Don't you think you should close the door when you're not watching the room?" I said.

"Didn't you check out?" she said.

"No. Can't you see there are things all over the room that belong to us?"

"People leave stuff all the time. I didn't check the drawers and closets yet." She was offhand, obviously not as worried as I was about someone who might be after the printouts, which were stacked in plain sight on the table by the window.

"I'm going to wait until you're done," I said. "I don't like the door open with our stuff in here." Snotty. I admit it.

She did a half-assed job on the beds. Served me right. And she was out of there in five minutes flat.

After she left, I carefully hid the printouts, a few here, a few there. Then I straightened out the beds and hung up the clothes that were lying around, most of them looked like Delia's. She must have packed for a week.

I was about to call Edith when Delia came in. "I forgot my wallet," she said. "I hid it and then didn't put it back in my purse."

"Why did you hide it? You were right in the room."

"Didn't you tell me that a couple of the women in the group were light-fingered? I was afraid one of them was Amy."

"Oh, there were two that we suspected. But Amy wasn't one of them," I lied. But Amy had recovered from that part of her life, I told myself. And I believed it.

"That's a relief." She dug the wallet out of the toe of a running shoe.

"If I were a thief, I would have looked there."

"Well you're not a thief. And all the thieves I know would never look there." Delia did not lack assertiveness.

I told her about the messages at the office.

"I talked to Nat," she said.

"You know Natasha hates to be called that." I wasn't going to lecture Delia, but she needed reminding sometimes. I picked up the phone.

"Who are you calling?" Delia said.

"Edith," I said. "I have to let her know I'm still working."

"Don't call her from here."

I put the phone down. "Why, for goodness sakes."

"They have a caller identification system. You don't want her to know where you are, do you?"

"Damn. I didn't know that. I almost called before."

"So did Amy. I told her to have Nat-ash-a call Edith." She said the syllables slowly.

"I'd better do the same. Thanks for telling me."

When breakfast and all the phone calls were finally made, we started work on the printouts. I worked on Greta's at first while Delia and Amy sorted out the huge pile of business files. There was little duplication in the printouts of the material I'd seen in Greta's terminal. But the sort of material was the same: names and addresses, musical groups, homework assignments, but not the same ones. It occurred to me that when she was working in the office, she did some of her work and when she was in her room, she did some more. But why different musical groups at home and in the office?

I looked at the names of the groups again. These were country and Western groups, not the heavy metal and punk stuff that she had listed at home.

Of course! In her grandmother's house she had a modicum of privacy. No older brother. No mother and father lurking. Maybe at Edith's she felt she could let go. After all, Edith and Heinz were novices on the computer, and by Edith's account, Greta and Eric were whizzes.

I wished now I had a printout of Greta's files from her room—or her backup disks.

When I couldn't glean anything more from Greta's papers,

I joined Delia and Amy in their search through the business files. It was boring work, but Amy made it seem less so, because she knew what the orders meant, had heard about some of the places that Hickory Hills ordered from, including some Asian monks who grew organic berries and dried them, and some small farmers who were eccentric as hell. One, Amy said, couldn't be contacted when he was sitting in his yard under his pyramid, and another wouldn't do business unless her astrologer told her it was the right day. With Amy's stories and all the odd names—Jim's Jersey Moo, manufacturer of organic cheeses; Ho Ho Ho Organic Farms; We Dig You Potatoes; Paws and Jaws Lotions—we almost enjoyed ourselves.

Hickory Hills carried a full line of organic foods, but they didn't raise all of the things they sold out of their mail order catalogue or the store. There was a huge file of certificates and documents of all kinds, Amy said, attesting to the purity and nonlethal qualities of the products they bought from others.

I was sure that Edith took care of quality control on the farm.

I was checking an order from a company called California Arbor Naturals for almonds and dried fruits when I remembered having seen the name before. Greta had a copy of the order in her personal files that I had seen on Monday.

I mentioned it to Delia.

"Why would she have that in her files? Did she have a lot of other business stuff in her personal files?"

"Not a lot. But some. Let's go through the paperwork and see what else we find with California Arbor Naturals on it."

We found about a year's worth of orders, but we couldn't find anything wrong with them. Amy remembered the name, said she thought she remembered seeing the organic certification in the file.

"What does this *E* mean?" I asked Amy. Each order had a letter code at the top left. The California Arbor Naturals orders all had an *E* on them.

"That means Eric handled the orders. They're trying to give him more responsibility, so he has certain companies that are his clients."

"Maybe the little shit is getting kickbacks," Delia said.

"I didn't react too positively to him, either," Amy said.

"But I don't know whether he would steal money from his family."

"Well, that makes three of us who are not fans of Eric the brat. Maybe Greta didn't like him either."

"No, they didn't get along," Amy said, "at all. They were always sniping at each other at dinner."

"Let me guess," I said. "Greta would be the one who would be told to shut up."

Amy's eyes shot wide, "Why, yes. Yes, that did happen quite a lot."

"I don't know why they think the sun rises and sets on Eric," I said.

"Primogeniture," Delia said.

I hadn't heard that word since elementary school. "If that's the reason," I said, "then that is where the sun rises and sets. What did Greta do when they gave her short shrift?"

Amy was deep in thought. "Come to think of it," she said, "I'm not surprised that Greta took off. The warning signs were there."

Delia and I said nothing. Amy had more.

"She got all the discipline. He got all the praise. They were delighted with his work. He's the one who signed up California Arbor Naturals. You know, the way they were with him, I kept thinking about how my family treated my brother."

I could see the pain in her face. An old wound was the worst.

"But you didn't run away," Delia said.

"No. I got married. The first day I no longer needed permission. My eighteenth birthday."

"I bet your folks were surprised," I said.

Amy smiled wistfully. "They were."

"Well, the Baeres can't figure out why Greta took off," Delia said.

An idea popped into my head that seemed so right. "Thanks, Amy," I said. "I think I know where Greta went."

"You do? Where?"

"I hope you don't mind, but I don't want to say anything yet."

"No, I don't mind," she said. She did; I could see it in her face.

The phone rang, and we all jumped. It was Natasha, which we should have been able to guess. The sheriff had called and told Natasha that the printouts had turned up. Someone had taken them by mistake, he'd said.

"What a cock-and-bull story that is," Delia said.

"Cock-and-bull story?" Amy said. "What's a cock-and-bull story?"

"Just an expression," Delia said. "My dad used to say that whenever he didn't believe something. I thought it was appropriate for the farm."

"I never heard that before," Amy said. "Cock-and-bull story. I wonder where that expression came from."

Ignoring Amy's foray into the history of language, I said, "I think you're right, Delia. What I'd like to know is why the sheriff thought he had to tell it."

"Maybe he wants you to call him," Delia said. "Maybe he knows that you won't believe it."

"What is this game? Are we bidding at bridge, saying one thing and meaning another?"

Delia shrugged.

"You don't trust the sheriff either?" Amy said. The "either" referred to my reluctance to tell her where I thought Greta was.

"It's not a matter of trust," I said. "I'm just trying to figure out what to do next. Do I call him? Have Natasha call him? Is he trying to tell us that we don't have to take precautions anymore? I have a lot of questions, Amy."

"Why don't you call your cop friend and have him escort us to the office?" Delia said. "We can call the sheriff from there. Then, if you're satisfied, we can all go home."

"Good idea," I said. "I'll call Ted from here." The reason it was such a good idea was that I would be including Ted in my job; he liked the private eye routine. Also, it would show how much I needed him. He needed to be needed; I knew that much about him.

"I'm not going home," Amy said.

"No, of course not," I said. "You'll stay with me until we go back to the farm."

"Greg knows where you live. He knows where the group meets. I'm not sure—"

"What do you want to do?" I said, realizing that Amy might be in danger and feeling guilty that I hadn't been keeping her welfare in mind. "Do you want to go out of town? Would you be interested in wearing a disguise?"

Amy smiled. "Yes. That's it. Then I'll be able to stay with you. What kind of disguise?"

"I've got a few things in my car," I said. "I'll get them after I call Ted." I headed for the door. I always have extra outfits in the car, mostly to change the way I look. This trip I was using them to change my clothes. The jeans I had started with on Sunday were getting stiff.

"You can call him from here," Delia said, her face plastered with undisguised curiosity.

I was what, for me, passes for cool. "I'm expecting to have an argument. I'd rather do it in private."

"Do you think he'll come and get us?" Delia said.

"Yes, I think he will, after I make up an excuse for ignoring him for almost two days."

"Jeez," Delia said, "don't let the guy run your life."

"I can use some lessons in that area," I said, and left.

Ten

I got hold of Ted at the precinct, where he and his partner, Roland, were finishing up the paperwork on an arrest they had made earlier. I could tell from his voice he was glad to hear from me. When he sounded like that, all I could think of was that sweet smile of his and the tender things he could do to make me forget my misgivings about the male side of life's dramatis personae.

I don't know why I had been so reluctant to call him. Probably it was something weird about me, rather than something he had done to make me feel that way. Maybe I would bring it up tonight at the group meeting. Maybe.

As I thought, he was happy to be asked to take Delia and Amy and me to the office. He asked a lot of questions about what had happened at the farm and the way the various cops had conducted themselves.

Basically, he agreed with Delia that the sheriff's message was a cock-and-bull story, but he called it horsefeathers, going Delia one better in the metaphor department.

"I don't blame you for getting out of there, Fran. Too many things coming at you from too many angles."

I asked if he had seen the all-points bulletin on Greg, and he said he hadn't. Ted knew about Amy and Greg from what I had told him, but he'd never met Greg. Still, he ventured an opinion that Greg was not the guy who killed Ben Grasse. "Sounds like a different kind of guy. The kind who gets loaded and lands in a county jail after he has been looking for his wife is not the kind who runs a pitchfork through somebody's heart and then moves the body to make it look like an accident." He shook his head. "Not the same at all. Forget about Greg. Tell Amy not to worry."

"You tell her," I said. "She's got reason to be scared."

"I'll look up that APB," he said, and I had to admit, if not audibly, that he had backed out of that confrontation in style.

We arranged for him to pick us up right after his shift that afternoon. "Mind if Roland comes along?" he said.

"Not at all. Two for the price of one. Maybe we can all go for pizza."

"Great."

I wondered why he wanted to bring Roland. When I mentioned that to Delia, she had the answer: "He didn't want to be outnumbered."

That made sense, but it never occurred to me. "I guess there's a lot I don't understand about men."

"What's to understand? Flatter them, feed them, fuck them."

Amy and I both laughed. I knew one of us would tell the group. And I knew Polly would use it to launch a lesson. I knew, too, that Polly would say that conclusions like that about the other gender would only serve to isolate us from it.

By the time Ted and Roland got to the motel to pick us up, Delia and I had Amy looking like she was ready to collect Social Security. My trusty gray wig over her beautiful blond hair immediately took the life out of her face. A few dark circles and lines on her face and she could have been my mother. I also had a coat that I lent her that looked like something my mother wore when I was a kid. The weather was a little too warm for the coat, but Amy said she didn't mind.

Delia did a great job on the facial makeup. I had to get right up close to see that the lines were makeup and not wrinkles. And when Amy started walking hunched over like Theodora Baere, Delia and I applauded.

"Have you considered a career in the theater?" Delia said. "I mean it. You actually tranformed yourself with that walk."

"I don't know anything about acting," Amy said.

"I'll let you know the next time I hear about auditions. You ought to try it."

The look on Amy's face was like Miss America when she hears the name of the first runner-up and she knows she's the one. The best moment came, though, when we met Ted and Roland in the lobby.

Ted said, ''Where's Amy?'' and he was looking right at her.

When we got to the office, it took Natasha about ten seconds to recognize her. ''Amy, my God, is that really you?' she said. ''Are you going to wear that tonight?''

Amy said she was, because Greg knew about the Tuesday meetings. But she didn't feel so good about the disguise that she wanted to go out for pizza in it. No amount of coaxing would change her mind, so we agreed to eat in the office. Ted and Roland went to get the pizza.

I caught Sheriff Castle at his desk in the county hall.

''I knew you'd call,'' he said. ''I'm glad you did.''

''What's with the printouts?''

He cleared his throat. ''Well, you have to understand the relationships . . .''

I cleared my throat. ''Do you have them now?'' I said. ''All of them?''

''I have them, but I have no way of telling if they're all here.''

''What about the secretary? How many copies did she make? Can you tell anything from that?''

''I did ask her. She didn't keep track.''

Well, at least he had asked her.

''So, who took them?''

''Hank.''

Good old Hank, I thought, friend of the family. ''Don't tell me. He told Edith and Edith asked him to get them for her.''

''You're pretty good.''

''So now the secret's out, and whoever wanted to destroy the computer data can probably figure out that copies were made.''

Then I told him about the California Arbor Naturals file that Greta had with her personal data and about my theory that Greta had backup disks somewhere. ''Is the computer system ruined?''

''We have someone working on it,'' he said. ''We may be

able to salvage some of the records. Seems there was a backup system that Heinz insisted on, but he didn't tell anyone, because he was ashamed to be such a technophobe." Tech-no-phobe is the way he said it. "Trouble is that Grasse was always late on Heinz's backup files, and he didn't make back-ups of everything."

"Now Heinz is gloating, no doubt."

"You might say that," the sheriff said. "When are you coming back this way? Now that everybody is watching everybody else, you ought to be fairly safe out here."

"Amy is still uneasy. Do you have any word about her husband's whereabouts?"

I heard papers shuffling. "They found his car," he said. "Impounded it."

"Where?"

"Erie, Pennsylvania."

"They found Greg's car in Erie," I told Amy.

"His cousin lives there," she said. I gave her the phone, and she told the sheriff everything she could remember about the cousin, including the fact that he had been in jail for assault and robbery.

Natasha and Delia and I exchanged looks, complete with rolling eyes and shaking heads.

When Amy was done, I arranged with the sheriff to go back to the farm the next day. I wanted to probe around in Greta's things to see if my theory about where Greta might be would hold up.

I didn't know what Delia and Amy wanted to do. Both of them talked to the sheriff, voicing their misgivings about coming back.

He came up with a plan to leave a man with each of us at all times. Delia could work for Edith and Heinz and try to reconstruct all the records on the new hardware that Sunset had paid for. The Baeres had hired some inputters, too, he said, and all the computer people would be working in one building. Amy, on the other hand, could do her usual chores, working alongside Edith.

Delia agreed. Amy said she'd go along, but she was half-hearted.

When Ted and Roland came back with the pizzas, neither

one of them was impressed with the sheriff's plan.

"He's let too many things get by him," Ted said. "And you told me yourself that he wasn't too thrilled with some of the guys he has working for him."

"Suppose he puts one of his duds on duty to guard you," Roland said. Roland was a pudgy carrot top with freckles who looked as innocent as a choirboy. He was anything but naive. "There's a lot falling between the cracks out there," he said. "We never got the APB on Amy's husband. The state police got it, and the FBI got it, but not the Buffalo police. At least, not until I asked about it."

"So how come they found his car in Pennsylvania?" I said.

Ted shrugged. "Go figure."

Amy was eating pizza and getting younger by the minute. Every time she wiped some oil or tomato off her face, she took off a couple of years on her napkin. "I still don't know whether to go back there. If I knew where Greg was, I'd feel safer." She rubbed off another year from around her mouth. "Do you mind if I call Edith?"

I shook my head, and Amy dropped the pizza crust in the pile and went to another desk to make her call.

It was obvious that Edith was trying to persuade her to come back. Amy held back and repeated her misgivings several times. Finally something was said that lifted the cloud on her brow, and she was smiling as she finished the conversation.

"Edith wants me to come back whenever I feel like it." Then she added, "She knows about me and Ben. She said that if someone hadn't already killed him, she would have done it when she heard he took me in with his sweet talk." Amy's smile was broad.

Amy found the mother she always wanted, I thought.

"So when are you going back?" Delia said.

"Tomorrow," Amy said. She turned her face toward Roland, then, and asked, "Could you take me to my apartment? Now that I'm here, I'd like to get more clothes and curlers and stuff like that. It's not far."

"We could all go, Amy. We have time before the meeting. Then if Greg is there with his criminal cousin, we'll have strength in numbers," I said.

"Not me," Delia said. "I have some business to do. I'll stay here."

Roland and Ted decided that they both would go, but they didn't want either Delia or me to go along.

"Fix up her disguise again," Roland said. He picked up Amy's napkin and held it up. "Unless you can rub this back on."

While Roland and Ted and Amy were gone, Delia went at the phone with gusto. She had a list that she was checking things off. I think she sold a couple of policies.

I called the Sunset appraiser, who was at his desk, having just returned from Hickory Hills. I gave him some information about the farm and the vandalism. Then I availed myself of Sunset's voice mail to bring my bill up to date. I would send a paper copy, too, just in case.

When Amy returned, much sooner than I expected, she was livid. "He's given up the apartment. Somebody else is living there. I don't know where my things are." She waved her arms around and brought her hands to rest on her hips, looking more pugnacious than I'd ever seen her. "That bastard. That fungus."

Roland smiled wryly. "She's been saying things like that for the last twenty minutes."

"And worse," Ted added.

We all tried to calm her down, reminding her of the state she was in when she left.

Finally, I said, "Amy, let's talk about this tonight with Polly."

"She won't know how to get my stuff. She'll just tell me how I'm supposed to get my mind in shape so I won't care that all the stuff is gone."

Amy looked very funny to me just then when she said that, standing there in her old lady outfit with her hands on her hips.

Apparently, Roland thought the same thing, because his next words were, "What does an old lady like you want with curlers, anyway?"

I began to giggle. I couldn't hold it in. One by one the others joined in until Amy's grim face started to soften and she laughed.

We all laughed. She laughed and laughed until she cried. I recognized the emotional roller coaster she had been riding the last few hours. I could barely contain my own tears.

Ted, Roland, and Delia waited for us in Ted's Jeep while Amy and Natasha and I went to the group meeting. Ted and Roland decided that to be on the safe side we should stay in the motel another night. Delia had her portable phone and continued to do her business as we rode and, I assume, as she waited with Ted and Roland. She had it on her ear when Amy and I went into the meeting and when we came back out.

Everybody was happy to see Amy since she hadn't been to a meeting in a couple of months. They all knew what she was doing because Polly kept in touch. Amy and I had enough to tell to keep the meeting going, but we weren't the only needy ones that night. The planets must have been in a bad configuration for marital felicity, because every woman there was grim faced.

"Maybe we need an extra meeting sometime soon," I said. "We could do one of those Saturday picnic meetings."

"Why don't they all come out to Hickory Hills?" Amy said. "We could hire Edith to make the picnic."

She told the others about Edith's meals and assured us that Edith regularly had group picnics out at the farm on weekends. I held back; I didn't think we should go there. The others, I think, caught my reluctance.

When Polly arrived, she had a very young, very small woman in tow. Her name was Teresa. Her face was bruised and cut, and she walked with a limp and carried one arm close to her body. She spoke little, and when she did, her words were heavy with a Latino accent. Polly spoke to her in Spanish, another skill Polly had that she hadn't ballyhooed. The conversation took forever because Teresa didn't understand much of what we said.

She had been beaten by her husband's brother and her husband did not defend her, she told Polly in a combination of Spanish and very elemental English. The beating had started when she put on lipstick to go out to her job in the morning. Nothing she said would make him stop.

We told her what Polly expected us to tell her, but since she didn't understand us, all the words came from Polly and

I wasn't sure they had the same weight as they would have had if she had heard each of us telling her that she had to get out of there, that she had to call the police, that the beating would get worse.

She said something about her family, which Polly translated to us. "Her family likes her husband."

"Teresa, the family is not getting beat up."

"The family's life is not in danger."

"Think of yourself first, Teresa."

We all said variations of the same thing. Polly translated.

Teresa looked skeptical.

"I think she has a double problem," I said. "She has the problem we all have, plus she is in a foreign place and she doesn't know people, doesn't have family, and doesn't know the rules here."

Natasha, simpatico as he was, got up and went over to Teresa and hugged her. There were tears in Natasha's eyes when she said, "I know, Teresa, I never felt at home anywhere."

I think we all felt the truth of that. Natasha was half black and half Thai, an orphan of the wars in Southeast Asia.

Teresa broke down and cried on Natasha's shoulder while the rest of us joined in the group grope. There were no dry eyes.

We all knew what it was like to feel that there was no place to turn, when we couldn't take the step even to save our lives, because to face up to the insult meant to lose the security of the situation we were in, however rotten it was.

My mind shifted at that juncture to Greta, and I tried to imagine what she felt, what she might do, where she might go. I hoped I would find a few more answers in her room with the split personality.

Hadn't I heard that abused children sometimes split off a part of themselves into another personality or into denial so great that they forget the abuse? Could it be that Greta, apparently a child of plenty, was a victim of abuse? Why should she leave? She had her own truck, an idyllic place to live, a healthy place, a family place.

But her mother talked about her bitterly, and her grandfather thought her spoiled. Her brother was too busy with his own inflated ego to do anything but lord it over her. Her only ally was Edith, and Edith, though well meaning, was a smothering presence. And what about her father?

I resolved to try to talk to Ernest about his daughter.

At the end of the meeting, Amy again brought up the subject of a Saturday picnic at Hickory Hills.

"I hate to douse the idea with cold water," Polly said, "but I don't want to go there. Not now. It's too soon."

Amy clung to the idea. "It's such a lovely place. It's been there for years and nothing like that has happened before."

"I'd love to go another time," Polly said. "I'm sure it is beautiful, and I love the kinds of foods they raise and their commitment to not polluting the earth." Polly was laying it on kind of thick, I thought, but she was trying to ease Amy's disappointment. Polly would not go to the farm; I could see that.

"If we want to go out into the country a ways," said Brenda, who worked for the phone company, "we could go to Sprague Brook Park, out near the ski areas." Brenda and her husband fought physically when they got drunk. They'd been in counseling together for several months.

"I've been there," Natasha said. "It's a terrific place."

Amy brightened, and so did Polly. None of us liked confrontation.

"We could still have Edith pack the meal," I said. "She does a bang-up job with food."

Amy smiled broadly.

"Done," Polly said. "I'm buying."

"Edith wouldn't charge me," Amy said.

Polly, for some reason, didn't want that either. "Let's keep it businesslike," she said. "If you tell her that you're getting it for an acquaintance, she won't feel obliged to furnish it gratis."

Amy let it go with a shrug, which I thought was a nice exercise in restraint for Amy. I don't know whether I would have been able to let go of it as easily.

Later, everybody put in their two cents about when to have the picnic, and the decision was made to have it a week from the coming Saturday.

On the way out, as we formed conversational knots, I got

Polly to myself for a few seconds and asked her what she thought about Amy and Hickory Hills.

"I think," Polly said, "that Amy is being swallowed up by that Edith person. It would be easy for Amy to go from one dependent situation to another."

"Oh," I said. "I was thinking how nice it was for Amy to have someone whom she admires who obviously likes her."

"When you put it that way, Fran, it sounds fine. Wonderful, even. But I've been talking to Amy since she's been out there, and, believe me, she's getting lost in that woman's apron."

Hadn't I just thought that Greta was being smothered? Why couldn't I see it with Amy? "I'll pay attention," I said. "Is there anything I can do?"

"Encourage her to do things independently of Edith."

Every once in a while, I would think about my own independence, and the niggling question would rear its ugly head: How dependent are you, Fran, on the group and on Polly? I knew that someday I would have to break away. But not yet.

Brenda approached then and told Polly that she had enrolled in a martial arts class.

Polly, only half joking, said, "Watch out that you don't become the batterer."

All the way back to the motel, I had the sensation of hair standing up on the back of my neck. I wasn't at all sure I wanted to go back to Hickory Hills.

Eleven

We got up early Wednesday and headed for the farm. The prickly sensation on my neck had not left me. Amy rode with me, and Delia followed. I could see her in my rearview mirror, talking on her phone.

"Look at Delia," I said. "She's always working."

Amy turned and waved. Delia took her other hand off the wheel briefly to wave back.

"I don't think she likes Edith," Amy said.

"That's not surprising."

"Why?"

"They're both strong personalities. Too much competition."

Amy said nothing for several beats. "You know, without Edith that farm would fall apart. She hired Ben and got that computer system going, even though she's really backward when it comes to using the computer."

"How did she happen to decide to do it, then?"

"She went to a class at the high school and learned what could be done."

"What about Ben? How did she find him?"

"She's known his family for years. He's from the same town that she and Heinz came from, Paradise."

"That's where Heinz's mother and sister live." I was thinking about the pictures of Greta with the older women, Grace and Hildegarde. I got the feeling again that that was where Greta would run to. But Edith had said that she had checked

83

with the women. Why would Edith lie? Or would Grace and Hildegarde lie to Edith?

"Yes. There's a German community there. Some of them are Amish. Some of Heinz's family, I think."

"What was Ben doing in Paradise before Edith hired him?"

"The same thing. Working on an organic foods farm, setting up a computer system. Of course, the Amish don't have computers. But not everybody there is Amish."

"Did he talk about Paradise much?"

"I didn't know him that long, Fran, but he mentioned it a couple of times when we would talk. You know, after."

I glanced over at Amy and realized that she was grieving for this man that she had known so short a time, and I wondered whether Amy's relationships were all doomed.

"Before you started to date him, did you talk to him much?"

"When I was alone in the office, he would come over to where I was working. He helped me a lot when I first started. I think that's why I got so good with the orders."

"Maybe you got so good because you're an organized and conscientious person."

I could feel Amy's smile before I looked at her and saw it. "That's nice of you to say," she said.

"It's true. You could do a lot of things. What about those auditions that Delia mentioned? Do you think you'll go try out?"

"God, I'd be so scared."

"Too scared?"

"I might try it," she said. "I've always had this secret dream about being a movie star. But a lot of girls have dreams like that, you know."

"It might be easier than you think. You might be one of those people who get in front of an audience and start to glow."

Amy giggled.

When we got to the farm, Edith was dispensing coffee cake to the temporary workers who had been hired to put her computer system back together.

Edith greeted us cordially and dished up the goodies for us

before we had a chance to refuse. Amy got an affectionate hug as soon as Edith put down her spatula.

It wasn't long before Delia was bossing the others around. I saw Edith watching her, but Edith did not interfere. Probably, I guessed, because Delia was getting things done in a way Edith herself might have done if she knew anything about setting up the computer files.

"Didn't you say you knew about the orders, Amy?" Delia said, pretending that she didn't know as much as she did about the system. But it seemed to me that Delia was too late with her attempt at duplicity and that Edith had already figured out that Delia knew a lot about the files already.

"Edith," I said, "could you spare a few minutes?" I needed to talk to her, and I thought Delia needed to be rid of her.

"Yes, yes," she said. She called one of the women who worked at the store to clean up, and we went outdoors, where the June sun was warm and the air smelled like new-mown hay.

Edith sniffed the air and said, "They're cutting the field behind the warehouse."

"Do you keep track of everything?" I said, before I had my brain in gear enough to say the same thing tactfully.

"Everything except the computers. I had Ben for that. Now, I don't know."

I told Edith that I thought it would be worth a trip to Paradise to see whether anybody there had seen Greta.

"I told you that was the first place I called," she said.

"But Greta spent many summers and vacations there. She might have made friends you never heard of. I think it's worth a try."

Edith shook her head. I think she didn't want to pay for the trip. After all, I wasn't costing her much. But I wasn't accomplishing much, either.

"There's no point in my continuing the job," I said, which was pretty brave for me. "I have to be able to follow my leads and my hunches."

"There are plenty of places to look around here," she said.

"But I don't think she's here. Tell you what," I said, "I'll only charge you for half the expenses if I don't find her there."

I had a great head for financial matters. Pro bono PI.

Edith looked at me intently. "All right," she said, slowly. She was still turning something over in her head. "If you feel that strongly about it, go. I'll pay."

"Great," I said. "I'll go tomorrow."

She stopped and cocked her head and looked around. "Let's walk around to the back of the warehouse. I want to see how the work is coming."

I followed her as she turned the corner of the building; I was feeling uneasy. The sheriff's deputies were inside and I hadn't asked one of them to accompany me. I saw no one else in the field, but I could not yet see behind the warehouse.

"I thought you said they were cutting," I said.

"Terry's supposed to be. But I don't see the tractor, and I don't hear it."

Neither do I, I thought.

Edith accelerated her pace. I was surprised how fast she could move all that bulk. The back of my neck was tingling with fear and dread. I didn't know whether to watch out for Edith or whether the both of us should watch out for someone else.

She was at the back corner of the building, looking at something behind it. She had stoppped. Her arms were in the air. I remember thinking that someone was holding a gun on her, but that was before the sound that came from her mouth, her chest, her gut, and maybe even her feet: half growl, half scream.

I stopped; my feet would not move me forward. A bitter taste backed up from my gorge.

Then Edith disappeared behind the warehouse at a trot.

My mouth was dry and I couldn't have produced a scream if it had occurred to me. Should I follow Edith or call the deputies? I followed Edith until I reached the corner where she had howled and saw why.

She was kneeling next to a pair of legs. The body attached to them was under a tractor wheel. She crawled around the wheel and peered under the axle.

"He's dead," she said. "Oh, no. Oh, no. We can't have this happening here." I guessed it wasn't one of the Baere men. Edith's sentiments concerned the future of the farm rather than the tragedy of the farmhand's death.

A huge breath of air escaped from my lips. I hadn't known I was holding it.

"Don't touch him," I said, my feet carrying me forward while my eyes darted away from what I knew I must see. It was Terry Kurtz. Squishy stuff scrawled next to his abdomen, blood drying in the sun, flies buzzing in the sweet, oxidizing liquids. But there was blood near his head, too. I looked closer and saw a deep gash at the back of his head. Did it get bumped as he fell under the wheel? I didn't see blood anywhere on the tractor. The tractor was not in gear, and the ignition was turned off. It didn't take a genius to figure out what had happened.

As I ran to call the deputies, I thought about what Edith said. How could the farm go on in the face of such an onslaught of disaster and death? And who was behind it? The evil was lurking right here, I thought, among the hills, fields, woodlands, and streams.

The sheriff was grim when he came into the store, where everyone had gathered, not because anyone had told us to, I thought, but because there was safety in numbers.

"Doc Farnham is on his way," the sheriff said. The sheriff had aged. Even the sparkle in his eyes was dulled.

I could imagine how he felt. Events seemed to overtake each investigation before it could get underway. The farm was under siege.

The sheriff had to be thinking what I was thinking. Terry Kurtz, the farmhand who smiled a lot, Terry, who had seen Theodora in the hay (literally) with Ben Grasse, had been silenced. Who else had Terry told besides the sheriff? Did Theodora want to silence him? Or was there something else? Someone else who wanted him dead? Or wanted them dead?

Edith was taking this latest death hard, or maybe it was the piling up of catastrophe that she was taking hard. In any event, she was absolutely silent, sitting in a corner with an expression on her face that warned all to keep their distance.

The sheriff was trying to question each of the farm's denizens quickly, before anybody had a chance to think up an excuse or change a story.

He questioned each one himself. One deputy, Jeff, the one with the red mustache who liked Amy, was in the room with the sheriff. The rest of the deputies were watching the assembled Baeres and farmworkers.

Theodora, her hand bandaged, sat between Ernest and Eric. They looked like the Grant Wood *American Gothic* painting plus one, looking straight ahead at nothing.

Heinz sat by the desk, shuffling papers and mumbling. The four women who worked at the store huddled in a group behind the counter, now and then picking up a dish or a package and moving it to another surface or shelf. They seemed to be waiting for instructions from Edith, but she wasn't paying attention to anything exterior.

I still had it in my mind that there might be something to be found in Greta's room, and I was looking for an opportunity to slip away while the forces of the law trotted out their machinery to deal with death.

The farmhands were questioned first and let go. They went back to whatever they had been doing before the deputies rounded them up. The day workers also went back to work.

I was getting edgy. I wanted out of there. When I tried to get the sheriff's attention on one of his trips into the store between questionings, he didn't look my way. I had the feeling that he was avoiding my eyes, that he felt somehow responsible that he couldn't keep the mayhem in check.

My opportunity came when Edith toppled over, chair and all. All activity stopped for a moment, all eyes were on the crumpled form on the floor. When people started moving toward her, I made my exit. It would be some time before I was missed. I stopped at my car in the lot next to the store. Wandering around the farm without my .38 didn't seem to be a good idea.

The deputies were all on the opposite side of the building and at the back. I had already decided that if I saw one of them, I would wave and smile. They were a friendly bunch. Too friendly. I didn't see anyone, though, and headed for the nearest woods.

I was still within sight of the road, trying to move from tree to tree in case anyone looked my way, when I saw Doc Farnham's car. I knew that would bring the deputies to the front of the store, so I went deeper into the woods, where the soft moss and pine needles cushioned my steps and where the sun didn't penetrate to warm the air. I shivered. Whether it was fear or cold, I couldn't tell.

The woods weren't deep enough to get me lost—they were more like islands of trees between the buildings and roads—but they were deep enough to hide in. I thought about who might have hidden in the farm woods: Greg was first on my list. But hadn't he been to Pennsylvania? Or maybe only his car went to Pennsylvania. Whoever had thrown the smoke bomb into the office where I was working could have hidden in the woods near the building. Those woods were separated from the ones I was in by the road that went from the store to the family compound.

Now that I was in the woods, I could see how easily someone could move from place to place and not be seen.

Crack.

The sound was nearby.

I stopped short and felt in my purse for my gun. I stood still, waiting for another sound. Nothing.

I tried a few tentative steps. Another crack. My hand clutched the .38 harder.

Several crackling sounds, coming closer.

Panting with fear, I put a tree between me and the sound. A movement a few yards away caught my eye. I blinked and squinted. It was seconds before my eyes could make out what it was. Then I saw it, a deer, a doe, her nose working trying to tell her what creature was near her.

A sweet-looking creature, large eyes, shiny coat; I hated the idea that someone would take a shot at her during hunting season. I brushed something, I don't know what, some feathery something, away from my face and she saw me. Her white tail bounced as she bounded away, her adrenaline going as fast as mine.

The silence returned when she was gone.

At one point I walked near the edge of the woods and could see another tractor in a field pulling a cart that was dropping something from behind it. I got a whiff and knew the manure spreaders were at it again.

There was no activity around the building where Amy lived,

and I crossed the road there. The window that had been smashed by the smoke bomb was already repaired. I didn't stop to check on the cleanup.

The woods on this side of the road had fewer pines, fewer needles on the ground, and more twigs from the maples, making my walk noisier than I wanted it to be. Still, no one was around to hear me; I told myself that, wanted to believe that.

However, at the rate the sheriff was turning people loose after he questioned them, I would have to hurry. They might even be bringing Edith back to the house right now, I thought.

I stayed in the cover of the trees as long as I could, but I would have to cross the clearing to get to Edith's place. A brisk pace, but not a hurried or sneaky pace was in order. If someone did see me, I should look like I was where I was supposed to be.

Once I was inside, I called out, "Hello. Anybody home?" and checked the downstairs. No one. Upstairs, too, was uninhabited. Greta's room had been cleaned up, but the fancy bedclothes were gone. Probably in the laundry. Also gone was the computer.

I tried to think like a teenager. Where would she hide backup disks or anything else secret that she wouldn't take with her? Mmmm. Her side of the room, not the side of the room that Edith had done over. I looked in the computer books and the fan magazines that were stashed between them. I went to her closet and opened the doors. The pictures that Edith hated were still there, the young alienated-looking men and women (or were they boys and girls?) glaring out from the graffiti littered set they had chosen for background.

There were some boxes on the shelves that yielded up a few letters and more pictures of snarling young people. Greta's secret life. I looked at the clothes hanging there: jeans, rugby shirts, jackets. I wondered what she had taken with her.

I checked her dresser drawers and found that the underwear drawer was empty except for a slip and a garter belt. So, she did have time to pack. A few pairs of socks, too few for a teenage girl, were in another drawer, along with one fussy nightgown, which looked like it was a present from her grandmother.

Hadn't someone told me that Greta had started wearing long

skirts recently? Back to the closet. No long skirts. There was enough to indicate that she had packed. What clinched it was there were no shoes except for a pair of pumps, the most un-Greta pair of shoes I could imagine, with little bows and sequins on the front. The next thing to know was whether anyone knew she was packing. And when she left.

The sound of a siren startled me. Were they taking Edith to a hospital? Or had the sheriff called in the state police again?

I felt that I was getting nowhere and that I had to hurry. There didn't seem to be anywhere else to look unless there was a secret compartment somewhere. That would appeal to a teenager, but where would she build one?

I looked again at the posters, the symbol of her rebellion. They were taped up with packing tape as if to dare anyone to try to take them down. Yes. As if to dare . . .

The posters were hung over panels in the closet doors. Maybe she had put something in the recesses behind them.

Damn. I heard someone on the porch. I didn't know whether to be afraid for my life or afraid to get caught in Greta's room.

I pulled the doors closed on the closet with me inside and started working on the tape on one side of one of the posters.

As I pulled at the tape, I listened. I didn't hear any more footsteps. Was someone standing still or creeping up the stairs? The tape was really on there. I didn't want to rip the poster and I didn't want anyone to know I had found anything—if I found anything.

It was getting hot in the closet, and I was about to risk opening the door a crack, when I heard a creak from the direction of the stairs. Whoever was in the house was sneaking around, just as I was. I opened my purse, pulled out the gun, and tucked it into my waistband. I always worried when I saw anybody do that on TV; putting a gun in one's pants seemed risky.

I stopped working on the poster and tried to breathe slowly, as if I weren't scared out of my wits. Where the two closet doors met, a slit of light knifed through the dark. I put my eye to the crack. I could see the doorway.

The creaks were coming closer. Now I could hear the shoe hitting the floor, less sneaky sounding, I thought. The footsteps passed the doorway. I could see a tall shape pass in the hall.

It looked like Eric. What was he doing here? I heard him go to the next room, Edith's and Heinz's, heard a drawer opening and closing. The footsteps were returning. I held my breath.

He didn't come into Greta's room, but as he went past, it looked like he was holding a wad of bills. I didn't know what to think of that. Had he stolen from his grandparents or had he been sent to get something? Were the bills his? When I heard him on the porch, I opened the closet and went to the window. Eric was walking nonchalantly toward the farmhouse.

I went back to the tape around the poster and managed to loosen one side easily, now that I wasn't working in the dark and the heat of the closet. I slipped my hand behind the poster and felt a cardboard square taped to the door. I worked the tape loose on it and pulled it out.

Eureka. It was a cardboard packet containing a computer disk.

I was congratulating myself when I heard more noise on the porch. This time nobody was sneaking around. This time I wanted to be out of there. But I wanted to check behind the other poster first.

I resealed the tape on the first poster and dropped the cardboard packet in my purse. As heavy footsteps came up the stairs, I closed myself in the closet again and started to pick at the edge of the tape on the other poster.

Heinz passed Greta's room and went to his own. I heard something that sounded like a body flopping on a bed. I waited and pulled at the tape. I heard no sound coming from the other room and pushed the closet open enough to give me air and light.

When I had the tape loosened, I reached inside and felt fabric. What? I pulled my hand out, holding bloody clothes, a blouse and a pair of lacy underpants. My knees grew weak.

It took all my concentration to push the clothes back behind the poster and seal the tape. My movements felt jerky and uncoordinated. I didn't know whether I was doing the right thing. I just knew I didn't want to handle those bloody things.

It seemed hours later that I heard snoring in the next room. I tiptoed down the stairs and looked out the windows to see which was the best route to escape undetected. The back, which led out to hills and trees and stream, was unpeopled and out of view of the other houses.

I needed to think, to clear my overloaded circuits. Bloody clothes in Greta's room, taped behind her poster. Was she the killer? She had disappeared the night Grasse was killed and had hidden the bloody clothes in her room. Why did only the blouse and underpants get bloody?

Those clothes would have to be tested before someone else found them. Who knows what the Baeres would do if they found them? The family seemed on the one hand to be a cohesive bunch and, on the other, to be hiding things from one another. And there was no unity about hiring me to find Greta. That was Edith's idea.

I decided that the clothes were safe, for now. If no one knew I had been in her room looking for something, no one would think there was something to be found there. I had to keep the disk a secret, but I also wanted to get a look at what was on it that made it worth hiding.

I had been walking around in the orchard behind Edith's and Heinz's house, my mind no longer occupied with hiding myself, when I heard a voice behind me.

"Stop right there, and don't move."

I lurched and let out a startled cry. I didn't recognize the voice.

"Put your hands up and turn around," he said.

When I turned, I faced the barrel of a shotgun held by a short fellow who had brown bristles sticking out from his ears and nose and face. He was wearing a uniform, not a deputy's.

"Who are you?" I said.

"I'm the one to ask the questions, gal," he said. His name tag said WORTH.

"So ask." I could feel his discomfort in wielding the gun.

"Pretty snippy, ain't you?"

"Yes."

He laughed. "Well, who are you?" he said.

I trotted out the big guns. "Fran Tremaine Kirk, private detective." I intimidated him and, I'm ashamed to say, I enjoyed it. "Edith hired me to find her granddaughter."

"Well she ain't here, is she?" he snapped. He didn't like being intimidated.

"I'll show you my ID if you'll put your gun down."

"No, you don't. I'm takin' you to Mr. Baere. March," he said, pointing the barrel toward the farmhouse, "and keep your hands high."

I felt like an actor in a horse opera. "When did they hire you?" I asked, assuming that the Baeres at some point had decided they needed private security.

"I just came on the job."

"That's why you haven't seen me around. I've been here on and off since Sunday."

"I'm still taking you to the Baeres."

"Fine," I said. "But let's hurry. My arms are getting tired."

"Put them behind your back where I can see them."

"Thanks," I said. I felt almost giddy at the ludicrous situation I found myself in, but I didn't think it would be wise to let myself smile or giggle. This guy Worth seemed jumpy, not the best person to entrust with a weapon. However, I wasn't as afraid as I might have been if I hadn't seen the safety in place on the shotgun. At least I didn't have to worry about the gun firing if he stumbled.

As we approached the back door of the farmhouse, Theodora appeared in the doorway.

"What?" she said.

"Mr. Worth thinks I'm an intruder," I said.

"It's okay, Harry," Theodora said and sighed. "I'm sorry, Fran," she said. "We just hired him. He doesn't know who belongs where."

"Better safe than sorry," Harry said.

"Yes. Thank you," Theodora said. "Come in, Fran. I think Edith would like to see you. Where did you go off to? I saw you run out when Edith fainted."

My story was ready. "I was getting claustrophobic in there with so many people, and I needed some air. That and the fact that I'd just seen a corpse made me feel faint, too. I took a walk, saw a deer. It's very peaceful in the woods."

"It's a good thing Harry didn't see you in the woods. He might have taken a shot at you."

Was she trying to scare me? Or was she trying to tell me not to poke around on the farm where I wasn't wanted? Then, because I do some things impulsively or because I don't have the patience I should have for the cat-and-mouse game, I said, "Terry saw you with Ben. You know that, don't you?"

If she'd had a gun, I thought, she might have used it in that split second before she shrouded herself with the ice of her self-control. "Who told you that?"

"It's not a secret," I said. If you're a killer, it's better for me that you don't think I'm the only one who knows.

Her shoulders rounded even more than usual. "I thought it was. I wish it was."

"You mean about Terry seeing you or your being with Ben?" Yes, that was bitchy.

She ignored the question. "We were so careful. I don't see why anybody would have seen us." She was fighting tears. "We went out in the field. It would be one chance in a million that someone would go to just that place. I've thought about this so many times."

"So you knew that Terry knew?"

"Yes. He . . . I was giving him money."

"Does the sheriff know this?"

"He'll think I killed him. Terry. Think I killed Terry."

Why had I suddenly become this woman's confidante? "Does anyone else know about the blackmail?"

"No. But Ernest suspected something. He asked questions about the money. I broke off with Ben, but Terry kept asking for more."

"You're going to have to clear this up with the sheriff. Maybe you'll be able to keep it from Ernest, but I don't know. The sheriff already knows that Terry saw you and Ben."

She gasped. The tears were winning the battle.

"Theo." The voice was Ernest's.

"I'm going," she said, "right now. I'll tell the sheriff."

She was gone when Ernest came into the mudroom.

"Where is she?" he said.

"She had to go back to the store," I said.

"She probably thinks I forgot the eggs. I forgot to put them in the ice box."

I smiled when I heard him say ice box. He misinterpreted the smile.

"This time I didn't forget to get them. I had them in my

hands when I went in to see Mama. I put them down in the living room and forgot them. Go see. They're still there.''

''Maybe you should put them in the fridge,'' I said, thinking that Ernest acted like an eight-year-old. I wondered what kind of reaction he would have if he knew what his wife had been doing.

He stood there with his hands hanging as if he didn't know what to do with them, then he put them in his pants pockets and took them back out. He finally crossed his arms in front of his chest and gave his shoulders a couple of shrugs. Definitely not at home in his skin.

''She went to the store?'' he said.

''Yes,'' I said.

''Did she go to get eggs?''

''She didn't say,'' I said.

''What do you want here?'' he said. What a way with social graces he had.

''I think your mother wants to see me,'' I said.

At that, he smiled. ''Okay. She's in the living room.''

He was nice looking when he smiled, but I wondered if much of anything was going on behind his eyes.

Twelve

Edith was propped up on the couch, a table beside her holding water, pills, tissues, and a pile of magazines, the top one being about farm wives. When I walked in, she pointed to a straight-backed chair and had me move it closer to the couch.

"How are you?" I said, noting that her color was better and that her old self was reemerging.

"I'm fine. I'll go back to my own house soon. Ernest and Theodora were worried so they set me up here. So much fuss."

"Well, you did faint. That would make me worry, too."

"It was just the shock. I can't believe these things are happening at Hickory Hills. We've made it such a wonderful place. We've worked so hard." Her tone was plaintive.

"What's behind it all?" I said. "Can you make a guess?"

"One thing does not seem connected to another. There's no rhyme or reason to it."

I didn't agree, but I went along. "Maybe you'll feel better if I find Greta."

"I hope you do. I'm worried about her."

"Do you remember whether you heard her packing Saturday night or in the early hours Sunday?"

"I haven't seen her since Saturday afternoon. But I thought she had gone out with her friends. I thought I heard her truck Saturday night, but I didn't see it there in the morning."

"What time Saturday night?"

"I don't know. I was used to hearing her truck come in

late, and then I would be able to fall into a deeper sleep because I knew she was home.''

''Could she have come home and then packed?''

''I wouldn't have been listening for that. Once I hear her truck, I fall asleep like a bear.''

I decided it was time to open the can of worms: ''Was Greta unhappy?''

''Aren't all teenagers unhappy?''

''She didn't have any special reason to be unhappy?''

''No, no, no. She has her family. We give her a good life.''

''Why wasn't she living with her mother and father, then?''

''It was just temporary. You know how mothers and daughters are sometimes.''

Yes, I guess I did. My own mother and I could barely speak to each other when I was a senior in high school. She didn't like my boyfriend, later my husband. She was right, but I didn't know that then.

''What about Eric? Did she get along with Eric?''

''Eric gets along with everyone. He doesn't fight with everyone.'' Implied in that was ''not the way Greta does.''

No, he just sneaks around, I thought. I wanted to tell her about seeing him in her house, but that would have told her that I was in the house. ''But he did fight with Greta.''

''When she started it, yes, he would fight with her.''

I wanted to blurt out my resentment on Greta's part for the favoritism that she was showing, but I reminded myself that getting her mad wouldn't help me get information out of her. Why I was feeling supportive of a wild young girl in whose room I had just found bloody clothing was something I wasn't ready to examine.

''What did they fight about?''

''They used to fight about Greta's friends. Last week they were arguing about the computer. She had found him in her room by her computer.''

''That was one fight she didn't start, then. If he was in her room without permission.'' I couldn't help putting in a word for her.

''We don't have permission. No locked doors here. We go in anybody's room unless the door is closed. Then we knock. That is the way it has always been.''

"If I were Greta, I wouldn't like my brother in my room."

"She didn't like it. She screamed at him."

"Did you hear anything she said?"

"They could hear her in the next county." Edith smiled. "She told him she would not tell him where something was and that she would do whatever she wanted with it."

"What was it that she was hiding from him?"

"I don't know. Eric said it belonged to him. When we told her to give it to him, she said it wasn't his."

"How did you settle it?" I knew Greta would get the worst of it before she told me.

"We took away her allowance for the week. That's why I didn't think she could go far in her truck. She wouldn't have money for the gas."

"Could she have gotten money from someone else, or could she have saved some money, or could she have taken some money from someplace where it is usually kept?" I thought again about Eric coming out of his grandparents' house with the wad of bills.

Edith looked flustered. "There is some money missing, but Greta wouldn't . . ."

I was glad to see that Edith's blind spots weren't confined to her grandson.

I asked her again about Greta and Theodora, and Edith told me a much-watered-down version of the story that I'd heard from Theodora about Greta's behavior.

I was curious about what Edith knew about Theodora and her trysts with Grasse. If Edith knew, maybe Greta was taken away because Theodora was a bad influence. But, no, if Edith knew, then why was Theodora paying Terry for his silence? Maybe Theodora was the key to all of the mayhem. But what did it all have to do with the vandalism to the computers? Or was that symbolic, someone saying: I killed Grasse and erased his work? But how did the farmhand, Terry Kurtz, fit into the picture? Was there another connection between Grasse and Terry Kurtz?

Before I left, Edith gave me a check for the trip to Paradise. She also told me about a "reasonable" motel where I could stay.

On my way out, I stopped in the kitchen, where Ernest was

sitting watching a game show on a small TV that was mounted on a corner shelf. What the hell, I thought, maybe I could get something out of a chat with him. I often avoided conversations with men, especially men who made me feel uneasy. But some days I was braver than others.

I started asking him about Greta's friends, since that seemed to be a subject on which there was some agreement.

"They're very nice girls," he said. "They come to the farm sometimes."

That was not what I was expecting. "What about boys? Does she have a boyfriend?"

"No, no. She's too young for a boyfriend."

What planet are you living on? "I know quite a few girls her age who have boyfriends." And girls a whole lot younger.

"She has boys who are friends, but not a boyfriend."

He kept looking at the TV as if something interesting was happening, so I gradually edged my way between him and the screen. "Your wife seems to think that Greta goes out with boys," I said. What the hell, the family was falling apart anyway, I might as well give it another nudge.

The absent expression on his face was replaced by one that resembled a Hollywood version of an evil alien. There was something unreal about the guy. "What right do you have to talk to my wife about my daughter?"

Now, there was a question. Where to start, regarding my rights? "I was hired to find her. She turned up missing the same day a man was killed here, and the police are interested in finding her, too. You've got to expect people to ask questions."

His hands were working, clasping, unclasping, wringing, clenching, and it looked like he was chewing on the inside of his lip. "Greta will come back. She didn't do anything. She's only mad because we took away her allowance."

The man was in deep denial, I thought, barely keeping the lid on. I wondered how much was registering, or, rather, how much he could afford to let register before he blew his top.

"What do you think happened to Ben Grasse?" I said.

He moved his head to one side so he could see the TV. I moved away so that he could see it without leaning over.

"I'll miss Ben," he said. "He was a good guy."

Jesus! Is this guy on Valium or what? "Who killed him?" I said, rather forcefully.

His eyes bugged out, and his hands came up in front of him as if he were afraid. "I didn't do it," he said.

"I'm sorry," I said. "I didn't mean to yell."

"I don't like people who holler," he said.

This part of the picture was weirder than the others. Ernest seemed to have the IQ of a slug and the emotions of a child. I left him gazing at the TV. The eggs were on the kitchen table.

Could he have fathered Eric and Greta? Had something happened to make him feebleminded or had he always been that way? I could see why Theodora wandered: something between the ears would be a nice change.

If he had always been like that, why did Theodora marry him? Of course. The farm. She wanted the farm. Edith and Heinz would have been happy to marry him off to anyone that looked strong enough to wield a hoe.

I was heading for the store, staying on the road so as not to surprise Harry "rent-a-cop" Worth. It was past lunchtime and the farm mealtime rhythms had been interrupted. Edith and Theodora were the keepers of the culinary clock, and they both had problems of their own this day. There would be food at the store, even if I had to buy it.

When I came in sight of the store I could see Heinz and Theodora on the porch arguing. As I got closer, I heard what they were arguing about. Heinz was telling her to go back to the farmhouse and get lunch ready, and she was telling him that she had to see the sheriff. When he wanted to know what she had to see the sheriff about, she wouldn't tell him. As I approached they covered the same ground twice. I don't know how much longer it would have gone on, but Theodora stopped talking when she finally saw me.

I felt silly smiling at them, but that's what I did.

"Are you hungry?" Heinz said, suddenly turning to me.

Theodora sighed and slumped. "Did you just leave the house?" she said, obviously trying to override Heinz's question.

"Yes," I said. And they were both satisfied.

"Is everyone all right?" she said before he could launch into his demand that she go make lunch.

"Yes, and Ernest wanted you to know that he got the eggs."

"Good," she said, and then turned to Heinz. "If I don't get back right away, you can make scrambled eggs."

Heinz looked indignant, but he was apparently tired of arguing. "Worthless witch," he mumbled as he walked away.

"I'm glad you came along," Theodora said. "I would have been here till dark arguing with him about making lunch."

"Couldn't you just walk away from him?"

She smiled ruefully. "I'd be afraid to try that."

"Is he violent?"

"Only with Ernest."

"He beats Ernest?"

Theodora frowned and looked away. "Forget it, will you. Just forget it."

She walked off and headed for the room where the sheriff had been questioning people, while I went to see how Delia and Amy were making out. The computer people had been set up in a room carved out of the warehouse behind the store. Since the farm sold a lot of products that had flour in them, the air in the warehouse was gritty. That was probably the rationale behind the separate room in the warehouse space: close enough to handle the orders and yet clean enough to keep the computers working.

Amy and Delia and the others were eating sandwiches, the smell of which made my mouth water. They smelled suspiciously like nonorganic, delicious deli food.

"Where did you get that?" I said.

Amy pointed to a table where there was a long board that bore the remains of a six-foot sandwich. There was plenty left, and I tucked into it without any more conversation. There also was, horror of horrors, Coke, Pepsi, 7Up, and Sprite, diet and regular. All Edith had to do was faint, and people began bringing these tainted foods onto her farm.

When I finally stopped chewing long enough to ask, I found out that the computer people had sent out for the stuff after they took a look at what was offered at the farm store.

One of them said, "I'd die without my daily dose of pesticides."

I thought that reaction was rather extreme, because Edith served some very good food, but I enjoyed the hero and Coke, nonetheless.

"We're going gangbusters on the data," Delia said. "These folks are fast and they are good." She said it loudly enough for them to hear.

"Amen," said a lean fellow with a ponytail who didn't lift his eyes from the screen.

"We aim to please," one of the women said.

"You should see us on the dance floor, after work," another guy, who looked like Sylvester Stallone, said.

"You should see us later, much later," said another woman, who was dressed in jeans and a low-cut blouse showing lots of cleavage.

"Do you all work together a lot?" I said.

"Every day. It's our business," said the Stallone look-alike. He got up and handed me a card. It said: THE EXTERMINATORS/ WE'LL GET THE BUGS OUT OF YOUR SYSTEM/ COMPUTER SPECIALISTS, PROGRAMMING WHIZZES, DEBUGGING ACES/ IF IT'S ELECTRONIC, WE CAN DO IT.

"Very impressive," I said, and tucked the card into my purse. It would go into my file for future reference.

When they all got back into their trances, I took the opportunity to get Amy aside. "What's with Ernest?" I said.

"He is a little peculiar," Amy said.

"A little? Does he ever speak like an intelligent adult?"

"I don't think he's stupid," she said. "He just acts that way."

"So if he acts that way, what does he do to make you think he's not?"

"He watches everything that goes on. If he likes you, he'll talk to you. He keeps track of things, like Edith."

"Why does he act so dumb, then?"

"He's afraid of Heinz. He hides sometimes when he knows Heinz is coming. If Heinz sneaks up on him, Ernest jumps."

"What does Heinz do to him? How come he's afraid?" I wondered how many of the family skeletons Amy knew about.

"I never saw him actually do anything. But it's peculiar the way he tries to sneak up on Ernest. And when Ernest jumps, Heinz gets this weird look on his face, sort of a mean smile.''

"Theodora said that Heinz beats him.''

Amy's hand flew to her mouth. "I heard something,'' she said. "Once, just as supper was starting, Heinz called Ernest away from the table. They went outside and Edith said we shouldn't wait, that we should start eating. Then we heard this awful howl, and Edith got up from the table and went outside, too.''

"Did anybody say anything?''

"They all kept on eating. But they were kind of quiet.''

"When they came back to the table, what did Ernest look like?''

"I didn't think anything of it at the time. But Ernest didn't come back to the table. Heinz came back. He looked cheerful. Edith said something about a sick dog and that Ernest was going to take care of it.''

"This family gets odder, the longer I stay around here. Don't they seem odd to you?''

"Since Sunday, they seem odd. Before that, I don't know, they seemed okay. Normal. But now, what you say makes me think I was ignoring things that I should have been paying attention to.''

"You know what Polly says about that,'' I said. Polly was always reminding us about the way we tried to keep life going in a normal fashion even when events were screaming at us.

I remembered going to work and taking uppers so that I could get through the day without falling asleep from exhaustion after my husband, Dick, had kept me awake all night, first, yelling at me, then hitting me, then trying to make up with me. Every time something like that happened, I would tell myself that I had to get through the day and the next day would be all right.

Just before we split up, there were days and days, one after another, of beatings, and never a good one in between.

I pressed Amy to try to recall other times when Ernest might have been beaten by Heinz. Once the floodgates opened, Amy remembered several incidents that pointed to that kind of abuse. Amy was upset about it, more so because she had not let herself notice the dark side of the events.

Amy remembered actually seeing Heinz strike Ernest in a barn, but, at the time, she interpreted what she saw as playful. "Heinz came out smiling," she said. "So I thought everything was hunky-dory."

"We ought to get Ernest to come to the group," I said, and though it was not at all out of the question that Ernest go to such a group, that Ernest get some serious help, we both burst out laughing.

Not very charitable. We had some growing to do in the area of understanding. I admit it.

I asked Amy to tell me her impressions of Heinz, his walloping of Ernest aside.

"He seems devoted to Edith. He can't do enough for her. She talks, he jumps. She told me he didn't want to get the computers. Neither did Theodora or Eric, she said. Edith said that she and Greta were the ones who wanted to modernize the farm's record keeping."

"Heinz," I said. "Tell me about Heinz."

Amy grinned. "I did wander, didn't I?"

I nodded.

"He works hard. He works with the milkers one day, the hayers another, the office people another. Sometimes he goes from the field to the office and has manure on his shoes. We complained about that once and he took his shoes off and put them outside the door."

"Does he have one special area that he is the best at?"

"He always takes care of the cows having calves. Stays up all night if he has to. And when there's a sick animal, he takes care of it. He seems to know when he has to call the vet. Edith says they lose very few animals because Heinz is so good with them."

"And Ernest," I said, "what does he do?"

"He takes care of the chickens. There are some other birds over in the coops, turkeys, pheasants, a peacock, and some others that I don't know the names of. Ernest takes care of them, too. I think they're his lobby. He stays out in the coops sometimes until they ring a bell for him to come to dinner."

"Maybe the birds make noise and Heinz can't sneak up on him out there," I said.

Amy looked at me quizzically, then smiled a tight little

smile. "You're thinking that this place is a crazy house, aren't you?"

"We have to make allowances for individuals. We can't assume that everybody who's a little different is crazy." I barely got the words out before we both were giggling.

"What's funny?" Delia said.

I guess Amy and I had been chatting too long and Delia wanted Amy to get back to work.

Amy kept her voice low and said to Delia, "I was just telling Fran about some of the things that go on here," she said, "and I realized that some of the stuff is whacky."

"What do you expect? It's a farm, for cry eye. Farmers like the smell of manure and have relationships with animals."

Leave it to Delia to put things in perspective.

"Have you got enough in the system to find out what's going on with California Arbor Naturals?" I said in a low voice to Delia. She had told me that we could run the data through some calisthenics and check on the account.

"We should be in shape by tonight," she said. "When the debuggers leave, we'll got at it."

Thirteen

The sheriff sent Deputy Jeff to fetch me. It was time to square things with the sheriff and maybe to get some information out of him about the Baeres. Jeff lingered, gaping at Amy, as I left the electronics room.

When I entered the little room at the back of the store, the sheriff was on the phone. "How long ago was that?" he said.

After a silence, he said, "Why didn't you hold him? We've had the APB out since Sunday."

Then he said, "You didn't? I can't figure that one."

When he hung up, he told me that Greg had been picked up in Buffalo Monday night and released Tuesday morning. "Damn snafu, if you ask me. They said they didn't get the all-points till yesterday."

"That's right," I said, and told him about Ted and Roland checking on it.

The sheriff started asking me questions about who Ted and Roland were, and I was vague, told him they were friends.

I was thinking that Amy was right to be afraid when she was in Buffalo on Tuesday. Who knew where Greg was and what he would do next?

When the sheriff asked how Edith and I happened to discover the body, I told him she wanted to check on the haying behind the warehouse.

He nodded, getting the impression that I was conveying, that it was a bit peculiar of her to suddenly want to go behind the warehouse.

"But at the time," I told the sheriff, "I didn't know whether

107

I should be afraid of Edith. Someone on this farm is a killer, and all of the Baeres are on my short list.''

Sheriff Castle nodded. "It's starting to look bad.''

"But if you'd heard her howl," I said, "you would have thought she was surprised at what she saw. Did she give you any reason for wanting to check on the haying?''

"I haven't had a chance to talk to her yet. She fainted. You remember that, don't you? It was just before you took your leave.''

He gave me a smart-ass look, as if to say, You didn't put anything over on me.

"I had a touch of claustrophobia," I said. "Too many bodies in the room and too many dead bodies, period." I gave him my best Victorian-lady-with-tight-corset smile. If I'd had a fan, I would have waved it in front of my face as if I had the vapors.

"Remember what I said about telling me if you find something that's important.''

I hoped my face wouldn't tell him that I was holding back. Whether Greta deserved such loyalty or not, I wasn't about to tell him what I found in her room, or even that I'd been in her room. "What about Kurtz?" I said. "It was another murder, wasn't it? Was he banged on the head and then dumped near the wheel before it rode over him?''

"That's what Les seems to think, too.''

"Les?''

"Doc Farnham.''

We compared notes on Theodora's story, and I asked him if he thought she did it.

"Good motive," he said. "The method is not one that I'd guess a woman would use, but it's possible. And she's strong enough.''

Since I had decided not to tell the sheriff about my visit to Greta's room, I couldn't very well tell him about Eric's visit to his grandparents' house. I did talk to the sheriff about Greta's position in the family and Ernest's relationship with Heinz.

The sheriff acted as if he knew nothing about either. "Looks like you picked up on more things in a few days than anybody in the county figured out in all the years they've lived here.''

I doubted that was true, but I pretended to go along. "Since I don't have to coexist with them, I have fewer qualms about stirring up a rat's nest."

"It does put a new light on the girl's disappearance. She might have been thinking about running away for a long time."

I didn't think so, but I wasn't about to tell him why just yet, and I still hadn't examined my motive for protecting Greta. I told myself that was part of my investigation. I was obliged to report such things to the police, I knew that, and I would, but I wanted to find Greta first. The next day, I thought, I would know where she was. I just hoped they didn't search her room and find my fingerprints all over the posters.

I had not let myself examine the possibility of Greta's being the killer of Ben Grasse despite the fact of the bloody clothes. Since I could see myself in Greta, I guess such a suspicion wasn't comfortable for me to harbor.

When the sheriff asked me how I was coming in my search for Greta, I paused before answering him and made him suspicious.

"If you know something, Fran, I hope you're not holding back."

"I don't know anything," I said. "I've got a hunch about where she might be. I'm going to check on that hunch tomorrow." That wasn't a total lie.

"Would you care to enlighten me about your hunch?"

I told him where I was going, and he had the same response that Edith had when I told her. "Nobody down there's seen her. We've checked that."

"It would have been nice if you'd told me," I said. But it wouldn't have changed my mind, I thought.

"How did I know you were going to go there to look for her?" His face was smug. He thought I was on the wrong track. Then his face softened, as if he were afraid of hurting my feelings. "If you find her," he said, "I want you to notify me right away."

"Immediately," I said. "Scout's honor." I held up my hand in a Girl Scout salute.

"So you're leaving again tomorrow? When do you expect to come back?"

"If I'm right, I'll be back Friday."

"Good," he said. "There's a country dinner at the Grange Hall. Young Mr. Jeff is going to ask Amy. Would you like to accompany me? There's square dancing afterward. Hank and his missus will be there, too."

Whoa. The sheriff asking for a date? This really complicates my life, I thought. But I said, "How nice. If I'm back by then, I'd love it. But I've never square-danced."

"It's easy. Even us hayseeds can do it. You'll call me early Friday and let me know?"

"Sure. Sure." Hayseeds, indeed. "While we're on the subject of hayseeds," I said, smiling my cutest smile, you know the way—eyes crinkled up, mouth slightly open, chin forward, shoulders lifted, the Marilyn Monroe style—"I wanted to ask you about the other farmhands. Would any of the others have a motive to kill Grasse or Kurtz?"

"The other two who live on the farm," he said, "were the ones I questioned most closely. One of them, Joseph, speaks very little English; he just arrived in this country from Poland. I didn't find anything I could sink my teeth into there. Since Joseph knows some German, Heinz is able to communicate with him.

"The other one, Bert, is a longtime hand here. Started working for the Baeres when he was a teenager. He's known them long enough to know about the family, but he's not involved with them. He keeps apart. He does his work and goes to the local bar at night. He dates a woman who also hangs out at the bar. His life is separate from the farm. So I didn't come up with anything. The day workers are mostly locals. There are some who have had dealings of one sort or another with the family, but I haven't found anything that might lead to murder. Not yet."

"What about Ben and Terry? Did they get along?"

"Bert said they knew each other before Ben came to the farm. Everybody else I asked about it said that wasn't true."

"What do you think about the family?" I said. "Any motives there that jump out at you, other than Theodora's?"

"If Theodora was playing with Grasse, and I don't doubt that, then Ernest has a motive."

"But Theodora doesn't think Ernest knows. That's why she

was paying Terry. By the way, when did you find out that Terry knew?''

"Sunday, when I questioned him after Grasse's death.''

"Does that seem to jibe with what a blackmailer would do: tell the sheriff and possibly kill the golden goose?'' I said.

"He didn't tell me about the blackmail. But I see what you mean. The currency of the blackmailer is information that nobody else has.'' The sheriff made a tent with his fingers.

Some of what Theodora told me came bobbing to the surface of the pool of memory. "Did she tell you how careful she and Grasse were about choosing the places where they, uh, played?''

"Yes, yes,'' the sheriff said. "I was just thinking about that myself.'' He seemed annoyed.

I had an unpleasant thought, which I blurted out. "Since this Grasse had the morals of a jackrabbit, do you think he was in on the blackmail?''

"It's not likely we'll find out about that now,'' the sheriff said, "but that makes more sense than Terry coming up with a blackmail scheme. Not that I knew him all that well, but he didn't seem the type for blackmail. If Grasse put him up to it, he might go along.'' He nodded.

"But since they're both dead,'' I said, "and if—''

"Makes you wonder if somebody else was in on it, too, doesn't it?''

A shiver ran through me. I imagined Theodora a pawn in a blackmail scheme, she all thrilled, going out to meet her lover, he plotting to bleed her dry, telling Terry where they would be. "You don't suppose there are photos somewhere,'' I said.

"Theodora didn't say Terry told her he had photos.''

"I never asked Theodora whether she told Grasse about the blackmail, did you?''

"She didn't. She said she broke it up, hoping that would stop the demands for money. But Terry kept asking her for money every week.''

"How long had this been going on?'' I said.

"The affair started soon after Grasse arrived on the farm. The blackmail started almost immediately. Theodora broke it off after about a month.''

"Grasse started his campaign with Amy right after she arrived. She didn't know it was a campaign; she thought he was being helpful."

"The Lord helps those who help themselves." The sheriff shrugged and looked down at a piece of paper on the desk. It looked like a list. "The computer," he said, "how are they coming? When are you going to check on that company?"

"Delia says they should have the bare bones in place by the time the day is over. She says we can set the system up to see how that company fits into the scheme of things," I said. I didn't say that I had found Greta's disk and would take a look at that.

"I'm going to leave a unit here to keep tabs on the computers," he said. "It would make it easier for us if you and Delia and Amy would have your dinner right there where the computers are. Then when you go to the apartment for the night, I'll put one man on the computers and another at your apartment. How's that?"

"Are they going to be able to talk to one another?" I didn't like the idea of being guarded by only one officer. Whoever had turned off the lights and the phones on Monday night knew his way around.

The sheriff tried to reassure me. "They'll have their two-way radios and the phone in the car. I'm leaving two of my best night men for the midnight shift. They're used to the shift, they don't get tired, and they can see in the dark." He smiled, as if to say, What more could you want?

My answer would be that a couple more men would be a good idea. After all, he had a crime wave going on right here on the farm. Probably more crime than in the rest of the county. I didn't smile back.

"Look," he said, "if something happens to you, I have no date for the dance." He tried again to coax a smile out of me.

"If something happens to me," I said, "I have more to lose than a date."

"I'm guaranteeing you'll be safe," he said. "I've got total confidence in the guys I've put on this detail."

He sounded like a politician. But I wasn't in any mood to be persuaded. I didn't like the odds. But Sheriff Castle wasn't going to change his mind either. He adopted a condescending attitude and repeated his assurances, patting me on the shoulder.

I shrank from his touch, and I sulked out.

When I got back to the computer room, Delia had a new group working, the usual farm office workers were inputting like a band of furies. The computer aces had packed their bags and ridden off. Delia was smiling.

"We're rolling. I just called Edith to tell her. She'll be here any minute."

"How did you manage it?"

"The tech people were really tooled up. And the system isn't that old, so it wasn't overloaded. By the end of the week, everything will be back to normal."

"Will you get a bonus?"

"No, I put in a bill for the job. It doesn't matter how long it takes. And the nice part of it is Sunset will cut the check that pays the bill. Indirectly, of course. But I might figure out a way to let Dresden know." Delia giggled.

"That shouldn't be much of a challenge," I said.

Amy had gotten up from her desk, where she had been hammering away with the other office workers. "How did your meeting with the sheriff go?" There was a merry twinkle in her eye.

"You knew he was going to ask me to the dance?"

"Jeff told me," Amy said.

"You're going to go out with the sheriff?" Delia said, too loudly.

"Shh," I said. "It's a dinner and dance on Friday night. Don't tell me he didn't fix you up with a date, too."

"Gee, I don't know whether to be hurt or relieved," Delia said. "But I'll try to make up my mind on my way to Buffalo tonight." She smiled and moved her eyebrows up and down.

"You're leaving? I thought we were going to do that research." I wasn't about to name the California company for fear that one of the office people would hear and word would get around.

"We'll do it before I go."

"When will we be able to do it?" I said, looking around the room full of people and waving one hand.

Delia looked at her watch and lowered her voice. "They'll be here till nine."

"I'll be staying here, too," Amy said. "We've got to catch up." She went back to the desk where she'd been working.

"We can work at Amy's," Delia said. "I've got a modem and a laptop that we can work on. The farm computer is set up for phone access."

"The sheriff has the guard duty set up so that we eat dinner here. I'll tell him there's been a change in plans and we'll get to work." Greta's disk was burning a hole in my pocketbook.

When I went to tell the sheriff, he handed me the phone. "Somebody's been trying to get hold of you," he said.

It was Ted. I blushed, because I hadn't been candid with the sheriff, and he was standing there listening. But I didn't owe the sheriff anything, I told myself. If I had any allegiance so far, it was to Ted. And even there, I wasn't engaged to him or anything. Those thoughts played around in my head as I tried to figure out what my stance should be.

"What's up, Ted?"

"I've been trying to reach you. They had Amy's husband in jail Monday night and then let him go."

"The sheriff found out about that today," I said. "There was a foul-up somewhere along the line. But thanks for letting us know."

"Good," he said. "At least you know about it. It was a good thing Roll and I went with you Tuesday night. He might have been in town."

Ted was trying to get into a conversational mode, and the sheriff was still standing there. I wanted to tell Ted there was no privacy, but felt awkward about saying that. "You're right about that," I said, which was not exactly the right thing to say. It wasn't chatty enough. I was standing on one foot, then the other, as if I had to go to the john. "Are you home?" I said.

"Yes."

"Let me call you back."

"Don't brush me off, Fran. You get over there and you don't call." Ted's tone was not plaintive, it was blaming. And I didn't like it. Even if he was right.

"I will. Give me about an hour." I tried to tamp down the

rritation I was feeling. Then it occurred to me that Ted had probably not heard that there was another murder. That would help explain to him why I hadn't called, I thought. "Another farmhand was killed," I said. "The sheriff's department has more work than it can handle."

"They need a few of Buffalo's finest over there," Ted said. "But, Fran, you be careful. Maybe you shouldn't stay there."

"I'm leaving tomorrow."

"Then I'll see you tomorrow night. I'm off duty."

"I'm not coming home." The sheriff was still standing there, trying to figure things out from one end of the conversation. I was trying to thwart that effort.

"When will you?" Ted was sulking again.

"I've got to go. I'll call you later," I said and hung up. I quickly told the sheriff where Delia and I would be for the next several hours and left before he could ask any questions.

When I went to get Delia, she was giving Edith the rundown on the progress.

Edith was smiling. "You're a miracle," she said. "I should have hired you to set up the system in the first place."

"Hindsight is always twenty-twenty," Delia said.

Gloom descended on Edith's face. "Who would have thought?" she said. I could have sworn there were tears welling up in that determined face.

I was itching to get started on the computer, but I didn't want to say anything in front of Edith. I hoped she would be finished with her inspection and go back to the house, but she was settling in, sitting at a desk, punching keys, scrolling through files. Hmmm. Pretty good for someone who knows nothing about the computer, I thought.

Several minutes later, Edith remembered, I guess, that she was supposed to be a computer illiterate. "I don't understand it," she said. "What does it mean?" One of the office workers went and sat next to her and started to punch keys for her.

Why would she have played dumb?

I signaled to Delia that we should get out of there, but she shook me off. Apparently she didn't want to leave while Edith was there. So we were stuck not wanting to let anyone know we were going to search the files and not being able to leave to do it. Then I remembered that the sheriff hadn't questioned

Edith yet, and I excused myself to tell the sheriff where she was. He was very obliging, and Delia and I got out of there posthaste.

The sun was setting behind the trees and I could feel the evening chill. Hank accompanied us to the apartment, and he settled himself downstairs in the little office, which had been cleaned up and emptied of computers and furniture except for a table and a few chairs.

Delia and I went upstairs and got to work. For a while.

Fourteen

Delia's little laptop looked too small to be able to do much of anything, but she assured me that it was dynamite. She hooked into the farm's main computer and gave me an electronic tour through the farm system, and then she started searching for the California Arbor Naturals entries that had been restored by the inputters.

She did some number crunching on several companies and then with Arbor Naturals.

"What are you looking for?" I said.

"Numbers that don't add up," she said, not looking at me, staring at columns sliding up the screen, the flickering light making eerie patterns on her face. The only sound in the room was the faint tick of the keys. Finally, she said: "There. You were right, Fran. Something's fishy with that account."

"How did you know how to find it?" I said.

"It's not a highly creative method," she said. "Any greedy dog could have done it."

She explained what she had done and how she had come to the conclusion that something was wrong. I only half understood. But the upshot was that there were duplicate records, and one set of records didn't jibe with the other. And when they were both put in the system, they looked all right unless you did the number crunching that Delia had just done.

"Is it something Grasse would have done, do you think?" I said.

"My guess is that if he were going to cheat, he would think of something more sophisticated."

"I thought you said it was a simple system," I said.

She punched a few more keys and smiled. "Not as simple as I thought at first. This system he set up has some nice wrinkles."

"So, now at least we know there was some hanky-panky, and someone had reason to try to muck up the computers to hide it. Maybe Eric. The sheriff's first thought was Eric because of the smoke bomb."

"California Arbor Naturals was his account. Makes sense," Delia said.

"What kind of discrepancy are you finding?" I said.

"Looks like a couple thou, and it was recent."

"How recent?"

"Two months, max."

I thought about the blackmail and wondered whether Theodora had gotten the money to pay Terry by fiddling with the accounts. But no, Theodora said that Ernest was asking questions about the money. How could he have found out about the account? I couldn't see Ernest doing with the computer what Delia had just done.

"If there was an audit at tax time," I said, "would the differences be discovered?"

"There are audits and there are audits," Delia said. "If the auditor just goes through the main account to see if the numbers add up, he wouldn't discover anything. He or she would have to go over the individual orders to pick up the differences."

"When the system was put back together from the printouts, were any files missing?" I said.

"I checked the printouts against the copies we had. Nothing missing. But our copies were out of our hands, so I can't guarantee that nothing is missing. All I can say is that nobody took anything when the printouts were taken from the sheriff's car."

"Hank gave them to Edith. Anybody in the family could have gone through them. Maybe there was nothing worth taking. But you don't think anything happened to them before they were copied, do you?" I said.

"Well, it could be just the way the debuggers arranged things, but when I checked to see how much was in the system, the number was bigger than it is now. So I don't feel comfortable saying for sure that we got it all back.''

"I have something that might make a difference," I said. Then I had to tell Delia about Greta's disk and how I got it, but before I did, I swore her to secrecy.

"Bloody clothes?" she said. "Do you think the kid killed Grasse?"

I shook my head. "I can't see her doing that. But when I find her, I think I'll know more about what happened to Grasse."

"Let's look at that disk," Delia said. Delia loved poking into other people's business. She was practically salivating as she put Greta's disk into the slot.

As the data scrolled by, my heart sank. "It's not Greta's disk," I said. "It looks like it's Grasse's." Could she have killed him, after all?

"Look! Here's the data on Arbor Naturals," Delia said, and the same numbers flew by, but in this case both sets of numbers were side by side.

"That means, at least, that Grasse knew about it. And Greta."

"Are you sure you want to find that kid? She may be dangerous."

"She must have known what was on the disk and that's why she hid it," I said, remembering what Edith told me about the fight Greta and Eric had. Something about the computer, she'd said.

"But there wasn't much money stolen," Delia said. "A couple thousand's not enough to kill for."

"If the computer trashing was about the money, Greta couldn't have done it. She was long gone," I said. But I remembered sneaking around in the woods and thinking how easy it was to hide. If she were sneaking around the farm now, she might fall into the hands of Harry Worth. "What else is on that disk?" I said.

"A bunch of names and addresses, a doctor, the county clerk, some Grasses some Baeres, but not from around here."

I looked over her shoulder and saw that the Baeres on Grasse's list were Hildegarde and Grace, Greta's favorite relatives.

The doctor, Peter Menkin, also had an address in Paradise. The Grasses, too. Neighbors all.

Then there were some short files, cryptic, like messages. One said, "Go soon." Another said "T.K." And another, "Plenty coming." Some files had only numbers in them. I couldn't tell what kind of numbers they were. Some could have been dates, others looked long enough to be drivers' license numbers. Were they messages from Grasse to someone? Greta? Why did Greta hide the disk?

While I was in Paradise searching for Greta, it wouldn't hurt to check on Grasse. I started to copy the data, but Delia stopped me. She had more technology to show off in the guise of a tiny printer, which she hooked up and had print the contents of the disk.

"Didn't you say you had to call Ted?" Delia reminded me.

"Damn, I forgot. And I hung up on him before. Damn. Well, I couldn't call him while the phone was hooked into the modem," I said. "He'll never believe that I got so interested in what I was doing that I forgot to call him."

"He may believe it, but it won't make him any happier. You're not supposed to forget your significant others."

We detached the phone from the modem and I picked up and waited for the dial tone. And waited. "Phone's dead."

"Not again," Delia said. "No way of telling how long it's been dead, since we've been using the disk and not accessing the main computer for the last hour."

"Well, we still have lights," I said, cheerfully, "and our protector downstairs."

That's when the lights went out.

"Jesus!" I shouted.

"Never mind Jesus, call Hank," Delia said.

I ran to the door and screamed Hank's name down the dark stairs. There was no answer. "Maybe's he's gone to check on the lights," I said.

I closed the door and locked it.

"Some protector," Delia said.

I was furious at the sheriff. Where was Hank?

"Where's my purse?" Delia said. "Help me find my purse."

"Why?"

"My phone is in my purse."

We crawled around the floor, feeling for the purse. "Where did you leave it, Delia. Think."

"How can I think when I'm scared shitless?"

Something hit the door, like a stone, something hard and not too big.

I heard Delia gasp a split second after I did. Was there another note on the door?

"Is this the same joker as last time?" she said. "I wonder what the note says this time."

But then another missile hit the door and zipped through it, hitting something in the room.

"Whatever that was went right through the door," I said. "He's not nailing up a note this time. He's shooting at us. Get behind something," I whispered, knocking over a chair. "Get down."

From my position on the floor, I pulled the laptop off the table and pushed the table over. The more thickness, the better, but I still wasn't sure it would be enough.

"Watch out, Fran," Delia whispered. "I'm knocking over these other chairs."

It occurred to me, that all our knocking over of furniture would tell the shooter where we were and tell him where to aim.

Another shot whizzed through the door and hit something close to us. It was a peculiar-sounding shot, but the missiles were coming through the door at great speed.

"Found it," Delia whispered. "It was on the chair."

"What?"

"The purse. I've got the phone."

Another shot. Closer. I heard something hit near me.

"After the next shot," I told Delia, "Run like hell for the bathroom. Put more wall between him and us. I'll follow."

Another shot. Delia ran. Then another. Closer together now. I didn't know whether it was safe to run or not. I was getting ready to get up and run when my hand hit something on the floor. I ran my fingers over it. A nail.

It took me a few seconds to connect. Then I realized that he was shooting at us with one of those carpenter's nail guns. I hunkered down, panting and trying to devise a prayer to whoever listened to such things. I started with an apology for not sending up conversations about anything else when I wasn't in trouble. Then I got to the business at hand: Let me live. Followed by promises to not be a stranger in the future.

I was sweating and praying, while the shooter kept spraying the room with nails. The shooting stopped and I heard something slam against the door and then a cracking sound.

He's coming in. Oh, no. He's coming in. I screamed and screamed. And then, because I knew I was a dead woman, I stopped screaming and somehow found my own purse and the .38. Don't ask me how I went from victim to fighter. It just happens to me. I'm not consistent.

I aimed at the door and shot.

Silence.

I shot again and heard a howl, followed by footsteps running down the stairs.

I stayed put. I hadn't heard a sound from Delia. I was panting and my heart was thumping as if it were trying to escape from my chest.

I don't know how long I stayed there, but the sound that finally pulled me to a standing position was the voice of Sheriff Castle.

"Fran. Fran. What's going on? Where are you?"

"Up here," I said.

"We're here," Delia said. "Thank God, the call got through. The damn operator was giving me . . ."

The sound of the sheriff's voice came from the other side of the door and shards of light were coming through the door. "What happened here?" In the beam of his flashlight, I saw the door half fall and half swing open.

He was practically inside, I thought. The shooter was that close.

"Here I am. No thanks to your guard," I said. "Someone was shooting nails at us. We could have been killed. We almost were."

"I heard a gun shot," he said. "Not a nail gun."

"That was me. I shot at him. Twice. I think I winged him."

"I didn't know you had a gun," he said. I wondered whether he was thinking that next time he wouldn't bother putting on a guard.

* * *

By the time the lights were back on, Delia and I had given the sheriff the story and several pieces of our minds.

As the sheriff was about to leave we heard a groan and a shape loomed up the hall and showed itself in the doorway. A bloody shape.

All three of us jumped. The sheriff and I grabbed our guns. And then we realized the bloody mess was Hank.

"Somebody hit me. Are you ladies all right?" Hank said, holding his bloody head, and then he fell in a heap.

It was ten o'clock before the ambulance had taken Hank away and the phones were working again. The wires had been cut this time.

The sheriff deputies were told to look for someone on the farm with some kind of surface cut that could have been made by a bullet grazing the skin. They came back and reported to the sheriff: Every one of the men on the farm had some kind of wound, the deputies said. All of them superficial, all of them recent.

The sheriff shook his head. "A farm's a dangerous place."

"Tell me about it," I said.

When Delia left, she insisted on leaving me her phone. When I protested, she said, "You'll need it more than I will. I'm taking a few days off. The Bahamas sound good."

Before he left the farm that night, I told the sheriff about California Arbor Naturals. I didn't know whether he'd get a chance to investigate it or not. I didn't know whether it had anything to do with people shooting through doors and killing off farmhands.

Amy and I had double guards that night. The next day, Amy was going away. She would stay with an aunt in Chicago, an aunt who had moved there recently and whose address Greg didn't know.

I would catch a flight to Philadelphia in the morning.

Fifteen

I got to the airport early next morning. The plane looked so small I almost didn't get on it. The weather was clear, though, so I figured we wouldn't get bounced around too much.

I was wrong. I went for the little bag a few times and held it in front of me. Flight attendants can spot infrequent fliers by their color. Mine was greenish. She gave me a peppermint Life Saver, and that helped.

The rental car was only slightly better than the plane. When I started it up, it sputtered. The mechanic assured me that the car was running fine. "It just needs to get warmed up." That didn't stop me from worrying.

According to the map, I had more than an hour's drive to Paradise. From the Philadelphia airport I headed north and then west and finally picked up Route 30 west. It ran through rolling country dotted with houses, barns, and silos. Horses pulled the plows of the Amish farmers, and no electric wires ran into their houses. I tried to imagine children being brought up without television: children reading, children playing checkers, playing tiddlywinks, playing games I never heard of, maybe even paper versions of Nintendo, who knows. Several times along the route I had to pass one of their black horse-drawn carriages, the bright orange triangle vibrating on the back, the driver serene in the face of the impatience of those with considerably more horsepower at their fingertips.

The Amish faces looked too stern for me, but maybe it was my notion of the severity of their lives that I was seeing. However, they weren't averse to making a little money from their idiosyncrasies; there were signs all over for Amish cooking, Amish quilts, Amish handicrafts.

When I got to Paradise, I drove around the town, looking for the addresses I'd brought. They were all within a mile of one another. There was a Grasse's Hardware, a Baere's Amish Restaurant with a neon sign in the window that told me right away that the people who ran the restaurant weren't Amish, and a Grasse's turkey farm. Doctor Menkin's office was right in the center of town near the Amish restaurant. Hildegarde and Grace Baere lived near the edge of town, right where the sign tells through traffic that speed is controlled by radar.

The Baere house was an older version of the farmhouse in Wyoming County: two stories, front porch, and an addition on the back that also had a porch. The back part, I guessed, housed the kitchen.

I drove by a couple of times, trying to spot Greta's pickup truck. It wasn't in the yard, but my guess was that it was in the barn. Finally, I pulled in the driveway. An old dog came out to greet me, barking and wagging his tail. I vaguely remembered a dog in some of the pictures taken of Greta when she was young and staying with her great-grandmother. He looked like a yellow lab, but he was so gray, it was hard to tell what color he started with. His back legs moved stiffly, and his left eye was frosted over. He was one of those dogs that look like they're smiling.

I stuck one foot out of the car door, figuring he'd get a whiff of Horace on my shoes, not to mention whatever animal scents I had picked up at Hickory Hills. He was interested and gave my shoes a good long sniff. As I walked toward the back door (on farms, the back door is the one everybody uses unless there's a wedding), he kept on sniffing, but he barked a couple of times to let me know he was on the job.

A gray head poked out the door. "Rover, that's enough. What do you think you're doing? That's no way to treat company." The accent was thick German, the *t*'s and *th*'s sounded like *d*'s. The rest of the gray personage moved onto the porch. She was wearing a long gray skirt. "What can I do for you?"

"I'm Fran Tremaine Kirk. Edith Baere hired me to find

Greta,'' I said. I held out my hand, but she acted as if she didn't see it.

"Oh, ja, come in, come in.''

She knew I was coming, I thought.

She smiled, and that's where the gray gave way to yellow— old teeth with most of the enamel eroded by years. But in her smile of a million wrinkles I could see the smooth-faced girl of eighty years before. "I am Greta's great-grandmother,'' she said. "Mother'' sounded like "mudder.''

"You're Heinz's mother?''

"Ja, ja. Grace Baere. And my daughter is here, Heinz's sister. Hilda,'' she called out, "we have company.''

Hildegarde looked like a female Heinz, large and loose limbed, except she had considerably more hair, gray and yellow, in a single braid down her back. Her skirt, too, was long and gray. She smiled shyly and said, "Hello, I'm Hildegarde.''

"Fran Tremaine Kirk,'' I said and held out my hand, which she took gingerly and gave a wisp of a handshake.

"Sit down, Mrs. Kirk,'' Grace said. "I have hot coffee on the stove. You want?''

"Yes, thank you,'' I said, and hoped that some rolls or bread would accompany the coffee. I needn't have worried. Heinz's mother was a match for Edith in rolling out the tablecloth for guests.

Sweet rolls with sugar frosting, cinnamon buns, plain rolls, all warm, were paraded out along with sliced ham, chunks of dark yellow cheese, a bowl of apple sauce, jars of jam that looked homemade, butter, and cream. Then there were the cookies—date filled, oatmeal-raisin drop cookies, rolled cookies cut into shapes, lace cookies drizzled with chocolate—a huge plate of them. I only wished I had just come in from the fields so that I could justify getting on the outside of more of that stuff.

The woman probably never heard of cholesterol.

Although neither of the women were fat, they ate with the abandon of teenagers.

They had been getting bulletins from Edith on what was happening at Hickory Hills. "She calls every day,'' Grace said. "What a shame. The farm is going to the devil.''

Hildegarde nodded.

"Has Greta contacted you at all?" I said.

Grace smiled and took another sweet roll. "No. No. We have not heard from her. You haven't heard from her, have you, Hilda?"

Hildegarde looked at the doorway to the kitchen and said, "No, I haven't heard anything. I hope she's all right."

I didn't believe either one of them. "When was the last time you spoke to Greta?"

"Sunday, no Saturday morning," Grace said.

"Did she tell you anything that made you think she was unhappy or she was planning to run away?"

"No, no. She talked about her computer that Edith put in her room. She likes the computer." Grace was winging it. I thought that if I stayed long enough, I would surely trip her up. She was a lousy liar.

"You and Hildegarde live here by yourselves?"

"Ja, ja. We have lived here by ourselves for over forty years, except for when little Greta would come to stay with us."

"You enjoyed her visits? She behaved herself?"

"She was never any trouble. Such a joy."

Hildegarde nodded all the while.

"Who owns Baere's Amish restaurant? Another relative?" I said.

"A long time ago. A brother of my husband and his wife had that place. No more." She waved her arm to dismiss the subject.

"Are there other Baeres in town now?"

"No. No more Baeres here," Grace said. "Some relatives still live not too far, but they live the old way, and we haven't seen them for a long time."

"They're very strict," Hildegarde said.

"Yes," Grace said, "strict."

I was getting the idea that there had been some bad feeling about the "old way" somewhere along the line.

"I guess you knew Ben Grasse," I said.

Grace's face sagged. "We knew him. He was here all the time when he was a little boy. A pretty boy. Blond and blue-eyed. We have pictures. Hilda, get the pictures of little Benny."

Hildegarde left the room and came back with an album that she handed to Grace. Grace showed me pictures of Ben.

"He looked like an angel," Grace said, "but he was a devil." She chuckled as if the deviltry was something she enjoyed. "You couldn't keep him away from the cookie jar."

His taste in sweets may have changed, I thought, but he still couldn't stay away from them. "Did he keep in touch with you as he got older?" I said.

"Not the way he did when he was little, but he always sent us cards on our birthdays. Didn't he, Hilda?"

Hildegarde nodded so much she put me in mind of those figures that ride in the back windows of cars.

"He used to get Greta presents, too, when she was a little tyke. Her birthday is in June," Hilda said. "It's soon. She . . . I hope you find her before her birthday." It was the longest bit of conversation she'd uttered, and what she almost said, I'm sure, would have told me that she knew where Greta was.

Of course, I thought. Greta's known Grasse all her life. She had a relationship with him that stretched back all the years she stayed in Paradise during vacations. A man who brought her birthday presents. A man about the age of her father.

I stayed a little longer and then offered to help clean up, but they insisted that they didn't need help.

I left, having gotten what I came for. I knew Greta was there. The reason I knew was that the drain basket on the sink drain had three of everything in it. Three forks, spoons, knives, cups, bowls, saucers. Grace and Hildegarde lived there alone, all right. And they always had that huge supply of homemade cookies, too.

Rover didn't bother to escort me to my car. He was curled up on a piece of rug on the porch. As I drove away, I saw a hand at the lace curtain in a front window.

I pondered my options. What next? A stakeout? No, the country is too open. Someone would call the Baeres and tell them a car was parked nearby, or they'd call the police and have them pick me up for loitering. Should I ask questions around town? Had everyone been told to keep mum? Or should I not let anyone know why I was there? Had Greta been going out or had she been lying low?

I drove around the town, which was a melding of new and

old, Amish and secular, rural and urban. Grasse's Hardware was on the corner of Main Street and Mile Strip Road. Out in front were garden tools and in the window were T-shirts with messages printed on them like I LIVE IN PARADISE and I SLEPT IN PARADISE and OUR MARRIAGE IS IN PARADISE—you get the idea.

While I was trying to decide what to do about Greta, I could find out about Grasse. I parked by a parking meter in front of the hardware store; for a nickle I could park for an hour.

The aisles were narrow, and the shelves were loaded inside the dimly lit store. At the back of the center aisle was a counter where the only customer was handing over some coins in exchange for something in a small brown bag. Behind the counter stood a man with salt-and-pepper hair and dark eyebrows. His face was long and horsey, his teeth, likewise.

"Can I help you?" he said.

"I'm not here to buy anything," I said, and introduced myself, told him why I was in town, and that I'd just come from the Baeres's house.

"Dieter Grasse," he said, holding out his hand. "Were you at the farm when my brother was killed?" I searched his face for a resemblance to the man whom I'd seen in person only once, and that was in death, with a pitchfork coming out of his chest.

"No, after." I decided not to tell him I'd seen the body.

"They're sending the body today," he said. "Visiting hours tommorrow, funeral Saturday." He looked a bit like Ben Grasse from up close, but the resemblance was slight. I was surprised, though, when he said Ben was his brother. He looked old enough to be Ben's father.

"Did you hear that another man was killed on the farm?"

"No. Another man killed? Do they have one of those serial killers loose up there?"

"I don't know," I said. "The other fellow's name was Terry Kurtz."

Dieter reacted to the name. "Poor fella," he said.

"I thought maybe Ben knew him from before he went to Hickory Hills."

"There's some Kurtzes over in Intercourse," he said. There was something he wasn't telling.

Lucky for me, I had seen the name of the town on the map, so I wasn't surprised. "Did Ben know anybody over there?" I couldn't bring myself to say, Did Ben know anybody in Intercourse. Not with the reputation he had.

"Can't say. He could have. But I never heard him talk about anybody name of Kurtz."

Dieter looked like he could talk all day, so I decided to chat him up. "Did you know Heinz and Edith when they lived here?"

"Sure. Heinz and I went to school together. We were friends. His family had more money than mine, but in those days that didn't make so much difference. The things we did for fun didn't cost so much."

"Do you still keep in touch with him?"

"No. Not since he left town. Haven't heard a word directly. But I hear about him. That's quite a farming business they have up there. I heard a lot about it from Ben."

He told me what he knew about the farm; how big it was, how many barns, how many head of cattle, what kind of house Heinz lived in, and where Ernest and Theodora and their children lived.

"I ought to go up and see it," he said. "Sounds like quite a place. Ben liked it there. He wanted to stay there."

"I thought they hired him to set up the computer programs and then he would be leaving."

"That's not what he told me. Just recently he told me he'd met a gal he could settle down with. He said she liked the farm, too."

Would that be Amy? I thought. Was Ben thinking about settling down with Amy?

"I don't know whether I believed him, though," he said. "Ben had an eye for the ladies."

His eye was not the part of his anatomy that came immediately to mind. "Were there a lot of kids in your family?" Then tactful as ever, I said, "Ben was younger than you, wasn't he?"

"He was Mom's last. A change baby. There were us three older kids and Ben, the baby."

I had to run that by a couple of times before I realized he

was saying that Ben was a change-of-life accident that happened to his mother.

"We're having a hard year," Dieter said. "Our sister, Lizzie, died less than a year ago, and now Ben. Fritz and I are the only ones left now, and Fritz has a bad heart. It's the end of the line. No children."

"Didn't I see a Grasse's turkey farm? I've seen a lot of signs around town with the name Grasse on them."

"The turkey farm is Fritz's. There used to be a lot of us, but we died out. Doc Menkin thinks maybe the water made us sterile." Dieter smiled as if to say that that theory was pure hogwash.

Farm metaphors are contagious.

Doctor Menkin was one of the names on the disk I figured was Ben's. But why would Ben put those names on the disk in the first place? They were names and addresses he would remember without writing them down. Did they have some special significance?

"Don't get Edith started on the subject of water," I said. "She won't water her vegetables with anything but the water from the spring on the farm."

He smiled. "That Edith. Always was a pistol. I used to go out with her. Heinz dated Lizzie, and we would double-date, go to a drive-in movie, and mush it up."

What a romantic. "What did Edith look like?"

"A beauty, golden haired, with a figure like a Venus. Heinz stole her away from me. It took me a long time to forgive him. Don't know as I have forgiven him, if it comes to that."

"Her granddaughter, Greta, the one I'm looking for, does she look like Edith did?"

"Almost, but not as good. Edith was something special."

"You haven't seen Greta around here lately, have you?"

"Not since last summer."

So Greta has been hiding out, I thought. I don't know why I was so sure that Greta was here in Paradise, but maybe it was because she looked so happy in the pictures with Grace and Hildegarde and she was so unhappy at home.

"Where does Fritz live?" I said. "Maybe I ought to go see him."

"He likes company," Dieter said. "But he don't talk as

much as me." Dieter laughed, showing the full length of his teeth. Very horsey. "Fritz and Marge live up on the hill. You could have got there cross lots from the Baeres's in no time. By road, you got to come into town and turn onto Mile Strip here, and then onto Valley View and go back up the same hill you come down." As he spoke he ran his finger on the roads on a map of Paradise hanging behind the counter. "Valley View is two blocks down that way," he said.

"Should I call and tell him I'm coming?" I said.

"You just go on ahead. I'll call him. He'll be there. If he's not in the house, he'll be out in the barn. The dog don't bite."

Valley View Road was aptly named. The valley stretched out below, like a cliché, the white church spire with the houses around it, and outside of town the rectangles of the fields in shades of green depending on the crops, hedgerows running between.

My nostrils told me when I was getting close to the turkey farm. And when I drove into the driveway, the birds announced my arrival. I could see a number of runs that came from the barn, each run had birds of a different size, all of them white. They fluttered and jumped, but none of them flew.

When I got out of the car, a dog began to bark, but I couldn't see it. I stood still, looking around, not wanting to be surprised by the dog, until I realized that the dog was in the house, punctuating his barks with scratches on the screen door.

As soon as I got to the porch, a woman showed up at the other side of the screen door. She was wiping her hands on her apron. When she opened the door to greet me, the dog shot out and began leaping on me, barking and wagging his tail as if I were his long-lost friend. He looked like a large fox terrier.

"Cut that out, Pilgrim," the woman said. Then she looked at me and said, "He'll calm down, but not much. I'm Marge Grasse. You the lady was just at the store?"

"Yes," I said, and gave her a card.

She stood there, reading every word on it, aloud. Then she put the card in her apron pocket. "A shame about Ben," she said. "I thought he would go places now that he knew about the computers."

Go places? The man was in his forties. Why, all of a sudden

was he going to go places? "I heard he worked on an organic farm here before he went to Hickory Hills."

"There's no organic farm in Paradise. He worked on the computers at an organic farm run by the State Corrections Department."

"That must have been good experience for him," I said.

"It was," she said. And then, because I wasn't catching on, she said, "But he didn't have much choice."

"In jail? He was in jail? What for?"

"Messing with a young girl. Statutory rape."

"Hell of a guy," I said, before I remembered that I was talking to his sister-in-law. Dieter, the nonstop talker, had been closemouthed on the subject of Ben's jail time.

But she was no fan of Ben Grasse. "He couldn't keep his pants zipped," she said. "But at least he wasn't fooling with babies anymore."

Maybe, I thought. "No one at Hickory Hills knew that he'd been in jail," I said.

"We didn't tell anybody. But he's dead now, so it doesn't matter. It can't hurt his future."

"When did he get out?" I said.

"End of last summer, just before Lizzie died. Lizzie took it hard, him being in jail."

"How did you keep something like that secret?"

"The girl's folks didn't want to make a thing out of it, so Ben just pleaded guilty and they whisked him off to jail."

"Simple as that." The voice came from behind me. I turned and saw another horse-faced man. This one, though, had skin grayer than Grace Baere's, but he was a score younger.

I was invited in after Fritz and I shook hands. Marge was no slouch when it came to putting out a spread for visitors, either. But her foods ran more to the healthy, and I figured that was because she was trying to keep her husband's weak heart going a little longer.

There were turkey sandwiches and tuna sandwiches on whole wheat bread and vegetables cut up for dipping. One dip was made from yogurt and the other was made of beans and spices. There was lemonade and iced tea to drink. Dessert was fruit and angel food cake. I figured I could clean out my arteries from the snack I'd had at the Baeres's.

Fritz and Marge wanted to know everything about Hickory Hills and the Baeres. What kind of food they raised and what kind of food they sold at the store were particularly interesting to Marge. Fritz asked about the barns and the cattle, but he was especially interested in what kind of birds they raised.

I told him what little I knew about Ernest's birds. At first I was reluctant to tell them about the mess the family was in, but after an hour or so of friendly conversation, I told them about the family dynamics. They laughed like maniacs when I told them about the way Edith ran things.

"Just like her," Marge said. "She had Heinz wrappped around her little finger just like she had Dieter."

Fritz chuckled. "She was in my class at school. Always was bossing us around."

When I asked them about Ben Grasse growing up in Paradise, they told me how he was everybody's baby, because the other children were all grown up when he arrived.

"Sure surprised my mom, having a new one after all the baby clothes were long gone from the attic," Fritz said.

"We were already married and hoping to have one of our own," Marge said. She looked at Fritz and patted him on the arm. He put his hand over hers and patted some more. I guessed they had consoled each other through the years. They seemed so comfortable with each other, I wanted to tell them how lucky they were. But that probably wouldn't have changed the way they felt about not having children.

Then I asked them if they'd seen Greta recently.

"No," Fritz said, "I haven't seen her, but she could be staying over there and I'd never see her." He pointed out the window toward a rise of ground.

I followed with my eyes in the direction he was pointing.

"They live right over the knoll. When Greta was a little tyke, she'd come toddling over that rise with Hilda right behind her. Greta always wanted to come and see the turkeys," Marge said. "What did she used to call them, Fritzie?"

"Tookeys," he said, and chuckled.

"Yes, tookeys," Marge said, and laughed right along with him.

"You wouldn't have seen a pickup truck over there recently, would you?" I said.

"No, I don't see anything over there unless I go up on that rise, and I don't have call to do that very often," Fritz said.

"We can see over there from upstairs, but we don't sleep upstairs anymore," Marge said. "We have plenty of room down here. And we don't have to heat up there in winter."

"That reminds me," I said. "I've got to get a place to sleep tonight. I'd better do that before everything's all booked up."

"No worry about getting booked up in Paradise," she said, but she was looking at Fritz. Some kind of silent communication was going on. Then she nodded. "You can stay here. We'd love to have you. We've got a nice room upstairs, and you'd have the upstairs bathroom to yourself."

I gathered that Fritz had signaled her that she should invite me. I had nothing but good vibes from these people, but I didn't want to impose on them. "Edith gave me the name of a motel, the Hay Den. She's paying my expenses."

"The Hay Den?" Marge said. "You don't want to stay there. It's next to the lumberyard and the bar. There's always somebody sleeping it off there, and none too quietly, either. They're always calling the sheriff."

I guess Edith wasn't sending me first class.

"You can pay us what you'd pay at the motel," Fritz said, " 'cept we'll throw in dinner." He smiled and showed his teeth. They were even longer than his brother's.

That sounded like an exceptional deal. The thought that I'd be close enough to spy on the Baeres also crossed my mind. "You folks are very kind," I said. "Will I bother you if I walk in the fields at night? I don't get a chance to do that very often."

"Did you do any walking at Hickory Hills?" Marge said. Her curiosity about the place was bottomless.

"I didn't feel safe walking around a place where two bodies turned up, both murdered."

"Two? Who was the other one?" Marge said.

"A farmhand named Terry Kurtz. I was there when the body was found under the tractor wheel."

"Ugh," Marge said.

"Say, Marge, we know Terry Kurtz, don't we?"

"Do we? Terry Kurtz? Oh, yes, Kurtz was the name of that fellow Ben brought here from prison. Ben used to stay with us after Mom died. And when he got out, he came here. Another fellow got out the same day, and he brought him here. We weren't too pleased about that.''

''Your own flesh and blood being in prison and then coming to live with you is one thing. But a stranger from prison living under your roof makes you uneasy,'' Fritz said.

''How long did he stay?''

Marge looked at Fritz and frowned. ''Seemed like a year,'' she said.

''Two weeks,'' Fritz said and smiled. ''It wasn't him, it was us that made it seem so long. He was polite and helped with the chores.''

''But we couldn't relax,'' Marge said.

''What was he in jail for?'' I said.

''A holdup. Shot somebody when he was a teenager. He was in jail for twenty years. Ben was in for ten. He was sure different when he came out,'' Marge said.

''He wanted to make something of himself,'' Fritz said.

''He was doing so well at Hickory Hills. He told us he was going to get a big job there.''

Big job? ''I didn't know that,'' I said.

''It was a secret, he told us. It was supposed to be announced soon.''

I wondered why I hadn't heard about it. That wasn't the kind of thing I expected the Baeres to keep secret. Other things, yes. But an appointment to a big job at the farm? I wondered who had promised him that.

Sixteen

I left Fritz and Marge after we had arranged for my over-night stay. I did ask Marge whether she needed any help with dinner, since my mother had taught me to offer help to my hostess if my hostess didn't have live-in help, and I didn't know many people with live-ins.

I remember my mother telling me that women had the best conversations in the kitchen while the men were waiting for the next course. Nowadays, the men are supposed to get up from their chairs and pick up the dishes, too. Some do, I'm told.

But my life doesn't lend itself to sit-down dinners. If life is a banquet, mine is fast food.

Marge didn't need any help, she said, and didn't need any-thing from the store. "Don't forget. We'll eat at seven," she said as I got into the car.

The first thing I did was to find a phone to call Sheriff Castle—I supposed I'd be calling him Dick after I'd square-danced with him a few times. The horrible thing was that my husband's name was Dick, and whenever I said the name, waves of old feelings nearly drowned me.

The sheriff picked up the phone on the second ring. He was glad to hear from me.

"We've got Miss Amy's husband," he said. "He came back out here."

"Ooh, I'm glad Amy was gone."

"He was up to no good. We found him on the farm. He went to the store and got friendly with one of the women. She told him everything she knew. Thank God, it wasn't much. After he left, she told one of the other women about him. She got suspicious and called us.''

"What did he say about Ben Grasse?''

"He didn't seem to know anything about Grasse or anything else that went on at the farm. But we've only just started talking to him,'' he said. "What have you dug up there?''

I told him what I'd learned about Grasse and Kurtz.

"This changes everything,'' he said. "Do you know whether Kurtz was using his real name?''

"It's the only name the folks here have. Did you get prints off the body?''

"Right,'' he said. "We'll take the prints and run them through the computer. Nobody's claimed the body.''

"Maybe you'll find some relatives,'' I said. "Do you think Kurtz and Grasse planned the blackmail scheme?''

"Wouldn't put it past them. A couple of cons in the pen planning their lives when they get out. They could have come up with something like this.''

"Have you found anything else in the computer that would link the two of them?''

"No, but we haven't gone through all the files.''

Then I asked the sheriff if he had heard anything about Ben getting a big job at the farm.

"No, I haven't,'' he said, "but I'll ask the Baeres about it and have the computer records checked for that. The troopers have lent us a computer maven. He's already got the California Arbor Naturals stuff all printed out and documented.''

"Delia got that in a couple of minutes,'' I said. I guess I was being snotty, but I knew where the credit for that belonged and it wasn't with the so-called maven from the state police.

"He did say that you women did a hell of a job.''

Yes, we did. "Tell him thank you.''

"He'll confront the Baeres with the data on the California account, one at a time.''

"That should be interesting,'' I said. Then I told him about the argument Greta and Eric had about something related to the computer. I also told him that Edith was a bit smarter about the computers than she was letting on. I still didn't tell him about the disk I'd found—or the bloody clothing.

"I guess you haven't found Greta yet, eh?" he said.

"No, but I think I'm on the right track."

"And you're still coming back tomorrow? For the square dance?"

"I hope so. I'm not certain, though. Maybe you should go with someone else. Someone who's sure."

"I'll take my chances," he said. "If you don't show up, there'll be other ladies to dance with."

"Even if I do show up," I said, "you might find dancing with one of the other women easier on your feet."

"You look pretty light on your feet to me," he said.

What a thing to say. I hadn't had someone say anything so odd or anything that pleased me so much in a long time. I didn't know how to respond, so I said, "Probably from running."

"Hey, you're a runner? Want to race me?"

"You run?"

"Ever since high school. Before everybody else was doing it."

We were getting away from the subject and into an area where our lives were apt to get intertwined. I was an old hand at avoiding intimacy. "Before I forget, Sheriff, will you let me know what you find out about Grasse and Kurtz from the records?"

He snapped to. He knew his job. "Will do," he said. "Call me back in a couple of hours and I'll have that for you. Will it help you find Greta?"

"Yes, I think so."

"I want to question her if you find her, don't forget that."

"Where are you looking for her?" I said.

"We're still tracking her through her friends."

"By the way," I said, "what are the girls wearing in high school now?"

"What? How should I know? What's that got to do with anything?"

"Greta started wearing long skirts recently. Sort of like the Amish down here wear and like her great-grandmother and great-aunt wear, as well. I wondered whether the girls up there were also wearing them or whether Greta had started her own style. And Heinz hated those long skirts. Maybe because some of his family used to be Amish.''

"What's that got to do with anything?"

"I don't know. I thought it was interesting. Maybe it would indicate she had been planning to leave.''

I was thinking that at one time I would have backed off if some man in authority had told me that my comments were irrelevant. One step forward for me.

"I'll have someone check that out," he said, but I could hear the amusement in his voice.

"Maybe your secretary will know," I said, "then you won't have to put a deputy on it.''

"I'll ask her when she comes back," he said. "You know, I would have never figured Grasse for an ex-con. Good work, Fran.''

"I wouldn't have, either."

"If you hadn't gone down there, we wouldn't have known. Maybe I ought to have someone go down there and see what else we can dig up on Grasse.''

"Maybe. Unless the killer is one of the Baeres right there on the farm.''

"There are no Baeres on the farm today."

"What do you mean?"

"They all took off this morning. Heinz had to go for some tests at Roswell Park in Buffalo. Edith went with him. Theodora and Ernest took Eric to a college up near Boston, one that Theodora visited last month. Seems he's decided he wants to go to college after all.''

"Who's running the farm?" If I had been sheriff, I would have tried to keep the Baeres at home, even if I did have Greg in custody.

"Edith left a list of instructions. Everybody has plenty to do.''

"Had these trips been planned all along?"

"They said so, but I didn't check up on them."

Why not? I thought. "Has Heinz been sick?" I hadn't noticed any sign of Heinz ailing.

"He's been having some pain, Edith told me."

"What did Heinz say?"

"Heinz? I never heard anything like that from him. He's not the type to complain about pain."

"He must have been having some, must have talked to a doctor about it. Why else would they be going to Roswell Park? That's where they treat cancers."

"I didn't ask," he said. "I'm beginning to think I'm too close to these people."

"I didn't mean . . ." I was embarrassed for the sheriff. He was missing the ball right and left. And yet, I thought, it took a big person to see his own shortcomings. "What I mean is, a lot's been happening." I was really trying to let him off the hook. Another step on the path to adulthood.

"Yeah," he said. "Call later and we'll have that information for you. If I'm not here, Mary will give you the information."

He hung up. Probably mad at me, probably mad at himself. But heck, he needed help and should have had the troopers in on it right from the start.

Next I went to see the doctor, Doctor Peter Menkin, whose name was on the disk that Greta had hidden. I didn't know what I was going to ask him, but I figured something would come to me.

The house was larger than most of the others in the town, with an addition on the left side that was clearly office space. It was white clapboard with black shutters and had a porch that wrapped around the right side. At one time, the porch probably wrapped all around; the house had the look of one whose symmetry had been broken up in the name of practicality.

A man about thirty-five or forty answered the door. With his round shaved head and small features, his face looked like a pink bowling ball resting on top of his bow tie, white collar and pin-striped three-piece suit.

"I'm Fran Tremaine Kirk," I said, "and I'm looking for Doctor Peter Menkin."

His smile revealed a set of even white teeth that made the pink bowling ball look absolutely handsome. "Junior or senior?" he said.

"I don't know."

"Well, I'm junior. Come on in."

I gave him my card and told him I was looking for Greta.

He had heard about Grasse's murder, said he had just come from examining the body before it was turned over to the funeral parlor. "Nasty, getting killed that way," he said.

"Could you tell whether he died right away?" I said. I don't know why I asked that. But it had something to do with Greta and those bloody clothes.

"He might have had a few minutes, maybe ten. But I'm guessing. Why?"

"I wondered whether he could have called for help."

"He died in a barn, I'm told, that was fairly distant from any of the houses there."

"Oh, who told you that?"

"His brother Dieter. He's making the arrangements."

"Do you have any idea why your name or your father's name would have been among Grasse's records?"

"Probably Dad. He was the family doctor around here for years. I just moved back to town and started working with Dad."

"Your father is probably the one I want to see. Is he home?"

"No, he's gone to the city to have his pacemaker checked." He smiled again. "Even doctors get sick. But he's already outlived his own father. Heart trouble takes the Menkin boys early."

I took another look at junior and realized that under that three-piece suit, the body was trim and fit.

"So you take care of yourself," I said.

"Try to," he said. "Now, what can I do for you?"

"I don't know. Is there anything about Ben Grasse that would be helpful for me to know?"

"You know he spent some time in jail?"

"Yes."

"He always had a reputation of being a lady-killer. And then he started fooling with younger and younger girls. When he hit on a twelve-year-old, everybody had had enough."

"How did he get that way?"

"I don't have the faintest. I went to school with him, and in elementary school he was just a kid like the rest of us. No better, no worse. It started in junior high. He chased and chased. His marks in school went down and he failed a grade. After that, I didn't see him much.''

"Hormones?" I said.

"You'd think so, but usually something else happens. Some kind of abuse that pushes the kid into a posture that's so extreme.''

The *A* word again, I thought. "Who would abuse him? He was the baby of the family. I thought they all doted on him.''

"That doesn't mean something like that didn't happen in the family. Mind you, I'm not saying it happened. I'm not saying it happened in the family. It could have been anybody he came into contact with.'' He lifted his arms with his palms turned up. "And it could be that it was all hormones.''

"Did your father treat him for some disorder? Is that why the name was in his files?''

"I'm afraid I can't help you. And Dad won't be home until late, nine-thirty at the earliest. Where are you staying? I'll have him call you when he comes in, unless it's really late. Then he'll call you in the morning.''

I told him where I'd be staying and gave him the number of Delia's portable phone.

"I've thought of getting one of those phones,'' he said. "But just about the time I decide to go for it, I get a phone call from someone I'd rather not talk to, and I think, why should I make it easy for assholes like that to find me?'' He smiled again and didn't apologize for his language. If anything, he should have apologized for his suit. It was the only phony thing about him.

He offered me a glass of white wine, "a terrific chardonnay,'' he said. It was the best offer I'd had all day, and I didn't think there'd be any alcohol at the Grasse table that night.

We sat in a room at the back of the house that looked out into a back yard blooming with lilacs, irises, and peonies.

"Nice yard,'' I said.

"My mom put in those perennials years ago,'' he said. "She died a few years ago. I'm sorry I wasn't living here then. I was in Africa. Didn't make the funeral. They couldn't find me.''

"You must have felt awful,'' I said.

"I did,'' he said. "I sure did.'' His head bobbed up and

down, and I was getting the bowling ball impression again. "Miss Kirk—is it 'miss'?"

"I was married," I said. "Not now. I use Ms. when I get the choice."

"Would you excuse me for a few minutes? I had to go to court today, and this suit is driving me nuts."

I laughed. "Go right ahead," I said.

"Help yourself to more wine. We might as well kill the bottle. Dad doesn't drink."

When young Doctor Menkin returned, the whole picture changed. In his khaki shorts and black T-shirt, the bowling-ball look had completely disappeared. His neck was long, his torso was the kind women drool over, and his legs were, well, let's just drop the whole thing. He was a hunk.

He asked me about myself, and I gave him the cleaned-up version of my life. I'm sure that he left out a few details when he gave me his biography, too.

I asked him about Paradise and why he'd come back to live here.

"I always knew I'd be a doctor and work with my dad. I didn't know that I would take so long to get here. But I'm here now, and Dad is glad to have me." He got up and filled our glasses while he talked. "The practice is too big for him to handle alone. And the records that he has to keep nowadays are very daunting."

I looked at my watch. I was so comfortable sitting there listening to this talkative young doctor that I was afraid I would lose track of time and be late for dinner.

"Am I keeping you?" he said. He didn't miss anything.

"No, but I want to be sure that I get back to Fritz and Marge Grasse's place before seven. I've been invited for dinner."

"Lucky you," he said. "Marge always was the best cook in town and now that she's cooking healthy, there's no place in town I'd rather eat." His smile widened and widened, his eyes disappearing into slits under his brows.

I cocked my head to one side. "Something funny?" I said.

"An inspiration. Marge is always asking me to dinner. And so long as she's cooking for company tonight, maybe today's the day to wangle an invitation."

Now it was my turn to smile. The guy was good company.

"You don't mind, do you?" he said.

"Not a bit. We could continue the conversation."

"My sentiments exactly," he said.

He called Marge and it was obvious from the end of the talk I heard that Marge was delighted to have him. He offered to bring a bottle of wine, though, and that was clearly declined.

When he put down the phone, he said, "Marge told me that she'd throw another potato in the pot."

"I'll bet," I said. "She's probably adding another course to the menu."

"Maybe more than one," he said. "She's inviting Dieter and Eileen, too."

I figured I'd know more than I wanted to about the Grasse family by the end of the evening. But I was wrong.

Seventeen

When I left young Doctor Menkin, who was Pete to me by that time, the town was closing down. Although the sun hadn't set, the stores were closed and the lights were on in the tavern next to the Hay Den. The Hay Den, which Edith had recommended for my overnight stay, was a seedy-looking place with the Vacancy sign hanging by one hook.

I was glad I wasn't staying there. Even in a quiet place like Paradise, it didn't look safe. And it definitely didn't look clean. Last season's leaves were still heaped against the buildings, papers blew across the parking lot, paint peels fluttered in the breeze, and the windows were cracked and filthy.

Its one saving grace was a collection of wooden figures on the neatly kept center lawn. They were whimsical without being cute: A cat rode a terrified dog, a woman with six little children was eating a watermelon, a fisherman with his creel overloaded was followed by a procession of cats, a mouse stood with a sword on a wedge of Swiss cheese.

I stopped the car and went into the motel office, where a sign said the wooden figures were sold. I thought I might find something I liked, and maybe something for Marge.

My first impression of the woman behind the counter was that she was one of those women you see one minute and forget the next. Brown hair, brownish eyes, no makeup, and every feature not ugly, not pretty. The part I could see of her over the counter was not fat or thin, and her dress was made of a printed fabric that didn't call attention to itself, either.

It wasn't until she walked out from behind the counter that

she became memorable. The normal top of her body was attached to a backside as big as a washtub. I could hear her pantyhose rubbing between her thighs as she walked, and the flesh on her ankles folded over her sneakers.

She showed me some smaller versions of the figures on the lawn; I thought they were priced ridiculously low. I bought the fisherman for Marge and the mouse for me. Then I bought the dog for Delia and the woman with the watermelon for Natasha. I could already hear Natasha's rich laugh.

I paid for the figures with my credit card, and when the woman saw my name, she said, "We have a reservation for you."

"Oh. I didn't make a reservation."

"Well someone did." She flipped through a file of cards and pulled one out. "See," she said. "It's paid for, too."

"I already made other arrangements," I said. "I'm sorry; I wasn't told about this."

She looked sulky.

"Would you mind telling me who paid for it?" I said.

"A company, let me see, Hickory Hills, Inc. That's who paid."

"If I hadn't stopped to buy these pieces, I wouldn't have known about it," I said.

"So you're not staying?"

"No, I've already got a place to stay."

"Nobody better be putting you up without a license," she said, belligerent as a guard dog. "So where are you staying?"

"There's no law that requires me to answer your question," I said. I didn't want to get Marge and Fritz in trouble, although I didn't think there was any law against having a guest overnight, even if she was paying. Probably it would be bad enough to get them on bad terms with this woman. "Now, if you'll give me my package, I'd like to leave."

"I'm not giving you your package until you tell me where you're staying."

I couldn't believe what I was hearing. I stood there trying to decide on the best tack to take. "If you don't give me my package," I said slowly, trying to sound more calm than I felt, "I will leave without it and tell the charge company what happened."

She looked so furious, I thought she was going to throw the package at me. She finally handed it over and said huffily, "Well, I don't care. I get to rent out a room and I don't have to bother cleaning it again."

I could have left it at that, but I was miffed. "Since you were notified before six o'clock, you should refund all or part of the money to Hickory Hills. I intend to tell them that you were notified."

If looks could kill, I would have been cut down. She stuck out her lip, lifted one shoulder, and turned away from me. "Don't ever come here again," she said.

I congratulated myself as I walked out the door for not answering her with any of the obvious replies. I wished that our conversation had gone better, because I never found out who did the figures.

I drove a comfortable distance away and spent a few minutes calming down before I called Sheriff Castle from the portable phone. He was ready.

"Terry Kurtz is Gerard Benton Kurtz from Ithaca, New York. He had a record of felonies in his teens before he turned killer. His sister is going to come and claim the body. In case I didn't tell you, Kurtz was dead before he was run over."

"Before? I thought maybe he was unconscious before and then somebody ran him over," I said.

"No, he was dead. The head wound killed him some time before he was run over."

"So somebody carried him there and dumped him and then ran him over?"

"Something like that," the sheriff said. "And those long skirts you asked about, Greta and a few of her friends were the only ones wearing them. The word is that Greta and her friends started fads like that before. Last year, it was capes."

"Thanks, Sheriff."

"Did you find Greta yet?"

"No."

"Did you find out anything else that I might like to know about?"

I told him what Pete Menkin had told me about Ben Grasse and his jack rabbit inclinations.

"He hadn't changed much, then, except that he wasn't fooling with jail bait.'' Then he asked again whether I'd be back in Wyoming County for the dinner dance.

"I'm still planning on it," I said.

"Good. By the way, that Buffalo cop's been calling here, wanting to know where you are. Should I tell him?"

Damn. "Tell him I'll call him as soon as I get a chance." I guess I'd be angry if someone was treating me the way I was treating Ted. I was definitely confused about what my behavior should be and what he was entitled to after sleeping with me one time.

I thought about last Saturday night and the warm and cuddly feeling I had Sunday morning, a feeling that dissipated like sugar disolving in water as soon as I got busy with this case. I'd have to talk to Polly about it. Maybe it wasn't normal. What did I know about normal?

Marge loved the wooden fisherman I'd bought her, and dinner was everything Pete said it would be, healthy and delicious. I told Marge that she ought to open a restaurant.

Pete agreed. "I'd eat there every day," he said.

Dieter and Eileen Grasse couldn't make it to dinner because Dieter was detained at the hardware store, but they showed up in time for dessert, which was almost a meal in itself.

Marge had made balls of frozen nonfat yogurt rolled in chopped nuts, served on a bed of fresh strawberries, surrounded by toasted fingers of angel food cake. She served a berry preserve with it, in case it wasn't sweet enough.

After dinner, the Grasses showed me pictures of Ben as a baby, and then as he grew. There were pictures of all the Grasses, including their sister, Lizzie, who had died. They all had those long teeth, a feature that was much less pronounced in Ben. They were all dark haired, before they were gray, and Ben was fair.

When I mentioned that I thought Ben looked different from the other kids, Fritz started to chuckle. "Folks around here used to say Mom jumped the fence for that one," he said.

"Even Pop said that, Fritzie," Marge said. "She was kidded about that all the time."

Apparently there was a whole repertoire of jokes about it, including the line that he was switched with a devil child at birth. Sometimes the nicest people—and the Grasses were nice people—have a cruel streak of which they're not aware. All those jokes would have been enough to warp a kid.

I watched Pete's face during the conversation, and I was sure it meant something significant to him. Maybe he was remembering being a boy with Ben. His expression was pained, as if he recalled something that made him uncomfortable.

He was the one who changed the subject. "We ought to be helping Fran, here, find Greta Baere," he said.

"What can we do?" Eileen said, looking at me.

"Tell me what you know about her," I said. "What kinds of things did she do while she was here?"

"I don't know anything she did," Marge said, "except come over and look at the turkeys."

"She liked the kittens, too," Eileen said. "She used to come over and play with the barn cats. Don't you remember when she got scratched and Grace came over like a fury, telling you not to let her play with the cats? Wild cats, she called them."

Marge laughed. "How could I forget that?"

"Grace was real protective about Greta," Eileen said.

"Treated her like she was her own child," Dieter said.

"Maybe that's why Greta liked to come here," I said.

"I know she used to run away when her folks came to take her back home," Fritz said.

"Sad," I said, "that she was so unhappy at home."

"Some kids will be unhappy no matter how good their home is. Like Ben," Fritz said.

Dieter nodded. "I'd have to say you're right about that."

And we were back again to Topic A: Ben Grasse.

"I just thought about something," Eileen said. "You remember when Ben was little? Well, where did he used to go when he was in a bad mood or he got into trouble?"

Dieter slammed his hand down on the table, which, thank providence, was a sturdy piece of oak. "Damned if you aren't right. He used to run to Gramma Grace. That's what he called her. That's what a lot of kids called her."

"You used to be over there all the time yourself," Fritz said to Dieter, "when you and Heinz were buddies."

"Well, she always had cookies and sweet rolls. It's a wonder Heinz wasn't fat as a toad."

"Heinz may be sick," I said.

Everybody looked my way, waiting.

"Edith took him to Roswell Park today. He's been having pain."

"It's hard to imagine Heinz sick. He was always the biggest, the healthiest, the strongest, had the most endurance," Dieter said.

"He was always the biggest pest," Marge said.

"Yeah," Eileen joined in, "he thought all the girls loved him. So full of himself."

"I thought all the girls did love him," Dieter said.

"You never saw me go out with him, did you?" Eileen said.

"That's why I liked you," he said, smiling at her and patting her on the shoulder.

"He sure didn't act like the other Amish boys," Marge said.

"I didn't know Heinz was Amish," I said. Pete was looking uncomfortable again. Then he looked at his watch, and it occurred to me that he was looking for a chance to leave because his father was expected home.

"The family left the community and moved into the house when Heinz and Hilda were teenagers," Fritz said. "Grace and Hilda still wear those skirts, but I never saw them with the bonnets."

"Why did they leave, I wonder?" I said.

"Heinz never said," Dieter answered. "But he had no patience with them. He used to get up behind their carriages and honk his horn and do anything he could think of to pester them."

"What about Heinz's father? He must have been the one to make the decision to move the family. Aren't they patriarchal?" Pete asked.

"The father was ailing when they left. He hung on for a few years before he died. Grace was the one that moved them out of there," Dieter said.

Pete stood up. "You know," he said, "this has been a lovely evening. I should leave soon, though. Dad will be getting home anytime now, if he isn't home already. Let me help you with the dishes, Marge.''

"Looka here," Dieter said. "These young fellows think they have to do the dishes."

"And he's a doctor," Eileen said. "And he's not too good to get his hands in dishwater."

Apparently the subject had come up at the Dieter and Eileen Grasse household.

"Nobody comes into my kitchen," Marge said, standing arms akimbo. "I don't want anything put in the wrong place."

Fritz chuckled. "You'll let me help, won't you, honey pot?"

"Only if you do as you're told," she said.

"That let's me out," Dieter said.

"I didn't hear you offer," Eileen said.

Pete stood there, not knowing what to say, finally settling on, "I'll just help clear the table and then I'll be off."

Everybody except Dieter got up and took dishes into the kitchen, and then Marge urged Pete to be on his way. I walked him to the door to remind him that I wanted to talk to his father before I left Paradise.

"I ran into something the other day in Dad's files," he said. "It may be important. Let me take another look. Come over tomorrow about ten."

"What is it?" I said. He looked so grave.

"Maybe it's the reason Dad was in Ben's files."

"Tell me. Don't keep me dangling."

"No. I may be wrong. I have to check it out."

All sorts of possibilities ran through my head: terrible illness; a death that wasn't reported; a child who was abused. I was cursing Pete for bringing it up and leaving me wondering.

After Pete left, we all, including Dieter, helped Marge clean up. She was definitely in charge, though, and not one dish was put in the cupboard without her say-so.

Dieter scrubbed the pans. "Just like KP," he said, "except the pans are smaller."

Eileen was smiling at him as if she'd been given a gift.

By nine-thirty, the kitchen was clean and Dieter and Eileen were getting ready to go home. Fritz walked them to the door and Marge handed me some towels.

"I forgot to put towels in the bathroom," she said. "I got so excited about Young Doc coming to dinner. What were you doing over there anyway?"

I told her about the names and numbers in Ben's files.

"The numbers could be from prison," she said.

"Do you have his number from then?"

"Sure. I used to write to him."

I retrieved my notebook from my purse and found the numbers, and Marge recited Ben's number from memory. One of the numbers, indeed, was his prison ID number.

"Thanks," I said. "I wish all mysteries were so easily solved." Then I showed her some of the other numbers and names.

She looked down the list, poking her finger on the page as she went along. "That's his birthday. That's Lizzie's birthday. I don't know what that date is. That's the phone number that Mom and Dad used to have." The woman was a walking memory bank. "That's the number up at the Baeres's. I don't recognize that number, but it looks like a prison number. Maybe it's Terry Kurtz's."

"If I had known you had all that information stored, I would have asked you about it sooner," I said.

"Marge doing her numbers tricks?" Fritz said as he walked in from the front hall.

"Numbers are easy for me," she said, "but it takes me all day to read a story in the newspaper; even a recipe takes me a long time."

I remembered the way she'd read my business card, slowly and out loud, word by word. "Do you remember my phone number from my card?"

She did. The woman was amazing.

"I can't forget numbers. They just stay there in my head."

"What about the numbers on this list that you don't recognize?" I said. "Do you have any idea what kind of numbers they are?"

"These, down here," she said, "are like numbers on property. This one could be a hospital number. Now I know. That's Lizzie's number from when she was in the hospital."

"You didn't see that number more than once, woman," Fritz said, as if he were chastising her.

"Neither did Ben. Why would he have put it in his files?" she said.

"You remember he complained about the treatment she got. Maybe he intended to follow up on his complaints," he said, yawning.

"We better get to bed," she said, ever vigilant where Fritz's health was concerned. "You don't need to lock the door when you come in from your walk, Fran. We never lock it."

"We wouldn't know how to get out of here if we found it locked," Fritz said.

"If Pilgrim wants to go with you, it's all right. He'll come back with you; just call him. We don't leave him out all night. Don't want him baying at the moon and disturbing the birds."

"One more thing," Fritz said. "Try to keep away from the pens or the turkeys will wake up and think it's time to be fed."

I went upstairs and put on my sweats. I was craving a run after all the eating I'd been doing. I felt healthier just getting into the workout clothes, but I'd have to start slowly after the meal I'd put away.

Pilgrim, who had followed me to my bedroom, sniffed at my clothes. He was making the acquaintance of Horace through his most potent sensory organ. When I went downstairs, Pilgrim was at my heel. Likewise when I went out the door.

The night was cool and starry, with the waxing moon just climbing from the horizon. As I put distance between me and the house, the landscape's shapes grew distinct, and the sounds and smells of night closed in on me.

I started to jog along slowly, getting used to the uneven terrain on a tractor road at the edge of a field. Pilgrim ran alongside me, leaping up at me every once in a while, as if to tell me he was having a good time.

As often happens when I run, my mind cleared itself out and I was there in the field and nothing else existed. Just my body moving through air.

When I picked up speed, Pilgrim took it to mean that he should run flat out, which he did and disappeared in the dark in front of me.

I called him, but he didn't come as Marge had said he would. That was my first surprise.

Eighteen

After I had run about a mile, I stopped to look around, to see where I'd come from and where I was going. I could no longer see the house or smell the turkeys. But I hadn't made any turns or come to any forks in the road, so I figured I wasn't lost. Pilgrim still hadn't showed up, but he knew his way around better than I did, so I wasn't worried about his getting lost. What I was worried about was having to stay up all night waiting for him to come home.

I could have run longer, but I had come out not only to run. I had some snooping to do.

I ran back along the tractor road, which was bordered by a hedgerow and a field that was already knee high with some kind of grain. I wouldn't have been able to see Pilgrim if he had been ten feet from me unless he was in the road.

My plan was to run over the hill to the Baeres's place and take a peek in the barn behind the house to see if Greta's truck was there. But the plan went awry.

As I got back in range of the turkey farm, I heard sounds in the hedgerow. Thrashing sounds, coming at me. I picked up my speed, knowing that I could outrun most people. But the sounds stayed with me, closer than before. I was sweating and trying to keep fear from overcoming reason. Fear ran away with me or else I might have been ready for what came next.

The crashing was next to me, and then something whacked me from the side, knocking me over and sending a burning pain from my ankle up my leg. Something was pounding on me, but between my terror and the darkness, discrimination had left me. I heard myself whimpering. From my spot on the ground, I looked up, expecting to see some ogre standing over me with a deadly weapon. But I couldn't see. A shape was directly on top of me.

In moments like that, reason surfaces slowly. When it did, I realized Pilgrim was licking my face. He had jumped up at me just as he had at the beginning of our outing, but with the increased speed, he bowled me over.

My ankle was screaming in pain and my face was wet with dog spit. I didn't know whether there was any other damage. He really bushwhacked me.

When I tried to stand up, my ankle wouldn't take the weight. I felt like bashing the dog, but I knew he was just being enthusiastic and was having a wonderful time. A stick would be good—not to bash the dog, but to help me stand— a stout one to use as a cane.

I was crawling along the hedgerow, feeling for a fallen limb, straining my eyes to see if any of the bushes would yield a branch thick enough, while Pilgrim thought it was great fun having me down on my hands and knees like a doggie playmate.

A polelike limb suddenly materialized, and I was stripping off the small branches, when I distinctly heard footsteps, human ones. I grabbed Pilgrim and held him close to me, hoping he would be quiet, but that is not the nature of dogs. He began to whine.

So I let him go, and he ran toward the footsteps, barking, while I cowered in the bushes. The footsteps stopped. The next thing I heard sounded like clapping and the barking stopped.

Had someone hurt the dog? I strained to hear. The footsteps started up again. And, yes, there were more footfalls than the human ones. So Pilgrim was all right. The human and the dog were coming in my direction.

What would happen if Pilgrim came back this way? Would he run into the bushes where I was hiding and give me away? Was the person someone I wanted to hide from?

As the shape loomed up the road, I saw that it was wearing a long skirt and playing with the dog. Greta? Could it be? It would make sense for her to come out at night, just to get some air and exercise.

Now, I thought, what do I do? How do I not scare her away?

I waited until she was closer to me, and then I called, "Pilgrim, is that you? Who's there? Somebody help me."

She stopped, and Pilgrim ran toward me. I tried another plaintive tone. "Pilgrim, you naughty dog, knocking me over. Now I can't walk."

Greta—I was sure it was she—said, "Who's there?"

"I'm hurt," I said. "I was jogging and the dog knocked me over. My ankle is twisted."

She came over to where I was sitting in the hedgerow and put a hand out to help me up.

I grabbed her hand and got about halfway, with my good foot on the ground along with the other knee.

"I found a stick on the ground. Let me get it."

"Here's a good one," she said, picking up the one I had been working on and steadying it while I pulled myself erect. "Who are you? What are you doing out here?"

"I was getting some exercise until Pilgrim maimed me. I'm Fran Tremaine Kirk," I said.

"Oh. You're the—" She let go of the stick and turned to go.

"Wait," I said. "I know you have good reason to hide."

"What do you know about it?" she said belligerently.

"I know that your family doesn't treat you well. I know that your brother is a brat. I know that your mother has not been acting right. I know that you always liked Grace and Hildegarde and felt loved here."

"Everybody knows that except my family." There was a touch of weepiness in her voice.

"I also found the disk and the bloody clothes," I said.

She wilted. Her shoulders rounded and her hands came up to her face as the sobs started to build.

I put one arm around her and leaned on the stick with the other hand. My ankle wasn't feeling as bad as I thought it would. I put a little weight on it.

Greta was a big girl, five ten easy. So it was awkward for her to cry on my five-seven shoulders. She did it anyway. Like a flood.

Pilgrim kept jumping up on her and whining, as if he

wanted to do something for her. Probably he thought that a face licking was just what she needed.

I kept telling her that I was sorry, and I was—sorry for her, sorry she was having such a rotten life, and sorry she reminded me of the rotten parts of my own life.

Finally, the waterworks slowed to a trickle and she said, "It's not your fault."

"It's not yours, either," I said.

"Some of it is," she said, and started wailing louder again.

"Do you think we can be heard?" I said.

She lifted her head off my shoulder and wiped her eyes on her sleeve. "There's no one around here," she said. "There's never anyone around here."

"But I'm here tonight," I said. "And you didn't expect that."

She thought about that for a minute. "We could go sit in my truck," she said.

"Where is it?"

"In the barn." She turned to walk away and then turned back. "Do you need help?"

"Thanks," I said. "I don't know."

After a few steps, several of them painful, I discovered that I could walk if I set my foot down straight and lifted it straight up without any twisting or bending at all—as if the whole foot was one solid block. I clopped along beside Greta, and she led the way, Pilgrim now leaping up at her every few steps.

When the door of her truck was opened, I got a good look at the girl I had been searching for. Her pictures did not do her justice; she was a great beauty. Besides having lovely features, her skin and hair seemed to glow. I couldn't tell much about her figure, because she was swathed in the long skirt, a billowy blouse, and a filmy scarf over her shoulders that hung to her thighs.

I started telling her about myself and how I came to be at Hickory Hills, thinking that would open her up when her turn came to talk. Then I told her about what had happened at the farm after she left. I left out the part about Edith hiring me to find her.

When I got to the computer mess, she erupted. "Damn that Eric. He was behind that. I know it."

"Why?"

"Because he didn't want anyone to find out what he'd been doing with that California company."

"Is that what you were fighting about before you left. The fight that got your allowance stopped?"

"Partly. He didn't know how much I knew, though. Ben knew, too." At that, she started to weep again, more quietly than before.

"What did you know?"

"Ben and I found the figures didn't match, and we called California a couple of times, pretending we were just verifying the orders we'd made. Eric was buying nonorganic fruits and nuts and charging Hickory Hills for organic. He was relabeling it when it came in."

"Did Edith find out about this?"

"I told him that I was going to tell her. He said if I did, he'd tell about Ben and me."

"Ben and you?" Oh, Lord, the leopard didn't change his spots. Here he was fooling with underage girls again. I began to wonder whether Theodora knew about Ben and her daughter. "How long had you been seeing Ben?"

"Almost since the first day he arrived. I knew him when I was a little kid. I always liked him. I used to dream about growing up and marrying him. We were going to . . ." She cried again.

What a complete and utter asshole, a rat, a slime ball. "Did he say he was going to marry you?"

"Of course. Why else would I . . . ."

"Why else would you what?"

"Never mind. It's nothing."

Sure it's nothing. "Why did you run away?"

"Because Ben was dead. Oh, God, I can't believe he's dead. Dead. Gone. Never coming back." She wept.

I waited a few seconds before I went on. "How did your blouse and pants get bloody?"

"He was lying on them, bleeding. So much blood." She choked back a deep sob. "We were lying there and I had to go to the bathroom. When I came back, he was still alive."

"Did he say anything? Say who did it?"

"When he saw me—I can still see him, bleeding and fighting for breath—he put his fingers to his lips to tell me to be quiet.''

"The killer must have been still there. What did you do?''

"I went to him. I put my face up close to his. He whispered to me, told me to destroy the disk. Then he—he died.''

"You didn't see anyone? He didn't tell you who did that to him?''

"No. He was trying to save me.''

"Was he lying on his back?''

"No. How could he be lying on his back with the, the . . .'' This was too much for her, and her sobbing became deep and irregular.

It was all I could do to not cry with her. "You've had more trouble than most people can take,'' I said, patting her on the back. We were sitting in the truck in the old barn, lit by stray moonbeams that found their way through the gritty barn windows. Pilgrim had curled up in the space behind the seat. He was a dog who knew his way around pickup trucks.

Whoever killed Ben must have come back after Greta left, must have come back to turn the body onto its back. "Did you leave right away?'' I said. "Did you call the police?''

"I don't remember anything after he died. I don't know what I did. The next thing I can remember is being in my room and packing.''

I didn't want to add to her trouble by telling her that her husband-to-be was also bedding her mother and Amy. But I didn't like the idea of her holding the creep in high esteem, either.

"Did you know that Ben spent time in jail?'' I said.

She stopped crying and turned toward me. "Why are you telling me such a rotten thing? The man's dead, for Pete's sake.''

"Because it's true, and it's something you should know. I think you deserved someone better.''

She was still weeping, but she was interested in what I had to say. I didn't want to shock her, but I did want her to knock off the halo he was wearing in her thoughts.

"I've been talking to people about Ben all day. He got into a lot of trouble because he fooled around with young girls. He was sent to jail because he was fooling around with a twelve-year-old.''

''Who told you that?'' She was angry again.

''Ben's brothers and sisters-in-law and Doctor Peter Menkin, Jr.''

''Oh,'' she said, and lapsed into a long silence.

I waited. At some point, I would have to tell her that the sheriff wanted to talk to her, but I didn't want to scare her off, to make her run away again.

''Ben wanted me to destroy the disk,'' she said. ''But I knew everything on it, except for those numbers. I didn't know what they were.''

''I know what some of them were.'' I told her about Marge and her way with numbers. She got a kick out of that.

''I never knew that about Marge,'' she said, a trace of a smile hovering at the corners of her mouth. ''But what were the numbers?''

I told her, and that didn't set too well. The halo was coming off in big chunks. She even sounded mad when she said, ''I want to find out what the rest of those numbers are. I want to know what the rest of the secrets are before—''

The sirens started at that moment.

''The whole town will be awake,'' she said. ''I've got to go. Come to the house tomorrow. I'll tell Grammy and Hildy that you know.''

And she was gone. And I was left to hobble back to the Grasse house with the irrepressible Pilgrim launching himself at me every couple of minutes.

When I got to the house, Marge and Fritz were standing on the back porch looking toward town. I turned to look in the same direction. The sky was orange.

''It's over by the lumberyard,'' Fritz said.

Then Marge noticed my peculiar gait. ''What happened to you?'' she said.

''I fell and twisted my foot.'' I didn't say that Pilgrim had knocked me over. I didn't want to get the dog in trouble even if he did need some training.

''Come on in,'' she said. ''I've got one of those elastic bandages.''

''That'll help,'' I said.

Fritz hollered after us. "Want to take a ride downtown and see what's burning?"

"Sure," Marge said. "Just take a minute to give Fran the bandage."

"Bring Fran and the bandage along," he said.

I sat in the little backseat of their pickup and bandaged my ankle while we drove to the fire. When we got there, it looked like a pep rally. The whole town was there.

I didn't know then that I was in for another shock that evening.

Nineteen

The voluteer firemen were passing us on the road as we made our way toward the blaze. Every time Fritz saw a blue light behind him, he pulled over.

"When I used to run to the fires," he said, "it used to make me mad when folks didn't get out of the way."

"What do you mean 'used to run to the fires'? You still do," Marge said.

Fritz just chuckled.

We were still a long block away from the spot where the engines were stopped when Marge said, "It's the motel. The Hay Den is burning."

I looked up the street and saw the wooden figures on the lawn, backlit by the flames.

"Good thing you didn't stay there," Fritz said.

We couldn't drive any closer, because of the traffic jam. The street was full of spectators, and the local police were shooing people away to make room for the volunteers. Soon the hoses were snaking along the road from the pumper, which was pulling water from a pond on the other side of the street.

Fritz and Marge wanted to get closer, but I didn't want to stand around on my sore ankle, so I stayed in the truck.

The crowd stood in a knot near the fire engine, talking to the firemen as they passed. The man wearing the white chief's hat was no other than Dieter, who stood near the crowd, pointing and waving his arms, which I interpreted as giving orders to the firemen. I wasn't close enough to make out what was said, although there was a lot of shouting going on and glass breaking and the rumble of engines.

Then there were screams from the crowd as a fireman carried a motionless body out of one of the rooms. That's when I noticed a couple of men sparsely dressed standing at the edge of the motel lawn. Guests, I thought, whose sleep had been interrupted. I wondered what it would have been like to have been awakened by someone shouting "Fire." Or, worse, by smoke or flames in the room I was sleeping in.

Marge and Fritz were chatting busily with the townfolk, and the fire did not seem to be getting more intense, although it was still burning. I felt my eyelids getting thick and my breathing getting slow and regular, so I leaned against the back window and let myself drift.

I was startled awake by a nasty whisper. "You, you're lucky you weren't in it."

My eyes snapped open and there framed in the driver's window of the pickup was the woman from the motel. The anger in her face was just as hot as it had been yesterday afternoon.

"Yes," I said, "I am lucky." Maybe I shouldn't have answered at all. It's a no-win situation when someone is that mad.

"So you're staying with Marge and Fritz," she said. Obviously, people were known by their trucks.

"I'm a private detective," I said. "I was called in when their brother was killed." The statement was notable for what it left out, but I wanted to justify my being at the Grasses's house. I didn't know what kind of clout she might have if people were renting to roomers without a license.

Her attitude changed immediately. "How much will you charge me to find out who set the fire?" she said.

"You think it was arson?"

"So does the chief. He said he smelled gasoline as soon as he got here."

"Where did it start?"

"Behind room Four. The room they reserved for you." Her face slid into a malevolent smile.

"What? You mean someone reserved a specific room for me?"

"Not exactly. They just asked which room was the quietest;

and I told them room Four, and that's the one they took.''

"Was anyone in the room tonight?''

She looked guarded. I guessed it was because she had been paid twice for the same room and wasn't intending to send any money back to Hickory Hills.

"Frankly,'' I said, "I don't give a hoot whether you refund them the money or not.''

The woman's face broke into a huge smile, which almost made her pretty. "I did rent it out,'' she said. "We were full up tonight. That hasn't happened in a coon's age. Heck of a night to have a fire.''

"Did you take the call from Hickory Hills?''

"Yes. Why?''

"Who made the reservation, a man or a woman?''

"Woman.''

"Anything peculiar about her voice or the way she talked?''

"No. She knew what she wanted. She didn't waste words.''

Edith, I thought. Then I had another thought that made me very uncomfortable: Would Edith have rented a specific room so she'd know where I was? Could she be trying to kill me? And why? Was there something down here I could find out that would be a threat to her? Would she have come here, or would she hire somebody to light the fire? Or was all this coincidence? "Even a wild theory,'' my husband used to say, "in this business could be true.'' He was a nasty wife-beating drunk, but he wasn't a bad private eye when he was sober.

"How much is it worth to you to find the arsonist?'' I said.

"I'll rip up that charge slip that you signed yesterday afternoon,'' she said, as if she were a queen doling out favors.

I didn't tell her that I thought the charge slip had probably burned up in the fire. Besides, the amount of the charge was less than a hundred dollars. I knew enough to charge more than that to find a culprit.

"My fees are higher than that, but don't worry, if I find out who did it, I'll tell you. Just tell me who does those figures on the lawn.''

"Oh, those. I do them in my spare time. I make a little money to go into the city once in a while.''

That blew me away. She was the last person in the world I would have guessed. "How long have you been doing them?''

"I've been doing things like that as long as I can remember but I just started putting them out on the lawn for sale since my husband left."

"Left?"

"He met a gal at the tavern, and they took off last year."

"Sorry," I said.

"He never did pull his weight," she said with a shrug.

I thought about the few things I knew about this woman and wondered whether she was nursing her pain with a lot of food. But I didn't dwell on her for long. The idea that Edith or someone from Hickory Hills was trying to put my lights out had me stewing. I decided to act as if it were true and watch my every step.

"Listen," I said to the woman, "if you should get a call from Hickory Hills or anywhere, and they want to know whether I was in the motel when it burned, don't come right out and tell them I wasn't there, will you?"

"I'll say you checked in and I don't know who was where when the fire started."

"Thanks," I said. "I appreciate it."

"The people that were in your room are in bad shape," she said. "They took them to the hospital."

"Do you have their names?"

"No. The records are in the fire. I don't know what's burned and what's not."

"Was it a man and a woman?"

"Yes."

"Good." That gives me some room, I thought. "Don't say anything to anyone. And do me a favor, will you? Tell Marge and Fritz not to say anything about my staying at their place." I didn't have much hope that they hadn't already blabbed it.

"I'll hurry," she said. She knew how fast news traveled in this town.

I saw her hurry away, that washtub backside of hers setting up tidal waves in her skirt. I pulled myself back into the darkest corner of the truck and watched as she cornered Marge and Fritz.

Their curiosity piqued, it wasn't long before they were on their way back to the truck. I was wishing I had my portable phone with me. I didn't think the sheriff would mind being waked up with what I had to tell him.

I told Marge and Fritz enough to persuade them to keep mum about where I was. Luckily, they hadn't mentioned it to anyone yet. They would tell Dieter to keep quiet, too, they said. That would be a more difficult proposition, they said, Dieter being the "motor-mouth" he was.

They went back to the crowd by the engine, and I could see Fritz talking to Dieter after a bit. Eileen materialized next to Marge, too, so I figured my bases were covered. Except for Pete, whom I didn't see in the crowd. But he didn't seem to be the type that tells everybody everything anyway. I kept my eyes on the crowd to see if anyone else I knew showed up, but no one did.

The pickup truck windows were open halfway, so when the morning breeze sprang up, I felt it. The firemen had sunk into a routine of hosing down the motel, and the bar and lumberyard, which were its neighbors. The flames that had been leaping into the sky were replaced by plumes of smoke, and some of the rooms had been searched thoroughly to make sure there were no bodies. Some of the undamaged furniture had been pulled out onto the lawn: a TV sat next to the figure of the mouse, a nightstand behind the fisherman.

The woman who ran the motel and made the figures sat forlornly on an empty crate next to a cutout woman in a hoop skirt.

I awoke to the bumping of the truck and the sounds of Marge and Fritz. I don't know how long I had been asleep, but the sun was up. "Good morning," I said.

"Sleeping beauty," Marge said. "The fire's out. They found a gas can out back, and the state police took it to their lab."

"The officers were having a hard time finding out who the guests were," Fritz said.

"The records all burned. And some of the guests just took off in their cars when it looked like they wouldn't be getting any sleep at the motel," Marge said.

"Some of them shouldn't have been there anyway," Fritz said.

"Those ones weren't there for sleeping," Marge said.

"How are the people they took to the hospital?" I said.

"Last I heard, they were critical," he said.

"Was anyone asking questions about who was in the motel?" I said.

"Just the officers," Marge said.

"I have an idea," I said. "Maybe you could help me." I told them my worry about the fire.

"So what's your idea? Is it a detective idea?" Marge said.

"Sort of. Is there any way I could get the car I rented somewhere near the motel, near enough that the police would start tracing it?" I was wishing I had gotten the idea sooner.

But Fritz had the answer. The parking lot for the bar was around behind the motel, and actually closer to the motel units than the motel's parking lot. He also knew a way to get there with the car that was "almost invisible," he said.

"The police hadn't even started on the cars in the lot," Marge said.

Marge and Fritz insisted that I stay at the house while they moved my car. While they were gone, I called the sheriff and told him about the fire.

"If it was one of the Baeres, I don't know which one, because none of them has come back to the farm."

"That gives me the willies," I said, "but I haven't seen any of them here."

"They know the area. They don't have to be seen."

I thought about Fritz taking an "invisible" route to put my car in the lot by the motel. "Have you started trying to find them or checked on where they've been?" I knew that was a snotty thing to ask, but the sheriff had been dropping the ball so many times.

"We haven't been able to verify anything they told us. No record of an appointment at Roswell Park. No appointment at the college. Nobody who works on the farm has heard anything about Heinz being sick or about Eric wanting to go to college."

"Another case of the bunch of them sticking together," I said. "I guess Greta was the odd man out."

Then I filled the sheriff in on what I knew. I gave him everything, but I asked him to leave Greta be for a while.

"I think she trusts me," I said. "I want her to feel safe, so she tells me the rest. There's something else she hasn't told me yet. But I think she will."

The sheriff acted miffed that I hadn't told him before about the bloody clothes.

"You would have issued a warrant for Greta's arrest and she would have been off God knows where," I said.

"I may still."

"I didn't give you all that information so you could louse up what I'm doing," I said, before I thought.

There was a deadness on the line. It's funny how you blurt things out and then you're stuck with them.

I tried to soften the remark. "Sorry," I said. "It's just that I haven't had much sleep and now I'm worried that someone could be after me. And Greta, too, for that matter."

"I can spread the word up here that you were in the fire and that nobody knows whether you took off or you're the woman in the hospital." Sometimes the man was positively reasonable.

"Thanks, Sheriff."

"Why don't you call me Dick?"

"Do you mind if I call you Richard?"

"What's the matter with Dick?"

"Guess what my husband's name was."

"Oh," he said. "Well, my mom calls me Richie. But I hate that."

"How about Rich?"

"That's better than 'Sheriff,' " he said, and laughed a low rumbling laugh. "So what are you going to do next?"

"Talk to Greta and to Pete and his father."

"Pete?"

"That's what everybody calls young Doctor Menkin." Here I was, feeling that the sheriff was on guard about my calling Pete "Pete." Was it that all men were jealous of your associations with other men, or was it the way I experienced it? The sheriff might have just been wondering who Pete was. After all, I hadn't referred to him as Pete when I was giving the sheriff the rundown on my activities.

I tied up the loose ends with him and hung up the phone just as Fritz and Marge were slamming the truck doors.

The switch had taken twenty minutes, and Marge and Fritz were giggling like a couple of kids when they came back.

"The only one saw us was Lois from the motel," Marge said. "And she's in on the secret."

So, her name was Lois.

"This won't have to go on long," I said. "I need a few hours to get some work done and then I'll be out of here."

"We'll miss you," Marge said. "You've been a lot of fun."

That brought a big grin to my face. The idea that I was a lot of fun. It was my turn to say something nice. Never let a compliment go unanswered, my mom used to say. "I couldn't have asked for better hosts or better food. I didn't get to try the bed," I said, "but I had a nice nap in your truck."

"What were you doing all night?" Marge said.

I told them about Greta. They were impressed that I had found her.

"You must be a hell of a detective," Fritz said. "I'll hire you if I need to find out something."

"So now you have two secrets," I said, "and you'll have to keep them until Greta and I are safe."

"That's easy. I wouldn't want anything to happen to either one of you," Marge said. "And the first thing I'll do to keep you safe and healthy is make you breakfast."

The mere mention of breakfast made me hungry. Marge insisted that she could do it all alone, so I went upstairs to take a shower.

The hot water running over me revived the cells that wanted to be in bed. I was looking forward to the caffeine, which I hoped she would have in this health-oriented house.

My ankle was okay while it was wrapped in the bandage. But it kicked up a little when I was in the shower. I wrapped it up again after I dried off. It felt almost okay, but I wasn't about to try any leaping or twisting.

I left the bathroom neat and folded my towel on the rack. Then I straightened the wrinkles that I'd made sitting on the bed, which I never got around to sleeping in, and put my clothes in my duffel and put the duffel in the closet. My mother read me that drill from some etiquette column: If your hostess doesn't have household help, make your bed and clean your room. Even though I had paid for the room, I still felt like a guest.

Marge had made a huge breakfast. She recited the menu and ingredients, which included a delicious omelet that she made with five egg whites and one yolk and bits of onion, green pepper, and mushrooms. There were fresh strawberries, homemade low-fat granola, whole wheat toast, preserves, and—thank God—real coffee, which she and Fritz allowed themselves one cup of every morning.

They would have lingered over that one cup for hours if I had been willing to join them, but I had to get over to the Baeres's before Greta got up and told "Grammy and Hildy" where I was and they picked up the phone to broadcast the news.

Marge, who would have made a wonderful mother, dug a cane out of the attic to ease my trip across meadows. I set out with my purse this time, figuring that Delia's phone would come in handy if I was confronted by anything dangerous. My .38 was in the purse, too, but I liked the idea of using the phone better.

The morning was sunny, but the air outside the house was still tinged with the odor of smoke—in addition to the turkeys, of course, but I was getting used to that.

With the cane and the bandage, I walked almost normal speed across the ground that I had hobbled over the night before. I thought about Greta and the horrible things that had happened to her. Poor kid. But maybe she could salvage a life out of it. She was young and very pretty, after all.

I was rehearsing what I would say to Grace and Hildegarde, because I figured Greta would be still in bed and wouldn't have told them that I knew she was there.

But what I saw behind the barn, where Greta and I had sat in her truck the night before, sent a shiver down my spine. I was too late.

Twenty

My first instinct was to hide. I looked around, knowing that the hedgerow was the tallest thing around, but I would have to travel over open ground to get to it. So I opted for the field of grain, in which I would have to lie down to conceal myself.

I lay on my side, disturbing as few of the shafts of grain as possible, thinking that I was glad that my sweats were gray and not red. If I lifted my head, I could see the truck from Hickory Hills parked behind the barn. It had a coating of road dust that made me wonder whether the distance between there and here had been traveled, at least partly, over dirt roads.

How had they found out where Greta was? I had just told the sheriff this morning. Maybe Grace or Hildegarde spilled the beans. And what do I do now? Of course, I didn't know which one or how many of the Baeres had driven the truck here.

Seeing that truck gave me the willies. I already had my suspicions about who started the Hay Den fire. The truck could easily have arrived in Paradise last night in time for whoever was driving it to burn down the motel.

I dialed Marge and Fritz on Delia's phone. It was easy to get to like the convenience of it.

"Would you do me a favor?" I said when Marge answered, and I asked her if she felt like risking a neighborly visit to the Baeres and told her what I thought the danger might be.

Marge was all excited. "Goody," she said. Really, she said, "Goody." "I'll take over some fruit bread that I make. Grace

172

is partial to my fruit bread. And Fritzie will walk over with me. Where are you?"

I told her and she giggled. The woman loved this game. I told them to pass me by as if I weren't there. I asked them to observe everything they could and tell me later.

In minutes, Marge and Fritz walked by, but they didn't ignore me. They looked and giggled as they passed. They needed more training. I lay there, wondering whether to stay where I was or to crawl back toward the turkey farm.

I waited for about a half hour longer and had just decided to go back when I heard voices coming my way. I flattened myself against the ground. The voices I heard belonged to Edith and Heinz, but I couldn't hear the conversation, only the stray word or two.

"Not there," Edith's voice.

"Hospital," Heinz.

"Doctor Menkin," Edith. That quickened my pulse, made me wonder if they were going to see the doctor.

I had to stop my imagination from running away with me. What was the best picture I could imagine? Heinz wanted to see his old family doctor instead of going to Roswell Park, so they had come down here. They hadn't been setting a trap for me at the Hay Den; some pyromaniac had set the fire. And they hadn't come down to get Greta and lock her up away from civilization until she became a pliant family member.

That's when I heard a whole snatch of conversation: "Do you think Mama is lying?" from Heinz.

What does that mean? I thought. Does that mean that they are still looking for Greta? Is she hiding again? Did they look for her truck? Why did they park behind the barn?

They got in the truck and drove around to the front of the barn to the driveway. I sat up in the grass. My clothes were damp from the dew.

I could see the top of the truck going down the road toward town. If Edith and Heinz were on their way to the Menkin house, I wanted to warn Pete and his dad. I dialed their number.

Pete said, "Thanks for letting us know. Dad and I have been talking about you and all the goings on at Hickory Hills. He wants to talk to you."

"About what?"

"Later," he said.

"Don't hang up," I said, and gave him a quick rundown on the events since he left the Grasses last night, including the fact that I was lying low. I didn't say how low I'd been lying for the past hour.

"Curiouser and curiouser," he said.

"Yeah."

"Tell you what, Dad and I'll come up to the turkey farm after Heinz and Edith leave here," Pete said.

"If that's where they're headed," I said. "I heard them mention your name is all."

"They're coming here," Pete said. "They just drove up. I'll see you later. Hold tight."

I figured that if they were there, I could hoist my bottom off the wet ground. There were muddy spots on the side of my sweats where I had been lying. I twisted around and pulled on my sweats to see the two round brown spots on my derriere. Great. I should buy myself a pair of camouflage fatigues if I'm going to play commando.

I heard Marge and Fritz coming my way. Marge's voice was running like sixty. Fritz, as usual, punctuated the conversation with chuckles.

When they came around the barn, Marge said, "No Greta in sight."

Fritz hushed her. "Wait till we don't have to shout."

"Did they say anything about Greta?" I said.

"Grace and Hildegarde were making out that it was a shame the girl disappeared," Marge said.

"They didn't even let on that Greta had been there," Fritz said.

"When did Heinz and Edith arrive? Did you get any idea?" I said.

Marge looked at Fritz. "Didn't it seem that they just got there, Fritzie?"

"Yeah. They were standing right by the door when we got there."

"They looked kind of tense," Marge said, "when we walked up onto the porch."

"That's when Grace offered coffee to the bunch of us. Like they hadn't been there long," Fritz said.

"We told them we hadn't seen you since last night," Marge said.

"Said you had reservations at the motel," Fritz said.

"What did Edith say about that?" I said.

"She made a fuss about you being a 'poor girl just doing her job,' " Marge said, doing a creditable imitation of Edith.

They were both beaming.

"Good," I said. "But what's happened to Greta?"

I went back to the barn, wiped off one of the windows, and put my face against the glass.

"What are you looking for?" Marge said.

"Greta's truck." It took a minute for my eyes to adjust to the darkness. "It's gone."

I wondered when she had left and when she'd decided to go. Had someone told her Edith and Heinz were on their way? Had she already hatched a getaway plan with Grace and Hildegarde? If I went to talk to them, would they open up? Had they told Edith and Heinz anything? Did she leave because I had found her? The idea that disturbed me most of all was that she might think I had betrayed her. She had too few people to trust as it was.

Somehow, the fact that Edith and Heinz were traveling in broad daylight and had shown up at the Menkins's made them seem less threatening. Still, I wasn't sure I wanted to confront them just yet. And they had parked behind the barn for some reason.

Then I remembered the "4WD" on the side of truck. Maybe they had approached from the back way. Maybe they had already searched for Greta's truck.

I started looking around the field and the road for fresh tire tracks. Marge and Fritz joined me in looking once they knew what I was doing.

Fritz turned out to be good at this. He went to where the truck had been parked and found a spot where he could get a look at the tread. He found it on the tractor road and followed it a quarter of a mile to where the grass in the field was flattened by parallel ruts leading to the main road.

"So," I said, "they were trying to sneak up on her." Something else occurred to me that made my paranoia flourish and grow. Maybe they were sneaking up on me. Maybe one of these people I trusted had been in communication with Edith and Heinz. I shivered.

Thank goodness the sun was shining. It took away some of that chill, and I looked at Marge and Fritz and said to myself, No. Not them.

Then I began to wonder about the mobile phone, how secure it was, whether Heinz and Edith had a phone in their car, whether someone could pick up my calls. Oh, the depths of my insecurity.

I decided that, in my present mood, I would call the sheriff from Marge and Fritz's place. I needed to tell him where Heinz and Edith were, if he didn't know already.

He didn't. "They could have been tailing you in Paradise yesterday," he said.

I thought about that, trying to remember where I'd been and whether I'd felt watched, not that I always pick up on vibes, but sometimes I do. "If they knew where I was, they didn't burn down the motel. And they would have gotten hold of Greta."

"They might have. You don't know where Greta is."

"But I don't think they do, either," I said. "Are you going to have them picked up?"

"What for? For not telling me where they were going?"

"Isn't there some law that you can tell people to not leave town until you're finished questioning them?"

"I have to live with these people," he said.

"And you're elected, and they donate to your campaign?" The sheriff was very quiet. I had guessed right.

"I'll notify the sheriff down there right away and have them escorted back," he said.

"What about Ernest and Theodora and Eric? Any sign of them?"

"They're due back tonight."

"Are you going to tell Theodora and Ernest about the scam Eric was running?"

"First thing."

I told the sheriff I'd keep in touch and that he could leave messages for me with Marge or Fritz.

I got the feeling that the sheriff was glad to have something on Eric. And I wondered what Eric's life would be like once his folks found out he had been cheating them. If the word got out that Hickory Hills was selling things marked organic that weren't organic, it would ruin the business that Theodora had mortgaged her soul for. Certainly, once the family found out about Eric, the ties would unravel.

Or would they circle the wagons and try to protect him and the business? Was that what was at the heart of what had happened at Hickory Hills? Had the family discovered Eric's game and then tried to cover his tracks? Eric must have known that Ben had found out. He could have killed him to shut him up, then messed up the computers, or had his friend mess up the computers, and then gone after Terry, because Terry knew about it too. Hmm. But how did he know that Terry was a buddy of Ben's?

No, that theory doesn't quite do it. Whoever threatened us the first time we were at Amy's wasn't a killer. And those threats were about the computer, I think.

There's something else, I thought, that I'm not getting. Something more dangerous.

I was in the hall at the front of the house, still sitting by the phone, when Marge came in.

"Hide," she said.

"What?"

"Edith and Heinz just drove in the driveway. Go on upstairs."

I was about to obey and go up the stairs, but my wariness made me distrust even Marge. "You go talk to them," I said, and pretended to go up the stairs. But as soon as she went toward the rear of the house, where the back door led onto the driveway, I scooted back down. When I heard the footsteps on the back porch, I let myself out the front door and made tracks out to the field on the side of the house, where I again was crawling on the wet ground to keep out of sight.

It was a way to keep weight off my ankle, though. I had left Marge's cane in the front hall. The ankle was not giving me a lot of trouble, but I didn't want to press my luck.

As soon as I was far enough away to feel somewhat safe, I called Pete again, to tell him where Edith and Heinz were.

The phone rang five times, and I figured I was too late, that Pete and his father had already left to come here. Maybe I could crawl out to the road and intercept them. I tried to remember the lay of the land, whether the field I was in was overgrown enough to get me to the road. Just as I was about to disconnect the call, Pete answered. He was breathless.

"They're here," I said. "Don't come here."

"Where are you now?" He was getting used to my calling him from rabbit warrens.

I told him which field I was in this time.

"Can you get over to Grace and Hilda's place from there?"

"I think so. But suppose they come back there?"

We worked out the logistics. I would crawl across the field to the ditch beside the road near Grace and Hildegarde's place. He would park there and wait until I had made my way there.

I could already feel my knees getting damp and muddy. By the time I was almost to the ditch, I had burdocks in my hair, crusted mud on the knees of my sweats, scratches on my hands and face, and a full bladder. The last item was easy to take care of. What could be more natural?

Once, years before, I had gone camping, and the counselor had one piece of good advice. "Pee downhill so it doesn't run onto your feet."

The mud, scratches, and burdocks I had to put up with for a while.

A car pulled up next to the ditch. I could see the MD plates. I dropped into the ditch, which was low enough so that I couldn't be seen from the Baeres's. The back door of the car swung open, and I got in, apologizing for the mud I was tracking in.

An older version of Pete, with a full head of white hair, turned around and greeted me. "Pete tells me you've been having some adventures. Who'd a thought it. Here in Paradise."

"It may be just my imagination running wild," I said.

"Ah, imagination. What a jolly ride it takes one on," Doctor Menkin, senior said. "You're a private detective, Pete tells me. Do you have a card? You never know when you might want to find out something you can't find any other way."

I smiled and dug out a card for him. Then I took the opportunity, what the heck, I had two doctors in the car with me, to ask them about my ankle. The two of them asked me questions about how I'd fallen, what it looked like, how much swelling there was, a ton of questions. They told me that what I was doing was the right thing and if I could stay off it, it would get better sooner.

"Fat chance of that," I said.

"In that case, just be sure you keep it wrapped securely," senior said.

"How do people make it clear which Peter they're talking to when you two are in the same room?"

They both laughed, and Junior said, "That hasn't been a problem for a while. But Mom used to call me Pete and Dad Sam."

"Sam?"

Senior turned round in his seat and looked at me. "My wife always loved the name, and when Pete was born, she started calling me Sam. She said it was a more fatherly name than Peter. Before long, almost everyone was calling me Sam." He smiled and got a faraway look on his face. "She's making Spanish rice for supper."

Pete gave a quick look around at me and then at his dad. "Dad?" he said. "Are you with us?"

Sam said nothing. The look on his face remained peaceful and distant.

"That's why I came home," Pete said. "It happens now and then. I have to be with him when he's with patients."

"But he went by himself yesterday to Philadelphia," I said, glancing at Sam as I spoke.

"No, I had the housekeeper take him." Pete shook his shiny head. "He's got a number of problems. He hates it when he wakes up and realizes he's been out of touch."

"I love Spanish rice," Sam said, still turned in his seat and looking at me.

"Dad," Pete said, "we're almost there."

Sam's face lost its contented smile, which was followed in quick succession by flashes of confusion and anger and then a look of profound sadness.

Pete pulled the car to a stop in the Baeres's driveway, and

father and son turned toward each another. Both of them had tears in their eyes.

"Why are we visiting them?" I said.

"We have something to tell them, and you, too. So we'll tell you all at once," Sam said. It was as if the incident in the car had never happened.

Grace and Hildegarde met us at the kitchen door. They were waiting for us, having been phoned by Pete.

"Come in, come in," Grace said. "We have coffee ready, and tea, too."

Sam wasted no time getting a place at the table and tucking his napkin over his tie. "I always slop something on it," he said.

"Good thing you don't wear it in surgery," Hildegarde said, surprising the heck out of me. Not only had she not been conversational when I met her before, but she definitely wasn't one to make jokes.

I didn't feel hungry, but I did take a piece of the fruit bread that Marge had brought over earlier. Pete and Sam dug in like trenchermen. I wondered when we were going to get around to the conversation that brought us all together.

We didn't get around to it until Sam and Pete slowed down their hand-over-fist intake. And all the while they ravaged the piles of sweet rolls, muffins, cookies, cakes, and pies, Grace nodded and smiled. I have to say, though, that for the amount they ate and the speed with which they ate it, they didn't splatter much around and they managed to keep their chins clean.

After a silent belch or two, Pete was ready with his revelations.

Twenty-one

"Greta is safe," Pete said.

Grace and Hildegarde looked at me. I thought they seemed embarrassed. After all, the last time I was here, they acted as if they hadn't seen her in months.

"Thank God," Hildegarde said. "I was so worried. She left us a note on her pillow."

"Where is she?" I asked Pete.

"She's at our place. We've hired a guard."

"Do you think you need a guard?"

"It made her feel better," Sam said. "She's been through hell."

I was glad that somebody else agreed with me that Greta needed pity more than criticism. "When did she leave?" I asked Grace and Hildegarde.

"Some time after her walk last night. I heard her come in, but I didn't hear her go out," Grace said.

"I didn't hear her truck, either," Hildegarde said.

"So you didn't know that I talked to her last night?" I said to Grace and Hildegarde.

"You did?" Grace said.

"No," Hildegarde said. "Did you scare her?"

"I don't know," I said.

"She was planning on coming to see us anyway," Pete said. "She wanted us to tell you—and you, too, Fran—where she was and also to tell you something she couldn't bring herself to tell you."

I knew there was something else. But why did she tell the

181

doctors and not her relatives? Grace and Hildegarde and I didn't say anything.

Pete had a flair for the dramatic and let the silence lengthen. It was sometime during that silence that I knew what he was going to say. I caught Grace's old watery eyes and found there a sort of recognition. We were both expecting and dreading the same thing.

It was Hildegarde who broke the silence, with, "Oh, no."

It was what I wanted to say, too, and I figured it was on the tip of Grace's tongue as well.

Finally, Pete said it. "Greta is pregnant. Late second trimester. She's trying to decide whether to have an abortion. That's why she came to us. Not that we'd do it, but we could find the right person to do it, if that's what she decides."

"And the father is Ben Grasse," I said.

"Apparently," Pete said.

Grace and Hildegarde gasped in unison.

"Ben and our little Greta?" Grace said.

"Little Benny and Greta?" Hildegarde said.

Since neither Ben nor Greta were little, I could only assume that they had stopped growing in the minds of Grace and Hildegarde, both of whom were moaning at the thought of such a union between the little people of their minds. A few minutes later, Grace came out of it and said firmly, "He shouldn't have done that. Greta is not of legal age."

Hildegarde took her cue. "He should go to jail for that. Oh, no, he can't. He's dead." She dabbed at her eyes with the corner of her apron.

I looked at Sam, and his attention seemed to be drifting. He didn't say anything this time, but having seen him do his otherworldly bit earlier, I recognized the expression on his face. Pete saw it, too, and covered for his dad by smiling at him and saying softly to the rest of us, "Deep in thought."

"Have you advised Greta as to what she ought to do?" I said. "Isn't there some kind of new law in Pennsylvania that makes abortion harder to get?"

"We're not advertising this," Pete said, "and we're not advising her. She says she has some money and can get more."

"She wouldn't have to worry about money," Grace said.

"No," Hildegarde echoed.

"She does feel very close to both of you," Pete said, nodding at the Baere women and smiling at them.

"And she wants me to keep the secret of her whereabouts?" I said, thinking about the fee I wouldn't make for finding her.

"Yes. She especially asked us to plead with you on that score. She said she would pay you whatever her grandmother would have paid."

I really ought to do business with my head instead of my heart. Delia would kill me if she knew how I was handling this. It's probably not even ethical, my brain angel said, to change clients in mid case. But, my coronary cherub said, how do you know that Edith isn't trying to kill you? Maybe Greta will watch out for your welfare better. The argument was already won, anyway. I just had to give lip service to letting my intellect override my instincts.

"Got any idea what she wants to do?" I said.

"Until Ben died, she was going to go through with it. She said they were going to marry and that Ben was excited about the baby being the only Grasse in his generation."

At this point, Sam joined us again. It was as if he had not skipped a beat. "The entire Grasse clan is dying out," Sam said. "All the males that would let me run tests on them— and I did this some years ago—were sterile."

Paradise was the place for Greta, I thought, and the people here were pulling together to protect her. I thought about a little Grasse baby, and imagined the love and doting that would be forthcoming from Marge and Fritz and Dieter and Eileen. But Greta had not decided yet what to do about the little Grasse-Baere she was carrying.

"Did Edith and Heinz come here looking for Greta?" I said to Grace.

"Ja. They were very angry. They said we were hiding her."

"But by the time they got here, Greta was gone and we didn't know where she was, so we didn't have to lie," Hildegarde said. "Well, we didn't have to lie very much."

Grace laughed. "I am not sure that Edith believed us, though."

"Neither am I," I said, and told her what I had overheard when I was hiding in the field.

I began to wonder again why Edith and Heinz had come to Paradise and if they were responsible for the motel fire. I didn't like the answers that kept popping up.

Suddenly I remembered that there was a couple in the hospital who had been injured in that fire. If Edith and/or Heinz thought that I was that woman, would they try to finish the job? Not long ago, they were still searching for me, I thought, at the turkey farm. Would their next stop be the hospital?

I caught Pete looking at me in a strange way, and realized that I had been lost in thought. Maybe I looked like his father when I drifted away from the conversation on my own thought waves.

"I have to call the cops," I said. "Got their number?"

"It's on the phone," Hildegarde said, "in the front hall."

I explained what I was calling about to the officer who answered, and he switched me to a Sergeant Hoffmann.

The sergeant came on the line talking. "We're already looking for those two," he said.

I told him that they had been at the turkey farm within the last half hour, and then tried to tell him what I thought about the motel fire and the danger to the woman in the hospital.

"You have no proof of this, do you, Ma'am."

"No, but I've been working on this case for most of this week and have reason to believe that the Baeres might harm that woman in the hospital."

He argued with me, and we went around and around for about five minutes. I told him about the computer mess, I told him my theory about keeping the organic scam quiet, I told him to check with Sheriff Castle, and finally I told him: "Look, their own granddaughter is afraid of them. She's hiding out here in Paradise."

"Greta is here? She's hiding from them?" His voice and the distance in it had changed completely.

I breathed a big sigh. Now, I thought, he believes me.

"Yes," I said.

"I'll send one car to the Grasse farm and another to the hospital," he said. "And I'd like you to come see me."

"What about?"

"Let's just say I have a special interest in Ben Grasse."

"Okay, let's say that," I said. "Do you know anything

about him that I'd like to know?'' I knew I was pushing buttons that cops don't like to have pushed. Most of them expected immediate obedience, or else you were resisting arrest and they could do whatever they thought necessary to get you under control.

But Sergeant Hoffmann was in control of his buttons. ''I think we might find a meeting mutually satisfying,'' he said. ''I have no cause to arrest you.'' Then he paused. ''Do I?''

''Nothing that I know of,'' I said, and then paused, ''unless I have multiple personalities and go around maiming and burning in the middle of the night.''

''By the way,'' he said, ''do you have a car?''

I knew right away what he was after. They had finally gotten around to tracing the plates on the car I'd rented. ''I left it behind the motel,'' I said.

''But you didn't stay there?''

''I was registered,'' I said. ''But maybe I'd better get to all this when I see you.''

It was almost noon, and I was beginning to think I wouldn't be back in Wyoming County for the dinner and dance. My internal clock was all messed up because I had had so little sleep and because the people in Paradise kept feeding me whenever I entered one of their houses. I didn't know when I'd be able to see the sergeant, and the sneaky thought occurred to me that I ought to get out of town and skip the meeting.

''I'll send a car for you,'' he said, ''and then take you to your car.''

So much for sneaking out of town. I still had to return the rental car. I hoped our talk wouldn't take too long. ''Great,'' I said. ''I'm at the Baeres's place.''

I told Pete and the others what Sergeant Hoffmann had said about wanting to see me, and Pete frowned. ''Hoffmann,'' he said. ''I think I know why he wants to talk to you.''

''Yes? Why?''

''His daughter. She was the twelve-year-old that finally got Ben in trouble with the law,'' Pete said.

Sam shook his head. ''Terrible,'' he said.

I didn't know what particular thing was the most terrible and was reluctant to ask.

Sam continued: "The child was never the same, mentally or physically."

Pete looked alarmed. "Maybe you shouldn't tell about it, Dad. Maybe it's a secret." Pete was obviously thinking that his dad was about to breach medical ethics. I was beginning to think that Sam's condition was a lot worse than Pete had let on up to now.

But this time, Sam was in fine form. "It was in the paper, everything but the girl's name. But everybody knew who it was anyway," Sam said.

Pete frowned. "I was away when it happened."

"It took years for the girl to get straightened out. She's okay now, but I'm sure her father doesn't want her to hear too much about Ben Grasse. The police didn't let him out of their sight much when he got out of jail."

"Small wonder he left town," Pete said.

"Men like that shouldn't be let to roam free," Sam said. "It's a sickness."

By the time the trooper got there to pick me up, Grace, Hildegarde, Pete, Sam, and I had agreed to keep Greta's secret as long as she wanted it kept. And by tacit agreement, we would keep her hidden.

Twenty-two

I had tried to brush some of the brown marks off my sweats, but they weren't budging. Good old farm mud, with those wonderful organic things breaking down in the soil! So, I was off to see Sergeant Hoffmann, dirt and all.

When I got in the state police car, I asked the trooper who got the dubious honor of picking me up whether Edith and Heinz had been found yet. I was wondering what had happened at the turkey farm after I left, so I asked the trooper whether he would mind if I used the mobile phone. He told me that I might get interference from the police radio, but that I was welcome to try.

At that moment some crackling came out of the dashboard, followed by a message about the "suspects wanted in Wyoming County." My ear wasn't tuned in to the noises coming from the radio, so I couldn't make out all the words.

While the message was still coming, I tried out the mobile phone and found it useless. When the radio fell silent, I asked the trooper what had happened.

"Those people were no longer at the turkey farm," he said, "but the Grasses are going to press charges against them when we pick them up."

"Press charges? What did they do?"

"Don't know exactly. Trespassing is all I heard."

I was itching to call Marge and Fritz, so I asked the trooper to let me out.

"We're almost there, Ma'am. Why don't you call from the barracks."

187

I was starting to get irritated, but just then we drove into the lot of the state police barracks. The door didn't open when I tried to get out. The doors on police cars, I remembered then, were controlled from the front. I was in the back, where prisoners sometimes ride.

The mobile phone was not working here, either. There was a big antenna rising from the building, from where, I assumed, the messages to the cars were dispatched. When I got inside, even though I was told that Sergeant Hoffmann was waiting for me, I insisted on making my call. Marge and Fritz had been through a lot on my behalf, and I was upset that Heinz and Edith had done something that would cause Fritz and Marge to want to press charges.

The voice that answered the phone belonged to neither one of them.

"I'd like to speak to Marge or Fritz," I said.

"Who is this?" the voice said.

"Well, who are you?" I said. "I'm calling Marge or Fritz Grasse and you're in their house."

"This is Officer Sean Monahan, state police," he said.

"This is Fran Tremaine Kirk," I said. "Can I speak to one of them?"

Marge got on the line. "Are you all right, Fran?"

"Yes."

"Where are you?"

I told her.

"Good. Then you're safe."

"What's going on?"

"Heinz and Edith marched in here looking for you."

"Did you tell them you hadn't seen me since last night?"

"Yes, but they insisted on searching the house for you. I was so worried they'd find you upstairs. They were like crazy people. Where did you go?"

Sometimes the crazy things my paranoia makes me do are just right. "I went out the front door as soon as they came in the house," I said. "Did you try to stop them from looking for me?"

"Yes, and they pushed Fritzie down. I was so worried that his heart would act up."

"Did they say why they wanted to find me?"

"They said Theodora told them you had something that belonged to them. They said they were going to press charges against you."

I thought about that for a minute and then decided that they weren't really going to press charges against me, but what they wanted was that disk. I wondered how Theodora knew I had it. Maybe Theodora hadn't told them anything at all.

Maybe there were some electronic goings-on that would have given away the existence of the disk. Maybe Delia could tell me about that. Oh, but Delia was going to take a vacation. Oh, but Delia wouldn't be out of touch, vacation or no.

I dropped that line of thought when it occurred to me that Eric knew about the disk. Hadn't he and Greta argued about it? But still, how would they know that I had it? But what else would Heinz and Edith think I had that belonged to them? And why would they be so ferocious about finding me?

"Is Fritz all right?" I said.

"He says so, but I'd feel better if he'd go to the hospital and let them have a look-see. Do you know what all this is about, Fran?" There was an edge to her voice. I guess playing private eye was one thing, but when someone hurt her Fritzie, there'd be hell to pay.

"I'm sorry, Marge, I didn't think you would be in danger. I wasn't even sure they were after me."

"Well, now you can be sure." She softened slightly.

"I'm hoping the troopers will nab them and I won't have to worry about them for a while. Did they say anything else?"

"They wanted to know whether we'd seen Greta. That was easy for us to answer, 'cause we haven't."

"It's just as well that Heinz and Edith didn't find her," I said. Or me, for that matter.

"What's gotten into that girl?" Marge said.

It was a question I wasn't about to answer. Nor did I think that Marge was prepared to hear about what had gotten into Greta.

I told Marge that I'd be back to the farm in a little while to pick up my things and change my clothes. When I mentioned my clothes, I tried to think where I'd put them, whether they were out of sight, or whether Edith and Heinz would have seen something of mine lying around in the upstairs bedroom or bathroom. Then I remembered that they were in my duffel and the duffel was in the closet. Chances were that Edith would not connect a duffel in the bottom of a closet to me, I thought. And maybe this was all moot. Maybe Edith and Heinz would be in custody soon.

Sergeant Rudy Hoffmann was standing at the door to his office, waiting for me. His uniform shirt was tailored to fit his tapered torso and was pressed to a fare-thee-well. His salt-and-pepper hair was brush cut, and his chin, nose, and cheekbones looked like they were chiseled from granite. His eyes were aquamarine and deep set; his thin lips drew back in a slightly crooked smile over large teeth, not unlike the horsey teeth of the Grasse family.

"Come in, Ms. Kirk," he said. "Would you like coffee?"

"No thanks," I said. "I've had plenty of coffee already today."

"You can't go anywhere in Paradise without somebody offering," he said, still smiling.

"I noticed. But it's the stuff they offer with the coffee that makes me want to get out of town before they have to roll me out."

"Ah, the Baeres, yes. But they're not as bad as they used to be. They used to make all this stuff with cream filling."

"Ugh. I'm glad they're better."

"So you're a private eye, Ms. Kirk."

I dug in my purse and pulled out my ID before he had a chance to ask me for it. He took it and looked it over and took it to his copying machine and made a copy of both sides. I knew he would have me checked out before I left.

As if on cue, a female officer came in, and he handed her the copies of my ID without a word.

"I hope you don't mind?" he said.

As if it would matter if I did. "No. You have your job, I have mine. But would you mind telling me whether you've picked up Heinz and Edith Baere yet?"

"No word on that yet, Ms. Kirk. But I'm hoping to hear from the officers at the hospital very soon."

"You heard what they did at the turkey farm, didn't you?"

"Yes, and I'm trying to decide whether to detain them here because of that. I've got a call in to Sheriff Castle in Wyoming

County to discuss it." Sergeant Hoffmann spoke slowly and clearly, as if he was used to talking to people with hearing problems. "Now, could you clear up for me what happened to you at the motel last night?"

I gave him the whole story, starting with my accidental discovery of the reservation for me and ending with the placement of the car in the lot behind the motel.

"So you wanted people to think you were the woman in the hospital, but then realized that the woman in the hospital might be in danger from them. . . . That is, if your theory about the motel fire and the Baeres's intentions were correct."

"That's about it."

"As a matter of fact, we did get a call from a female this morning, who identified herself as a secretary at Hickory Hills and asked whether you were in the fire at the Hay Den."

"If she was calling from Hickory Hills, how did they know about the fire? It's not exactly the kind of thing that makes the national morning news."

He smiled. "That's exactly what the officer who took the call thought. So she kept her on the line and traced the call to a pay phone at a gas station here in Paradise."

"So why did you give me a hard time about going to the hospital to protect the woman?"

"Ah, yes. I was stalling."

"Tracing my call." I was thinking if a guy like Hoffmann had been doing Sheriff Castle's job, there might have been fewer slipups.

I spent the next hour talking about what had happened at Hickory Hills, and the sergeant more than once after asking what the law enforcement people had done shook his head and tsked, tsked.

"I would like to talk to Greta," he said. "Do you think you could arrange it?"

"She took off again," I said. "And right now, I don't know where she is." I brought him up to speed on Greta, leaving out the pregnancy and the fact that she was holed up at the Menkins's. In reality, the job I had been hired to do was done. I had found Greta. But since I had to keep that fact secret, I had to pretend to continue looking.

Hoffmann was interested in Ben Grasse's computer disk and

asked to see the numbers that Marge had run through her number-crunching mind. I dug out my notebook and told him which numbers Marge had identified.

"I have a personal interest in anything to do with Ben Grasse," he said.

I waited, not knowing whether to repeat what I'd heard.

"Ah, he, ah, has a tendency to like young women, and my daughter was one of the young women who crossed his path, unfortunately. She has made progress, but it has been a struggle for her."

I decided to end his agonizingly slow revelation. "The Menkins told me a little about that this morning," I said.

"Old Doc Menkin knows about everybody," he said. "But he's always been the soul of discretion. He probably didn't tell you that my daughter was injured by Grasse, made pregnant, and spent time in a padded cell." Hoffmann's jaw was clenching as he spoke.

"What happened to the pregnancy?"

"Doc Menkin took care of it. He handled it quietly. My daughter is still troubled by that. When she sees the pictures that some of the demonstrators carry outside abortion clinics, she runs for the Valium."

"I guess you try to shield her from things that will hurt her."

"This murder has her all upset again. The last few nights, when I go home and she's watching TV, she doesn't blink. She throws up after every meal. So, yes, I try to shield her."

He stopped talking and shifted his attention to the numbers I had listed in my notebook, with the notes I had made about what Marge had said. He took the notebook to the copy machine and then stopped. "Do you mind? We may be able to give you some help, or it might help us."

"What are you looking for?"

"Nothing in particular, but I want to make sure that Grasse doesn't get away with anything, even now. I've been following his trail for years. I kept track of his activities in jail, too."

"So you knew that Terry Kurtz had a job at Hickory Hills and that Grasse met Terry in jail?"

"I knew, but they didn't seem to be doing anything wrong. But now that I know about Kurtz blackmailing Theodora, it

wouldn't surprise me if they were working that racket together. So these are birthdays,'' he said, hunched over his copy
of my notebook. "And this is his number in prison." He
opened his top drawer and pulled out a thick folder. "Ah, this
is Kurtz's number."

"What do these other numbers mean? Marge said they were
like some of the numbers at town hall, but she wasn't sure.
Do they look like property numbers?"

"Ah, yes. File numbers. They could be file numbers." He
called in the female officer again and asked her to have
someone run down these numbers at town hall. "Maybe he
was planning to get hold of some property some way. I
wouldn't put anything past him."

I was getting bored sitting and waiting for other people to
do the work. I wanted to get my car, get my clothes, and go
see Greta. I also wanted to avoid Edith and Heinz, and was
hoping they'd get picked up soon. Then I could get on a plane
and go back to Cheektowaga. I could skip the dance in Wyoming County and go straight home and call Ted.

The phone rang on Rudy Hoffmann's desk. "Hoffmann,"
he said. "How long ago?" He frowned. "Is she all right?"
He had picked up a pencil and was pressing on the middle of
it with his thumb while holding it in his fingers. It snapped.
Then he snapped: "Put out the APB."

When he cradled the phone, he was already shouting. He
was telling his troops to mobilize to find Edith and Heinz,
who had eluded the troopers sent to find them at the hospital.
After the orders had been given, he turned to me. "Sorry,"
he said, "they got a look at the woman in the hospital, but
they didn't do anything to her."

"How come?"

"Maybe because she weighs three hundred pounds." His
crooked mouth drew back over his teeth and he laughed. The
sound was not unlike the whinny of a horse. It went with the
teeth.

"I have gained some weight since I've been in Paradise,"
I said. I was thinking that I'd have to watch my step. Lord
only knows where Heinz and Edith were. "Well, I guess now
we know they're looking for me or for the disk."

"You have that with you?" he said. "I could make a copy of that, too."

"For your file?"

He nodded. "I've been chasing after him so long, it's going to feel funny now that he's dead."

"You'll go to the funeral parlor tonight?"

"Wouldn't miss it," he said.

And then, because I'm nosey and prone to blurting out things that sane and polite people let lie, I said, "Are you, by any chance, related to the Grasses?"

"Ben was my cousin," he said. "His mother was my mother's older sister. Why did you ask?"

"There's a family resemblance."

"I look like Ben? You think that?" He leaned forward in his chair in a pose that I thought was designed to intimidate me. But I am not always sure about my interpretations where men are concerned. They don't have to do much to put me on my guard, to frighten me.

I answered and tried to act as if my heart wasn't pounding. "No. I thought you looked a bit like Dieter and Fritz and their sister, Elizabeth. Ben doesn't look as much like them as you do."

"I don't how that family spawned a one like Ben. The rest of them are salt of the earth. Their sister, Lizzie, was a peach, sweet as they come."

"Maybe they spoiled him because he was the youngest."

"They did that. But I always thought there was more to it."

The female officer came back into the office with a puzzled look on her face. "They do have numbers like this in town hall," she said, "but they're numbers on sections of the file room."

"That's why they stuck in Marge's mind," I said. "She claims that when she sees numbers, they take up residence in her head and stay there."

Hoffmann started to laugh. "Ah, that's right. Marge used to do those number tricks at the fair. She was a whizz. I forgot about that."

"Did they say what sections of the files those numbers are on?" I figured that Ben must have had a reason for listing them.

"No, only that those numbers are there," she said.

"Thanks," Hoffmann said to the officer, and then to me: "What do you think?"

"I think I'd like to check it out."

"We'll send someone with you. While you're in my territory, I don't want anything to happen to you."

"And when I leave?"

He laughed. "You're on your own."

Before I left with the female officer, I called my office in Buffalo and gave Natasha a brief synopsis of my travels. Mostly I wanted to alert her that Edith and Heinz might go there looking for me, and I didn't want her to get hurt.

"Frances," she said in her liquid alto, "you are always being chased by demons."

"Some are real," I said.

"I hear you, girl. And I'll be careful. I'll lock the door and I'll alert the folks downstairs."

"You could call the police, too," I said. "The troopers down here have put out an APB on them."

"Speaking of policemen," she said, "the blue-eyed one has been asking about you."

"I feel guilty about that."

"Don't."

"Don't?"

"No. Don't. He has to do some adapting. You have a job to do."

Now there was a point of view. Instead of apologizing and whining and making excuses, I could assert myself. I wondered how Ted would react. "I could try on that attitude, but I don't know whether it would fit me," I said.

"Squeeze into it," she said. "It'll be liberating."

"That's for sure."

Natasha told me that Delia had, indeed, taken off for St. Martin, but that she called in every day. "She'll be back Monday," Natasha said, and then she told me not to worry about the office or the dating service. "Everything's going along as usual. A few spats at the house, a minor plumbing problem downstairs in the beauty parlor that left us without water in our bathroom, and one little thing, I'm in love."

"Natasha! What? When? Who?"

"Don't laugh," she said.

"I promise. Even if you tell me it's Donald Duck."

"It's Donald Duck."

"I'm not laughing."

"They just hired him downstairs."

"At Looks? What does he do?"

"He's a colorist."

"A colorist?"

"Yeah. He dyes hair."

"So what's he like?"

"Not too tall, about five nine, and he moves like a cat. He used to be a dancer, he's Jewish, Italian-Jewish, and he's very smart."

"He sounds wonderful. I can't wait to meet him."

"You will, Frances."

"What's his name?"

"Anthony." When she said it, it sounded like song. "Anthony Cordero." Love, I thought. It's wonderful. I would have liked to see the way the sparks had flown when she met Anthony. "Oh, one more thing. The new woman at the group. Teresa, you remember her?"

"It seems like ages ago, but I do remember. What's up with her?"

"She's at the shelter. She left the guy and his brother."

"I didn't think she was that tough. Good for her."

"I don't think it was tough. She managed to run away when the brother came at her with a knife."

"I hate these stories. I really do." I was hyperventilating and sweating and getting the chills all at once.

"You don't hate stories, Frances. I know what you hate. We've both had narrow escapes."

"You're right. You're right." A small sob burst from my chest.

"Polly is pulling all the strings she can to get her some support. English lessons, job training. All she knows now is cleaning houses. The men were sending her out to clean, because they couldn't get any work. They're all illegal."

"God, the woman has nothing but problems. I suppose with all that, things are even worse for her back in her own country."

"You said it. I'll tell you the rest when you get home."

"Depressing. How does she even get up in the morning carrying that load?"

"Polly will work wonders, wait and see."

"I know she'll try."

When I hung up, I gave myself a minute to talk myself down. Getting agitated over other people's problems wouldn't solve theirs or mine. That's what I told myself. Acting on my good advice was another story.

The female officer, who now had on her uniform jacket was standing next to me, tapping her foot. I don't think she was aware that she was doing it. She wanted to be on her way and I was holding her up.

But we didn't go to town hall. An alarm came in about a shooting at the Menkins's. I got a ride with Sergeant Hoffmann, and on the way I told him that Doctor Menkin's name had been listed on Grasse's disk.

"Why didn't you tell me sooner?" he said.

"I didn't think that he was in danger because his name was on the disk," I said. "Besides, Grace and Hildegarde and the other Grasses were on the disk, too."

He frowned. "What else was on that disk? Didn't you say that he told Greta to destroy it?"

"That's what she told me. The data on the California company that Eric was working his racket with was on the disk, too."

"I'd like to plug that disk in and see what's on it."

"No problem," I said, and dug into my purse. But it wasn't there. "It must be in my duffel at the Grasses's," I said.

Twenty-three

So much for secrets. When we, the troopers and I, arrived at the Menkins's, Greta was in the living room crying. Pete was administering to Sam, who was on the floor of the doctor's office, bleeding from the head.

The ambulance arrived just after we did. Pete had told them what equipment to bring, and before they loaded Sam onto the gurney, they hooked him up to an IV and a some kind of breathing apparatus.

Pete told Sergeant Hoffmann what had happened while Sam was wheeled out. Sam had gotten a call and met someone in his office. Pete heard the shot, and when he went into the office, no one was there except Sam.

Pete had delivered this information so breathlessly that I thought he was going to pass out.

"Are you all right, Pete?" Sergeant Hoffmann said.

Pete stood still and his shoulders sagged. "No. I'm not," he said, and started to cry out loud like a little kid cries, with his mouth open, making a loud howl, with tears and boogers running down his face.

The sergeant put his arm around Pete and walked him into the living room and sat him down. "You did everything you could do. The emergency crew brought what you told them to bring. The surgeon is on his way to the emergency room."

"I should have gone into the office with him. He didn't want me to. He said it would only take a minute. Who could have done this to him? Why?"

"Are you sure you didn't see anyone, hear anything?"

Hoffmann looked over at Greta. First at her face and then at her body. He didn't miss anything. He got the picture faster than the rest of us had. "Greta, did you see or hear anything?"

"I saw a pickup truck out front," she said, her eyes wide, her face wet. "It looked like Grandmother's."

"Did you see anyone get in or out?"

"No. When I saw it, I ran upstairs to hide. I thought they were coming in to look for me."

"And when you came back down," Hoffmann said, "was the truck still there?"

"I heard the shot and Pete was hollering. Then I came down. Pete was helping Sam, so I called the police."

"I've got to go," Pete said. "I want to be with him. Fran, will you stay here with Greta?"

"Let me have an officer drive you," Hoffmann said, "and I'll leave an officer here, too."

After Pete left, Hoffmann said, "I don't understand why none of our guys have picked up Heinz and Edith yet."

"I think I can help," I said. "I don't think they're using the roads. They have four-wheel drive. This morning Fritz found their tracks on the old tractor road and going through the field behind the Baeres's."

"Of course," he said. "The old Indian trails. That's what every kid in Paradise calls them. That's how they did it. But now that they've shot someone, they'll be on their way out of town, I expect."

"Unless there's more they have to do," I said, looking at Greta, who was not looking my way.

"I'm going to put up a helicopter," he said and walked to the phone in the hall and began dialing.

I wanted to get my car and my clothes and get out of town. There was no longer any reason for me to be in Paradise, and I didn't like the idea of being a target.

"Fran," Greta said. "Pete said the police are going to want to talk to me about the night Ben died." She was wearing jeans and her stomach was definitely noticeable. The other night when I saw her, she had been wearing the long skirt. Maybe that's why she started wearing long skirts.

"Yes," I said. "You were there. They'll want to talk to you about it. There might be something you forgot."

"I can't think of anything else. But I want to know who killed him."

"So do the police," I said.

"Will you help?" she said.

"You want to hire me?"

"Yes. I have money. I can pay you."

"What money?"

"Ben's money. He told me where it was."

"How much was there? Or am I being too nosey?"

"A lot. Enough to pay you."

"But the cops are already working on this."

"The cops were trying to find me, too. But you found me."

"I just don't want to take your money for nothing," I said.

"It won't be for nothing."

Sergeant Hoffmann came back from the front hall. "We'll find them, now," he said. "I'll leave an officer outside. Now, Greta, I don't want you taking off again. Just stay put. We'll take care of you."

"Okay," Greta said.

When Hoffmann was gone, I asked Greta about the hiding place where Ben had cached his money. "Was there anything else in it?" I said.

"Lots of stuff, but I was in a hurry. I just took some of the money. There's plenty more there."

She told me that Ben's hiding place was in the barn where he was killed. I figured that if the hiding place hadn't been found yet, another day or so wouldn't make it any more likely to be found. I still had to get my car, get my clothes, and make a side trip to town hall before I got on the plane back to Buffalo.

"Are you going to the funeral tomorrow?" I said.

"Only if they've found Grandmother and Grandfather," she said. "I don't want them to take me back to the farm."

"What are you going to do about the—" I stopped short of calling it baby, because I wasn't sure what she wanted to do "—the pregnancy."

"Hildy called me. She said she would take care of me and leave everything she had to me and the child. She doesn't want me to have an abortion."

"But you're so young," I said. "You haven't even finished high school. A baby's a big responsibility."

"Hildy said she would help me. She said the Grasses would help me, too. She said the baby would be rich." Greta smiled. "Who ever heard of a rich baby?" she said.

I talked to her for a while, hoping that her decision would be made because she wanted the child and so that she wouldn't resent the child once it was born. She was definitely leaning toward keeping it when I left.

I walked out the back door and through the lots to the motel, where the car was parked. There were other cars in the lot, too, probably at the bar, I thought.

I kept my eye out for pickup trucks, which, in that area, kept me pretty busy. There were more of them than cars. Everything seemed calm and normal, and I saw no sign of Edith and Heinz or their truck. The helicopter was patrolling overhead, and there was heavy machinery cleaning up at the motel.

I got in the car and drove toward the turkey farm, thinking that there had been plenty of motives for the killing of Grasse, and probably for the killing of Kurtz. But I couldn't figure out why anybody would shoot at Sam. I was assuming it was Edith or Heinz who had done that, but, then, nobody was sure about that either.

I drove past the turkey farm once, before I circled back and drove in the driveway. Fritz's truck was gone and there was no police car either, despite the fact that Hoffmann had said someone would be staying with Marge and Fritz.

I pulled my car around to the back of the house so that it wouldn't be visible from the road. When I got out, I got a chill when I saw the tread marks in the ground. They looked like the ones I'd seen that morning from Heinz and Edith's truck.

Before I went into the house, I checked around the barns and outbuildings for any other sign of them, but the tread marks went one way: over the hill toward the Baeres's place and toward the tractor road where we had seen the tread marks earlier.

I went in the back door of the house and was greeted by a

wonderful aroma, but no sound. In the kitchen a huge pot was simmering, but Marge wasn't there.

I looked in all the downstairs rooms before I went upstairs to the room where I was supposed to have slept, but hadn't. I had one hand on my gun as I crept around upstairs. I had not heard a sound and I didn't feel especially spooked, but I didn't feel that I could let my guard down, either.

When I was satisfied that I was alone, I grabbed my duffel and started downstairs. I was halfway down when I heard a creak, which sent shock waves through my body. I stopped on the stairs and listened. Another creak. It was coming from the living room, the archway to which was just at the foot of the stairs.

If I didn't have a sprained ankle, I thought, I would vault over the railing and make a break for the back door.

Then I heard the strangest sound, and it took me several seconds to identify it. "Pilgrim," I said. The sound was that of a dog yawning. Pilgrim came toddling up the stairs to greet me.

He probably hadn't barked when I came in, because he knew me. But I didn't remember seeing him when I checked the rooms earlier. I looked in the living room again. There was only one way into it other than the windows. Pilgrim looked at me, and then jumped back onto the couch to continue his nap. He curled himself up in a corner and tucked his head behind one of the pillows. I looked at him and then looked again. He looked like just another pillow in the corner of the couch. So much for being sharp-eyed, I thought.

I breathed deeply when I was back behind the wheel of the car. So far, so good. I wondered where Fritz and Marge had gone, but thought maybe they were at the hospital getting Fritz checked up. Marge had said she wanted him to do that.

As I drove back toward town, the sky was boiling up a storm. The clouds were almost black and the wind had started to sweep leaves and dirt across the road and whip at the tree branches.

Since it was almost three o'clock and a Friday, I wondered whether the folks who worked at town hall were about to leave for the weekend. But there were plenty of cars still parked in the lot in front of the one-story brick building, so the weekend hadn't started yet.

Even though I was in a hurry, I took a minute to check on the cars and trucks that were already there. Then I found a spot where my car was almost out of sight from the road, behind a van parked at an angle.

Big drops of rain mixed with hail pelted me as I ran from the car to the building. When I got inside and was confronted by a clerk behind a counter, I stammered. I hadn't concocted a story, so I had to tell the truth. Or part of it.

I gave the clerk the numbers that I was interested in finding, and she smiled.

"Those again?" she said. "Come with me."

Those again? Who else had been looking for them? I followed her down a set of metal stairs to a high-ceilinged basement that was furnished with shelves and more shelves. We walked down one of the aisles and she pointed to the end of one row of shelves.

"There's one of your numbers," she said.

"What's on that shelf?" I said.

"That's property maps."

"Do you know what property, and where it's located?"

"Umm, that would be the northwest corner."

I thought for a minute. North? Which way was north? Country people always do that to you. They start talking north-south. Suburban and city folk have to think twice to tell you where the sun rises.

She finally got down a map of the town and showed me the area covered on the shelves. There was nothing in that area that rang a bell. I kept wondering who else had wanted to see where those numbers were and whether anything stored in that area was important.

Then she showed me the other number on a set of shelves in another section of the records room. That was vital statistics, birth and death certificates, marriage licenses, from 1940 to the present. I didn't know what to make of that. But just because Marge associated these numbers with the ones on the disk didn't mean that they were connected. The numbers on the disk could refer to something entirely different.

"I can't leave you down here alone," the clerk said. "If

there's a volume you want to look over, I can let you look at it in the reading room."

I looked at my notebook again, at the list of numbers. There was only one date on the list that might be in one of the volumes on the shelf, and that was Ben Grasse's birthday, so I asked for that volume. She took it off the shelf and put a marker in the place of the missing volume.

"Do you remember who else was looking for these numbers?" I said.

"A woman, I think it was. About a month ago. I can check the records for you if it's important. People don't often come in here looking for the numbers on the shelves. They usually know what they want. Those numbers on the shelves don't mean anything except for us to find our way around down here."

"So that's why you remembered?"

"Yes."

When we got upstairs, she filled out a form, which detailed who took which volume and when.

"Did the woman who was looking for those numbers take out this volume?" I asked.

The clerk scratched her head and frowned. "I can't remember. And I usually remember stuff like that." She started to go through a file next to the counter. "Now I remember. It was a busy day. A lot of the high school kids were in here for some project. It was a madhouse in here. That's why I'm having trouble with that day. Here. Here it is."

She handed me three forms like the one she had just filled out for me. Each was for a volume taken out by Mary Jones on the same day. One of the volumes was the one I was taking.

"Thanks," I said. "Mary Jones. I'm afraid I don't know her."

"I don't think that was her real name," the clerk said. "I remember her now."

No Shinola, Sherlock. "Is that so? Why?" I said.

"Just the way she acted."

"Well, thanks for looking her up. I appreciate it."

Then she led me to the reading room, which was a tiny

cubbyhole with barely enough room for the table and two chairs that were its only furnishings. There was one window, but it didn't let in much light, because outside it had become quite dark. The clerk turned on the overhead fluorescent lights, which blinked annoyingly.

"Tornado warnings," the clerk said. "It sure looks like twister weather."

"Is this building safe?"

"It's never been in a tornado, so I couldn't tell you."

"What will you do if a tornado hits?" I said.

"Head for the cellar," she said, smiling as if a tornado wouldn't dare hit the town hall. "Bring the book to the desk when you're done," she said.

Distracted by the weather, I kept one eye on the window. The sky was a deep purple and the wind was howling and beating against the pane.

I didn't expect to find anything, but I went through the motions. I opened the big cloth-bound tome and was hit with the smell of mildew and musk. Dust danced up from the pages as I flipped through the big volume. The old entries were made in different colored inks that didn't seem to have any significance. There were several different handwritings, one was small and neat, another was florid and large, and still another was more like printing than writing, but plain, no loops or curlicues.

It looked like the clerks would save up the births for a week and then one of them would enter them all. Maybe they didn't work full-time and only came in once a week to enter the vital statistics.

Ben Grasse's birth date was right where it was supposed to be, and I was about to close the book.

I slammed it back open, and looked again at the entry: "Mother's maiden name, Elizabeth Grasse." But she was his sister, wasn't she? His mother's maiden name couldn't have been Grasse. Next to the entry that called for the father's name, the record was blank.

My head was spinning. How could this have sat here all these years and Dieter and Fritz not known that Ben wasn't their brother but their nephew? Or did they know and keep the secret? And what was all the joking about the mother jumping the fence because Ben didn't look like the others? And did the other person looking for shelf numbers also look into this volume?

My heart was racing as I copied the information. And when I got to the doctor's name, I asked myself a few more questions. Dr. Peter Menkin had delivered Ben. So he must have known.

I was just getting up to return the book, when there was a tremendous crash and the lights went out. I looked out into the hall, wondering whether I'd see a tree hanging through the roof.

Several flashlights were already in use, and I heard the voice of the clerk, saying, "Those numbers are downstairs. I'll show you when the lights go back on. The other woman was looking for the same numbers."

"What other woman?" The voice was Edith's. I wasn't about to hang around. I closed the door and jammed it shut with a chair. Damn. I would have to jump. My ankle would not take that. I'd have to try to land on my other foot. I threw my purse out of the window and crawled out onto the ledge and let down my legs and then my torso and finally hung there by my arms. I prayed as I let myself down and then let go.

That was the longest split second I've ever experienced. The drop, it turned out, was only a couple of feet. A piece of cake. A perfect landing on my good foot. I listened for a moment to see if anyone was coming into the reading room yet. Nothing.

I stayed close to the building behind the plantings and ducked as I went by the windows. I was behind the town hall and my car was at the front. The rain was coming down in sheets and I was getting soaked.

When I got to the side of the building, I could see my car. I would have to cross an open space to get to it. The van that I had hidden it behind was gone. I didn't know whether to risk it or stay where I was and call the troopers with the portable phone. The helicopter certainly wasn't up looking for Edith and Heinz in this weather.

I tried to put my mind in gear. Where were Edith and Heinz? Where was the clerk? Where was the reading room? I went over the route I had taken in the building and decided that I was some distance from where they were likely to be.

I looked again at the car to see whether there was any danger in going to it. There was the possibility that Edith and Heinz had found my car and trashed it, flattened the tires, disabled the ignition, something. But what were the chances that they knew what my rental car looked like? Where would they have seen it?

I decided to walk, not run to my car. I would pretend to be an older person. It would be easier on my ankle anyway. I found a scarf balled up in the corner of my purse and tied it around my head. Then I hunched my shoulders and tottered to the car.

Once at the car, I looked back at the building, and now I could barely see it through the deluge. I felt relatively safe. My clothes were soaked, and I hated the idea of drenching the car seat, so I took a minute to dump out my duffel and put the duffel on the seat.

I dumped it out carefully so that I wouldn't be too rough on the computer disk, which I had promised to give to Sergeant Hoffmann. The clothes slid out, rolled up the way I usually packed them, then my other shoes, then the toiletries case. No disk. I looked inside the bag. Not there. It was gone.

Someone had taken it. Who? Who had been in the house at the turkey farm? Who had gone upstairs? Did Edith and Heinz search my things this morning when they went upstairs to look for me? Would anyone else have taken it? Marge? Fritz? Dieter? Eileen? Pete? The troopers? Hadn't I told Hoffmann that the disk was in my duffel? Had someone taken the disk and then followed the number trail?

I started up and drove away slowly, trying to continue the senior citizen role I had adopted. After about a block, I speeded up. I couldn't floor the accelerator, which was what I wanted to do, because the visibility was lousy.

If Edith and Heinz had taken the disk, that would explain their appearance at town hall. But they would have had to put the disk into a computer. How? Then I remembered the little computer that Delia had used, and Edith punching up the programs like a pro when she dropped her pose as computer illiterate for a minute back at the farm.

But why would they shoot Dr. Menkin and then go to the town hall to follow the number trail?

Instead of calling the troopers, I went directly to the barracks to tell them where I had left Edith.

But the troopers were otherwise engaged.

Twenty-four

The troopers's barracks were deserted except for the officer doing the dispatching, and he was overwhelmed with calls about the storm. I tried to get his attention, waving and thumping on the ledge that separated him from the front desk.

He raised his eyebrows at me and put a finger in the air.

Finally, I yelled. "This is an emergency. Those people might be the ones who shot Doctor Menkin."

He put everyone on hold and listened to me. Then he put out the message to "all units." While I was standing there dripping, Sergeant Hoffmann came in.

"What are you doing here? You're soaked to the skin."

I blurted out everything at once.

"Just a minute," he said, and stepped over to the dispatch desk and spoke briefly to the dispatcher before he made his own calls to his officers. The dispatcher got up and yielded his chair.

The dispatcher went out the door at the back of the room and came back several minutes later with a shopping bag.

He handed the bag to me and said, "Some of this stuff might fit you. It ain't pretty but it's dry and clean."

The sergeant was still picking up one phone, then another, then a mike. I couldn't tell what was happening except for the fact that some officers were at the town hall and the Hickory Hills truck was there, too.

The dispatch officer showed me the way to the ladies' room, where I peeled off my wet—and dirty—sweats and picked through the clothes in the bag. I donned a pair of jeans, which actually fit pretty well except for being about three inches too long, and an old trooper's shirt, from which the insignia had been removed, leaving a darker gray patch.

I dried my hair a bit under the hot-air hand dryer and felt almost human.

When I went back to the front desk, the dispatcher was back at his post. I gave him the bag with the rest of the clothes and thanked him again.

"Sergeant's in his office," he said.

"So tell me again, slowly, what you've got on Ben Grasse," he said.

"First, can you tell me how Sam is?"

"I just came from there. Pete was feeling hopeful when I left."

"And is someone still outside the Menkin house keeping an eye on Greta?"

"In this mess, don't ask me where anybody is. But, yes, those were the orders."

The sergeant gave me a steaming cup of coffee, which I gratefully accepted.

"The doughnuts are getting a little long in the tooth," he said, "but they're still edible."

I picked out a sugared cruller and dunked it in the coffee to soften it. I can't tell you how delicious that tasted.

The sergeant waited until I stopped eating like a wolf and then asked, "What's this about Ben's mother?"

I apparently hadn't been very coherent before. When I told him about the birth record, he couldn't stay in his chair. He jumped up. "How could that have been sitting there that long and nobody—I—Are you sure?"

I laid out my notebook for him and showed him what I had copied.

"Jesus!" He paced the room. "And the father's name was blank? You're sure?"

"Maybe you ought to go have a look at it yourself."

"No, no. I didn't mean that. So the numbers you had from that disk were on the side of the shelves. Do you think Edith and Heinz were after the same thing?"

I had forgotten to tell him that the disk had been lifted from my duffel. I told him then.

"So the Baeres are traveling around with a computer, you think?"

"Well, if they're the ones who took the disk and then they decided to go to town hall, it could be that they have a computer."

"But how did they know where to find the numbers? Marge is the one who told you where she'd seen numbers like that."

"They used to live around here. Maybe they remembered."

"Or they followed you."

"But I heard the clerk tell Heinz and Edith that the other woman—meaning me—was looking for those numbers." Then I was jolted by the memory of the clerk telling me about the woman who had been there before.

The sergeant caught the look on my face and said, "What?"

"There was a woman who asked the clerk about the same numbers. About a month ago."

"I'm going to call over to town hall," he said, "and make sure they keep that book under wraps. Where did you leave it?"

"In the reading room. I jumped out the window when I heard Edith's voice."

He laughed. "You're a piece of work."

"What would you do?"

"I'm a policeman; I'd confront them."

"With your gun drawn, no doubt."

"Not a doubt in the world. Especially since we don't know what these two have done so far."

"Could you check to see if you've got them in custody yet?" I wanted to get out of there. There was something nagging at me. Something wasn't right with the scenario. Edith was a lot of things, but I couldn't see her putting a slug into Sam's head. Maybe Sheriff Castle's assessment of Edith had rubbed off onto me. Maybe I shouldn't have run away. Maybe I should have confronted Edith and Heinz. No. Heinz was something else again. I didn't trust him.

I went through the cast of characters and put them one by one through my trust meter. It was probably not a coincidence that more men failed the test than women. I tried to tell myself that more men commit violent crime than women. But there was that doubt in the back of my mind that I couldn't really do my job the way I should with the bias I felt against men. I was always able to think the worst of them.

I then defended myself and told the critical part of me that I was working on my faults. Didn't I go to the battered women's group every Tuesday night? Didn't we talk about the way we relate to men?

Miss Critical had an answer for that, too. Aren't there always more rotten men to hear about when you go to a battered women's group? Maybe you ought to see a therapist. Maybe you should go to a different kind of group.

Sergeant Hoffmann was talking to me. "They're on their way here now."

"Who?"

"Edith and Heinz. We've got them."

I felt a great weight lift off me. A weight that I didn't even know I had been carrying.

"I want to go see Greta," I said, "before I get on the plane to go back to Buffalo."

"Now you're going to leave? After you've stirred up all this stuff?"

"It should make great conversation at the funeral parlor tonight," I said.

"You've got a twisted sense of humor," he said. But he was smiling.

"Seriously," I said, "I don't think Fritz and Dieter knew that Ben wasn't their brother. Maybe they ought to be brought together and told gently."

"There's no way to tell them gently."

"No, I guess not," I said. "I feel sorry for them. But you know what they say about lies. 'What a tangled web we weave . . . '"

He joined me with the rest: "'When first we practice to deceive.'" Then he said, "Tell you what. Before you leave tonight, maybe around five-thirty or so, we'll get the Grasses all together up at the turkey farm. They've been living with these lies a long time. We should give them the truth gently."

"You want me to be there?"

"You're the one who found it. It's the least you can do."

I did not need anyone putting a guilt trip on me. I felt guilty enough already.

"Okay," I said, "but first I go to see Greta."

"I'll tell the officer there to expect you," he said.

As I drove away from the barracks, I passed two police cars and the Hickory Hills pickup truck. I assumed that neither Edith nor Heinz was driving the truck. I couldn't see which car they were riding in, because the rain was still hammering down.

At the Menkin house, the officer got out of his car—wearing a slicker that I envied—and came over to where I had parked. I was waiting for the rain to let up enough to let me make a run for the front door. It wasn't happening. Since my duffel was already wet on one side, I used it to keep some of the rain off. The officer escorted me, and when we were both on the front porch, he asked me for my ID.

Good, I thought, they're doing their jobs. It made me feel safer, too.

Greta came to the door before I rang the bell. I was still putting my ID back in my wallet. She looked more pregnant than ever, I thought. But then, maybe I was looking at her differently from the way I had before I knew.

Once inside, I told her that Edith and Heinz had been picked up by the cops.

"Poor Grandma," she said.

"Poor? Weren't you worried that she was after you?"

"Yes, but that was because I didn't want to go back to the farm."

I was interested in Greta's feelings about Edith, because my own feelings were so ambivalent. "And now?"

"Now, I don't have to go back."

"What's different?"

"I'm going to be eighteen tomorrow. Then they can't make me go back. They can't tell me to do anything."

"Happy birthday," I said. It was the saddest happy birthday I ever uttered.

Greta didn't miss the tone of voice. "Yes," she said. "Thanks." And then, probably because she was Edith's granddaughter, she said, "Can I get you something to eat?"

"Yes," I said. "I could use some fruit and vegetables. I've been eating too many sweet rolls and doughnuts."

"Grandma Grace can make those things in her sleep. But I was making a salad and hot dogs when you got here. That okay?"

"Great," I said. "Let me give you a hand."

"I'm almost done. I made extra because I didn't know when Pete was coming."

"In that case, I'll make a phone call," I said to her back.

"Go ahead. The phone's in the front hall."

I dialed Sheriff Castle's number, but I didn't know what to expect. He might be home getting ready for the dance, I thought.

"Castle." He was still at his desk.

"Hi."

"Where are you?"

"Paradise. How are things going there?"

"The farm's running, but there aren't any Baeres on it."

"Theodora and the bunch aren't back?"

"Haven't heard word one from any of them today."

"There's news from down here," I said, and gave him the story. Even that I'd found Greta.

When I was done, he said, "Damn. I should have kept all of them right here. Why'd they shoot the doctor?"

"Nobody saw the shooting," I said. "Greta saw the truck."

"Jesus, all this information just brings up more questions," he said. "The only thing that we have for sure is that now we know where Greta is."

We? What's this we stuff? "Let me give you some phone numbers, so you can reach me." I gave him the portable phone number and the numbers of places I might be. "I'm still going to try to get out of here tonight. I just hope the weather clears up."

"We're getting some nasty weather here, too. Maybe you want to wait until tomorrow. Your job is done anyway."

"Not quite," I said. "I'm still working for one of the Baeres."

"Which one?"

"Greta."

"You getting paid?"

"I expect to." I didn't tell him about the money Greta had found in Ben's secret cache.

"What's she want you to do?"

"Find out who killed Ben."

He laughed. "Let me know when you do. It'll make my job easier." His tone was belittling and I didn't like it.

"I'll let you know as soon as I find out anything," I said. My voice was pure ice.

He cleared his throat. "By the way," he said, "that policeman from Buffalo was out here today looking for you." I didn't respond. "I told him where you were. Was that all right?"

"Of course," I said. Just thinking about Ted made me feel guilty. And I knew the sheriff was trying to figure out who Ted was in my life. But, heck, so was I.

"I just wondered," he said.

"Wondered what?" I wanted to make him feel uncomfortable.

"Wondered what kind of girl you were."

"I'm not a girl," I said, calmly, matter-of-factly. "I'm a woman. And I don't know what you mean."

"You do so." He was almost shouting. Losing it.

"Sheriff," I said, "I'll call you later." And I hung up.

Even though I had controlled my voice, I wasn't calm. He had irritated me. He was trying to get under my skin and he had succeeded.

Ted's the one I ought to call, I thought. Just to tell him I'm all right and still working on the case.

I dialed his house and got his machine and told him just that, and added that I missed him. I didn't mention anything about his being at Hickory Hills, mainly because I didn't like the idea that he had chased me out there. That was something we were going to have to work out. I had a job and he had a job, and sometimes the jobs came first. That was the posture that Natasha had told me to try on. Maybe I could fit into it with a nip here and a tuck there.

I was tossing some ideas around about my relationship to Ted and where it was going, if anywhere, when Greta called me to eat.

She was no slouch when it came to putting out a meal,

either. And she wasn't even eighteen. The hot dog rolls were toasted, the hot dogs were done to a turn, the salad was heavy on ingredients, and the dressing looked and smelled delicious. There was also fruit salad, pickles and olives, and a bowl of home fries.

"Oh, that looks good," I said, "and I'm starved." Getting soaked must have made me hungry.

Greta's appetite wasn't petite, either, and the leftovers were sparse.

"If Pete comes back, we'll have to rustle up something else for him," I said.

"I wish he'd call," she said. "I tried to get him at the hospital, but they wouldn't tell me anything and they couldn't get him on the phone."

"The last I heard was that Sam was doing better."

"Good, good," she said. Her face was clouding up. "I hope nobody shot him because I was here."

"That's not a good enough reason, unless somebody's crazy. You know anybody that crazy?"

"I don't know anymore," she said. "Everything's crazy." Tears were running down her face, but she wasn't sobbing.

"Greta, I have something else to tell you. And it might have something to do with Sam being shot, or it might not. In any case, it's something you'll want to know.

She wiped her face with a paper napkin. "More craziness?" she said.

"It's pretty crazy," I said. "But it was a secret for a long time."

When I told her, she frowned and shook her head. "How could people do that? The mother raised the baby as if it was hers? That would be like my mother raising this baby as if it was my sister or brother. Gee. God. What was it like for Ben's mother to have to pretend she was his sister? Do you think Ben knew?"

"Yes. That's why those numbers were on the disk."

"What numbers?" she said.

"You know, the ones on Ben's disk."

"I never paid attention to any numbers," she said.

I got out my notebook and showed her the numbers and what I had learned about them from Marge and what I had found out about them at the town hall. "This number is on some shelves at the town hall, but I don't know what their connection is to Ben," I said, showing her the number in the notebook.

"That's the combination to his safe," she said. "But he stopped using it. He said it wasn't safe." She smiled wryly.

"But it's a number at the town hall."

"No, it's not. See the *L* after the first two digits? That means left."

I laughed. "Well, there are a bunch of shelves downstairs at the town hall. Come to think of it, they're on the left as you get to the bottom of the stairs."

"I never paid attention to that file on the disk. But maybe that's because I was too busy working on Eric's numbers on that California racket he was pulling."

"Well that clears up another mystery. But Ben never told you about his mother?"

"Maybe he was trying to tell me." At that moment, she looked as if her mind was somewhere else. "That night. He was hinting around. Saying things about how some parents keep secrets. I thought he meant that he and I were keeping secrets not telling anyone I was pregnant."

"But he never did come right out and tell you."

"No. It's so weird."

We had cleaned up the kitchen and I was looking at my watch. It was almost time for me to meet the Grasses at the turkey farm. "Are you interested in going to the turkey farm while I tell the Grasses who Ben's mother was?"

"Are you sure they don't know?"

"Pretty sure."

"I don't want to see them," she said. "I'm not sure I want them to know about this yet." She patted her stomach with her hand.

"I know they'd get a kick out of it, but I don't think you should go through with it just to please other people."

"I just don't know what to do. Do you think a baby would grow up like its father? The things I've heard about Ben are so, so awful."

I didn't remind her that someone in her family might be even more awful. There was something else I didn't say to her. And that was that I wanted to take a look in Doc Menkin's old files to see if his records matched the ones at the town hall.

I just told Greta that I had to look in the doctor's files for something that Pete wanted, and that satisfied her. Pete had told me earlier that he had found something that might be important. So I felt almost entitled to look around. Almost.

Greta turned on the TV and sat quietly, rubbing her belly.

When I went into the office, I closed the blinds and went searching. The file cabinets lined the office walls, six drawers high. The recent files were down below and were all dated and clearly marked, while the older stuff was on top. I tried out one of the swivel chairs and decided that I could make it work if I was careful, but it would be hard to see the top drawer.

After going through one cabinet from that perch, I realized it was hard on my ankle whenever the chair started to swivel and I moved my feet to keep the chair straight.

I looked around to see if I could find something to keep the chair from turning. In my search, I opened a narrow closet, and found, instead, a stepladder, which made the job faster.

Time was flying, and I was going to be late getting to the turkey farm, but I figured that Sergeant Hoffmann would tell them if I was too late. I didn't really need to be the one who told them.

I was still trying to figure out the filing system for the old records. There seemed to be groups of files with people with the same ailment, and other groups of files by family, and others by age. But I didn't run across the Grasses in any of them.

But I was only about halfway through the drawers. Then I remembered that Sam had said something about the Grasses. That he had tested them. That the men were sterile.

I went back to the drawers where I'd seen the ailments and looked for sterility, and bingo, there was a list of Grasses. This file was cross-referenced to other files that were numbered, and I finally found the Grasse family.

There were a lot of them when Sam started his practice, but many of them were old. All the diseases and deaths were there, but few births. The women went on to have a few children, but, they weren't Grasses any more. The men of Fritz and Dieter's generation had no children.

I kept going through the records until I found the copy of the birth record of Ben Grasse.

Born to Elizabeth Grasse, age 19, on April 25, 1949.

The next entry got my skin crawling.

Twenty-five

My hands were shaking when I took the sheet from the file. I turned on the copy machine and waited for its little red light to go on, thinking all the while what this meant to Greta, to Fritz and Marge, to Dieter and Eileen, and to the folks at Hickory Hills.

The entry stood out as if it was written in fire: Father: Heinz Baere, age 21.

But that information wasn't in the town records.

How long had Ben Grasse known this? What kind of man would impregnate Greta, knowing she was his own neice? Then I remembered that this was the man who had done the same thing to his cousin, Sergeant Hoffmann's daughter. Could this be the reason he was killed? Was he blackmailing Heinz? Was Sam shot because he knew? But who else knew about it?

Now I was in a hurry to get to the turkey farm. I wanted to watch the faces when they were told, watch to see who was surprised.

As I was putting the papers together, I noticed a pile of copies next to the copy machine. The name Grasse caught my eye and I kept on reading. It was a health record for Genevieve Grasse. It showed the births of her three children, Dieter, Fritz and Elizabeth. Then it showed a hysterectomy in 1945.

That's what Pete had found. That's what he wanted to show me.

I returned the files I had copied to their drawers and put the ladder in the closet. Then I called the turkey farm.

Marge answered. "Where are you, Fran? We're waiting for you."

"I'll be there in ten minutes or less," I said. "Will you put Sergeant Hoffmann on the phone?"

I heard her call, "Rudy, Fran's on the phone. She wants to talk to you."

He also gave me the business about being late.

"I've got more information," I said. "Can you get Grace and Hildegarde to come over?"

"Probably. But why?"

"Meet me in the driveway and I'll tell you before I tell the others." I didn't want to risk saying it out loud. I wanted to cut Greta a little slack.

When I told Hoffmann what I'd found, he blew a gasket. "God, if the guy were still alive, I'd kill him myself."

He fumed for a few minutes, and when we were ready to go in, I told him that I wanted to see what reaction the Baeres had to the news.

"They were wondering why you wanted them here. I hope Grace's heart can take it."

"What about Fritz's heart?"

"Maybe we ought to have a medical unit here," he said, and he was only half joking.

Everybody was sitting around the dining room table, and Marge had the board groaning. I didn't notice what she had this time, though; I was too wired.

Marge offered me a cup of coffee, which I took, and then I took a couple of cookies. She said they were low fat.

The others were sipping and nibbling and looking at me and then at Sergeant Hoffmann. They talked about the terrible weather, which had let up in the last hour, and sat uneasily in their chairs.

After I took one sip and one nibble to be polite, I started talking. I took them step by step through what I had done. Before I dropped the bomb, I told them that I had found surprising news.

They all followed right along. Not one of them seemed edgy or more nervous than the others. Hoffmann was studying the faces and postures, too.

Then I told them what I had found in town hall.

"Mom's name wasn't Elizabeth," Dieter said.

"Lizzie?" Fritz said.

"Oh my," Eileen said.

"Poor Lizzie," Marge said.

Grace said nothing. She patted her lip with her napkin.

Hildegarde said, "Lizzie was sick that year."

As the realization sunk in, Dieter and Fritz went from surprise to anger.

"How could they have kept such a secret?" Fritz said.

"You're right, Hilda. That spring Lizzie spent in her room. We weren't allowed to go in. She had something that might be catching, Mom told us," Dieter said.

"And we made all those jokes about Mom jumping the fence," Fritz said. "And they kept quiet. Damn."

The conversation continued for a while until they realized that I was sitting on the edge of my chair.

"What else?" Marge said.

"There's more?" Fritz said.

Grace bit her lip.

I said to Grace, "Do you know the rest?"

"Ja, I do, I think. But it was not supposed to be. They got money. I gave them money."

"Money?" Fritz said. "Money for what?"

Grace's composure was slipping. "Tell them," she said. "I did not know until now."

"Mama," Hildegarde said, "what didn't you know?"

"Heinz was the father," I said.

That started an argument between Dieter and Grace about what a bad kid Heinz was. The others made comments about how Ben really did take after Heinz. No one seemed to have any advanced knowledge about it except Grace.

"No sense fighting about it now," Rudy Hoffmann said.

"Grace," Fritz said, "why did you say you knew what Fran was going to say?"

"When Lizzie was in the family way," Grace said, "your mother came to see me." Grace was red eyed and breathing hard. "We decided she should not have the child. I gave them money to take her to a doctor who did such things. Plus I gave them more. Much more."

We all sat silent.

Finally Fritz said, "That was the year the folks paid off the mortgage and fixed up the house."

"I told Heinz he had embarrassed me too much," Grace said. "He left town with Edith."

"I wasn't too fond of Heinz before," Dieter said. "What a snake in the grass. Knocks up my sister and then steals my girl."

"Did you ever suspect what the Grasses did?" I asked Grace.

"After Benny was born, sometimes I saw in him . . . but they were my neighbors. We made an agreement. What could I say?"

Suddenly Hildegarde gasped. "Greta."

My mouth opened. I wanted to tell her not to say what she was going to say. But it was already too late, because Grace, too, was hyperventilating.

"She can't have that child," Grace said.

"What child?" Marge said. "Is Greta pregnant?"

"Who's the father?" Dieter said.

And then, a collective "Oh."

"Did Ben know?" Eileen said.

"Yes," I said. "He knew."

"I'm feeling sick at my stomach," Eileen said.

"Does Greta know about this?" Dieter said.

"Only about Lizzie," I said.

"That means Heinz would be the baby's grandfather on one side and great-grandfather on the other side," Marge said.

"I wouldn't blame her for not wanting to keep it," Dieter said. His eyes were brim full. "But it sure would be nice to have a little Grasse."

At that point, I felt I had to speak up for Greta. "Please," I said, "don't tell her you know about the baby. She didn't want anybody to know yet. I don't think she should have pressure put on her to have it or not to have it. She's only going to be eighteen tomorrow."

"I'm sorry," Hildegarde said. "I shouldn't have said anything."

"Me also," Grace said. "We were supposed to keep her secret."

"Do you think somebody found out about her baby and killed Ben because of it?" Fritz said.

"It's possible," I said.

After a while, I excused myself and called Sergeant Hoffmann aside. I wanted to know about Sam and I wanted to know about Edith and Heinz.

"Pete says they got the bullet and a tumor, too. If he makes it, the shooting will have been a blessing in disguise. If he makes it."

"Was that what was causing those lapses?"

"I didn't know anything about those lapses. Pete just mentioned tonight that he had been having little spells. He's hoping that the tumor was the cause."

"And Edith and Heinz?" I said. "Did you tell Grace and Hilda that you arrested them?"

"I was gentle," he said. "I told them that the sheriff in New York wanted to talk to them and that we were going to escort them back to the farm. That much is true, but I didn't tell Grace and Hilda that we're questioning them about Sam's shooting."

"So they know about Sam?"

"Are you kidding? In this town?"

"Ben's parentage was a secret in this town," I reminded him.

"But there was no ambulance out in front of the house when he was born. Or when he was conceived," he said.

"Have you gotten anything from Edith and Heinz yet?"

"They claim they didn't do it. We tested their hands for residue, and we searched the truck with a fine-tooth comb. No gun. No sign that either of them fired a gun lately. They could be telling the truth."

"What about the truck? Greta saw the truck," I said.

"They claim they weren't there."

"Is Greta mistaken? Or lying?"

"I don't know," he said, "but we're not done questioning Edith and Heinz. We're going through the whole day with them, step by step, trying to account for everything."

"When did they arrive in town? Were they here in time to set the motel fire?" I said.

"They said they arrived this morning and went right to Grace and Hilda's place."

The back of my neck was getting prickly. If I'd been a cat, my back would have been arched and my hair would have been standing up straight. I had motives and suspects up the kazoo. And every day, it seemed, there was another crime, and they were all connected in one way or another.

I was looking forward to the flight back to Buffalo. Maybe I'd have time to think.

I said my good-byes to the Baeres and the Grasses, and wished them luck. They teased me about turning their town upside down.

"It was upside down all along," I said. "You just got used to it that way."

"Just let me know the next time you're coming," Dieter said, "so I can go to bed and stay there."

Eileen poked him. "Stop that, Dee, she's just doing her work. She's not the one who kept the secret all those years."

Dieter shook his head. "I can't get over it. The folks keeping this a secret."

"I wonder when Ben found out," I said.

"I'll bet Lizzie told him before she died," Marge said. "Remember, Fritzie, he spent all that time with her in the hospital?"

"And he left town not long after she died," Dieter said.

"And went to live with his father," Marge said.

"I don't know when or if he told Heinz what he'd found out," I said.

"Heinz didn't know he had another son," Grace said.

"If Edith found out," Dieter said, "I wouldn't put murder past her. She'd want her son to inherit everything. If Heinz had any intention at all of giving anything to Ben, Edith would do what the old queens used to do, kill off the children who pretended to the throne." Dieter's tone was bitter. All the revelations must have opened the old wounds.

Grace was getting agitated again, and she looked weak and tired.

"Mama," Hildegarde said, "I think we should go home."

"I'll drive you," Sergeant Hoffmann said.

"But it's just over the hill," Hildegarde said.

"And it may be too far for Grace to walk," he said.

As we left, I reminded the Grasses again to keep Greta's secret until she was ready to divulge it, if ever.

"Maybe we can learn to keep secrets, too," Dieter said.

"Yeah," Fritz said with a wry smile, "it runs in the family."

I called Sheriff Castle again while I was driving back to the Menkin house. He had already been in contact with Sergeant Hoffmann and the state police in both New York and Pennsylvania. They were working on a plan to get Edith and Heinz back to New York after they figured out what to charge them with in Paradise. The sheriff said he was going to put them under house arrest when they returned. There was no word from the younger Baere family yet, he said.

"What time do you think you'll be getting back tonight?" he said.

"Before I turn into a pumpkin," I said.

"If you get back any time before midnight, drop in at the dance. We'll be going strong until the wee hours."

I couldn't imagine partying when I got back, and said so.

"You don't know what you're missing," he said.

And I didn't care, but I didn't say that. "I'm wrung out," I said.

Since it was a fairly short drive, there wasn't enough time to finish my calls, so I stopped a few blocks from the Menkins's and made the rest of them. I had to check on Horace and the office. Maybe I'd call Ted when I got back to Buffalo.

When I drove up in front of the doctors' house, there were a lot of lights on. When I was intercepted by the officer on guard, he told me Pete was home.

Pete looked gray and haggard, but he smiled when I walked in. "I think he's going to be okay," he said, "maybe even better than before."

"Hoffmann told me about the tumor," I said. "Fate does some strange things."

"What a day," he said.

"Ditto," I said.

We both sat down and sank into the cushions on the couch as if the moves had been choreographed. I thought it was funny, but I didn't bother to look at him to see whether he was smiling, too. I was suddenly overcome with exhaustion. And the softness of the couch seemed to invite me to close my eyes.

I was thinking that I should try to persuade Greta to go back to New York with me before Sheriff Castle sent someone down to pick her up. But I would just keep my eyes closed for a while.

The next thing I knew Greta was calling my name. When I opened my eyes, she was standing in front of the couch and smiling.

"What?" I said.

There was a groan next to me.

"You two have been sleeping there for an hour," she said. "You want some coffee?"

"I'm going to hit the sack," Pete said.

"I've got to get back to Buffalo," I said. "And, Greta, maybe you should come with me."

Greta frowned. "I don't want to go back there."

"You don't have to go to the farm," I said. "You can stay with me. We can stay in a motel. But the police up there want to talk to you."

"Will they arrest me?"

"Tell them what you told me. Tell them everything. I don't think they'll arrest you."

"But they might?"

"Anything's possible, but I don't think they will."

"If I don't go back with you?"

"Sometime soon, they'll send someone to get you and take you back there. You can run away again, but then they'll surely arrest you when they finally do find you."

"And meanwhile," Pete said, "you need to be seeing a doctor whether you keep the baby or not."

Pete seemed to be wide awake, now, so it seemed the right time to tell him about Ben's parents and to tell Greta who Ben's father was.

"Sit down," I said to Greta. Pete was still sitting.

First I asked Pete whether the record of the hysterectomy was what he wanted to tell me about.

"Oh, yes. I forgot all about it. But as soon as I saw it, I knew his mother wasn't—"

Then I gave Pete the information from the town hall records. Greta sat quietly. That was the part she already knew.

Then I went through what I had found in Doctor Menkin's files. I spoke slowly and didn't raise my voice. I didn't know what kind of reaction I would get from Greta.

Pete was shocked. Greta did not cry this time. She sat still and said nothing for a long time, while Pete ruminated on the upshot of this, and what would have happened if people had known sooner.

Finally, Greta said, "I can't have this baby. My grandfather was Ben's father." A look of disgust came over her face. "How could Ben have done this?" She was no longer feeling sad or sorry. Now she was angry. "Can you find someone to do the, the operation?" she said to Pete.

"Yes," he said.

"I mean now, tonight," she said. "Right away."

"I don't know," he said. "It can wait another day or two, can't it?"

"No," she said.

"Aren't there some regulations? Some paperwork? Some procedures?" I said.

"No, no," Greta said. "I've got to get rid of this—this monster."

Pete looked worried. Greta had been under a tremendous strain. "Greta," he said, "listen to me. I'm going to take care of you. I'll see what I can do tonight. Don't worry."

It was the right thing to say to Greta. What he was going to do to make good on his words was what I was wondering.

Pete went to the phone and started chasing down a doctor. When he found him, he told him the situation.

Greta sat there peacefully, listening. It seemed to me that her reactions were all screwed up.

I had one more thing to talk to her about, but I didn't want to set her off again. I needed her to get specific on how to find Ben's secret cache.

I talked around the subject for a few minutes. The talk served two purposes. One was to get her talking about the hiding place and the other was to distract her from what Pete was saying, which was that she wasn't going to have the procedure that night, because the procedure that was used at her stage of pregnancy took a lot longer than an early abortion.

She tried to listen to me and Pete at the same time, but finally gave in and talked to me. When I asked her to tell me where Ben had hidden his money and important papers, she didn't even blink when she told me.

"I guess Sheriff Castle can wait a day or two to talk to you," I said.

"Yes," she said. "Now I'm not going to be a mother. But my life won't be the way it was."

"You can go back to school," I said.

She smiled again. "Yes, here, in Paradise."

I was thinking that she was glad she was going to get a chance to be a child again. I didn't think this decision was going to be a cause of great regret as she got older. But what did I know? I was glad it wasn't a decision I had to make.

When Pete got off the phone, he told Greta to pack a bag for the hospital.

When she was upstairs, he said, "We can't do it tonight, but we can start getting her ready. And I'll give her something to make her sleep. We'll start the first thing in the morning."

I looked at him, at the lines in his face, and felt sorry for him. "You've been through a lot today, too," I said.

He looked at me and smiled. His smile really did a job on his face. "Yeah," he said. "I need somebody to take care of me."

I had to look at him twice to read his meaning. After all, I hardly knew him. I realized he was sending out a feeler, like a bug sensing his environment.

The possibilities spun around in my head, and I didn't know what I felt about him. I had trouble with my feelings in a lot of areas. So I answered the words and not the feelings. "You do," I said. "Especially since you spend so much time caring for others."

I said good-bye to Pete and Greta and told them I'd call. Just as I was starting to feel safe in Paradise, I was going to leave for Hickory Hills, where safety was a scarce commodity.

Twenty-six

When I got on the plane, I had a double seat to myself so I spread out my notes and added to the jottings about what had happened in Paradise and the people I'd met there.

I wondered about good and evil and whether some people had sprung from bad seed. What else would account for the way Ben turned out when he was surrounded by people who seemed so good?

And Heinz, what of him? Dieter felt wronged by him. Certainly Ernest was Heinz's victim. But Heinz's mother and sister seemed to be innocents, too.

Maybe Grace was wrong in the first place, trying to get her son out of the predicament he was in. Hadn't Dieter said that the Baeres had more money than the Grasses? Maybe Grace didn't want her son marrying someone she thought was beneath him.

But that was so long ago. And were the murders at Hickory Hills a direct result of that long-ago decision?

I had to shake myself to get myself on the trail. I got out my notebook and wrote: Two murders, Terry and Ben; one attempted murder, Sam; one fire (maybe connected), me; the threat nailed to Amy's door; the smoke bomb and the vandalism to the farm computers; the attack on Delia and me with the nail gun; Edith and Heinz and their invasion of Marge and Fritz's house, the theft of the disk, their visit to Grace and Hildegarde, their trail through the back roads, their visit to the town hall.

If they didn't shoot at Sam, who did? Someone in Paradise? Someone else from Hickory Hills? Where were Theodora, Ernest, and Eric? Could they have come to Paradise?

What were the motives? There were plenty of secrets that had been uncovered. If someone had killed to keep them, he or she would have to do a whole lot of killing to hide those facts now.

I was getting nowhere, but at least I was organized. It was going on ten-thirty, and we got the notice to buckle up. I could see the runways lit up beneath us, and I tensed up as I always do during takeoffs and landings. If I grasp the armrest with all my strength, it makes the landing go smoothly. It has worked so far.

As soon as I was in the terminal, I called Mrs. Klune—on a pay phone, because I couldn't bring myself to use the portable for a nonbusiness use—to see if I could pick up Horace, but there was no answer at the Klune house. She had said that the family was going camping for the weekend and that they'd take Horace with them if I didn't get back before they left.

The thought of Horace going camping with the Klunes and romping among pine trees made me sort of jealous. I never did things like that with him, and I was always going off and leaving him in Wally Klune's care. I didn't give him such a good time, especially when I was busy. Instead of being jealous and begrudging the dog and the people a little quality time, I thought, I should be grateful for people who love the dog so much.

That got me thinking about people who can't share friends or can't stand to have their spouses acting friendly to other people. And that, naturally, led to thoughts of my husband and how he would accuse me of flirting if I so much as smiled at another man and how he would show his displeasure with his fists.

I dwelt on these unpleasantries as I drove home to Maple Street, Cheektowaga, the house that used to be my mother's, the house she moved out of so that Dick and I would have a "nice place to live."

Now it was where I lived with Horace and where one night almost a week ago I'd had a man in my bed, a man I thought I loved. But all this week, while I was working, I didn't treat him like a lover. I don't know why I couldn't make the time to keep in touch with him. I told myself I was too busy.

Probably he'd had enough of me already.

Then it hit me: Is that what I wanted? To drive him away?

I immediately stored that thought with others of its type under the heading: THINGS I CAN'T DEAL WITH, and I went back to my ruminations about Hickory Hills.

The lights hooked to the timer were on in my house, and everything looked okay when the garage door slid open. I felt a chill, though, being in the house without Horace. I depended on him to sound the alarm if anything was wrong.

With my hand on my gun, I closed the garage and got out of the car and started my inspection of the house. I even looked in the attic, I was so spooked. Lucky, I thought, I don't have a basement.

When I finally got around to thinking about having a snack and going to bed, it was midnight. And, again, I hadn't called Ted. Was it too late? Was he working the late shift? I didn't remember.

I warmed up some milk. Even though I hated warm milk, I thought it would help me sleep. Wrong. I tossed.

Just as my eyelids were getting heavy, and that tired, relaxed feeling was finally overtaking me, I heard something bang on my bedroom window. My eyes snapped open.

Somebody from Hickory Hills had been waiting for me, I was certain. All my panic systems were operating, blood rushing, breath coming fast, hands sweating, alimentary canal on the verge of disgorging its contents one way or the other.

I couldn't remember where I had put the gun. My purse. Where was it? The gun was in the purse. Wasn't it? Or did I put it somewhere else after I had searched the house?

I slid out of bed on the side away from the window and shoved the pillows under the covers to create the illusion of a sleeping form. Maybe that would buy me some time. Then crawled out of the bedroom to look for the gun.

Wait. Why not call the police? Why not run screaming into the street? Why not go to the garage and get in the car? Whoever it was was at the back of the house. Suppose it was a kid trying his first burglary. Did I want to shoot him?

Get real, Fran, I told myself. It's you against him. He might have a gun, too.

I stood in the hallway next to the bedroom, trying to clear my head. I waited for another noise, but heard nothing. Then I remembered where the gun was: in the night table next to the bed. Back in the bedroom.

I crawled back, grabbed the gun and a flashlight, flicked on the light and shined it at the window, taking aim at the same time.

I didn't shoot.

The face at the window was Ted's.

He had seen that the pattern of lights in the house was different, had looked in the garage and seen my car, and then had come knocking on my window. I told him I had had him in my sights and that he'd better ring the bell next time.

Much later, I told Ted all about what I'd been doing. It was touching to see how he enjoyed being included in my work. We stayed up the rest of the night going over everything that had happened. We were high on the chase and high on each other.

He didn't say a word about my not calling him, didn't say a word about going out to Hickory Hills looking for me.

He told me he loved me more times than I've ever been told. Come to think of it, had I ever been told? By my mother? By Dick?

Over coffee, Ted told me who his favorite suspect was at Hickory Hils. "Heinz was the one with the big secret," he said.

"But all these years he didn't know. And when he found out, would he kill his son?"

"Maybe he didn't find out. Maybe Ben hadn't gotten around to telling him that."

"Then why would he kill him?" I said.

"Because he had found out that some of the food they were selling wasn't organic. Because he found out about Greta. Because he found out about Theodora."

"Those motives work for the others, too."

"You're right. But, you know, I want him to be guilty."

"Why?"

"Maybe because he seems to be the start of it all. Maybe because he beats up on his son." Ted got a cloud over his face just then that told me more about him than his words. I got a picture of him getting beaten by his father, and it was clear that he harbored resentment.

He caught me looking at him, and our eyes locked. We knew a lot about each other in that look, but we couldn't find the words. I wondered what Polly would say about a couple of abused people looking to each other for solace.

We got tangled up with each other again, and this time there were colored lights and sirens blowing. It was a brand-new experience for me: sex that was more than closeness, sex that was actually thrilling. The only word I could think of to describe the experience was "Oh."

We fell asleep with our limbs curled around parts of each other and didn't wake up until three in the afternoon.

Ted took one look at the clock and practically shot out of bed. "Four o'clock shift," he said, and kissed me and went to the door.

"Button your shirt," I said. "What will the neigbors think?"

He smiled, buttoned his shirt, kissed me again, and was gone.

My inclination was to loll around the house and munch potato chips and moon over Ted, and I let myself do that for about five minutes before I called Natasha to catch up on what was happening at the office.

Since it was Saturday and my office was closed, I called her at the house where she lived with the dating service women.

"Frances, where have you been?"

I filled her in on my activities since I'd spoken to her.

"Ted has been going crazy. Have you called him?"

"He just left," I said.

"Ooooh," she said. "A long night."

"How do you know he didn't come over this morning?"

"Mmmm, I think it's your voice."

Just what I need. A friend who reads my voice when she's not reading my mind. "And my voice is telling you what time Ted came to my house."

"Are you denying that he spent the night?"

"Damn it, Natasha, that's none of your business."

"I thought so," she said. Her voice was full of smiles. So voices do tell something. Too bad I can't learn to control mine.

Natasha, always the diplomat, changed the subject. "Mrs. Klune left a message for you at the office yesterday. She said your message machine was making weird noises."

"I wondered why the message light wasn't on last night. Maybe I'd better check the machine."

"Maybe the tape's full. Probably with messages from Ted. Anyway, Mrs. Klune wanted me to tell you that they were leaving to go camping earlier than they expected. She said not to worry about Horace. They bought him a bed and a blanket and he'll be sleeping in the tent with them."

"I'll bet Horace will have a blast."

"Pete Dresden from Sunset called. He has something for you to investigate, but it can wait. You're to call him early next week. And a woman called, wouldn't give her name but she said she works at Hickory Hills and wants to talk to you."

"Did she say anything about her work schedule? I mean when can I see her?"

"No, but she did say that if you tell Sheriff Castle when you're going to be at Hickory Hills, she'll find out about it."

"What? She knows whatever the sheriff knows?"

"Sounds like that's what she meant."

"Peculiar. Maybe I should be careful about what I say to the sheriff."

Natasha had a message from Delia, who was still romping in the sunshine, and another from Amy, who was going stir-crazy at her aunt's house and wanted to know when she could come back.

I told Natasha to tell Amy that Greg had been arrested but that it wasn't a good idea for her to go back to Hickory Hills just yet. If Amy gave Polly a call, she would get the same advice.

The office was running fine, Natasha said. The fax machine had malfunctioned, but she'd had it repaired. And yesterday a woman had had a heart attack downstairs at the beauty parlor while she was having her hair dyed.

"They put her on the stretcher with that goo still clinging

to her head. It was getting all over the sheet. Finally, they decided to back up the stretcher to one of the sinks and wash the stuff off. So they were working on her to stabilize her while one of the wash girls was nervous as hell and washing the dye off her hair. What a scene.''

''What happened to the woman? Is she going to survive?''

''I don't know,'' Natasha said. ''They took her away in the ambulance.''

''I'll bet the beauty parlor was buzzing all afternoon. Who was doing her hair?'' I remembered that Natasha's new friend was a colorist.

''My friend Tony. They were giving him a hard way to go all afternoon. They were calling him the killer colorist.''

''Is nothing sacred?''

''Not much,'' she said.

When I hung up, I thought over whether to call the sheriff. The mystery woman had left such a strange message, I wasn't sure how to interpret it. I decided not to call. I would just head out there and go straight to Ben's hiding place and see what else interesting was left.

I checked my message machine and rewound the entire tape. It was full. When I played it back, there were a few old messages from last week, but much of the tape was full of long silences and then hang ups. I wondered whether Ted had done it, but he had said nothing about that, nor had he said anything about going to Hickory Hills or about leaving all those messages at the office.

At the end there was a half a message from Mrs. Klune: ''Hello, Fran, this is Clara Klune, we'll be lea—''

I would definitely have to have a talk with Ted.

Next, I called Pete in Paradise to check on Greta.

''She's coming out of it,'' he said. ''She probably wouldn't have gone to term, anyway. She has a problem, and there were problems with the fetus.''

I didn't press him on what the problems were. I was glad that she was all right. ''When can she travel? The police up here want to talk to her.''

''I think Rudy has made some arrangement to talk to her here. He'll question her and send the tape to the sheriff up there.''

"I'll bet she's happy about that," I said.

"I haven't told her yet, but I'm sure she will be. And speaking of travel," he said, "I have to be in Buffalo next week. I was hoping you could have dinner with me."

"Ah, when?" What was going through my mind was that I could have dinner with him only if Ted were working. Then I thought that going to dinner with Pete was not the thing to do. Then I wondered whether I should go out with Pete just to see what he was like. After all, I had very little experience with men.

But, my strict self said, do you have to get all your experience in a couple of weeks?

"What night would be good for you?" he said. "My plans are flexible."

He's making it hard for me to say no. "Can I check my schedule and get back to you?"

"Sure," he said. He sounded happy. Maybe he'd expected me to say no outright.

When I hung up, I called Sergeant Hoffmann, but he wasn't in and no one would give me any information over the phone about Heinz and Edith. So I left a message and said I'd call back later.

The day was slipping away, and I still had plenty I wanted to do, so I tidied up the house and gave it "a lick and a promise," as my mother used to say when she did anything half-assed.

I packed enough food to keep me from starving and a sleeping bag and camping equipment, in case I had to rough it. But I had no clear plan about what I wanted to do. I did know that I had to get a look at Ben's secret hiding place and that I didn't want the Baeres to know where I was, if I could help it. I also packed everything I owned that I could use to disguise myself, including my mustache kit.

I drove over to the We Have It car rental place on Union Road and rented a pickup truck with four-wheel drive and a cap that fit over the bed. I figured I might be doing some camping.

The salesman assured me that the truck I rented was the best one he had because, "You can get from the cab to the back right through the winda, here. See how big this winda is?''

Why anybody would want to crawl through the ''winda'' when it was such a short walk from the cab to the back was something he did not explain. But I would have reason to remember the sales pitch and furnish my own explanations.

Twenty-seven

I parked my car at the back of the rental lot and stashed my stuff in the back of the pickup. There was plenty of room for all my gear and sleeping room besides.

It was almost five-thirty by the time I was on the road back to Hickory Hills. There was still plenty of daylight, and I would have to wait until dark before I made my way to the barn, but I could find a good spot for the truck while there was still some light.

Greta had described the spot where I'd find Ben's things, and she seemed pretty precise about it. I hoped her directions were adequate.

I drove out Route 20A until I got to a spot that was fairly deserted. Then I put on a pair of glasses with plain glass in them and tucked my hair up into a baseball cap. The jeans and running shoes I was wearing would be okay, but I added a bulky jacket. I wished I had a full-length mirror. What I was trying to look like was a farmhand at Hickory Hills. As long as nobody got too close, I was okay.

As I drove the rest of the way, I hatched a plan to get to Ben's cache. After that, I hadn't the slightest idea what to do next. Maybe then I'd call the sheriff.

When I got to the farm, I didn't use the entrance that I'd used the first day I arrived. God, it was less than a week ago. A week ago tonight, I thought, Ben Grasse was still alive, making his larcenous plans, not to mention his licentious plans.

There was no sign of any sheriff's cars near the main entrance or on any of the roads that circled the farm. I even drove partway up the road to the store but saw nobody. I assumed the store was already closed and that the farm offices were shut down for the weekend.

I remembered the location of the barn where Ben was killed, and I drove around the perimeter of the farm until I got to a spot that was behind that barn. The road I was on was the one the coroner had come in on that first day. I looked for a place to park where the truck wouldn't be noticed.

The first place I found was perfect. Except that when I got out and looked around, I discovered that the place was littered with beer cans, food wrappers, and some unmentionables that told the story of an often-used lover's lane.

Since it was Saturday night, I figured I'd have company before too long. I left that spot and went looking for a place that was less obvious. I slowed down where the road ran over the creek and noticed that some fishermen were on the stream and had a tent set up. Several trucks were parked along the road and I could see a few more in the woods near the stream.

Even though I was farther from the barn than I intended, the parking was good. I turned off into the woods on the side of the stream closer to the barn, switched into four-wheel drive, and churned my way in the woods until I was out of sight of the other trucks and in an area where the underbrush was heavier. It was a lot darker in the woods than out on the road. If anyone saw me, I hoped that I would pass for just another fisherman.

Before I headed for the barn where Ben had hidden his most private belongings, I jammed the stuff I needed into the pockets of my jacket, because fishermen don't carry purses as a rule. I chose a path that ran near the edge of the woods and not far from the road. These were deeper woods than the ones that ran between the buildings on the farm, and I didn't want to get lost. I took my bearings so that I could find my way back.

As I walked, a car and a truck with fishermen pulled over and parked. I realized that on the other side of the road the stream ran parallel to the road for some distance. I probably could have parked closer to the barn and still looked like a fisherman, I thought, but I didn't want to go back. Of course, the only thing fisherman-like about me was the truck parked by the stream. I had no tackle, no boots, no net, no creel, no hat with flies in the band, no can of worms, unless you count the mess at Hickory Hills.

Ben's cache might not yield anything that would give me a clue to his killer, but it was the only chance I had at this stage. I wondered whether the Baeres who were innocent knew who the guilty one was. Or was there a conspiracy? Of two? Of three? Of all of them? No, not Greta, she couldn't have. Or could she?

I was getting tired of going over the same old ground. I just didn't know who'd killed Ben or Terry. The computer mess was easier. That was probably Eric, maybe in connivance with his friend Hiram Cody. Maybe the first threat nailed to Amy's door was Eric, too. However, the second time the lights went out at Amy's apartment, the attacker was serious. That was more than a kid caught with his hand in the cookie jar. There must have been more at stake. And that was when Delia and I were looking at Ben's disk. But who knew? And how?

At that point, I got a terrible feeling, and a lot of my assumptions started to crumble. I knew of only one person who knew we had the disk. And that was the sheriff. Maybe he wasn't just a bumbler, maybe he was—what? A killer? What was his connection? And what about the woman who called and said she would know when I was coming to the farm if I told the sheriff? Was she trying to warn me about a leak?

I truly felt on my own. There was not a soul I felt I could trust anywhere within miles of this place.

The trees were thinning out, and there was a field ahead. If I was going to continue to make my way parallel to the road, I would have to walk in the field. I was reminded of the time I had spent getting soggy in the field in Paradise and wasn't looking forward to crawling amid the thigh-high crop of whatever it was. But that's what I did.

I even took off my baseball cap and tied a scarf on my head and tucked pieces of grain in it. Real commando. When I poked my head up every now and then, I wanted to be invisible.

The light was fading and a breeze had sprung up, making the grain in the field bend and wave. At one point I flushed a pheasant and I worried that I'd given myself away, so I stayed put for a few minutes.

As I closed in on the barn, I heard voices and tried to hear what was being said, but the wind carried only a word or two in my direction. I raised my head to see who it was and where they were headed. I didn't recognize them and figured they were some of the day workers who didn't live on the farm. I watched as they got into a truck and drove away.

There were no more sounds except the wind in the grain. I crawled closer to the barn and realized that I wouldn't have to cross much open space to get to the small door at the back of the barn. The big door, where they drove the trucks in to unload the hay, was on the other side of the building. I remembered last Sunday, looking through that big doorway and seeing Ben lying there with the tines of the pitchfork sticking through his shirt.

Before I got up and made for the door, I went over the directions Greta had given me on the location of Ben's hiding place. I was feeling less confident about finding it. She had told me to go in the big door and go to the right corner, then go along the side wall to the fourth upright. Down near the floor, at the side of the upright, she said, feel the wood and find a rectangular cut. That's a cover that you can pry off with a knife.

If Greta told anyone else about the cache, all they'd have to do is wait there for me. How paranoid ought I to be? But wait. She hired me. Hmm. But so had her grandmother, and look how that worked out.

I was wishing I knew where Edith and Heinz were. I would feel safer if they were still in Pennsylvania, I thought.

I looked around and didn't see any place from which someone could be watching me, except back in the woods. But that was some distance, now, and if I walked as if I belonged here, I thought, no one would think anything was awry.

I stood up and walked casually to the door. But when I pushed on it, something was holding it closed; it was barricaded or barred at the bottom. Damn. So much for keeping out of sight.

I walked around the side of the barn, looking for another door, but the side had no entrance. There was nobody around that I could see, and few places for anyone to hide, except for the fields. Someone lying in one of the fields could see me, if someone were lying in wait. But I hadn't told anyone I was coming.

Then it occurred to me that it was a good idea to walk around the barn before going inside anyway. And I gave myself a talking-to on the subject of casing a building before entering it. It was a lesson that my husband had taught me during one of the first cases I worked on with him. I felt stupid. I could have looked at a lot of the building without leaving the safety of the field.

Well, no harm done, I thought, there's no one around. The breeze was steady, making waves in the grain. A few birds were still foraging, probably the ones with chicks in the nest that were never satisfied. Nature gave no hint of evil or remorse.

I took a slow walk around the barn and then slid open one of the big doors and went inside. Once the door was closed and before my eyes grew accustomed to the low light, I couldn't see anything.

Slowly the shapes of the piled hay stood out. And high in the air, the big tongs that lifted the hay off the truck caught the last light through the windows near the peak. The tongs hung from a pulley on a track that moved along the barn's roof ridge. I looked toward the corner where I expected to see the door that wouldn't budge, but it wasn't there. Was the hay too high? Then I remembered that on my tour around the barn, the land had dropped away on the side where the small door was. So there was another level under the haymow, or under part of it.

Ben's cache would be to my right, and I started moving that way, keeping near the wall in case someone should come in. The hay was starting to bother my nose, and I was afraid that I was going to sneeze. I don't know why I thought I had to be quiet if there was no one around to hear.

The hay was quite high in the barn, and walking in it was a chore. I prayed there weren't any pitchforks lying loose. Even a needle in the haystack was not a comforting thought. It wasn't exactly quiet walking through it, either. The hay made a swishing sound as I pressed it down and then lifted my foot to take another step. Not quiet at all. I tried getting down on all fours to see if it was a quieter way of moving through the hay and discovered that it was easier and somewhat more quiet because I didn't have to lift my feet. I slid across the surface, which packed down gradually.

I was almost to the fourth upright on the side of the barn when I heard a thump. As I cowered in the hay, I had visions of a shadow bearing down on me with a pitchfork ready to spear me. How long I waited, I don't know, only that there was no longer any light coming through the high windows by the time I let myself move again. More slowly now, and almost noiselessly.

At the fourth upright, I had to worm my way down to the floor to get to the spot where I was supposed to feel the groove in the wood. I was fingering the wood carefully, because the wood was rough and splintery. I was just about buried in the hay, and I found the dust and dryness almost overpowering.

When I saw the flash, I stopped moving my hand. At first, I thought that a thunderstorm had come up. The second flash told me that someone was in the barn with a flashlight.

The kind of breathing you do when you're afraid, those little gasps that help your body keep up with the rush of adrenaline, is impossible when you're practically interred in a haymow. I flet like I was going to pass out from lack of oxygen. Then I felt like I was going to sneeze and pushed my finger hard against my upper lip.

The light was coming closer. I could hear the swish of the hay as whoever it was walked through it. I began wondering if Greta had told someone else where to look for Ben's things. The light was strafing the hay above me, and I was flat against the floor.

Then I could feel the pressure of the hay moving as the person moved right next to me. I was afraid to breathe. I could hear him, or her, breathing, sort of like a panting.

Then I felt something brush against my face and I almost screamed. My eyes must have been popping out like Ping Pong balls. I knew my body couldn't take much more. My stomach was aching, and I was afraid it was going to start growling. I didn't know what was next to my cheek, and my worst fear was that it was a rat or a mouse getting ready to taste me. I didn't know whether I could keep silent for that.

Whatever it was rubbed against my cheek again, harder this time. A cat, I thought, a cat wanting to be petted. But there was no way I could move. That's when my stomach gurgled and I thought the jig was up. The light flashed toward me. I could see a pant leg in the light. Still, I didn't move. But the cat did. It jumped up from the floor onto the top of the hay.

I heard the person gasp, but still I couldn't tell who it was. Not even what gender. "Psst," the person said, shooing the cat. But mostly what I was hearing was the thunder of my heart.

The light moved away from where I was, but the person continued to look for whatever was the object of the search. The cat meowed now and again, and I was grateful for the noise it made. Whoever it was stayed in the barn for a long time, shining the light around the edge of the barn. I was sure that the search was for Ben's hiding place and wondered how many people knew about it.

Greta said Ben told her where it was when he was dying. He could have told the other women he slept with, too: Amy, Theodora, and whoever.

My heart was pumping at a more normal rate, even though the person had not yet left the barn. Suddenly the door of the barn rumbled open and some light cut through the dark. I thought that meant the searcher was going to exit. But next I heard whispers that sounded angry. Then bumping sounds and cracking sounds. Someone was being hit, maybe blows were being traded. Was Heinz beating up on Ernest again? I didn't even know whether Heinz was here and not in Paradise.

Finally there was an "oof," and the fighting stopped. One person was panting. A light shone toward the roof and then there was a squeak and a rumble. The tongs were swaying, then descending, fast. They hit the hay not too far from where I was lying.

Maybe I should move, I thought. Were those tongs meant for me?

The tongs were then lifted, but they were no longer empty. They held a load of hay. I was baffled. Was someone redistributing the hay? The tongs came down again, this time not so fast, and then they were hauled up, up, very slowly about halfway up.

When the light from the flashlight hit the hay, I understood why the ascent had been so slow. The tongs not only held the hay, but jutting from the hay was a leg.

It was all I could do to keep silent. Another body.

Then the door of the barn closed and everything was quiet, and dark. The cat was meowing, probably protesting that she wanted to get out of the barn.

I was in a sweat to get out of there now. Although I couldn't see it, I imagined the body swinging overhead. I resumed my search for the groove in the wood, trying to keep my mind on my task and work methodically lower and lower toward the floor. The surface was so rough that I wasn't sure I would be able to detect the groove if I did touch it.

My hand was right next to the floor when I detected a horizontal groove. My mind told me it couldn't be the top of the door, it had to be the bottom, but I hadn't found anything above it. I stuck my knife blade into the groove and started prying. A small rectangle slid out from the surface of the wood. It's so small, I thought, not much could be hidden here.

Gently, I pulled at the rectangle and a block came off in my hand. I pulled out my small flashlight and shined the light into the hole. It was a lot bigger inside. My pockets were already loaded, but I found room for the stuff that was in the hole. A small bound notebook, a handkerchief, and money, a lot of it. There were also some loose papers that I quietly bunched together and pocketed. I poked around in the hole again to satisfy myself that it was empty, and found myself running my fingers against a smoothness that didn't feel like wood. Gently I palpated the surface until I came to its edge, where I started to scratch.

Tape, I thought. Something's taped there. It must have taken hours to do, it was so smooth.

I scratched until I got an edge and pulled at the tape. Before I had finished pulling away the tape, I knew that what it had concealed was another computer disk. Once I had pulled it free, I replaced the block.

Now all I have to do is work my way over to the door and get out of here, I thought. I was wrong again.

Twenty-eight

First I heard the sounds, the crackling, and seconds later, I saw the flickering light. A fire. A fire in a hay barn would be fast and hot. I scrambled up onto the hay. Get out, get out, was the urgent scream I heard inside my head.

I didn't have to bother being quiet. The flames made enough noise to cover my moves in the hay. Before I got to the door, I could see that the entire doorway was already engulfed in fire. There was no way to get to it.

The floor in front of the door was stained, a dark wet stain that was starting to bubble close to the door. Another stain farther back from the door was still growing. Blood was dripping from the body held by the tongs.

When I looked up, I could see that some of the hay had dropped off and more of the body was exposed. It was a very large body. There were not many people on this farm who were that size.

Another murder, I thought, but I didn't dwell on anything too long. I knew that it would be only minutes before the fire would go up like a Christmas tree.

There are only two ways out of here, I thought. Do I let down the body, hoist myself on the tongs, slide over to one of the high windows, kick it out and then hope I don't die jumping to the ground? Or do I find the door at the back? The one that I know is there, but don't know how to get to.

I said several prayers of unknown origin and took off for the back of the barn. More hay was starting to burn and the place was getting hot. When I got to the back corner, where

I thought I'd find a stairway and found nothing, I had visions of a roasted, charcoaled lump that was me. I was crying and pawing at the floor, thinking that I should have tried to open the big doors even though they were burning. Better a few burns than being burnt to a crisp.

The flames were racing toward me, consuming, gulping the hay in its path. Bits of flaming hay rose in the air on the thermals. The updraft was causing the body to spin. All I could think of was a barbecue. Parts of the roof were starting to burn, and the heat was intense.

I don't want to die like this.

Who said prayers don't work? At that instant, I felt a ring in the floor and hope took hold where despair had been the sole occupant. I pulled, and up came a trap door.

Thank you, God.

I didn't wait to look down in the hole. I just jumped. The door came down by itself. The jump wasn't far, but far enough to aggravate the ankle that was just curing itself. Down there it was still blissfully cool, and when I shined my flashlight, I could see that what was keeping the door to the outside closed was a couple of feed bags.

The pain was terrific when I put my weight on my foot, but I thought that pain was preferable to the pain of being toasted alive. At the second that I was about to burst out the door and to freedom, I heard the meow. The cat. I couldn't leave the cat, could I?

By now, I realized that there was a ladder to the trap door which, had I taken it, would have spared my ankle. I climbed up the ladder, wincing each time I put down my damaged foot. I pushed up the trap door an inch or so—it was heavy pushing it up—and saw the eyes shining at me through the crack. Another heave and the cat shot through the opening.

She took off out the door with me and crouched next to me when I fell to the ground once I had reached the field of grain.

As I lay there panting and crying and cuddling the cat, the barn exploded and flames shot high into the sky. I heard the siren in the distance. It would be too late to save much of anything by the time the volunteers arrived.

I was almost sure the body in the barn was Ernest. But was he the one who had been searching the barn? And who had killed him and set the fire? And where was the killer now?

When I sat up and peeked over the top of the grain, the breeze was carrying sparks across to the field in front of the barn. I could feel the heat from my perch in the grain, and thought I'd better crawl back to the woods and my truck.

I didn't want to hang around and be blamed for the fire, not to mention the murder. Crawling was better than walking anyway with my ankle pinging the way it was.

The cat walked under me, around me, and next to me as I made my way through the field. I think she thought it was some kind of game. Then just as suddenly as she had appeared in the barn, she disappeared in the field. Some unwary prey was no doubt near. I missed her. I think I was already harboring visions of her and Horace getting to know one another.

When I got to the woods, I limped along with the help of a stick that I'd picked up. There was just enough light at the edge of the woods so that I didn't use a flashlight. I didn't want to call attention to myself in any way, if I could help it.

When I got back to the truck, I crawled in the back and locked myself in, wrapped myself in the sleeping bag and shivered for I don't know how long. I may have slept. I don't know.

Hunger was what finally brought me to my senses. I turned on the flashlight briefly, so that I could find the bag with the food. Cheese and crackers and water never tasted so good, and the apple was as good as a chocolate soufflé.

Back to work, I told myself, and I emptied my pockets of the hoard from Ben's box. I put the disk into the box where I had stored the disguises; it was the only box I had. Then I looked through the loose papers.

They were copies of the in-house orders and the corresponding invoices from California Arbor Naturals. It was obvious from the dates what was going on. Ben had been building a case. Maybe he felt he had to because the family treated Eric as such a fair-haired boy. But if something like that got out, it would put Hickory Hills out of business. Maybe Ben had another motive.

But if the scam was as small as Delia said it was, why was Ben doing all the documenting that he seemed to be doing? Was there something else going on?

I tucked the papers in the box next to the disk and flipped open the small bound notebook that Ben thought it necessary to hide. The entries were short and abbreviated—some indecipherable. "Gr wonderful," was not hard to understand, however. Nor was "Amy swt."

I went back to the beginning of the book, and the first entry—the reason, perhaps, that he started the book—was, "Lizzie tells dth bed, she is moth. Fath is Grace Baere's son, Heinz. Hardly know him."

I read through the little book, heartbroken sometimes, disgusted at others. There were notes on the California Naturals deception, on his affairs with women—many more than I had heard about—and on some dealings with Terry Kurtz. It certainly opened up the field of suspects. There were dates, too, showing when he started an affair and when he ended it. "Intro" was the word he used for the first date. "Bye" was the kiss-off word. The dates that Greta had given me coincided with the ones in the notebook. There were notes, too, that referred to business that had been transacted before Ben started to work on the farm. Why?

The only woman he spoke about repeatedly with fondness was Greta. The notes seemed to indicate that he did intend to marry her. Then it hit me. There were no notes on Theodora. Why would he leave her out of his notes? Or had somebody edited the notes already? Why would she lie about having had an affair with him? And Terry Kurtz? He lied, too, if that was the case. He had told the sheriff about seeing Theodora with Ben.

I read on. A few days before he was killed, Ben apparently had told Heinz that he was his son. "H.B. did not believe me," the diary said.

I was almost to the end of the notes when I heard voices right next to the truck. I switched off the tiny light that I was using to read.

"Come on, baby," a slurred voice said. "We saw you."

"We just want to have a little fun." Another voice, also drunken.

"We got some nice wine," said a third voice.

I'll bet, I thought, but I said nothing. They would go away if I did not answer, I thought.

"Come on out and play."

"Come out, come out, whoever you are."

"We're not going to hurt you. We'll be so gentle."

And then they started banging on the side of the truck. Hard.

I couldn't believe what was happening. This sort of thing didn't happen. This cave-man mentality was a thing of another time, another place. But all my denial didn't make the reality go away.

"Get away or I'll shoot," I said.

"You'd shoot us?"

"Such a pretty thing?"

"We don't want you to bang us." That comment was followed by loud, lewd laughter.

Clearly they were too drunk to be dissuaded. And too horny.

I had the phone and I had the gun. The phone would be too slow and the gun would be too final. I was as scared of them as I've ever been on the trail of criminals.

They kept shouting that they were going to give me a good time. They didn't call it rape.

I didn't know there was any adrenaline left in my body after what I'd been through at the barn, but it was there, making my heart race, sending shocks through my limbs.

I had to get out of there. They were banging harder on the truck and now were trying to break in. Lucky they were too drunk to be immediately effective.

Then I remembered the window (yes, the "winda") in the back of the cab that the salesman had been so proud of, and I made a dive for it. I was through it in no time. It *was* a big window, thank heaven. They didn't even know I had moved.

I started the engine, and their shouts grew louder.

"Hey, where you going?"

"Don't be a sorehead."

Because I had driven into a patch of undergrowth that I didn't think I'd be able to drive through, even with the four-wheel drive, I shifted into reverse.

As I backed up they shouted curses.

Since I had weaved my way into the woods, I knew I couldn't keep backing up or I'd hit a tree. I switched on the headlights to find my way out.

There in the beams were three lumbering drunks. And just

to show me what I was missing, each one had unzipped his fly and displayed his penis. They waved them at me, laughing and calling me names, some derogatory, some sweet talking.

I retched, I cried, I cursed as I drove out of the woods, frightened, degraded, disgusted. It was not a night that would help me straighten out my relationships with men.

All I saw was the yellow line down the middle of the road. I didn't know which way I was going, didn't notice any of the signs, just kept driving. When I finally got around to noticing my surroundings, I was at a crossroad where an all-night diner beckoned travelers with its neon sign saying EATS, and under that, using the same giant letter *E*, ELSIE'S.

I pulled into the lot and turned off the engine. It took me several minutes to remember where my purse, my wallet, my comb, and all the necessaries were. I had to get in the back again to find everything, some of it having been tossed around as I made my escape.

My first stop after I hobbled into Elsie's was the bathroom, where I combed my hair and washed soot off my face. There was too much hay imbedded in my clothing to get myself looking lint free, but I made a stab at it. Then I sat at a table by a window from which I could look at the road. I was tired and confused and needed some hot food.

Elsie's was the kind of place that never heard of cholesterol, and I enjoyed every bite of my hamburger steak with brown gravy and french fries. I slathered butter on the warm rolls, and when I ate the apple pie à la mode, I realized the piecrust was made with butter and lard.

The waitress was round and ruddy and was full of chatter. She enjoyed seeing me eat.

"You look like you need it," she said.

It turned out she was Elsie, and when I asked her if there was a motel nearby, she told me that she rented rooms in her house right behind the diner. When I seemed reluctant, she told me that I would be safe. She knew what I needed to hear.

Before an hour had passed, I was tucked into a big bed with sweet-smelling sheets. Elsie had given me a room with a lock on the door and its own bathroom. I fell asleep with the notes from Ben's book swirling in my brain along with visions of naked men using their huge penises as weapons.

When I awoke it was broad daylight, and I could hear the hum of traffic on the road in front of the diner. My dreams were still with me and Ben's killer had walked through them. But I didn't want to believe my dream.

Twenty-nine

My ankle was so swollen I had to loosen the laces of my running shoe, but at least it didn't hurt too much and the elastic bandage gave me enough support to walk almost normally.

Elsie set out a huge breakfast for me in her kitchen, and the two of us must have talked almost an hour while we ate. She was a widow and had gotten a lump-sum payment from her husband's retirement fund and used it to open the diner.

"You took a big chance," I said.

"Yes," she said, "but I knew I could work hard and cook good. I've been at it for ten years now, still working hard and still slaving over a hot stove."

I told her more about my life than I do most people, even after I've known them for a while. I also told her about the drunks the night before.

"You ought to report them. There's a bunch like that that's been attacking women around these parts."

I was reluctant to tell her that I didn't think reporting it to the sheriff would do much good. That I thought the sheriff wasn't doing his job right. "I'll tell the troopers about it later," I said.

She looked at me as if she were going to ask me something but said nothing.

When she left to work in the diner, I was lingering over my coffee. I had arranged with Elsie to use her phone, for a modest fee. So I called Sheriff Castle.

"Where have you been? I expected you yesterday," he said.

254

"I had some business that needed attending to," I said. Well, I wasn't lying. "What's new?"

"Ernest is dead."

So, it *was* Ernest. "When?"

"Last night. Somebody stabbed him in the same barn Ben was killed in. Then they hoisted him in the air and set fire to the barn. What a blaze."

"Hoisted him?" I was trying to give appropriate responses.

"On the hay lift."

I weighed what I should say next and decided to err on the side of stupid. "What hay lift?"

"There are these big tongs that run on a pulley from the barn roof. They use them to lift big loads of hay and place them in the loft."

"And Ernest was up there?" I said.

"Just like a barbecue," the sheriff said. "He was cooked."

"But you said somebody stabbed him."

"First. Before they cooked him."

"Was the barn burned to cover the murder?"

"Looks like it. There wasn't much left of Ernest."

"How did you know it was murder? And how did you know who it was?"

"He was missing. And Theodora told us which of his teeth had gold caps on. Doc Farnham found the stab wound."

"What about Heinz and Edith? Where are they?"

"They got back yesterday. They're under house arrest." Sure, I thought, the way the family was under house arrest before, when the computers got vandalized.

"And Eric?"

"He's with Theodora."

"How are they taking it?"

"Everybody's doing okay except Heinz. The doctor had to dope him up."

Love takes many forms, I thought. "Has anyone called Greta to tell her?"

"They tried. Couldn't get hold of her. I guess she took off again."

I thought that was peculiar. Surely if one of Baeres had called Grace and Hildegarde, they would have been able to find Greta. Unless. Unless Greta had given instructions again that she didn't want her folks to know where she was. And now that she was eighteen, she didn't have to ask her folks's permission for anything. "Maybe I can find her again."

"Do you want to tell her about her dad, or do you want to give me her phone number and I'll tell her?"

"I didn't say I had her phone number. I said I think I can find her. I'll let you know."

"You're going to have to tell me what you know, Fran. I can't have pieces of information floating around that I don't know about. There's been too many killings."

My translation of his protest was: The troopers are getting ready to step in.

"I told you that I don't have her phone number." Icy was the way I'd have described my voice. Then, although my timing was not the greatest, I asked him what I'd been waiting to ask. "Is there anyone at Hickory Hills you are confiding in or who would know everything you know about what's gone on?"

He hesitated just long enough to convince me that there was such a someone. "Why do you ask that?" he said.

I told him about the woman who called the office and what she had told Natasha.

"That sure beats all," he said. "So where are you? Are you coming out to the farm?"

"I'm at my office in Buffalo," I said. "I'll be out later today."

"Too bad you missed the dance," he said. "I think you would have enjoyed it."

"Well, I was keeping busy in Paradise," I said. I didn't mention that he could have saved me some trouble by keeping the Baeres at home.

The sheriff seemed chatty and even put me on hold for a minute, "While I get rid of this other call."

He gave me more details on the dance and then on the fire and on the volunteer firemen who put it out, and about Doc Farnham when he examined the body found in the fire, and about the firemen poking through the remains of the barn and bringing in dogs to see if there were any other bodies.

That sent up a red flag for me, and I wondered who had given the firemen the idea that someone else was in the barn.

If someone had seen me go into the barn, that someone knew I was still in the barn, and that someone was hoping that I would die in the flames, too. That person may not have known who it was, but just that someone was in the barn, and whoever it was didn't matter.

Then I remembered the whispering when the third person entered the barn. Were they whispering because they knew someone else was already there?

It was probably too much to ask the sheriff not to tell anyone that he had heard from me, but I asked him anyway.

"What's the big secret?" he said.

"I think someone is trying to kill me."

"Someone here?" He was a little too innocent.

"Yes." I shouldn't have bothered asking him. He would probably blat it out to the woman who said she knew everything the sheriff knew. I tried to remember the women I'd seen working behind the counter and in the office at the farm. I didn't remember any one of them getting special attention from the sheriff or giving him special attention either. "I'll see you later," I said.

After I looked through Ben's diary one more time—finishing it this time without being interrupted by horny drunks—I wondered again about the night that Ben was killed and about what Greta had seen that night. Now I was wondering again what had happened to Greta.

Greta was still in the hospital, I was told by the housekeeper when I called Pete Menkin's number in Paradise.

"She's having some trouble," the woman said.

"Where can I reach Pete," I said, "to ask him more about her condition?"

She gave me a number at the hospital. After I was switched from one office to another, and put on hold while they paged Pete, he came on the line.

"Fran," he said, "I'm glad you called." I wasn't ready to give him my answer about having dinner with him, and I was getting ready to tell him so. But he wasn't thinking about our date. "Greta is not good. I wanted to ask you about talking to her folks."

"What happened?"

"She was getting along fine, and then Hildegarde came to

visit her and, according to Hildegarde, they were just talking
when Greta started shrieking. We haven't been able to get a
word out of her since.''

"There's no point in calling her family right now," I said,
and told him what had happened at the farm.

"Lord," he said, "what else can happen to the poor kid?''

"Do me a favor and don't tell anyone where she is.''

"A lot of people know already.''

"Move her somewhere else.''

"Is she in danger?''

"Probably.''

"From whom?''

"I'm not sure.''

When I hung up, I just sat there, trying to figure out what
to do next. Going to Hickory Hills would be dangerous. And
I didn't know how deeply the sheriff was involved. I had important evidence in my truck, which could be destroyed if it
fell into the wrong hands. And I didn't know how clean the
sheriff's hands were.

I thought back to his early reluctance to call in the state
police and wondered whether he was in cahoots with someone
from the beginning. Was the date he asked me on just a ruse
to get information from me?

And what about the New York state police? Were they cor-
rupt, too? Could I get them to believe me? After all, I was the
outsider, and the Baeres had been running the farm about thirty
years, they employed a lot of local people, and maybe even
contributed to political campaigns.

That's when I decided to call Rudy Hoffmann in Paradise
and see what he could set up for me. Maybe give me an entree
to the New York troopers. Maybe make me more believable.
Maybe find out how reliable the troopers here were. If the
state police were getting impatient with the way the sheriff
was conducting the investigation, maybe they would be glad
to hear from me.

Lucky. I got Sergeant Hoffmann on the phone right away,
and he was a good listener when it came to the adventures of
Ben Grasse. I read him the diary and told him what my theory
was, what my fears were about the sheriff, and what my wor-
ries were about the troopers. Hoffmann, being the thorough

police officer that he was, recorded my call. Oh, he didn't tell me he was doing it, but when someone asks you to repeat things several times during a conversation or asks you to speak more slowly, it does arouse your suspicions.

"I don't think you have to worry about the state boys, and that's not just because I'm a state policeman. They've been working night and day on a federal case and their manpower is maxed out. Stay put. I'll call you back within the hour."

The notion breezed through my mind that I might not be able to trust him either, but I whisked that one away. I felt pretty secure about the sergeant. So I gave him the phone number.

Since I had a little time before the sergeant was likely to call back, I packed my stuff back in the truck and spent a few minutes straightening out my gear. It was while I was crawling around in the back of the truck that I saw the sheriff's car pull into the lot. The sheriff got out and went into the diner.

Damn. How did he find me? Did Sergeant Hoffmann call him and tell him where I was? I canceled the second thought. There wasn't enough time for that to have happened unless the sheriff was right down the road when he got the call.

Stupid. That's what I called myself. The sheriff had traced my call. That's why he kept me on the line so long telling me all that nonsense. Stupid.

What would Elsie say if the sheriff asked her about me? After all, she hardly knew me. Would she keep quiet? Maybe she wouldn't think it was a good idea to keep quiet when the sheriff asked her questions.

I watched the sheriff take a booth, the same one I had sat in the night before. He was probably looking for my car. Maybe he thought I'd left already.

There was just a chance with Elsie, I thought, and dialed the phone number from the portable.

I could see Elsie going to the phone. "Elsie's. Good morning."

"Morning, Elsie. Please don't mention my name, this is Fran."

"Ah, yes. What can I do for you?"

She was terrific.

I told her then about the sheriff and my suspicions that he

wasn't exactly doing his duty and that I thought he had traced my call. "You could do me a favor, maybe even save my life."

"That bad?" she said. "I've never known that stuff to be that noxious."

"I'm not sure if he is that bad or whether he has gotten himself in deeper than he intended. I'm willing to give him the benefit of the doubt, but not right now."

She said, "Uh-huh," and, "I see." And then she added, "No, we don't ordinarily cook with that stuff, but where are your headquarters? If I ever want to order some of that stuff, I'll need to know."

"I'm in my truck, looking right at you from the back window."

She seemed to be in my corner, and I told her what I'd like her to say to the sheriff if he asked about me. I also told her I was expecting a call from Sergeant Hoffmann.

When I hung up, I saw her go over to the table where the sheriff was sitting. I didn't know whether to take off or to trust her. I watched them talking as my blood pressure zoomed. When he got up and hurried to the door, I dove for cover under my sleeping bag and rolled over against the side of the truck. I lay there panting and trying to hear over the pounding in my ears.

I heard a car screech out of the lot, and when I got the nerve to peek out the window, his car was gone.

I called Elsie back.

"Thanks," I said.

"Well, you were right about him wanting to know about you. He described you and said you were wanted for questioning. I'll tell you, when he said that, I almost told him where you were."

"Why didn't you?"

"Instinct. I thought you were telling the truth. And more important, I thought he was lying."

"Thanks for everything, Elsie. When this is over, I'll come back and tell you the whole story. That is, if I live through it." Then I asked her to give me a signal when the call came in from Pennsylvania and to tell Sergeant Hoffmann that I would call him right back.

When I called Rudy Hoffmann, he gave me directions to the New York state troopers's barracks and said they were expecting me. He didn't like it at all that the sheriff had come looking for me. "What are you driving?" he said. "Do you have any way of disguising yourself?"

At that point, I didn't know whether to tell him. I didn't know whom to trust. While I hesitated, he got the message.

"Look," he said, "I wasn't going to tell you this, because the state cops are still working on it. But they don't like the way things are going at Hickory Hills at all. I told them about you and what you've found. I think you should call them and have them come and pick you up. Don't give the sheriff another chance at you."

I got a chill thinking of myself on these country roads and being picked up by the sheriff. But I knew myself well enough to know that if I didn't do something, anything, pretty soon, I was going to be paralyzed by my fears. "I'm sorry," I said. "It's hard to trust anyone once . . ."

"Yeah," he said, "tell that to the young girls that Ben messed with. An older man, a father figure, messing with their minds and their bodies."

"I'll go right to the barracks," I said.

"Do you want to tell me where you are? I'd like to have someone keeping tabs on you."

At that point, there was static on my line and then a voice saying, "Calling Sheriff Castle. Do you read me, Sheriff?"

"What was that?" Rudy said.

"I'm on the portable. I guess it's interference."

"Yes, and that means you can be heard by others," he said. "Hang up and get out of there. Call me later."

I cleared the call, put the phone in my jacket pocket, and cowered in the corner of the truck, pawing through my stuff looking for my disguises.

The first thing I came to in the bag of other identities was my trusty old gray wig. It would do. That and the glasses. Then my hand hit a set of teeth that fit over my own and made me look gap-toothed and buck-toothed and changed the look of my jaw. Good. Then I put on a hat with a brim and looked in the mirror. It would do.

Since it was broad daylight, I didn't know whether to move

to the truck's cab via the window as I had the night before. So I got out and walked around. Elsie was watching as I got in the truck. I waved at her. She waved back and her face was one great big grin. I guess my disguise was funnier than I thought.

If the sheriff heard the phone call, how much did he hear? I know he didn't hear me while I was talking to Elsie and he was in the diner. But what about the second time I called her? And what did I say to Sergeant Hoffmann that would give me away?

I was wasting too much time speculating, I told myself. Get moving. I waved to Elsie again and drove away. The barracks were not in the same direction as the farm, but farther east in the same direction that Elsie had sent the sheriff. I hoped I wouldn't run into him, disguise or no.

If he had heard me talking to Rudy Hoffmann, he might just wait on the road near the barracks, I thought. I reached for my map and tried to find an alternate route, while I kept driving. If he knew I was at the diner, he would station himself between the diner and the barracks.

With that in mind, I made a U-turn and headed back west toward the next crossroad. I would go north and then go east until I found a road that was past the barracks. Then I'd go south and back west to the state police.

Of course, the sheriff might not have heard any of the conversations. But if he heard all of them, he might figure out what I would do to elude him.

I dialed the sheriff's office and was surprised when he answered. Oh. Either he has a portable or his phone is patched into his car. "Sheriff," I said, "it's Fran."

"Yes, Fran. Where are you?"

"I'm on my way to the farm. Can you meet me there? I'd like to talk to you before I talk to the Baeres."

"Did you find Greta?"

"She's on the move again. Nobody down there knows where she went this time. She told me when I saw her that after she turned eighteen, she wasn't going to live with her family anymore."

"Theodora wants to see her."

"Oh?"

"She wants Greta to come to Ernest's funeral," he said.

"Of course. Well, I can't help you on that. I found her once, but I couldn't hold her."

"I could arrest you for not turning her over to the police," he said. There was a nasty edge to his voice.

"But I did turn her over. Call Sergeant Rudy Hoffmann of the Pennsylvania state police, he'll tell you. Didn't he take a statement from Greta and send it to you?"

"No," he said. He was lying. Maybe to give himself an excuse to take me into custody. God only knows what would happen then.

"Call the sergeant," I said. "I have been dealing straight with you." Liar, liar, your pants are on fire.

"Where are you now?" he said.

"I just went through Orchard Park."

"I'll meet you at the farm," he said.

Just as I hung up, I saw a sheriff's car in my rearview mirror. The red light was spinning. When it got behind me, I could see the sheriff.

He's found me, I thought.

He turned on his siren.

Do I run or do I pull over?

He pulled out and came up next to me. I looked over at him. He looked at me and looked away and kept going.

I exhaled and after he was out of sight, I made another U-turn and headed for the state police barracks. I didn't need to take the roundabout route after all.

But I hadn't seen the last of Sheriff Castle that day.

Thirty

I had driven about five miles from the diner when I saw the sign indicating that the state police offices were AHEAD 1 MILE. Relief began seeping into my system, and I smiled. I tore off my hat and wig when I had the barracks in sight. The teeth came next.

I was tucking the teeth into my purse when a sheriff's car came out of nowhere and pulled me over. The barracks were only a hundred yards away. Screaming distance if anybody were outside to hear. But although there were several patrol cars in the lot, there was no one outside. I cursed myself for taking off the disguise.

Where had the car been hiding? Why didn't I see it? I looked in my rearview mirror and saw an outdoor advertising sign and remembered all the cartoons with cops hiding behind such signs. Was that where he was?

In the side mirror I saw a deputy approaching with his gun drawn. If I were ever going to have a heart attack, that would have been the time. I looked again at the deputy and saw that it was Jeff, the one who had the crush on Amy. Could he really have his gun drawn to capture me? What on earth had anyone said to him? What were his orders?

"Put your hands on the wheel," he said.

"What's going on, Jeff? Why the heavy artillery?"

"Orders," he said. "Keep your hands on the wheel." He was acting very scared of me, scared enough to shoot.

"Look," I said, "I'm on my way to the state police.

264

They're expecting me. I have some important evidence for them.''

''No you don't. I'm not going to believe any of your stories.''

''It's true. Jeff, listen to me. The sheriff is not on the up-and-up. He's trying to keep me from going to the troopers.''

''Ha. You expect me to believe that? After you withheld evidence, took evidence out of the county, and interfered with the sheriff's investigation?''

''Is that what I'm being charged with?''

''Just get out of the car, move slowly, and keep your hands up.''

Please, state troopers, come out, I prayed.

''Lean against the truck and spread 'em.''

''This is not necessary,'' I said. ''Your sheriff is out of line. Believe me, when this is over, he is going to lose his job.''

''Quiet.'' Jeff ran his hands lightly over me. I could see he was blushing. ''Put your hands behind you.''

''You're going to cuff me?''

''Put your hands behind you. You have the right to remain silent,'' he said and gave me the rest of the Miranda.

''There's absolutely no reason to arrest me,'' I said. ''I want an attorney, immediately.''

''Sheriff said to bring you to the farm.''

''What? Don't you know how dangerous that is for me? You trying to get me killed or what?''

I thought Jeff paid attention to what I said, but he didn't change his plan. He put me in the backseat of his car, closed the partition, and got on the radio. The conversation was animated, at least the end of it that I could see. And when it was over, he went to my truck and started pulling things out of it and putting them in the trunk of the patrol car.

My gun, my ID, my disguises, the money and papers and notebook that I'd taken from the hiding place in the barn, my food and my sleeping bag, everything that I had installed in the truck was transferred. Then he drove the truck to the state police parking lot, left it there, and went inside, presumably to tell them that he had arrested a dangerous criminal and was leaving the criminal's vehicle in their lot.

He even got a ride back to his car from one of the troopers.

When Jeff was getting in his car and the trooper looked in at me, I mouthed the word "help," even though I didn't think it would do me much good. The trooper didn't react; he just drove off.

On the way to the farm, I started having a panic attack. I was sure that going back there meant death. I already had the dishonor part. Imagining all sorts of ways to die, my mind had lost all its ability to reason.

Jeff had opened the partition to keep track of the sounds I was making, I guess. He had been checking me out in the rearview mirror, and I'm sure I didn't look too healthy.

It was when we passed Elsie's that I made myself take hold and try to persuade Jeff that the sheriff was not functioning like a law enforcement official. I told him that the troopers were already suspicious and that he, Jeff, could do himself a favor if he at least contacted the troopers to try to verify my story.

Jeff was my only hope. I even played the Amy card, telling him that he ought to check with Amy to see what kind of person I was. His face went through a variety of expressions that seemed to indicate indecisiveness, but he said nothing that verified that perception.

The jitters came back in full force when we turned into the driveway to the farm.

"So where is the sheriff?" I said. "You'd better not turn me over to any of the Baeres. One of them is a killer. At least one of them."

"The sheriff is waiting for you at the store," he said.

"Who else is there?"

"I don't know."

Now that Jeff was talking to me, I thought maybe I'd get some answers. "Did he tell you why he wanted you to bring me here rather than take me to the sheriff's office or the county jail?"

"He said you took some things from the farm that should be returned."

"I did take some things from the farm, but they belonged to Ben Grasse, not anyone on the farm."

"Maybe you don't know who they belonged to."

"Maybe you don't."

"That's enough conversation," he said.

"Do me a favor, will you, Jeff? Please call the troopers. If you don't, the next body you'll find will be mine."

"Nobody wants to kill you. You're just being paranoid."

"I swear I'll come back to haunt you. Every shadow you see will have me in it." I was trying everything to get his attention.

Only one car was in the parking lot by the store, the sheriff's car. Maybe that meant he was alone. Maybe he would listen to reason. As Jeff pulled into the lot, the sheriff came out of the store. He stood there with his hands on his hips and a big smart-ass smile on his face. I knew he had outsmarted me and I didn't like the feeling. But more than that, I was afraid.

"Good work," he said to Jeff, and he herded me into the store after instructing Jeff to move the stuff he had taken from me to the trunk of his car.

The sheriff had me sit on a straight-backed chair, and he recuffed my hands around the back of the chair.

It wasn't until after Jeff had left that Theodora came out from where she was hiding. If I was scared before, I was terrified now, because Theodora was my prime candidate for killer of the month.

"Did you get the stuff she stole, Dickie?" she said. And another piece of the puzzle fell into place. Theodora had been orchestrating everything from the sheriff's pillow. And then, some of the oddities that had been occurring from the beginning began to make sense, including the removal of the computer printouts from the sheriff's car.

"It's in my trunk," he said.

"Give me your keys," she said, and he handed her the keys.

When she had gone out, I said, "You're letting her tamper with evidence, Sheriff."

He suddenly got a peculiar look on his face, a combination of guilt and surprise. Could he have been so lovesick that he didn't realize what he was doing? Or was he in on some scheme with Theodora to take over the farm?

Out in the parking lot a sudden flash of light was followed by flames.

"That will be the notebook she's burning up," I said.

"What notebook?" he said. "She said you stole some papers from the barn."

"The notebook that Ben Grasse kept. The notebook that would have told you a lot of what you want to know. If—if you want to know."

"Of course, I want to know," he said. But he wasn't convincing. He went to the door and shouted, "What are you doing, Theo? You can't burn that stuff we took from Fran. It's evidence."

The only answer was manic laughter. The sheriff started toward her as she turned to come back into the store. She was carrying my purse, and I knew why.

"My gun is in that purse, Sheriff." I hoped he would take the purse away from her before she made her move.

But Theodora knew where the sheriff's gun was, and it was not hanging from his waist but was on a desk a good ten feet from where he was standing when she took out my gun and pointed it at him.

I almost felt sorry for him when he realized the kind of fool he had been. His face told a story of sunlight reaching into a foul corner that had purposely been left dark.

"Theo, what's this about?" he said.

She smiled and said, "It's about an hour too early for us to take our walk."

"What walk?"

The weather was getting threatening, and in an hour any walk would be in the rain, was my guess.

"Lie down on the floor, Dickie."

The sheriff lay down as if he had no more will, like a beaten dog. Once he was down, she had him roll onto his stomach and she cuffed his hands.

"Did you start going out with the sheriff before or after you planned Ben's death?" I said.

"Shut up," she said.

"Theo, you told me Ernest killed Grasse because he found out about your fling with him."

"Is that what she told you? She just burned up the evidence that said different. There was no affair with Grasse."

"But Terry told me . . ." he said. It was almost a whine.

"Terry told you because Theodora put him up to it. And later he was of no more use to her."

Theodora was waving the gun. "I told you to shut up, Miss Private Eye."

"That notebook she just burned," I went on despite Theodora's threat, "told all about Ben's affairs. Theodora wasn't in it, but some of her deals were."

"What notebook?" the sheriff said.

"The one I found in the barn along with a lot of money. Where's the money, Theodora?"

"When did you find it?" the sheriff said.

Theodora stood there waiting for me to speak. I knew it wouldn't make any difference whether she knew everything I knew, because I was sure her intent would be the same. "I was in the barn the night it burned. I barely escaped."

"Too bad you did," she said.

"You had more than one reason for burning the barn, didn't you?" I said to her.

The sheriff watched her, sadness and anger flashing across his face. "Did you kill all of them, Theo? And now do you mean to kill Fran and me, too?"

Her face turned ugly, her lips curled in a hard snarl, and her eyes got narrow and flinty. "It gets easier with practice."

"Did you kill Ben because he was onto your swindle? That was what the blackmail was about, wasn't it? Or did you have to get rid of Ben because you found out he was Ernest's half-brother and he might have a claim on the farm?"

"What?" the sheriff said.

"I could shoot you right now," she said, "so you'd better close your mouth."

"But your plan isn't to shoot me now, is it?" I didn't know what her plan was, but shooting me in the store was not her style. She'd have something more complicated plotted, like burning down a motel. Besides, I was trying to delay whatever plan she might have made. My hope was that Jeff would call the troopers, or that the troopers would come looking for me when I didn't arrive at the barracks as Sergeant Hoffmann had said I would.

"No," she said, "that isn't my plan."

"Theo, for God's sake, whatever you've done, I can help

you." The sheriff was trying to save his own skin.

"Not even you can keep her out of jail," I said.

"I don't intend to go to jail," she said.

"No, she's probably got a lot of other money stashed away in addition to Ben's money that I found in the barn. She probably has her reservations all made, too, now that there aren't any more people around who believe her. Even Ernest was doubting, wasn't he?"

I watched her as I spoke, and she verified what I had guessed. If Eric was taking money out of the farm with his little scam, I was sure that a further look into the affairs of the farm would uncover a much larger and more pervasive scam that Theodora had been running, probably for a long time.

Ben's computer system probably had put an end to her embezzling money from the farm. The wonder was that despite it all, the farm was making money and prospering.

"Did Greta tell you where to find Ben's things?" Theodora said. At that moment, I was glad that I had told Pete to hide Greta. I didn't know what Theodora intended to do to her daughter after she had disposed of the sheriff and me.

"That night in the barn," I said to Theodora, "did Greta see you kill Ben? Is that why she ran away?"

Theodora stood up very straight and tossed her head. "Nobody saw me," she said.

"Theo!" the sheriff said.

"What difference does it make now?" she said.

"And Terry Kurtz? What had he done?" the sheriff said.

"He was in on it with Ben."

"The blackmail," I said.

"Yes, and did you know they were in jail together?" she said, as if she had just displayed a jewel that she had been saving.

"Did you find that out when you took your trip to Pennsylvania? Before you killed him?"

"He was her uncle, for God's sake." Theodora's tone was indignant.

"How did Heinz and Edith find out?"

"Ben told Heinz. But Heinz didn't believe him."

"What did you tell Edith and Heinz to get them to go to Paradise?"

She smiled. "That Ben had put phony records in the town hall about Heinz being his father."

"But the town hall records didn't say that."

She smiled. "Not any more."

"So that's what you did on your trip to Paradise last month. And then you followed Heinz and Edith down there and stayed out of sight."

"They were supposed to stay at the motel overnight. They weren't supposed to go around playing detective. That was their idea."

"What were they supposed to do?" I said, but the answer came to me before her face told me the story. Heinz and Edith were supposed to perish in the motel fire along with me.

"Where are Heinz and Edith and Eric, sheriff?" I said.

"They're being guarded at the big house."

"Good plan," I said. "Maybe they'll live through this."

"There won't be anything left, anyway," she said.

"Where were Ernest and Eric while you were in Paradise?"

"None of your business."

"Well, what are you going to do with Eric, now?"

"Nothing. That's enough talk," she said. "Get up and walk." She waved her gun at the sheriff, who rolled himself around trying to stand up without the use of his hands. I think he was acting more helpless than he was, but I admired his deception.

"Damn it, Theo, I can't get up."

She helped him, and as he rose to his feet, he charged her, knocking her down and knocking the gun out of her hand. It landed on the floor by her feet.

Then he backed up to the desk where his gun was and picked up his gun behind his back and twisted around so that he was pointing the gun at her while he was only half facing her, and she was sitting on the floor near me looking stunned.

"Stay where you are," he said to her. "Fran, can you get out of that chair?"

I was working my arms up around the back of the chair. He hadn't attached the cuffs to the chair; he had only wrapped my arms around the back of it. It wasn't difficult to get up, but I knocked the chair over as I stood.

Theodora was quick. In that second when the sheriff was distracted by the falling chair, she pushed me over and grabbed the gun. The sheriff might have had time to shoot her, but I don't think he wanted to.

She wasn't troubled by such disinclination. She shot him in the arm and the gun dropped on the floor. Blood, a lot of it, started running out of him with great force.

"You've hit a big blood vessel, Theodora. You've got to tie up that wound, or he'll die."

"You get over in the corner," she said, "and I'll tie it up."

I was relieved by her reaction, because once she started shooting, she might have just kept on until we were both bleeding all over the store. I was still on the floor where I'd fallen when she knocked me over, so I walked over to the corner on my knees.

She worked quickly and with some skill to wrap the sheriff's arm. And as she pressed the bandage on his arm and wrapped it with gauze from the office first aid kit, I saw a tender expression pass over the sheriff's face. Her touch still did that to him, I thought, despite what he had found out.

When she was done, she walked us out to the sheriff's car and had us get into the backseat. I didn't know where she was taking us, but any hope I had had died. Who would be able to find me before she could do me in?

The rain had started, and was coming down heavily before we got out of the parking lot. She took a farm road, and I remembered the territory from the night before when I had gone to the barn. She pulled off the road onto a narrow lane that led down through the woods to the creek.

She stopped the car and got out and walked to the creek, a narrow rivulet that curled its way along the creek bed.

She came back to the car and instructed us to get out. She was already soaked, and it didn't take long before all of us were dripping.

"Are you going to shoot us here?" I said.

"I'm not going to shoot you," she said.

Should I be relieved? I wondered.

She marched us down the bank to the creek and then downstream a short way to a small bridge that connected two farm roads. She tied us to the upright that rose from the middle of the creek to support the bridge. Our arms were still cuffed behind us and our backs were pressed against the upright. Our feet were in the stream. She wrapped us round and round with rope. I didn't know where the rope had come from, but I guessed she had planned this all along.

"Now what?" I said, when she had finished wrapping us, mummy style.

"You'll see," she said. She walked back to the car, the sheriff and I turning our heads to the side to watch her.

"She means to drown us," the sheriff said when she'd gone.

"How's she going to do that?"

"When it rains this hard, the creek runs over this bridge. All we can do is watch the water rise."

"Why didn't she just shoot us? It would have been quicker."

"I think she's changing her MO."

"Huh? Why?"

"I remember we had a talk one night before all this started. She asked me about criminals. I told her that they have ways of working that trip them up. Like fingerprints are distinct, so are the methods that criminals use."

"Oh." Theodora was a novice who had gotten instruction on crime from the county's chief crime fighter. "So you're a good teacher," I said, thinking about Ernest rotating in the hay tongs.

"I never suspected," he said. There was a catch in his voice.

I tried to move my arms, my shoulders, my hips. Everything was held tightly by the coils of rope. "How did you get involved with her in the first place?" I said.

"Oh, God, I was stupid," he said.

Yeah. "What did she tell you?"

"She said Ernest had a fatal illness—cancer, she said. But nobody knew about it but her and Ernest. She would say things like, 'Do you think God will forgive me for loving you while I'm still married?' I, I believed her."

The rain was pelting the trees and running down on us from

between the boards of the bridge. I don't know whether I was imagining it or not, but the rope seemed to be getting tighter.

"Who did she say killed Terry?"

"Ernest. She said she told Ernest about the blackmail and Ernest killed him. She confessed to me that she helped Ernest put Terry's body under the tractor."

"When did she tell you all of this?" I wondered how much he believed.

"Today. Just today. She'd been away."

"Away, but not where she said she was. She was in Paradise burning up a motel and then taking a shot at Doctor Menkin. She meant to take over the farm."

"What do you know about Doctor Menkin?"

"He's an old-fashioned family doctor, why?"

"Theodora mentioned him once."

I wondered what kind of lie she had made up about the old doctor. "What did she say?"

"She said there was a lot of bad feeling toward him. Said he messed with little girls. Said someday somebody would go after him."

"When did she tell you that?"

"Quite a while ago."

"She had long-range plans," I said, and tried to imagine how Theodora would have proceeded if the sheriff had not been seduced by her.

"Tell me again why she shot the doctor."

"Because his records, which are in a mess, by the way, showed that Heinz was Ben's father. She probably didn't want any of the Grasse's making a claim on the farm once Heinz was dead."

"But Heinz wasn't dead. He didn't die in the fire."

"She would find another way."

"I'm sorry, Fran. I'm really sorry."

Sorry for yourself, too, I thought. But I said, "How's your arm?"

"Numb," he said. "I can't feel anything."

"The ropes are getting tighter," I said. I was sure now.

"Let's pull against them," he said.

We pulled away from the post, and when we did I could feel the ropes digging into my flesh; but it did seem, when we stopped pulling, that the ropes were a bit looser.

That's when I looked down at my feet and couldn't see them, because the water, roiling and muddy, was climbing up my calf.

"Let's pull some more," I said.

We pulled together and separately. It didn't seem that the rope would ever get loose enough to release us, but it did relieve the pressure that had been building as the rope got wet and tightened.

"Ouch," the sheriff said after I had pulled rather strenuously. "What have you got in your pocket?"

In my pocket? What? "Oh," I said. "Maybe there's a chance."

"Chance of what?"

"The mobile phone. It's still in my pocket."

"Some lousy police officer Jeff is, leaving a suspect with a phone."

"I take that back about your being a good teacher," I said.

We actually laughed, there under the bridge with water rising.

"If the phone's still dry, maybe I can dial 911," I said. But I got no answer. The sheriff was slumped forward, making the ropes tighter than ever and making it unlikely that I could work my pocket into place to get my hands into it.

"Sheriff, wake up," I hollered. Then I tried, "Dickie, wake up."

Believe it or not, it worked.

"What? Is that you, Theo?"

"Stand up straight," I said.

He straightened up and moaned.

"Hold on," I said, and pulled on the fabric of my jacket, trying to get the left pocket back to where my hands were and sliding my right arm as far around my body as I could so that my left arm had room to work. "Don't pass out on me again, Sheriff."

"No, no," he mumbled and I feared he was going out again.

"Holler," I said. "Maybe some of those fishermen are around here." Maybe if he hollered, he would keep from passing out again.

"Help, help, help," he yelled whenever the thunder ceased.

My hands were wet, my jacket was wet, and the phone felt wet when I finally got my hands in the pocket. I tried to visualize where all the buttons were that I'd pushed without thought when I'd been able to see them. I groped for the button that turned it on.

The sheriff continued to yell, albeit more weakly than before, as I hit the buttons and prayed that I had remembered right. Even if I did get someone on the line, I wouldn't be able to hear anything, so I just started talking as if someone had answered. "Help, we're going to drown. This is Fran Tremaine Kirk. Sheriff Dick Castle and I are tied under a bridge on Hickory Hills Farm. The water is rising. We're north of the store and a little west." I hoped I had the directions right. "Help."

I kept hiking up the jacket as the water rose and kept repeating some variation of my plea while the sheriff was shouting, "Help," every time I stopped to take a breath.

When the water got to our chests, we stopped.

Thirty-one

All the things I had tried to do to save myself had failed. I hadn't been able to persuade Jeff to call the troopers. My frantic phone call hadn't worked; I didn't even know whether I had dialed the right digits. And I guessed that the troopers hadn't come looking for me, either.

Where had Theodora gone with all the money she had hoarded and the money from Ben's cache? Had she gone to look for Greta? Or was she on her way to some foreign country?

Sheriff Castle was unconscious, his head drooping forward perilously close to the rushing water. I found that I could lift his head by pulling against the ropes. But the water was still rising, and that ploy would not work much longer. The cold was getting to me, too, and maybe I was getting delirious, because I kept hearing my mother saying, "Frances, you have to get out of the water. Your lips are turning blue."

All the tugging on the ropes that the sheriff and I had done had loosened them enough to let the sheriff droop, but not enough to free us. I kept on pulling away from the upright to keep the ropes tight against the sheriff's chest and keep his head up. I developed a sort of rhythm of pulling against the ropes.

Inhale, pull, relax, breathe out. Inhale, pull, relax, breathe out. I was saying the words out loud in a quavering voice that I didn't recognize. It seemed that my voice had gotten louder, and it took some confusing minutes to realize that the thunder had stopped and the rain had let up.

With what was left of my reason, I remembered thinking that even after it stops raining, the runoff continues, so the water would keep rising.

I shifted my weight from one numb foot to the other and realized that my feet were no longer bound. I must have shifted the rope, I thought. If the rope had shifted up, maybe I could get it to shift down.

I wriggled my shoulders and thought that the bonds slipped lower. Then I stopped. If I worked the ropes lower, the sheriff's head would fall in the water. I changed my strategy and started to wriggle my legs, kicking out first one then the other, then stepping on the rope and pulling down on it.

With great effort, I pulled myself out of the delirium that was pleasantly overtaking me. I told myself to fight it to the end, not to give in to it.

Kick, kick, pull, step. Kick, kick, pull, step. As the rope slid down, it became looser because it was binding a narrower part of our bodies. I began to hope again, but the water was still rising and the sheriff's head was still drooping.

"Damn it, wake up, Sheriff," I screamed. "I'm doing all the damn work."

"Cold," he said.

My heart did a flip. He was awake. "Hold up your head." I screamed at him again, since that seemed to keep him awake.

"Okay, okay," he said.

"Now hold still. I've got something working."

"What?"

"Just hold still until I tell you to do something."

"Bossy," he said.

"Good. You're recovering your wits. Do you think you could lift your feet and step on the ropes that are down around your ankles?"

I felt the ropes tug as he moved his feet, and then as he stepped out of the bottom ropes, I felt the ropes above it get looser still.

"Okay, now let's pull out away from the post," I said.

We did and there was suddenly space between us and the post.

"Now I'm going to work on the bottom again," I said. "Kick, kick, pull, step."

"What?" he said.

"Nothing. Don't do anything yet."

I did my step a few more times and pulled a couple more rounds of the rope down under my feet. Then I told the sheriff to step over the rope on his ankles.

We did this a few more times, and the ropes holding us were almost loose enough to wriggle out of but not quite. And the water now was up to my chin and swirling and splashing. I took in a few mouthfuls while I was giving the sheriff instructions.

"You pull out on your side and I'll stay close to the pole," he said. "Maybe there's enough slack so that you can climb out."

I started to climb over the ropes, pulling them down, but the water was so high and my hands were still cuffed. The sheriff had another couple of inches before the water got to his nose, but I was at zero.

I hopped up and took a breath and then stepped up on a few more rounds of the rope. I did this a few times, and suddenly the rope went all slack and I was free. I jumped up and down, grabbing a breath when my head was above water and trying to hop my way to the edge of the creek bed. The sheriff was somewhere, but I didn't know where and I couldn't help him now. I could barely help myself.

On the next hop, I felt the ground beneath me. Then I dug my foot in closer to the shore, and my head was clear and I gasped for breath. But I was still in the rising stream and didn't know how I was going to climb out.

Exhaustion was overtaking me, noises were going off in my head and my eyes were seeing flashing lights. My whole body was numb. I kept searching for higher ground with my feet, digging my feet into the muddy bank, and working my way up higher. When I got high enough to rest my head and shoulders on the bank, I rested and breathed.

It was then that I felt a hand on my shoulder and I let out a yell that was primal, frightened, discouraged. I was sure that Theodora had returned to toss me back into the drink.

"Here, we've got you," a voice said. The voice was calm, strong, even kind.

Then another voice. Jeff's. "The sheriff. Where's the sheriff?"

I heard some shouting and more lights flashed.

"We've got him," Jeff said, "just in time."

The calm voice over my head said, "We've been looking for you all over the farm. Lucky you called."

"Lucky," I said, and collapsed into tears, maybe hysteria, maybe just plain relief, but I remember nothing more about that day.

Thirty-two

A vase full of red roses dominated the view when I next opened my eyes. I was in a beige room in a narrow bed with clean white sheets and a warm blanket. There were other flowers in the room and the sun was slanting through the one large window. If those clues weren't enough, the smell told me I was in a hospital.

When I lifted my head, another head raised up from its perch on a pair of familiar arms resting on the side of my bed. It was Ted.

He blinked. "You're awake," he said.

"So are you."

"I guess you're your old self," he said, and he smiled that little-boy smile of his and ran his hand through my hair. A touch never felt so good.

"Where am I?"

"In the hospital," he said with a sly smile.

"Gee thanks for the information."

A woman wearing a name tag walked into the room. The tag said MOLLY GARVIN, RN. She said, "Good morning. Ah, you're awake."

I was getting the distinct impression that I had been asleep for a long time. "What day is it, anyway?"

"Tuesday," Ted said.

"What happened to Monday?" I said. "Did somebody dope me up?"

"You were right, Mr. Zwiatek," she said to Ted. "She is a tiger."

"Nobody answered my question," I said.

Molly Garvin, RN, said, "When you came in, you were suffering from exposure, your body temperature was down a few degrees, and you were very restless. The doctor gave you a normal dose of sedative, expecting you to sleep maybe a little late yesterday. But you just kept on sleeping. Like Rip van Winkle," she said. "Have you been under a lot of stress or have you been going on too little sleep?"

"Guilty," I said, "on both counts. But I feel great now. I want to get out of here."

With that, I sat up in bed and turned my body and dropped my legs over the side. Then I didn't feel so great. Dizzy, is what I felt.

"Take it slow," the nurse said. "You'll be okay, but you might be a little light-headed at first."

"I noticed." I eased myself off the bed with Ted and Molly on either side of me. A blast of cool air hit my back, and I realized that the hospital gown was untied.

Molly got me a more attractive hospital gown, one that overlapped when it was tied, and after I had gone to the bathroom and was settled in the chair, I had a few questions for Ted.

He was ready for me. "The sheriff's department called Delia and Delia called me," he said. Edith Baere had Delia's number. And through the wonder of electronics, Delia never misses a message, no matter where she is.

"What happened to the sheriff?" I said.

"He's down the hall. There's a guard on him."

"How's his arm?"

"It's all bandaged up."

"You've seen him?"

"He told me all about what happened. He's in big trouble, but he said he's just glad to be alive. He said you saved him. It must have been rough out there. I wish I could have been with you. I hate the idea of you being in trouble and I can't help you."

"I wish you were there, too. Believe me, I don't like being in trouble."

"I guess it's hard to stay out of when the sheriff is crooked."

"I bet he'd hate to hear that word used to describe him."

"It's the word he used himself."

The sheriff was giving himself no quarter, I thought. Somewhere in my tangle of emotions, there was pity for him, even though his double-dealing almost got me killed. "Did they catch Theodora?"

"State cops picked her up as she was boarding a plane for Montreal."

"Good. Now Greta is safe. Has anybody got any news from her?"

"You do. A Federal Express envelope came for you yesterday." He brought it to me.

In the package were two envelopes. In one was a check for more than I figured she owed me, but the note with it said,

Dear Fran,

 I hope this is enough. If not, let me know. Don't tell me it's too much. It couldn't be.

Greta

The other envelope contained a note from Pete.

Fran,

 Glad you came out of this mess all right. Dad is doing well, really, his old self again, no memory lapses. Theodora did him a favor, but that is not what she intended.

 Greta is fine, now, talking about everything with the hospital shrink and then telling it all to me. She's a delightful girl. I wish I were twenty years younger.

 What set her off was that she remembered her mother ramming the pitchfork through Ben. She said she watched Theodora turn Ben over. He was talking to Theodora and Theodora told him that he would never get a chance to tell what he knew about the money she took from the farm.

 I won't be getting to Buffalo anytime soon, after all, but when I do, I'll call you.

I gave the letter to Ted to read and thought that maybe Pete and Greta might get together, despite their ages. After all, she had fallen in love with Ben. It seemed to me that Pete would be a better deal for her.

When Ted was done reading, he said, "Poor kid. Her life really got turned upside down."

I didn't tell him what I had heard about Greta's life before she met Ben. I didn't tell him that her life could have turned out worse.

"What's happening at Hickory Hills?" I said.

"The story about the nonorganic foods sold as organic went out over the TV along with the story about all the murders. Theodora has been charged with the killings, and the Wyoming County DA is investigating the organic fraud."

Nurse Molly came back into the room carrying another envelope. "For you," she said. "You get a lot of mail for a person who sleeps all the time."

"Thanks," I said, and took the letter that bore the return address of Hickory Hills Farm, Organic Foods Since 1965.

The letter said,

Dear Ms. Kirk,

Enclosed please find a check for your work in finding my granddaughter. I am very sorry that the job put you in so much danger. We suspected that money was being taken, but we didn't know that our own daughter-in-law was so treacherous. I hope she gets what she deserves.

Yours truly,
Edith Baere

Her check was not as generous as Greta's, but it covered the time I'd spent looking for Greta.

I thought about the people at Hickory Hills, the people who for all the world seemed like a big happy family. But they were eating all their pure and natural foods in a room full of toxic secrets.

And then I had a deep yearning to see the women from the battered women's group, women who had been to the bottom of the pit and were trying to do something about their lives, women who, when they laughed, filled a room with their joy.